VERGIL'S *AENEID*:

The Essential Books

VERGIL'S *AENEID*:

The Essential Books

translated from the Latin
with notes and Introduction
by
Barry B. Powell

New York   Oxford
OXFORD UNIVERSITY PRESS

Oxford University Press is a department of the University of Oxford.
It furthers the University's objective of excellence in research,
scholarship, and education by publishing worldwide.

Oxford   New York
Auckland   Cape Town   Dar es Salaam   Hong Kong   Karachi
Kuala Lumpur   Madrid   Melbourne   Mexico City   Nairobi
New Delhi   Shanghai   Taipei   Toronto

With offices in
Argentina   Austria   Brazil   Chile   Czech Republic   France   Greece
Guatemala   Hungary   Italy   Japan   Poland   Portugal   Singapore
South Korea   Switzerland   Thailand   Turkey   Ukraine   Vietnam

Copyright © 2016 by Oxford University Press

For titles covered by Section 112 of the US Higher Education
Opportunity Act, please visit www.oup.com/us/he for the
latest information about pricing and alternate formats.

Published by Oxford University Press
198 Madison Avenue, New York, New York 10016
http://www.oup.com

Oxford is a registered trademark of Oxford University Press.

All rights reserved. No part of this publication may be reproduced,
stored in a retrieval system, or transmitted, in any form or by any means,
electronic, mechanical, photocopying, recording, or otherwise,
without the prior permission of Oxford University Press.

Library of Congress Cataloging-in-Publication Data
Virgil, author.
 [Aeneid. Selections. English]
 Vergil's Aeneid : the essential books / translated from the Latin with notes and introduction by Barry B. Powell.
   pages cm
 Includes bibliographical references and index.
 ISBN 978-0-19-020496-9
 I. Powell, Barry B., translator II. Title.
 PA6807.A5P69134   2015
 873'.01--dc23
                                                                    2015002141

To W. S. Anderson, who showed the way

Contents

List of Maps and Figures   ix
Foreword   xi
Acknowledgments   xv
About the Translator   xvi
Maps   xvii
Timeline of Roman History Through Augustus   xxii
Genealogical Chart   xxiv

Introduction   1
BOOK 1: The Shores of Africa   17
BOOK 2: The Fall of Troy   48
BOOK 4: The Death of Dido   77
BOOK 6: Descent into the Underworld   101
BOOK 7: The Seeds of War (lines 1–120; 230–389; 659–end)   138
BOOK 8: The Shield of Aeneas (lines 1–176; 352–end)   150
BOOK 9: Turnus Besieges the Trojan Camp (lines 152–391)   173
BOOK 10: The Deaths of Pallas, Lausus, and Mezentius
           (lines 1–116; 408–552; 626–end)   182
BOOK 11: The Glory of Camilla (lines 416–704)   199
BOOK 12: The Death of Turnus (lines 384–end)   209

Bibliography   225
Credits   227
Index/Glossary   229

List of Maps and Figures

Maps

MAP I: The Troad xvi
MAP II: The Mediterranean xvii
MAP III: Aeneas' Journey xviii
MAP IV: Italy xix
MAP V: Rome xx

Figures

I.1. *Vergil and the Muses*, Roman mosaic, AD third century 3
I.2. *Pietas*, Roman coin, AD 138 12
1.1. *Juno Asking Aeolus to Release the Winds*, by Boucher, 1769 21
1.2. *Venus Appears to Aeneas*, by da Cortona, 1631 30
1.3. *Dido Building Carthage*, by Turner, 1815 38
1.4. *Aeneas Introducing Cupid Dressed as Ascanius to Dido*, by Tiepolo, 1757 46
2.1. *Aeneas Telling Dido of His Misfortunes at Troy*, by Guérin, 1815 49
2.2. *Laocoön and His Sons*, by anonymous ancient artist, c. first century BC/AD first century 57
2.3. *The Laocoön*, by El Greco, 1610–1614 58
2.4. *The Rape of Cassandra*, by Langlois, 1810 64
2.5. *Helen Saved by Venus from the Wrath of Aeneas*, by Sablet, 1779 70
2.6. *Aeneas Fleeing Troy*, by Batoni, 1750 74
4.1. *Aeneas and Dido*, Roman mosaic, c. AD 340 82
4.2. *Aeneas and Dido*, from the commentary on Vergil by Servius, 1469 84
4.3. *Mercury Orders Aeneas to Leave Dido*, by Samachini, c. 1570 87
4.4. *Dido's Death*, by Rubens, c. 1630 99
6.1. *Daedalus, Pasiphaë, and Icarus*, fresco from Pompeii, c. AD 60 103
6.2A. *Passageway to the Sibyl's cave*, c. 500 BC 106
6.2B. *The Sibyl's cave* 107
6.3. *Hecatê*, by Blake, 1795 112
6.4. *Aeneas, the Sibyl, and Charon*, by Crespi, c. 1695 118
6.5. *Aeneas and the Sybil in the Underworld*, by Master of the Aeneid, c. 1530 126
6.6. *Aeneas and His Father in the Elysian Fields*, by Conca, 1735 130

7.1. *The Sibyl Takes Aeneas to His Companions* (top); and *Aeneas' Departure from Cumae* (bottom), from the *Eneide* by Heinrich von Veldeke, c. 1220   139
7.2. *Allecto Rousing Amata Against Aeneas*, woodblock print, sixteenth century   147
8.1. *Aeneas and Ascanius Discover the Sow with Thirty Piglets*, Roman relief, c. AD 150   153
8.2. *Aeneas with King Evander and Pallas*, by da Cortona, 1654   156
8.3. *Venus Asking Vulcan for Arms for Aeneas*, by Spranger, 1610   160
8.4. *Aeneas Receiving the Arms of Vulcan*, by de Lairesse, 1668   167
9.1. *Euryalus and Nisus at the Trojan Council*, Vatican Vergil, c. 400   176
10.1. *Jupiter and Juno*, by Figino, c. 1590   186
10.2. *Aeneas Kills Lausus*, illustration by Hollar (1607–1677)   196
11.1. *Camilla and Metabus Escaping into Exile*, woodcut illustration from Steinhöwel's translation of Boccaccio's *De mulieribus claris*, c. 1474   202
11.2. *Camilla Slaying the Son of Aunus*, illustration by Hollar (1607–1677)   205
11.3. *The Death of Camilla*, by Carlandi, 1810–1814   207
12.1. *Aeneas in Combat*, illustration from von Veldeke, c. 1220   211
12.2. *The Death of Turnus*, by Giordano, 1688   222

Foreword

Very few people have translated both Homer's *Iliad* and *Odyssey* and Vergil's *Aeneid*, as Barry Powell has now so successfully done. The epics are not just in different languages: they come from different universes. Homer's expanding Greek world of the eighth century BC was home to an aggressive seafaring warrior culture that eagerly drank in oral songs about their counterparts in a glamorous but long-lost world of gods and heroes, a world that came alive only in the songs of the bards. Almost eight hundred years later, Vergil wrote for a highly literate imperial ruling class. His audience were masters not only of the Greek-speaking East but of Western Europe and Northern Africa: they were biliterate and bilingual, reading and writing and speaking both Latin and Greek, and they were heirs to Greek and Roman political and literary traditions going back hundreds of years. Vergil's epic, despite feeling very Homeric in fundamental ways from its first words on, is a radically different kind of document from the song of Homer that was captured at the end of the Dark Ages by a literate scribe.

Once you have read and reread Homer you can start to feel that every aspect of human experience is in the *Iliad* and the *Odyssey* somewhere. Yet not everything is in Homer, and Vergil's epic concentrates on aspects of human experience that were simply not part of the world of Homer and his audience. Most importantly, there is no history in Homer. Homer's heroes live in the dim past, and his song makes that past come alive for the moment, so that there is a "past" in Homer, but Homer has no conception of a historical framework for human experience. The heroes are then, and the audience is now, but Homer has no concern with establishing a continuity between that "then" and this "now." Homer's heroes look ahead a generation, to their children, and they have a vague idea that they may live in song if they do glorious enough deeds, but there is no interest in how human experience is part of an institution that spans many generations, or in how the experience of a society or a state is given meaningful shape by the work of historical retrospective.

Vergil, by contrast, lived in a world where the writing of history had been flourishing for four hundred years, ever since the first Greek historian Herodotus, and in the *Aeneid* history is everywhere—not just in the banal sense that the poem is about Roman history, but also in the sense that it is about how history is constructed and shaped, how history is made comprehensible and meaningful, how people make sense of their past. The poem's first sentence already charts the historical plot, taking us in one sweep of seven lines from Homer's Troy to Augustus's Rome. Barry Powell breaks the opening Latin sentence into three English sentences in order to make it readable for a modern audience, but the fourth word in the original Latin sentence is *Troiae* and the last word is *Romae*. These two layers of time are felt all the way through the poem, from the distant past of Aeneas' heroic and quasi-mythical time, over eleven hundred years before Vergil, down to the "now" of Augustus's Rome, when Vergil was writing the poem between 30 and 19 BC.

The link between these two time frames is provided by the bloodline link between Aeneas' son Iulus and the patrician clan of the Iulii, who said that the name of their clan came from this man and who had been bragging about the connection for a long time before the birth of Julius Caesar, the adoptive father of Augustus. To us, the fact that this particular family came out on top after the bloody collapse of the Republic is just an accident, but it is hard to imagine that it looked that way to Augustus or Vergil. Any other of the top hundred families could have emerged victorious from the civil wars, after all: the fact that it was the family who claimed descent from the grandson of Venus is to us a fantastic fluke, an outrageous statistical improbability, yet Vergil constructs the pattern of history in such a way that the link between the first founder and the current ruler appears to be the inevitable end of the entire progression of Roman history.

The period of the poem's composition, then, was one that made it necessary to reconsider the patterns of Roman history. No one at the time could know what the future held, but it was obvious to Vergil and his contemporaries that Caesar's adopted son, renamed Augustus in 27 BC, would be the supreme figure in any conceivable order. These were years of ongoing political experimentation, as Augustus and the new governing class felt their way toward a symbiosis that would prevent recurrence of anarchy while avoiding the appearance of outright monarchy, and that would respect the Romans' traditional veneration of inherited tradition while allowing for the creation of unprecedented political and social patterns.

The story of Aeneas—moving from one continent to another, undergoing and enforcing great transformations in the process—transplants these contemporary Augustan preoccupations with transition, continuity, and change into the remote time of the poem's action. In the course of the poem we move from the East to the West, from Troy to Italy, as Aeneas moves from being a Trojan toward being something else, a kind of Roman in embryo. Even in such minor matters as sacrificing with his head covered Aeneas is starting to behave in distinctively Roman ways; above all, in advocating the amalgamation of national groups into larger units with a new identity he anticipates the political genius of the historical Romans. The poem's migratory movement, together with its wholesale assimilation of Homer, acts out another great transition, the transition of Greek culture to Italy: just as the people of ancient Italy become the inheritors of Troy, so the people of Vergil's Italy become the inheritors of Greece. The very location of the poem in time is transitional, at the pivot between myth and history: the poem's characters are moving out of the era of Homer into the era of what Vergil would have considered non-fabulous history.

The beginning and end of the poem's vast time scales are linked, then, by the family connection between Aeneas and Augustus—fortuitous to us, no doubt providential to many people at the time. Vergil strengthens these links throughout the poem, binding together the moment of origin and the contemporary end result. In this way, the poem participates in both of the dominant ways of constructing history, the aetiological (from Greek *aition*, "cause," "beginning") and the teleological (from Greek *telos*, "end," "purpose," "goal," "accomplishment"). The poem, that is to say, explains the present state of affairs not only by referring it to its origins (everything in the world is the way it is because of the "beginning," the *aition*, which is narrated in the poem), but also by describing the present as the outcome, the fulfillment, the *telos*, of all previous experience. In the historical plot of the *Aeneid*, Aeneas (the *aition*) and Augustus (the *telos*) are joined together as the cause and the purpose by a mutually self-reinforcing explanatory scheme. Book 8 is the most condensed embodiment of this theme, packed as it is with aetiological explanations of all kinds, and culminating in the image of Augustus as the inheritor of the historical process set in motion by Aeneas. The shield that Aeneas receives from his mother at the end of Book 8, with its depiction of Augustus' triumph over Antony and Cleopatra, is an icon of the poem itself. When the master craftsman, the divine image-maker Vulcan, makes this shield, he works on fluid amorphous stuff ("The bronze and gold flow in streams"), and he beats it into meaningful shape. Vergil does the same, making a unified, meaningful shape out of the fluidity of the past, a round shape, the shield, a world, in fact *the* world, the world of Rome and Augustus. The power of the *Aeneid* to impose its meaning and shape upon history is an image of Augustus's power to impose his meaning and shape upon history.

Set against these powerful structures of triumphalism and linear progress, however, are countervailing currents of flux, instability, and mutability. Cyclical patterns also pervade the poem, of which some are potentially beneficial in nature (the return of the Golden Age), while some destabilize faith in the durability or value of human establishments. When Aeneas goes to the site of the future city of Rome in Book 8, for example, he sees there ruins of earlier settlements, when Rome is still centuries in the future, and he wanders through scenes of rustic pastoralism that are all too close to the images of post-imperial desolation that Greek poets had associated with the former glories of Homer's Mycenae or Argos—all too close, as well, to the fate that overtook the metropolis in the Middle Ages. Similarly, the poem cannot shut out the future beyond Augustus. The parade of Roman history at the end of Book 6 closes not with Augustus, but with the death in 23 BC of his designated heir, Marcellus, leaving the forward impetus of Roman history uncontained, as the audience is left wondering what or who will follow Augustus now that this future has been removed.

In all these ways the *Aeneid* is a great poem of history, both as lived experience and as something constructed by people responding to the needs of society. If it is radically different from Homer in this respect, the presence of Homer is still always felt. The very first line puts the relationship with the original epics on display, for "arms" (*arma*) looks to Homer's *Iliad*, while "the man" (*uirum*) looks to Homer's *Odyssey*, whose first word is "man" (*andra*). Vergil often explicitly reminds us of Homeric passages, using language that calls attention to his poetic operation. When Aeneas speaks to his son for the only time in the poem, for example, as he goes to fight Turnus in the middle of Book 12, he puts on his armor, kisses his son through his helmet, and says, "When you are mature, remember: Let your father Aeneas/and your uncle Hector inspire you by their example." In telling his son to "remember" the example of Hector, Aeneas is also instructing the reader to remember *Iliad* Book 6, where Hector likewise kisses his son. As this case shows, however, the departures from Homer are regularly the real point of the imitation. In Homer, Hector's baby son cries when he sees his father, unrecognizable in his battle equipment and helmet, so that Hector takes off his helmet to cradle the boy in his arms and pray for his future glory. In Vergil, this human moment is reversed, as the "Roman" hero puts on his helmet before he kisses his son, interposing a barrier of iron between himself and his child in an almost exaggeratedly metaphorical gesture.

As we may see from the example of the Greekless Dante, to whom Homer was only a name, it is possible to read Vergil without knowing a word of Homer and still penetrate to the core of the poem, but readers of Barry Powell's splendid new *Aeneid*, who may also read his splendid *Iliad* and *Odyssey*, would be depriving themselves of a great deal if they did not do so.

Denis Feeney
Princeton University

Acknowledgments

I would like to thank my wife, who read the entire manuscript with an eagle's eye and made more suggestions and corrections than I can count.

I also wish to thank the following readers, in addition to those who wished to remain anonymous, who read early samples of the translations. I have taken advantage of their wise recommendations and am very grateful for their suggestions: Richard Thomas, Harvard University; Leah Kronenberg, Rutgers University; Laurel Fulkerson, Florida State University; Jennifer Rea, University of Florida; Christopher Brunelle, St. Olaf College; Sarah Spence, University of Georgia; W. Marshall Johnston, Fresno Pacific University; Christine Perkell, Emory University; and Jan Verstraete, Montclair State University.

As with my other translations with Oxford University Press, I am grateful for the support and expert editing provided by Charles Cavaliere, executive editor, and Marianne Paul, production editor. Christi Sheehan and Francelle Carapetyan also provided invaluable assistance.

About the Translator

BARRY B. POWELL is the Halls-Bascom Professor of Classics Emeritus at the University of Wisconsin–Madison, where he taught for thirty-four years. He is the author of the widely used textbook *Classical Myth* (8th ed., 2014) and many other books. His *A Short Introduction to Classical Myth* (2001, translated into German) is a summary study of the topic. *Homer and the Origin of the Greek Alphabet* (1991, translated into modern Greek) advances the thesis that a single man invented the Greek alphabet expressly in order to record the poems of Homer. *Writing and the Origins of Greek Literature* (2003) develops the consequence of this thesis. His critical study *Homer* (2nd ed., 2004, translated into Italian) is widely read as an introduction for philologists, historians, and students of literature. *A New Companion to Homer* (1997, with Ian Morris, translated into modern Greek) is a comprehensive review of modern scholarship on Homer. His *The Greeks: History, Culture, Society* (2nd ed., 2009, with Ian Morris, translated into Chinese) is a complete review widely used in college courses. His *Writing: Theory and History of the Technology of Civilization* (2009, translated into Arabic) attempts to create a scientific terminology and taxonomy for the study of writing. His textbook *World Myth* appeared in 2014, and his translations of the *Iliad* and the *Odyssey* appeared in 2013 and 2014. He has published on the poetry of Vergil and other Latin poets of the imperial period. He has also written novels, poetry, and a screenplay.

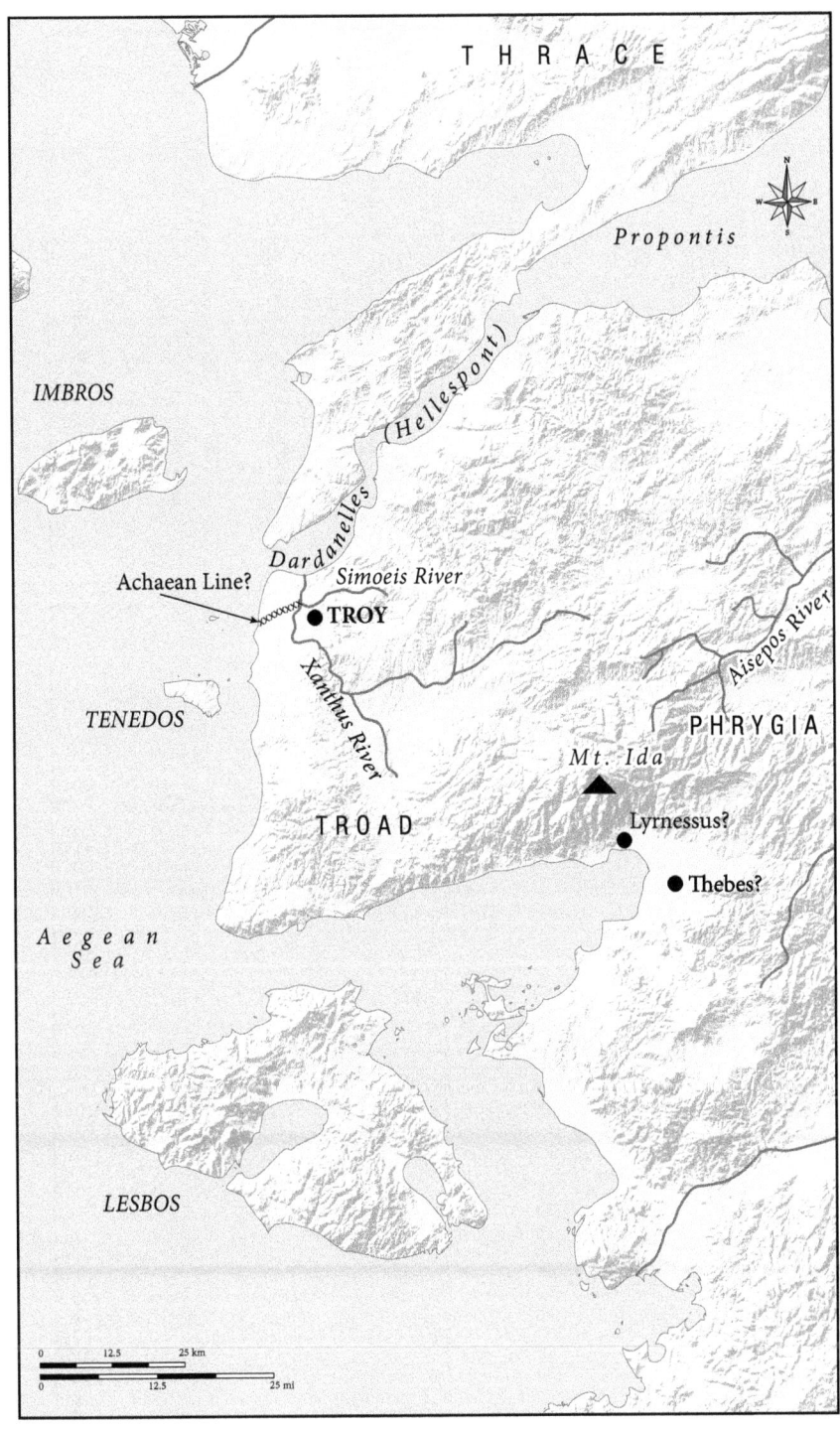

MAP I The Troad

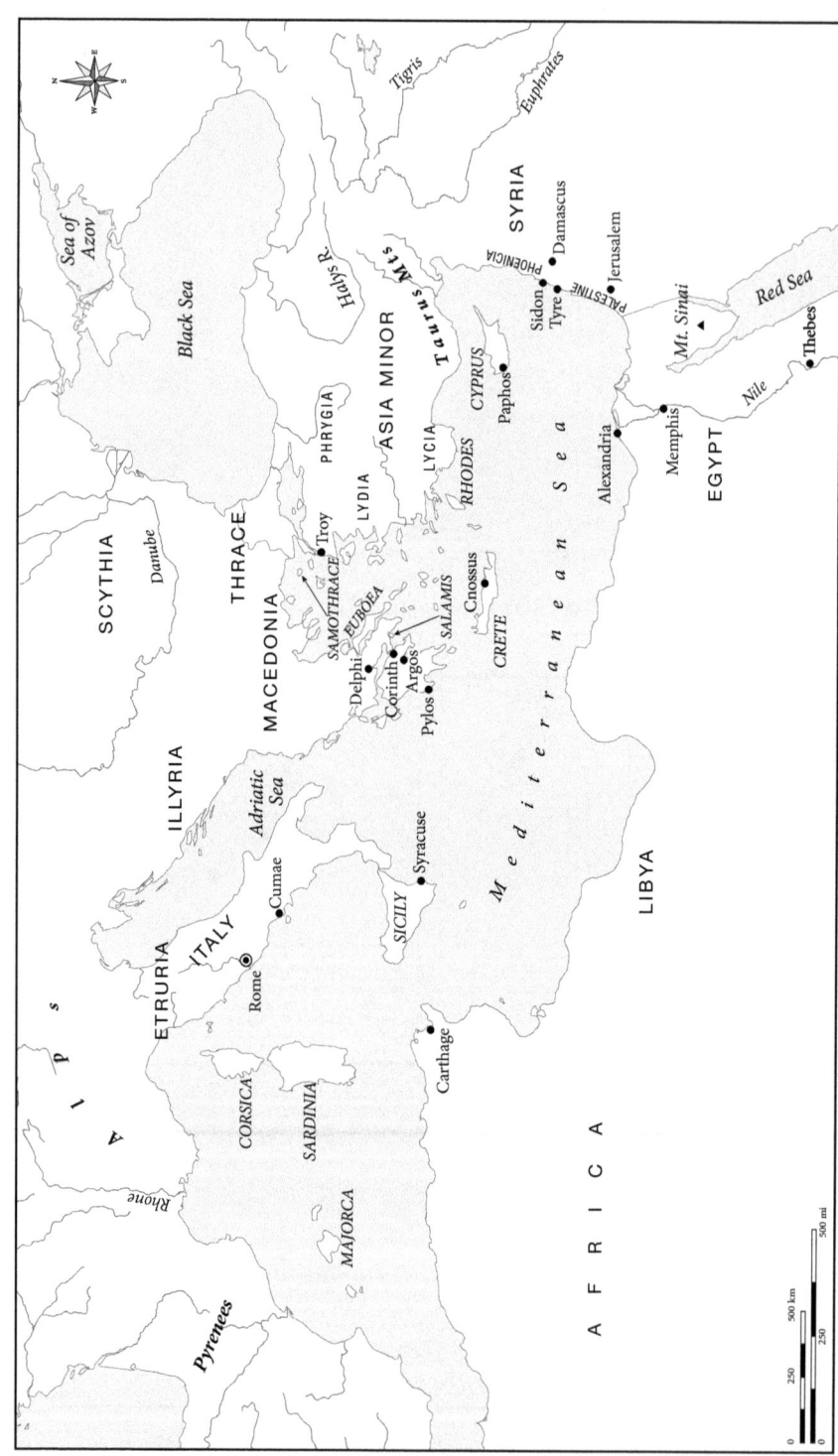

MAP II The Mediterranean

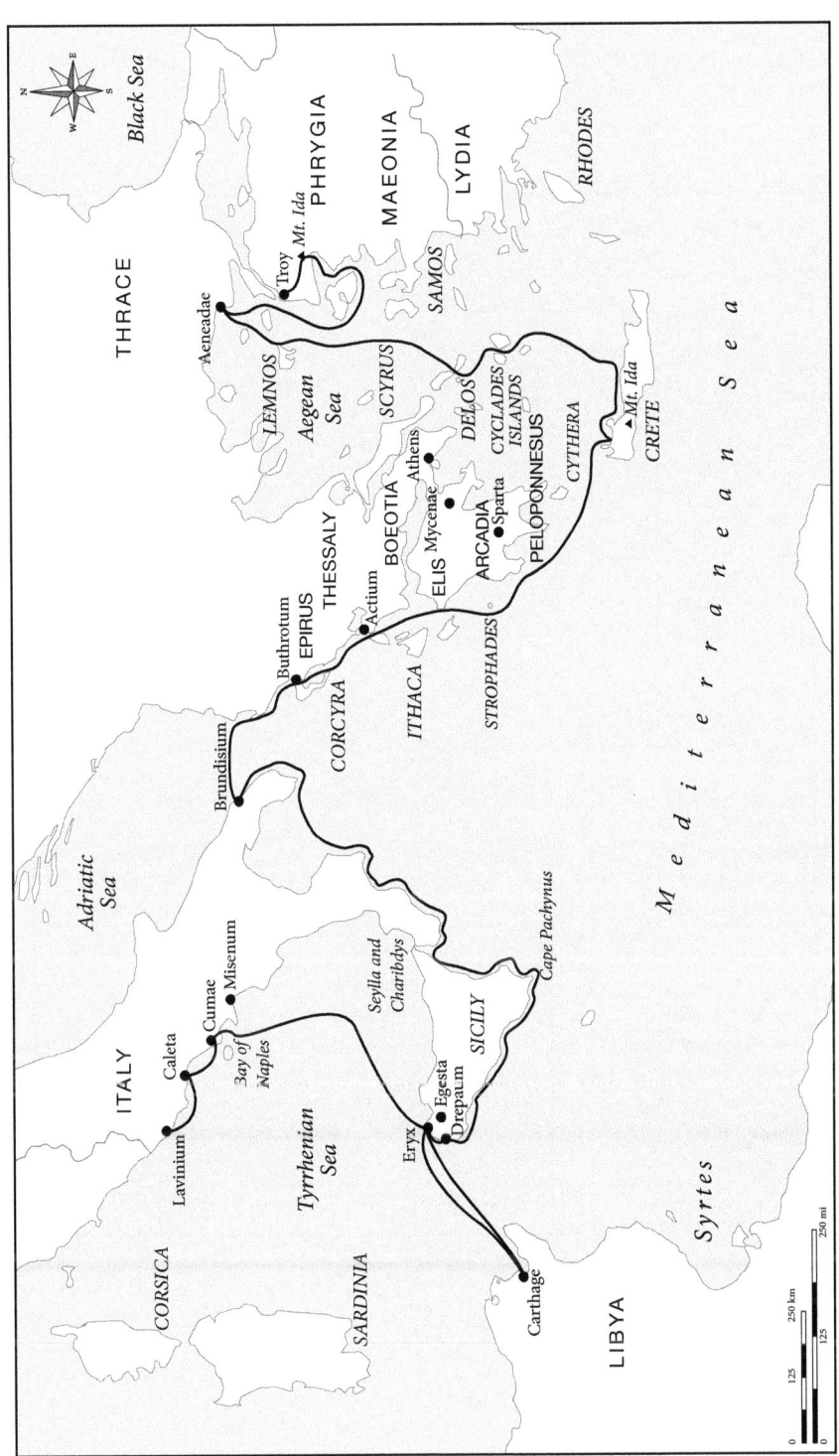

MAP III Aeneas' Journey

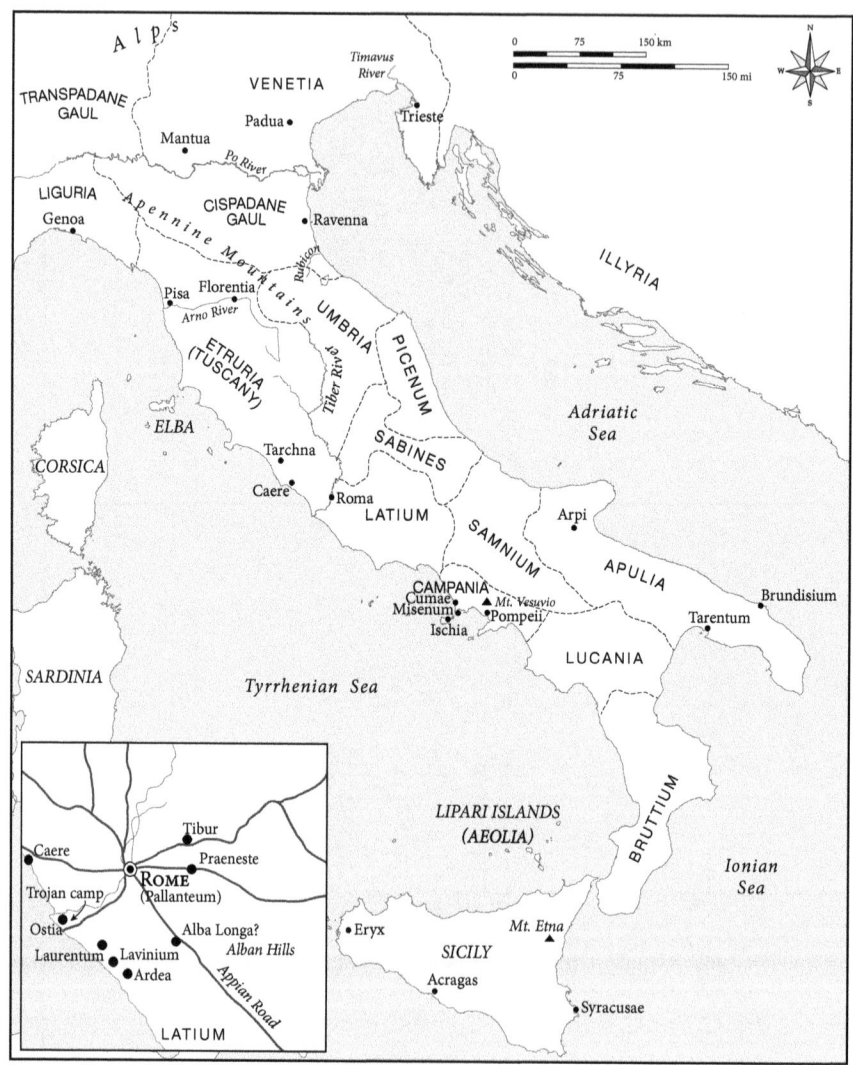

MAP IV   Italy

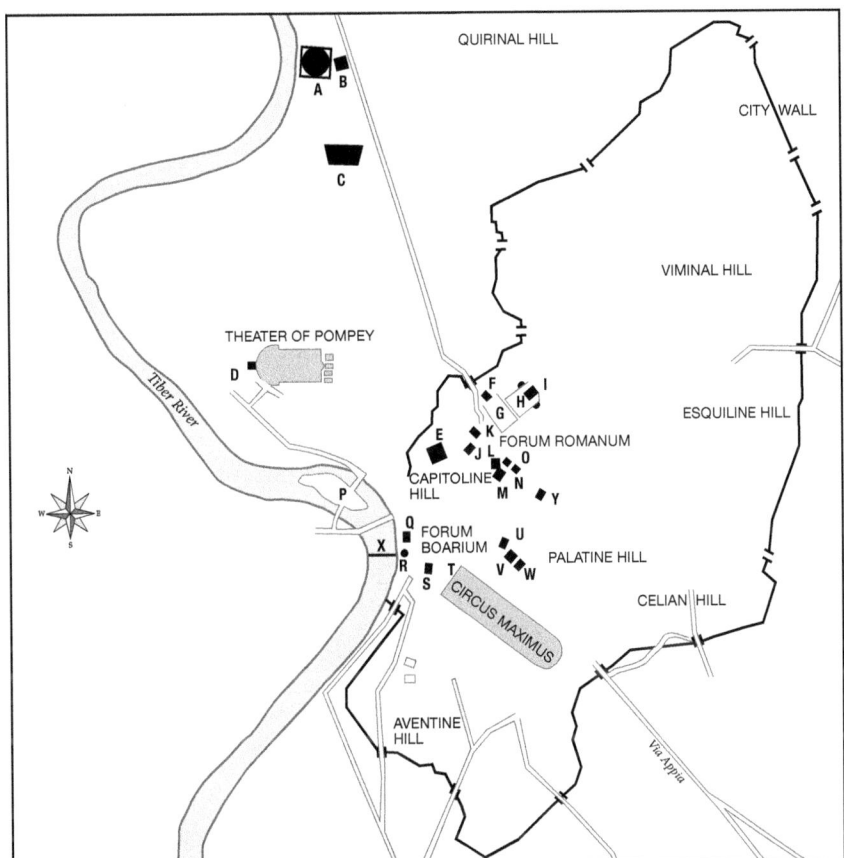

A. Mausoleum of Augustus; B. *Ara Pacis Augustae* ("Altar of Augustan Peace"); C. *Horologium Augusti* ("sundial of Augustus"); D. Temple of Venus Victrix ("conqueror"); E. Temple of Jupiter Optimus Maximus ("best, greatest"); F. Temple of Venus Genetrix ("begetter"); G. Forum of Caesar; H. Forum of Augustus; I. Temple of Mars Ultor ("avenger"); J. Temple of Saturn; K. Temple of Concord; L. Temple of the Divine Julius Caesar; M. Temple of Castor and Pollux; N. Temple of Vesta; O. Regia ("king's house"); P. Temple of Aesculapius; Q. Temple of Portunus; R. Temple of Hercules Victor (? "conqueror"); S. *Ara Maxima* ("greatest altar"); T. Temple of Hercules Invictus (*Herculis invicti ara maxima*); U. Temple of the Magna Mater ("great mother"); V. House of Augustus; W. Temple of Apollo on the Palatine; X. *Pons Sublicius*; Y. Arch of Titus.

MAP V Imperial Rome

Timeline of Roman History Through Augustus

753 BC	Foundation of Rome
390 BC	Rome is sacked by the Gauls
264–241 BC	First Punic War
218–202 BC	Second Punic War
168 BC	Romans win the Macedonian War, conquering Greece
149–146 BC	Third Punic War
133–120 BC	The reforming Gracchi brothers are murdered
71 BC	Spartacus is killed and his rebel army destroyed
70 BC	Vergil is born in the Po Valley
63 BC	Octavian is born
60 BC	Pompey, Crassus, and Caesar collude to share power
58–50 BC	Caesar conquers Gaul
49 BC	Caesar crosses the Rubicon in order to take Rome
48 BC	Caesar destroys the senatorial armies under Pompey at the battle of Pharsalus in Greece
44 BC	Caesar elects himself dictator, and in March is killed by Brutus and Cassius
42 BC	Octavian and Marc Antony destroy the senatorial armies under Brutus and Cassius and divide the world between themselves

31 BC	Battle of Actium in which Octavian triumphs over Antony and Cleopatra
30 BC	Antony and Cleopatra commit suicide
27 BC	Octavian's name is changed to Augustus, becoming Rome's first emperor
19 BC	Vergil dies at Brindisi
13 BC	Augustus dedicates the *Ara Pacis*, "Altar of Peace," in the Roman Forum
AD 14	Augustus dies

Genealogical Chart

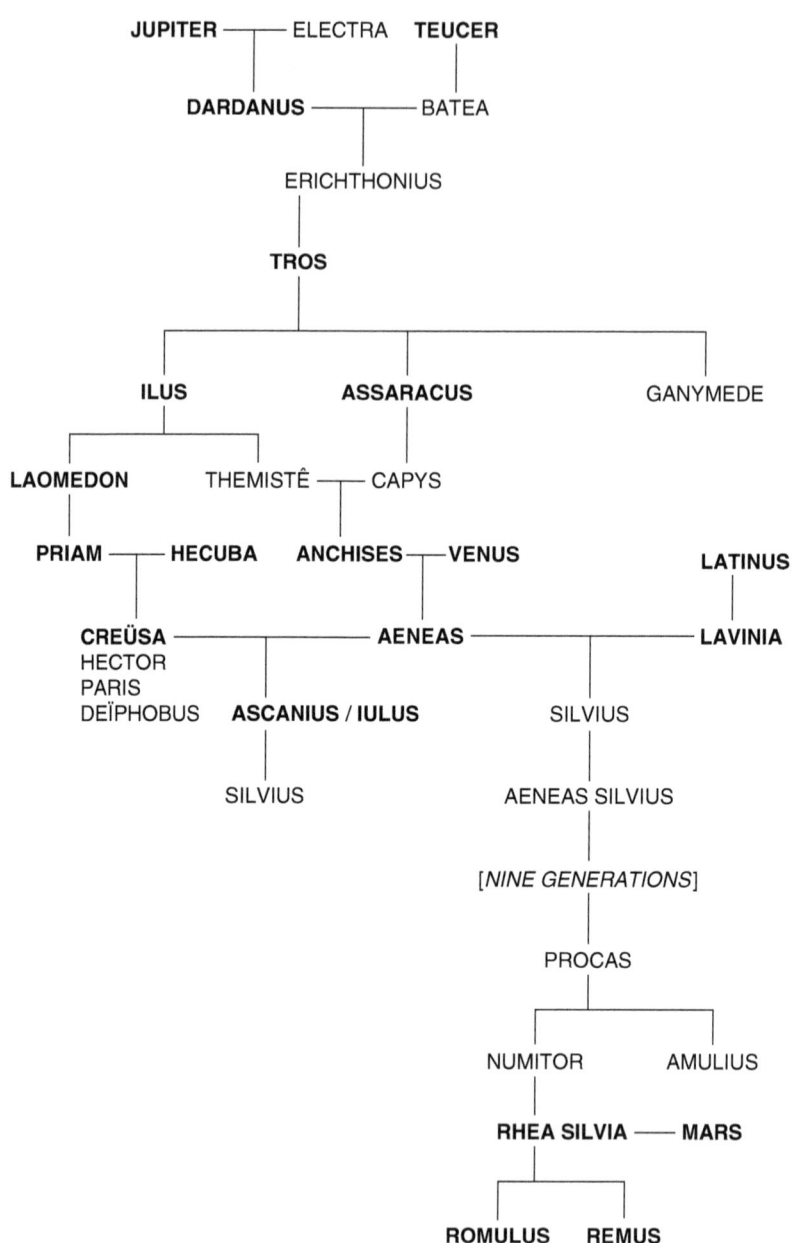

VERGIL'S *AENEID*:

The Essential Books

Introduction

The *Aeneid* is a difficult poem. To understand, and enjoy, this poem, you must have a lust for knowledge of the past, to know how it was in the days of Roman ascendancy over the world, in the household of Augustus (63 BC–AD 14), the first Roman emperor, who held absolute power over everything that happened in the state. This poem is dedicated to his power and his place in the world.

In Rome before Augustus—originally named Octavian but called Augustus ("the one who increases") after 27 BC—power was shared by a class of Roman nobles, perhaps forty families. These were the Roman senators, the "elders," who had forged Roman power over five hundred years, competing among themselves for status and position. Under the leadership of this highly competent class, Roman power, entangled in endless wars at first in Italy, then in the West, then in the East, had expanded until it encompassed all of the Mediterranean world and much of the hinterland. The system worked brilliantly for five hundred years, but then it did not work. The stakes had grown too high. There was too much wealth and too much power, and both drifted into the hands of a few men, who struggled with one another, each to be the boss of all.

With an army at their backs, only law and respect for Roman traditions held the warlords in check until Julius Caesar crossed the Rubicon River on January 10, 49 BC, with his men under arms. That was against the law. He justified his breaking of the law by noting, with undoubted truth, that if he returned to Rome unprotected, his enemies would kill him. There are always good reasons for breaking the law, when it suits you. When Caesar crossed the Rubicon, he said, "The die is cast" (*iacta alea est*). Truly it was. Now not law, but naked power would have the final say.

THE PURPOSE OF ROMAN POWER

The societies that the Romans met in their drive for power in the last days of antiquity were very old, using nonalphabetic writing systems of their own that went back three thousand years. These ethnic enclaves—for example, in Egypt and Persia—were proud of their identities and defensive of them. Such ancient peoples were well organized, immensely wealthy, and numerous. Their patterns of political behavior were always the same. A great man would arise, attract a following, lead his armies forth, slaughter the enemy, and take everything. So Thutmosis III slaughtered the Canaanites in the second millennium BC, leading his people, the Egyptians, to victory. But the sons of the great man would be less than their fathers, less than Alexander. Empires rose, then fell, as their leaders died and their families decayed.

The Roman system of conquest was different and more efficient, a form of government wherein a self-sacrificing, idealistic oligarchy warred against much less efficient foreign forms of government, usually monarchical. Depending on leaders drawn by election from the senatorial class, and not on great men who would suddenly arise on their own merits and as suddenly fall, the Roman system was superior to those of its enemies. The Roman commanders were elected, and their power was not absolute because they needed always to obey the laws enacted by the senate—for example, do not cross the Rubicon with your men under arms.

In morality the Romans admired nobility, and in intellectual matters they admired the law. To the Roman the law was all. When Julius Caesar crossed the Rubicon, he gave his personal enemies an intellectual basis for assassination. The next-to-last words of Julius Caesar are reported to be *ista quidem vis set*, "This is violence": violence is against the law. (His last words were directed to his treacherous friend Brutus, spoken in Greek: *kai su teknon*, "You too, my child?")

The Romans triumphed over all the particularisms, the racial and ethnic hatreds, of other peoples by offering them a rule under impartial law. Written in alphabetic characters that everyone could understand, the law applied to all, even to the small governing class. If you didn't like it, the Romans legions would make that a matter of indifference. As for your religion, no one cared about that, so long as you didn't preach against Roman power. The Roman was willing to die for this way of life, and many did.

Augustus did not obtain absolute power by legal means, as everybody knew, but by destroying his rivals in power. Yet it was prudent to pretend that he had followed the law, that the world itself was governed by law, the law of Fate. What had happened in the first century BC in the terrible civil wars first between Julius Caesar and Pompey the Great, and then between Octavian (Augustus) and Marc Antony, however ugly and vile and hateful, had to turn out this way—that is why it did so turn out. All that took place happened in accordance with the universal law that permeates all being, that destined Augustus to come to his ascendancy.

There can be no doubt that Vergil (70–19 BC) wrote the *Aeneid* under direct political influence. Augustus knew that if he were to be seen as not just one more warlord, but as a man of destiny intended by the forces that rule the cosmos to wield Roman power, to benefit the world, to shed happiness on all, then he needed a *vates*, a "prophet," to proclaim these truths.

Augustus needed somebody to say such things, but not in an obvious and stupid way. He needed somebody who really believed them, someone whose words could be repeated by loyal Romans everywhere, whose words could become the basis for Roman education and could tell a Roman who he was, where he had come from, and where he was destined to go. Fate had designed these sufferings. They were for a purpose. The Romans were for a purpose. Otherwise all that had happened was just one more gang war, and one more warlord bullying his enemies. Augustus and his propagandistic program stand firmly behind the *Aeneid*, and we can never forget it.

FIGURE I.1 Vergil and the Muses, Roman mosaic, AD third century. The poet is dressed in a Roman toga and sits between Clio and Melpomenê, the Muses of history and tragedy, reading lines 8–9 of his *Aeneid*, where he invokes the Muses. The Latin reads: *Musa, mihi causas memora, quo numine laeso quidve*, "O Muse, tell to me the causes, her divinity [Juno's] being offended by what, or [suffering] what …" Clio holds a papyrus with some history text on it; Melpomenê holds a tragic mask. Vergil is like a third Muse, the Muse of epic poetry.

ROMAN HISTORY

Exactly how *did* a small village on the Tiber become the center of one of the largest empires the world has ever known, and the most successful? Many have wondered about this extraordinary and unparalleled development in human history.

By the eighth century BC, the metal-rich hills of Italy's western coast, inhabited by indigenous non–Indo-European Etruscans, had become a magnet for Greek colonists and Phoenician traders. One of the oldest known inscriptions (c. 740 BC) in the Greek alphabet was found on a small island in the Bay of

Naples. In dactylic hexameters, it already refers to a famous cup owned by Nestor in Homer's *Iliad*. Homer's poems were evidently known in the far West within a generation of Homer's having created them around 800 BC.

Rome's appetite for territory and resources suited its equally voracious appetite for cultural forms, especially Greek and Etruscan ones. It was characteristic of Rome to take over cultural forms from other peoples and remake them as her own, for the essence of being a Roman was a love of law and a love of noble conduct, not an ability to paint pretty pictures.

Archaeological investigation shows that the ancestors of the Romans entered the Italian peninsula as early as 1800 BC. By 1000 BC, they had occupied the land south of the Tiber, bordered by the sea and inland to the later site of Rome. These were the Latini (la-**tēn**-ē), a tribal people who gave their name to LATIUM (**lā**-shum), the territory west of the central Apennine range and south of the Tiber River as far as the fertile plain of CAMPANIA. Campania is like a flat bowl lined by mountains behind the BAY OF NAPLES and its coastal settlements of Greeks, especially at CUMAE (see MAPS III, IV).[1]

Cumae was the first western Greek colony, made up of Greek settlers from the long island of EUBOEA ("good for cows") just east of mainland Greece (see Map II). Euboea was a backwater by the classical period of the fifth century BC, when ATHENS was dominant, but in the early days of Greek history the Euboeans were the richest and most powerful Greeks, the earliest possessors of the Greek alphabet. At Cumae, the founder of the Roman race, Aeneas, son of Anchises, descends into the underworld to learn the secrets of Rome's destiny, tied to the world of the Greeks.

The plain of Latium is north of Campania and cut off from Campania by an extension of the central Apennine range that runs down the spine of Italy, then wheels around in a spur to touch the coast, separating Latium from Campania. Dominating Latium on the south and east are the ALBAN HILLS, where many important Latin towns rose up in the sixth and fifth centuries BC, including ALBA LONGA at the western edge of the hills (see inset, Map IV).

Alba Longa is by tradition the first Roman town, founded in legend by Iulus (ī-**ū**-lus), the son of Aeneas, claimed as an ancestor by the Julian clan to which Julius Caesar and Augustus belonged. LAVINIUM, named after Aeneas' bride Lavinia, lay more toward the coast but also figures in stories about the early Roman people. Hundreds of years later, Romulus and Remus, descendants of Aeneas, will be born in Alba Longa. Exposed as infants, they will be nourished by a she-wolf and grow up to found the city of Rome around 750 BC, according to the conventional (and imaginary) date.

Reconstructing early Roman history is a kind of game of coming out the way you want, but nonetheless, working backward from legendary accounts, supported to some extent by archaeological finds, we can say that in its early days

---

[1] It will be my practice to put in SMALL CAPITALS the names of places that are on one of the five maps at the beginning of this book the first time the term appears in the Introduction or in a book of the poem.

Rome was ruled by kings. The latest king, however, was not a Roman, but was from ETRURIA, the land north of the Tiber River. The Etruscans were a strange people who spoke a non–Indo-European language of unknown affinity. They were believed to have come from the East at some time, but modern researchers have been unable to confirm this tradition. They deeply influenced the Romans, and much of what we think of as Roman is really Etruscan.

Perhaps about 500 BC an alliance of wealthy landowning Latin families, the patricians (from *patres*, "fathers"), destroyed the foreign Etruscan monarchy and took power into their own hands. They founded the Roman Republic (*res publica*, "public affair"). Thereafter the patricians met together in the senate, the "body of old men," to pass laws and decide on peace and war. Those excluded from this very small and privileged class were called *plebeians*, "commoners," who, especially in the fourth century BC, struggled to gain their own representation and voice in affairs of the state. The plebeian struggle met with real but limited success.

Under the Republic, elections, normally fixed, were held among the members of the ruling patrician oligarchy. The legislative branch held the power, whereas the weaker executive branch consisted of two consuls, elected annually. The power of the consuls was checked by their short term of office and by the power of veto each held over the other. But a consul did possess *imperium*, the "power" to command the army and enforce the law, including imposition of the death penalty. The symbol of *imperium* was the *fasces*, an ax surrounded by a bundle of rods. The rods were for whipping and the ax for beheading. (From this word comes the modern term "fascism," because the twentieth-century Italian political leader Benito Mussolini claimed to be reconstructing the ancient Roman state.)

In the third and second centuries BC, Rome fought its deadliest foe during the terrible Punic Wars, between 264 BC and 146 BC, against the aggressive and expansionist power of Carthage in North Africa. The Carthaginians were a Semitic-speaking people from the Levant. These wars were the largest and deadliest ever fought on this planet, up to that time. During the invasion of Hannibal in the Second Punic War (218–203 BC), it appeared that Rome would be destroyed. During this period the senate showed its coolness under fire and the threat of destruction, its versatility, and its ability to function in response to catastrophe and to be victorious. These qualities greatly enhanced the prestige and power of the senate, as well as the wealth of the Roman ruling class.

After the Punic Wars, the Roman state took over virtually the entire Mediterranean world, not only the old Greek states, but also what had once been the great kingdoms of the East. Having set up a government controlled by small cliques belonging to a restricted social class, the patrician families fabricated legendary traditions about their ancestors to justify their monopoly on power. Thus Julius Caesar (100–44 BC), a key figure in the disintegration of the Republic, claimed descent directly from Iulus, the son of Aeneas, whose mother was Venus.

But Caesar was in his enemies' eyes a man who placed personal ambition before the interests of the state—that is, the interests of the privileged patrician class. Backed by legions hardened by long and harsh campaigns in Gaul (France),

Julius Caesar marched on Rome in 49 BC. He swept all before him with brilliance and ruthless efficiency. He destroyed his rival Pompey (106–48 BC), the enemy warlord and his former son-in-law, and in defiance of Roman tradition became absolute master of the state.

Julius Caesar reformed the calendar and centralized the bureaucracy, then forgave his enemies in a conspicuous gesture of Roman *clementia*, "forgiveness of one's enemies," to prove that he was an honorable Roman after all. In return for the favor, a broad conspiracy of senators murdered him in the theater of Pompey on the Ides of March (March 15) in 44 BC. Not so coincidentally, Caesar's friend Marcus Brutus, a leader in the conspiracy against Caesar, claimed descent from an earlier tyrant-slayer also named Brutus, an alleged founder of the patrician oligarchic Republic five hundred years before.

With the murder of Caesar the state fell into chaos and came under threat from outside. The traditional carriers of Roman value, the senators, had lost their credibility. They may have made Rome great, but in their murderous greed, lust for power, and immorality they had become the enemies of stability.

Caesar's patrician enemies thought that his death would restore the Republic and the power of the senatorial oligarchy, but Caesar's party pulled together under Marc Antony (83–30 BC), one of his generals, and the young Octavian (63 BC–AD 14), later Augustus, his great-nephew and adoptive heir. These two men rallied the Caesarian legions behind them. If the name was Caesar, the cause was just—so thought the legions, as they destroyed the senatorial armies led by the conspirators Brutus and Cassius.

All power in the state now fell into the hands of Antony and Octavian. Everything was different, nothing could ever be the same. Marc Antony took the East and Octavian the West, where Rome was, where the real power lay. Antony succumbed to the charms of the Egyptian queen Cleopatra, descended from a general of Alexander the Great, and according to the official version, was corrupted by the evil and seductive charms of Eastern ways, and by a scheming, desperate woman who wanted Roman power.

Matters came to a head in a great naval battle between the two superpowers in 31 BC at ACTIUM on the northwestern shore of Greece. Octavian was victorious. Cleopatra and Antony fled to Egypt where in the next year, to avoid capture, they took their own lives, in 30 BC.

All power was now in the hands of a single man, Octavian. No one really wanted to challenge his power. Historians call this transformation the Roman Revolution, when power, *imperium*, passed from an elite oligarchy to a kind of monarchy. Roman society continued to be governed by its ruling class, but now under the jealous supervision of one man.

We might say that Octavian/Augustus was trapped by his own success. He had not wanted to be a tyrant, the king of all, and he would not take the title *rex*, "king." He called himself *princeps civitatis*, "first citizen of the state," the origin of our word "prince." He ruled over the principate. The old patrician oligarchic Republic had given way to a new quasi-monarchy. Modern historians call this new monarchy the Roman "empire," a period when *imperium* resided permanently in the hands of a single man and not with the representatives of a privileged social class.

Augustus calmed the remains of the old senatorial party, which under the empire remained an advisory elite, by retaining the outward trappings of Republican government. The religious, artistic, and literary program he sponsored was heavily propagandistic, with the aim of making the new regime appear to be a continuation of the old Republic that in reality had ceased to exist. Writers in this period, in searching for a tradition of national origin, often allude to the tales of early Rome, linking the present political situation with a mythical past.

Vergil is no exception.

THE ROMAN ADOPTION OF GREEK LITERARY FORMS

The Romans inherited the western Greek alphabet from the Etruscans, who took it from the Euboean Greeks living around the Bay of Naples, perhaps around 700 BC. Oddly, the Etruscans seem to have used the alphabet only for ritual calendars and for the writing of names—especially odd because they had a close familiarity with Greek myths and seem to have been able to read Greek. In any event, the Etruscans passed the technology to the Romans, whom they lived with and ruled for a while.

The Romans immediately began to experiment with writing down their own language, Latin. Other Italic people did the same, as well as several Eastern peoples, but written Latin became highly developed with elaborate rules and expected modes of expression. Literary Latin seems to appear in the third century BC. One of its pioneers was a man named Livius Andronicus (c. 280/260 BC–c. 200 BC), in fact a Greek, who wrote a Latin version of portions of the *Odyssey* using a native Latin meter called the Saturnian. The rules of the Saturnian are not well understood. Latin literature, then, begins with translation, practically unknown in other ancient literate traditions.

All the while, the Roman aristocracy was going to school to learn the Greek alphabet and read Homer, much as the Greeks did. A writer named Ennius (c. 239 BC–c. 169 BC), who overlapped with Livius Andronicus, was the first to shape Latin into the metrical pattern of Homer, that is, into dactylic hexameter. The dactylic hexameter is the most important meter in the history of Western literacy, so it is worth knowing the basics.

The basic pattern of dactylic hexameter in standard notation is:

Dactyl is Greek for finger, so *dactylic hexameter* means a line consisting of "six feet" (*hexameter*), each of which is a "finger long" (*dactylic*), that is, a long and two shorts. A foot is one finger, a sequence of three vowels in which the first is long and the next two short, or the two short vowels are resolved into one long vowel. Complex rules govern which vowels can be considered "long" and which "short," depending on the vowel's intrinsic nature and its position in relation to other consonants. If this sounds complicated, it is complicated, but Ennius first worked out the rules to impose this rhythm on the Latin language. All subsequent hexametric poetry in Latin descends from his innovations.

In fact the breakdown of the meter into "feet" is a convention of literacy that Homer himself could not have understood. Probably the Greek line consists of units brought together by an unconscious feeling. Vergil is using the meter in a self-conscious way that is basically unlike the usage of Homer, who is Vergil's model. We must remember that Homer no doubt dictated the *Iliad* and the *Odyssey* over months to a scribe, but that Vergil after working on the *Aeneid* for ten years was still not done. This situation fairly defines the difference between Vergil and Homer. Homer's poetry is the voice of a singer who lived long ago, and Vergil's poetry is the calculated creation of a man speaking to highly educated, snobbish possessors of worldly power.

Latin doesn't fit into the *dactylic hexameter* verse very well, and Ennius showed great ingenuity and cleverness in getting the verse to scan. Only fragments of Ennius' works survive, but his influence on Vergil's Latin is overriding. He wrote the *Annales*, an epic poem in eighteen books that covered Roman history from the fall of Troy (supposedly in 1184 BC) down to the second century BC. The *Annales* was a standard school text for Roman schoolchildren until it was supplanted by Vergil's *Aeneid*. About six hundred lines survive of the *Annales*, and a copy was among the Latin rolls of an incinerated library found in Herculaneum, buried in AD 79 in the same explosion that destroyed Pompeii.

Through his education, Vergil was steeped in the *Iliad* and the *Odyssey*, but these poems were to him, and to Vergil's audience, not easy to read. They are a very odd Greek, filled with arcane allusions that cry out for explication but promise rich rewards to the scholar who can penetrate them. Vergil and his audience had penetrated them, and in the *Aeneid* he rewards their education at every turn.

ROMAN RELIGION

The story of the *Aeneid* is much preoccupied with the behavior of the gods and their dealings with their mortal favorites. The gods stand firmly behind the story: It is Jupiter's will that Aeneas found a new race in Italy, which happens also to be fated, and although his powerful wife Juno opposes the project, in the end she must give in. Jupiter does make some concessions, however: the new race will forget its past, including its names and its language.

The religious behavior of these Roman gods is entirely Greek, a poetic affectation. Religion is belief and the course of action that follows from belief, a system of assumptions about how external powers affect our behavior and the things we do to maintain good relations with these external powers. Greek religion regarded its deities as endowed with superhuman powers and, in general, with immortality, but in poetry the Greek anthropomorphic gods also possessed a human psychology. They desired, lied, deceived, struggled, loved, hated, and took revenge. Many helped the humans they favored. Native Roman deities, by contrast, were in practice mostly personifications of qualities and were strictly limited in their function. Many such deities had only the right to refuse or assent to requests in accordance with a legal formula. Although Vergil has Hellenized his gods in accord with Greek poetic practice, his bias to see great powers as abstractions without personalities constantly peeks through.

Native Roman religion was formal, legal, and contractual: *do ut des*, "I give that you might give to me." In a legally binding contract both parties give something in order to receive something in return. Such a notion, applied to the gods, removed native Roman divinities from moral responsibility. The priest is not a holy man but a member of the ruling elite, acting as a lawyer for the Roman people to ensure that the gods fulfill their side of the contract. Julius Caesar held the title of *pontifex maximus*, "greatest bridge-builder," the highest religious office in the state.

These Roman deities were called *numina*, "nodders" (singular *numen*), from the Latin verb *nuo*, which means "nod" and hence "assent." The *numina* were spirits that could inhabit almost any object or serve almost any function, large or small, and they could be dealt with on a legal basis. The *numina* could also be the spirits of the dead, although the universal human ghost cult, whereby the spirits of the dead are venerated and considered effective, was a competing influence. There are many *numina* in the *Aeneid*. Vergil's story is about a man who does his part, fulfills his side of the contract with Fate, and in return is given what he contracted for: to be the founder of a new city and a new race.

The *numina* could be dealt with through *sacrificium*, a "making set-apart," a sacrifice. *Sacrificium* was a legal transfer of something into the ownership of the *numen*, who was then expected to fulfill his or her side of the bargain. In the closing lines of the *Aeneid*, as Aeneas kills his enemy Turnus, he uses the language of sacrifice, as if Turnus is a gift to the spirit of Aeneas' dead friend Pallas (*Pallas te ... immolate*) and to the project of founding the Roman race. Aeneas' killing of Turnus has puzzled readers, but it is a form of sacrifice in accordance with good Roman procedure, with an expected outcome.

The will of the *numina* was revealed through divination, at which the Romans were adept (thanks to their Etruscan teachers), and all proceedings required the "nod" of the invisible powers. All that happens to Aeneas has been repeatedly prophesied and foretold. He has received the "nod" of the powers that invest the world. He is only fulfilling the will of Fate in his adventures and in his eventual victory. Augustus is the new Aeneas, the founder of a New Rome, the fulfiller of prophecy, doing what he has to do because it was fated to be done.

Although the Roman *numina* were remote and colorless, some took on roles of service to the state and the family and enjoyed a central place in Roman civic and home life, and in the *Aeneid*. One of the best-known state *numina* was Janus (**jā**-nus), "gate," in origin perhaps a *numen* of bridges, hence of going forth and returning. He was represented as a man with two faces, one looking forward, the other back, hence the name of January (but in Vergil Janus is the first king in Latium). Jupiter was the *numen* of the Roman state, and his eagle appeared on the Roman standards carried into battle.

In origin the Penates (pe-**nat**-ēz) protected a household's things and especially its food—*penus* means "cupboard," the origin of our pantry—but later the Penates became identified with the welfare of the Roman state, viewed as a family writ large. Hector's ghost entrusts the Trojan Penates to Aeneas as he flees burning Troy, and the Penates play an important role in the *Aeneid*. In Rome the Penates were under the protection of the Vestal Virgins.

Similar to the Penates were the protective spirits called Lares (**lar**-ēz, singular Lar), the name apparently derived from the Etruscan word for a ghost. The Lares probably began as protective ghosts of the fertile field, then came to protect all kinds of places: the household, streets, even whole cities.

Vesta was protective *numen* of the household hearth (like the Greek Hestia), and because the state was a family writ large, of the eternal fire that stood for Rome itself. Six Vestal Virgins served her, protecting this sacred flame that Aeneas had brought from Troy itself, along with the Trojan Penates. The Vestals, chosen at the age of seven from the great families, served for thirty years in their round temple in the Roman Forum, after which they could marry, although few did. If a Vestal was caught having sexual relations, she was buried alive in a tomb containing a loaf of bread, a jug of water, and a lighted lamp. The mother of Romulus and Remus was a Vestal Virgin raped by Mars. Vesta, among the most sacred and revered deities in Roman religion, remained an abstract *numen* throughout Roman history.

ROMAN DEITIES EQUATED WITH GREEK DEITIES

When the Roman poets fell under the influence of the Greeks living in southern Italy, they began to think of these bloodless abstractions, the *numina*, as being like the anthropomorphic gods of the Greeks. It is hard to tell a story about an abstraction. There were also important political motivations for such identifications. Augustus claimed to be a descendant of Venus through Aeneas, and this meant a being with personality rather than the principle of fecundity, although that principle was strong too: Augustus, "he who increases," the descendant of Venus, will make the world bloom again.

The first syllable of the name of Jupiter (also called Jove, spelled Juppiter in Latin), originally a *numen* of the bright sky overhead, is etymologically identical to Zeus in its first syllable. He must descend from the common cultural, linguistic, and racial heritage shared by all speakers of Indo-European languages, although we cannot identify any specific Roman stories about him. Worshiped in many manifestations, Jupiter became the incarnation of the striking power of the Roman state.

He was the son of Saturn, in origin a harvest *numen* equated with the Greek Cronus. Juno was the *numen* who presided over women as members of the family and was easily equated with Hera. In the *Aeneid* she hates the Trojans because Paris, a Trojan prince, had scorned her in a beauty contest. Minerva, an Etruscan goddess, was *numen* of handicrafts, hence associated with the Greek Athena. In the *Aeneid* she is often called Pallas, after her Greek epithet, Pallas Athena. Ceres, *numen* of wheat, was from an early time equated with Demeter. In the *Aeneid* Ceres can mean simply "grain." Diana, the Roman Artemis, was perhaps in origin a spirit of the wood. She is often mentioned in the *Aeneid*.

Mercury has no ancient Italian heritage but is Hermes introduced to the Latins under a title indicating his commercial activities (*merx* is Latin for "merchandise"). In the *Aeneid* he is Zeus' messenger. Vulcan's name is not Latin. Identified with Hephaestus, he may have come from the eastern Mediterranean, from where the Etruscans may have come too. He was a god of volcanic and other forms of fire. In the *Aeneid* he makes magical armor for Aeneas in his smithy. Neptune was the *numen* of water, although not specifically the sea until he came to be identified with Poseidon. Apollo was never successfully identified with a Latin *numen*, but kept his ancient name and nature, coming early to Latium through Etruria and the Greek colonies of southern Italy.

Mars, assimilated to the Greek Ares, was associated with the wolf and may have been a primordial god of war. He gave his name to the month of March, a good time for military operations. Dionysus was usually known by his Greek name Bacchus, although he was also called Liber, "the freer" from care. Faunus (**fa**-nus), perhaps "kindly one," is named euphemistically, for he was ordinarily *numen* of the unreasoning terror of the lonely forest and was identified with Pan. In Vergil Faunus is the father of Latinus.

Venus seems once to have been a *numen* of fresh water, especially springs, perhaps from the Latin word for "pleasant," *venustus*. She is Aphrodite. In the *Aeneid*, she has been fully anthropomorphized from *numen* to goddess and functions as would any Greek god in the poems of Homer, protecting her son Aeneas in his trials.

To Hercules belongs the earliest foreign cult at Rome, and in the *Aeneid* he is a great hero who fought a monster on the very site of future Rome. The form of his name reflects Western Greek pronunciation, as does Ulysses, the Latin form of Odysseus. Dis, the Roman Hades, is an abbreviation of Latin *dives*, "riches," a translation of the Greek Pluto ("enricher"), a euphemism for Hades. Vergil also calls him Orcus, who was probably an Etruscan demon of death. Proserpina is a Latin form of Persephone.

Though Vergil has anthropomorphized the principal gods, the *numina* show their faces in the *Aeneid*. Hence we hear of the great god Rumor, and Storm, and all kinds of abstractions that live near the gates of the underworld. *Pietas*, the principle of righteous conduct toward one's father, family, and state, is a *numen* who drives the moral narrative forward, and she was often represented on coins.

FIGURE I.2 *Pietas*, **Roman coin, AD 138.** This coin was minted by the Emperor Antoninus Pius (AD 86–161). *Pietas*, labeled, is shown as a goddess holding an incense burner (?) in one hand over an altar and a sacrificial animal in her other hand. The ritual implies obedience to rule through the legal contract that the sacrifice enforces: I am obedient to authority, and authority protects me.

Vergil strongly emphasizes how close to the world of the gods are the events he portrays. Aeneas is himself the son of Venus, and Turnus is the son of the goddess Venilia. King Iarbas in Africa is a son of Jupiter. Acestes in Sicily is the son of the Sicilian river-god Crinisus by a Trojan woman named Egesta. King Evander from Arcadia is the son of Mercury and a nymph. The Trojan Misenus is the son of the wind-god Aeolus. Latinus is the son of Faunus. Again and again the gods appear in person, pretending to be mortals so they may participate in the action. At one point, Cupid pretends to be Aeneas' son so he may get close to Dido and bedevil her with passion for Aeneas.

In this world, gods and humans intermingle in a magical and stylized landscape, in a very Roman world.

THE MEANING OF THE *AENEID*: AN EPIC OF NATIONAL REBIRTH

The *Aeneid* is a modern poem, laboriously composed in writing over many years. The *Aeneid* makes self-conscious use of the mythical tradition to justify present conditions in the world at a time when alphabetic literacy was the medium by which everything was controlled, including all thinking about how the world was made. It is never just a story, but always an explanation of the problems that Romans faced and the moral and political solutions that gave them ascendancy over the world.

Thus characters and events in Vergil's myths have various levels of meaning; they stand for more than meets the eye. All events and characters are subordinated to Vergil's patriotic purpose of satisfying Rome's need for a tradition of national origin, a tale telling in the language of legend how this great empire was made. Its story of far away and long ago, when cows munched grass on the Palatine hill, satisfied contemporary literary taste for an escapist setting while making it possible for Vergil to proclaim, in symbolic form, the divine necessity of Rome's conquest of the world and of Augustus' ascendancy in it.

Vergil shows his hero as obedient to his country above all other obligations. Aeneas, called *pius*—that is, embodying *pietas*—may appear to be heartless for placing his duty to found Rome above his love for Dido, but the *pius* man must do his duty to the divine command, regardless of consequences to his personal life. He does what he must do, the only behavior that admits the possibility of human happiness, according to Stoic teaching. For the founding of empire, one must place personal interests behind those of the state.

The Trojan women who tire of wandering and are left in Sicily are not worthy of empire. We must purge the weak before the great task can begin. Palinurus, the helmsman who falls from the ship off the Bay of Naples, is not just a member of the crew, but stands for every noble Roman who gave his life, at divine behest, that Rome might be great. The individual will perish, but empire will grow. The youths Pallas, Nisus, and Euryalus all die, for the necessity of empire kills the young. But still the empire grows.

Vergil's complex myth places empire in the context of a divine plan for human history while glorifying the moral qualities necessary for the foundation of empire. The quality of *pietas*, devotion to duty, is the most important positive quality in a ruler. Vergil also shows what features a ruler should *not* have. Aeneas during his seven years of wandering has purged himself of the material and sexual excess that the exotic eastern city of Troy symbolized in ancient literature. He spurns the glorious new city that Dido is building and rejects his passion for her, so like that between Paris and Helen, who in placing personal desire above communal good gave rise to the catastrophic Trojan War.

In Dido, Vergil embodies many mythical and historical associations. Dido is not only like Helen of Troy, who gave in to her passion, but also like Circe and Calypso in the *Odyssey*, enchantresses who sought to sway the hero from his purpose. She is also like Euripides' savage Medea, who represents all that is Eastern, foreign, and barbaric. In the Dido sequence Vergil depends heavily on Apollonius of Rhodes' treatment of the love between Medea and Jason. In Dido the contemporary Roman reader would also recognize Cleopatra, who seduced Marc Antony and turned him against Augustus and Rome.

Dido represents the moral failings of broken faith and Eastern passion. Although she swore to her dead husband Sychaeus that she would have no other, she sleeps with Aeneas. Instead of transcending her heartbreak and pain (as a true Roman woman would), she takes her life in an act of vindictive self-destruction. Dido also is an incarnation of Carthage, Rome's greatest enemy, in the working-out of Dido's curse on Aeneas and his descendants.

The Romans were an amalgam of many clans and tribes whose primitive tribal identities were submerged in the greater being of the state. In Vergil's poem, Latinus the Latin, Tarchon the Etruscan, and Evander the Greek stand for the peoples fused into Rome. All work together toward the common enterprise. The brutal Mezentius, the incarnation of egotism and self-pride, must fall, and so must Camilla, who stands for "natural man," humans living in tribal groups in harmony with nature: noble, but doomed. Brazen and hot-headed, Turnus is too like Achilles or Alexander the Great or Marc Antony to survive. He stands for national pride, which must succumb to the universalism of empire. Morally, he is not wrong—he may be right. After all, he is engaged to Lavinia before Aeneas appears and carries her off as his bride. Still, Turnus the Italian must lose because he opposes the pattern of Fate. The personal and local pride that Turnus represents must give way if empire is to bestow its many benefits on humankind.

THE *AENEID* IN ART

European artists again and again have tried their hand at illustrating scenes from the *Aeneid*. Some reproductions of these paintings accompany this translation. Such scenes show how Europeans constantly reconceived events in the *Aeneid*, a poem that educated both artists and their sponsors. There are ancient illustrations of this work beginning in the fourth century AD, with pictures in a manuscript and on a tile floor in England. These illustrations are Roman in style, with simplified backgrounds and clear presentations of events. The with figures are often labeled. Medieval representations show Dido as a lady in a royal house and Aeneas as a knight.

At the beginning of the European Renaissance, around 1300 BC, art switched from a conceptual framework, in which thought governs the illustration, to a perceptual tradition, in which people and things look like "they really do." Illustrations of the *Aeneid* from the Italian Renaissance of the fourteenth and fifteenth centuries are rare, but there are many from the Mannerist period of the sixteenth century when elongated forms, strange poses, odd perspectives, unusual settings, and dramatic lighting replaced the calm dignity of the Renaissance.

But the dominant tradition by far of illustrations of the *Aeneid* begins in the seventeenth century with the introduction of the so-called Baroque style in which figures are exuberant, colorful, filled with action, and realistic in proportions. The Baroque style lasted until the late eighteenth century, when the Rococo style developed in reaction to the pretensions of the Baroque. Rococo artists used a more jocular and florid approach, often adopting playful subjects.

In the late eighteenth and early nineteenth centuries a competing artistic movement to Rococo arose called Neoclassical, coinciding with the Age of

Enlightenment, which drew its inspiration from the classical art of ancient Greece and ancient Rome. In turn the Neoclassical competed, in the nineteenth century, with the Romantic style, which first appeared in landscape painting, seascapes, and illustrations from history and myth. The Romantic movement advocated heightened emotion as a source of aesthetic pleasure, and Romantic art emphasizes terror, awe, and especially those emotions aroused by beholding the beauty of untamed nature.

It is hard to find an illustration from the *Aeneid* in Modern art, which began with the Impressionists of the late nineteenth century and has undergone a complex development. The absence of illustrations from the Modern period reflects the radical decline in influence of the poem, while the abundant illustrations between the sixteenth and the nineteenth centuries AD reflect the *Aeneid*'s dramatic influence on the intellectual life of Europe during this period. Artists during this time were more interested in the events in the first half of the poem, especially the romance of Dido and Aeneas, which was made into a famous opera by Henry Purcell in 1688. They were least interested in events from the second half of the poem; most of the pictures in Books 7–12 come from illustrated books.

VERGIL'S LATIN AND THIS TRANSLATION

Few today are familiar with the events of the *Aeneid*, even the story of Dido, whereas for hundred of years these stories formed part of the intellectual furniture of all men and women educated in the West. Vergil's influence may have abated with the decline of Latin education and the modern absence of a class of people who can read the Latin with appreciation, yet his poem stands as the most influential poem in the Western literary tradition, and anyone curious about this tradition must become familiar with it. I hope that this abbreviated translation will help the student achieve this familiarity.

Because in many respects the *Aeneid* is a study in *pietas*—the proper respect one must show to father, family, and country—I include forms of *pius* in the declined Latin form wherever it appears, so that the reader may follow Vergil's thought. Unlike *fatum* or *fata* (pl.), which I translate "Fate" or "the fates," *pius* has a broad range of meanings and has to be translated in many ways. In general, however, I render it "dutiful."

Latin has a small vocabulary, especially when compared with Greek, and therefore a few words must mean many things. This fact creates a style of expression utterly unlike modern English. The meaning dances behind the words, rather than resides in the words, as it does in Greek or English. The effect is not friendly to what we take to be clear expression, and every Latin student knows passages in Vergil where one knows what all the words mean, and understands how they are related grammatically, but still cannot say what the sentence means. That's when you need to go to the commentaries, to see what the great Latinists of the past thought about the meaning of the sentence. Unsurprisingly, they often disagree, and in reading Vergil in Latin you come to realize that there is always a fuzzy edge to his meaning, sometimes just beyond one's grasp, heightening poetic effect but challenging the intellect. In fact Vergil can be so difficult that one wonders that his poetry was widely read and loved. But read it was, and loved it was.

Vergil's style has created a tradition in translation where the translator feels free to express a personal notion of what is poetic, beautiful, or elegant. In this translation I have resisted the temptation to do this, placing meaning as much as possible in the Latin words, although admittedly this meaning is elusive. I have elected a plain modern English style, because I think this best explains what Vergil is reaching for in his poetic imagery. This is Vergil as he is, not as we wish he were.

When two vowels written together are to be pronounced separately, I place a dieresis over the second vowel, hence Laocoön. For the pronunciation of ancient names, consult the Index/Glossary. Emphasized syllables are bolded, "lā-**ok**-o-on."

The *Aeneid* is never funny, but dark and understated, always sober and high-toned, even operatic in its expression of strong emotion. Yet the language has a spare elegance, describing, the world from a distance. Hence this translation is spare, not luxuriant. The *Aeneid* is, after all, the handbook of empire.

Standard publications used for this translation are by F. A. Hirtzel, ed., *P. Vergili Maronis Opera* (Oxford, 1900); and by R. A. B. Mynors, ed., *P. Vergili Maronis Opera* (Oxford, 1969).

BOOK 1. *The Shores of Africa*

I sing of arms and of the man who first came from
the coasts of Troy, exiled by Fate, to the Lavinian
shores. That man was much tossed about on land
and on the deep by the might of the gods, because Juno
would not forget her rage. And he suffered much from war   5
to found the city and bring his gods to LATIUM,
whence came the Latin race, the fathers of ALBA LONGA,
and the high walls of ROME.°

invocation to the Muse

                       O Muse, remind me
of the causes—because of what insult to her divine power,
suffering what exactly, did the queen of the gods   10
drive on a man famous for his sense of duty [*pietate*]°
to withstand so many disasters, so many pains?
Do the gods hold such anger in their hearts?°

the anger of Juno

                                   There was
an ancient city, CARTHAGE, settled by colonists from TYRE,

---

8 *Rome*: Vergil invokes the *Iliad* with "arms" (*arma*) and the *Odyssey* with "man" (*virum*); "man" (*andra*) is the first word of the *Odyssey*. The whole poem is an elaborate literary allusion to Homer and the tradition that Homer represented. Aeneas founded the city of LAVINIUM (see inset, Map IV), hence "the Lavinian shores." From Lavinium, Aeneas' son Ascanius will go on to found Alba Longa, "the long white [city]," probably at the foot of the Alban hills twelve miles southeast of Rome in Latium (its location is not certain). Romulus and Remus will come from Alba Longa. The gods that Aeneas carries are the Penates, "spirits of the pantry," important in Roman religion. In their public role they protected the Roman state, thought of as the household writ large. The Penates had no equivalent in Greek religion. The Roman goddess Juno functions like the Greek goddess Hera.

11 *sense of duty*: The Latin is the untranslatable *pietas*, which means "sense of duty," "religious behavior," "loyalty," "devotion," or "filial piety" (see Introduction). In general I will render it "dutiful," but will alert the reader when forms of *pietas* appear so that the reader may follow Vergil's thought.

13 *in their hearts*: Juno is angry with Aeneas not so much because of anything he has done, but because he is a Trojan, a race she despises, and because his descendants one thousand years later—the Romans—will destroy her favorite city, Carthage (in 146 BC). But Aeneas has Fate on his side and will triumph, no matter what Juno does. Historically Juno (the Greek Hera) was equivalent to the Phoenician goddess Tanit, a goddess of fertility and prosperity. Tanit, along with Baal Hammon (probably "Lord Amon," the Egyptian god), were the two most prominent gods in historical Carthage.

15 opposite Italy and the harbors of the TIBER, rich in wealth
and excellent in the study of savage war.° Juno is said
to have cherished this city more than any other on earth,
including SAMOS.° Here were her armor, here her chariot.
The goddess wanted Carthage to hold power over
20 all other peoples—if only Fate would allow it!

    Even then she cared for Carthage, she favored her.
But she heard that an offshoot of Trojan blood would come
who would one day overturn her Tyrian towers—that from
this line would come a people wide of rule and proud in war,
25 who would one day come to destroy LIBYA.° For the Fates
had spun it so.

    Fearing this, the daughter of Saturn
was aware of that earlier war when she had helped
the Argives at TROY.° She could not let go of the causes
of her anger or shake the terrible pain from her heart.
30 The Judgment of Paris was always on her mind, and the injury
done to her beauty so despised—by that hated race!—
and the honors given to Ganymede when Jupiter
snatched him away.°

    Infuriated by these things
still more, she kept the Trojans far from Latium,
35 tossed everywhere over all the sea—those who were
left after the Danaäns° and savage Achilles were through

---

16 *...war*: Carthage, Rome's deadliest foe in the third to second centuries BC, was a Phoenician colony in North Africa close to modern Tunis. Its name means "newtown" in Semitic language (Naples is Greek Neapolis, "newtown"). In legend, Carthage was founded by Elissa, known as Dido (perhaps Phoenician for "virgin"), a princess of TYRE, the great Semitic-speaking emporium on the east coast of the Mediterranean, located in modern-day Lebanon. She likely to be a historical figure lived sometime in the late ninth century BC, too late for her to have met Aeneas: the traditional date of the Trojan War was c. 1200 BC.

18 *Samos*: An island very near the coast of modern Turkey where Hera (Juno) had one of the oldest temples in Greece, begun in the eighth century BC. Hera inherited the reverence paid Eastern fertility goddesses from time immemorial, a cult that spilled over from the mainland to Samos.

25 *destroy Libya*: "Libya" is Carthage, defeated in the three Punic (Phoenician) Wars of 264–241 BC, 218–201 BC, and 149–146 BC.

28 *...at Troy*: Juno (Hera) is the daughter of Saturn (Greek Cronus). The "Argives" are simply the Greeks. Hera/Juno also had a famous temple near ARGOS on the Argive plain in the PELOPONNESUS.

33 *him away*: The Judgment of Paris refers to the time when the Trojan prince Paris judged Aphrodite/Venus to be more beautiful than Hera/Juno and Athena/Minerva. His reward was Helen, the most beautiful woman in the world. Paris' abduction of Helen then caused the Trojan War. Zeus/Jupiter snatched up the very beautiful Ganymede, another Trojan prince, to be his cupbearer—that is, the object of his love interest.

36 *Danaäns*: Homer calls the Greeks "Danaäns," "Argives," and "Achaeans" indifferently; he never calls them "Greeks," a word taken from a northwest tribe of Greeks with whom the Romans came into contact at an early time. Vergil uses all these names, as well as "Greeks," to refer to the Greeks.

with them. They wandered throughout the many years,
driven by the Fates, around every sea. So great a labor
it was to found the Roman race!
       SICILY was scarcely
out of sight. Joyfully the Trojans turned their sails   40
toward the open sea. The bronze on their prows
cut through the swells of the salt sea when Juno,
savoring the endless hurt in her heart, said this
to herself: "So, am I to pull back from my design,
beaten down? Can I then not turn away this Teucrian   45
king° from Italy? Of course Fate forbids it! But Pallas°
could burn the ships of the Argives and drown the men
in the sea—all on account of the offense of one man,
the madness of that Ajax son of Oïleus!° She herself,
casting the sudden fire of Jove° from the clouds,   50
blasted his boats and overturned the sea with winds.
She took him up in a whirlwind as he spewed out
flames from his breast, transfixed. She stuck him on
a sharp crag.
    "But *I*, who move as queen of the gods,
the sister and wife of Jove—I've been at war with one   55
people for so many years!° Who will respect the godhead
of Juno after this, or will come a suppliant to place
offerings on my altars?"

Juno persuades Aeolus the wind-king to send a storm

       Speaking such words, the goddess,
with anger flaming in her heart, came to AEOLIA,°
fatherland of clouds, a place rife with the raging   60
blasts of the wind. Here in a vast cave King Aeolus
commanded the tempestuous winds and the roaring

---

46 *Teucrian king*: Teucer was the first, or one of the first, Trojan kings. Hence Teucrian means simply "Trojan," and Teucria is Troy. See Genealogical Chart.

46 *Pallas*: Minerva (Athena).

49 *son of Oïleus*: In Homer there are two Ajaxes: the son of Telamon, or the Greater Ajax, and the son of Oïleus, or the Lesser Ajax. They often fought side by side but were unrelated. During the sack of the city the Lesser Ajax, son of Oïleus, raped Cassandra, a daughter of Priam, as she clung to an image of Athena (Minerva), and for this crime he was punished by shipwreck and death.

50 *Jove*: Jupiter.

56 *many years*: The ten years of the Trojan War.

59 *Aeolia*: In *Odyssey* Book 10 Odysseus visits the floating island of Aeolus, whose winds his treacherous companions release from sacks hidden in the boat. The winds blow Odysseus back to Aeolus' island. But in Vergil, Aeolus is Juno's ally in trying to thwart the dictates of Fate—to keep Aeneas from founding the Roman race. Vergil (Book 8) identifies Aeolia with one of the LIPARI ISLANDS northeast of Sicily (Map IV).

tempests: He bound them in chains and held them
imprisoned. Indignant, with a huge roar they boomed
65 through the secret places of the mountain. But Aeolus
sits in his lofty stronghold, scepter in hand, and he calms
their spirit and moderates their anger. If he did not,
in their speed they would surely bear away with them
the seas and the land and the deep sky. They would sweep
70 them through the winds.
                              But Jove, the all-powerful father,
hid them in dark caves, fearing just this, and imposed
a massive mountain upon them, and he gave them a king
who would know how, under definite agreement, to control
them by now tightening, now relaxing the reins, as he was told.
75 Juno spoke to him with these suppliant words:
"Aeolus—for the father of gods and the king of men
has given you the power to calm the waves and to raise
them up with the wind—a people hostile to me sails
on the TYRRHENIAN SEA carrying Ilium and the conquered
80 Penates to Italy.° Throw your power into the winds
and smash the ships, driving them under the water,
or fling them everywhere and throw their bodies on the sea!
I have twice seven nymphs of outstanding beauty, but the best
in beauty is the lovely Deïopeä.° I will join her to you
85 in permanent wedlock. I will call her your own so that
she might pass years with you in repayment for your great
service, and that she might make you a father with beautiful
children."
           Aeolus answered her with these words:
"Your task, my queen, is to seek out what you desire;
90 mine to do what you command. I owe to you this kingdom,
to you this scepter and Jove's good will. You give me
a place on the couch at the meals of the gods, you give
me power over the clouds and the storms."

Aeneas' fleet is broken up

                              When he had said
these things, he turned his spear and struck the side
95 of the hollow mountain. The winds, as if set in an armed
array, rush out where he had made a door, and they blast
the earth with storm. They lay upon the sea and from

---

80 *... to Italy*: The Tyrrhenian Sea, named after the Etruscans, lies off the west coast of Italy between Sicily and Sardinia (Map IV). Ilium is another name for Troy.

84 *Deïopeä*: Otherwise unknown.

FIGURE 1.1 *Juno Asking Aeolus to Release the Winds*, **1769, by François Boucher (1703–1770).** Boucher was a French painter in the Rococo style best known for his sensual paintings on classical themes, his allegories, and his pastoral scenes. He was one of the most celebrated artists of the eighteenth century. Here Juno speaks to Aeolus while she offers the nymph Deïopeä as his wife. Cupids surround her, symbolizing sexual attraction, while the king of the winds, draped only in a red cloth, holds the scepter of command in his right hand. In his left hand he holds the chains that imprison the winds in a cave. Two winds are even now escaping. In the sea are Nereids (nymphs of the sea), large fish, and shells. To the left of the picture can be seen a prow of one of Aeneas' ships. Oil on canvas.

its lowest depths upturn all—East Wind and South Wind
together, and the Southwest Wind thick with storm.
100 They roll huge waves toward the shore.
                                                                             There follow
the shouts of men and the screech of cables. At once
clouds obscure the sky and day from the Trojans' eyes.
Black night lies upon the sea. From pole to pole
the thunder cracks. The sky lights up with constant fire,
105 and all conspire to bring instant death to the men.
    Aeneas' limbs are loosened with a sudden chill.
He moans and, raising his two upturned hands to the stars,
he cries out: "Three and four-times blessed were those
who met death in sight of their fathers beneath the high
110 walls of Troy! O Son of Tydeus °—bravest of the Danaän
race! I wish that I could have fallen to you on the plain
of Ilium, and that I might have poured out my spirit,
cut down by your right hand, there where savage Hector
lies dead by the spear of Aeacides, and huge Sarpedon—
115 where the Simoeis rolls so many shields and helmets
and the powerful bodies of men."°
                                              As he shouted out
these words, a screaming blast from the north hit
his sail head-on and drove the waves as high
as the stars. The oars were shattered, the prows spun
around, the ships turned sideways to the waves.
120 A sheer mountain of water fell in a heap. Some
of the men hang from the top of the wave, for others
the gaping surge reveals the earth at the bottom
of the sea, and the flood rages with sand.
                                          South Wind
snatches up three ships and twists them against hidden
125 rocks—the Italians call these rocks the Altars, standing
in the midst of the sea, a huge ridge on the top of the sea.
Three ships East Wind pushes from deep water
into the shoals of the SYRTES,° terrible to see,
and dashes them in the shallow water, piling them
130 under a mound of sand.

---

110 *Son of Tydeus*: Diomedes, one of the greatest Greek fighters at Troy. In the *Iliad*, Diomedes nearly kills Aeneas, but his mother Venus (Aphrodite) saves him (*Iliad* Book 5).

116 *... of men*: Aeacides is Achilles, the grandson of Aeacus. Sarpedon, fighting on the Trojan side, was a son of Zeus/Jupiter killed by Patroclus (*Iliad* Book 16). Simoeis is one of the rivers that cross the Trojan plain.

128 *Syrtes*: Quicksands off the coast of North Africa.

                    One ship, which carried
the Lycians and the faithful Orontes,° was hit in the stern
by a gigantic swell of water coming down from a peak,
right before Aeneas' eyes. The captain is shaken out
and falls headfirst, but the wave twists the ship round
and round, three times in the same place, and the rapid   135
whirlpool devours it in the maelstrom.
                            Here and there
appear those swimming in the immense raging abyss,
and the arms of men and planks and Trojan treasure
lie on the waves. Now the storm has overcome the strong
ship of Ilioneus, now the ship of brave Achates,   140
and that in which Abas rode, and the ship of old Aletes.°
All of them let in the dangerous rain, their side-joints
loosened, and cracks opened wide.

Neptune intervenes

                        Meanwhile, Neptune
saw the sea tossed with a great roar, and the storm let
loose, and the quiet waters cast up from the lowest depths. 145
He was profoundly disturbed, and looking out over the deep
he raised up his calm head over the top of the waves.
He sees the fleet of Aeneas thrown about over all the sea
and the Trojans overwhelmed by the whitecaps and the ruin
of the sky. The deceits of Juno, and her wrath, were no secret   150
to her brother.
                He calls East Wind and West Wind to him,
and he speaks as follows: "Are you so proud of your birth?
That now—you winds!—you confound heaven and earth
without my approval? That you dare to heap up such great
confusion? Why you—! but it is better to calm the waves   155
that you have stirred up. Later you shall pay me for your
crimes with a harsher punishment. But hasten your flight
and report this to your king: Not to him, but to me was given
by lot the sovereignty over the sea and the dread trident!°

---

131   *...Orontes*: The Lycians were Trojan allies who lived in southern Asia Minor (modern-day Turkey). Orontes was their captain; he appears in the underworld in Book 6.

140–141   *Ilioneus...Aletes*: Ilioneus will represent the Trojans to Dido later in this book, and to Latinus in Book 7; Achates, Aeneas' right-hand man, will accompany Aeneas to Carthage and also plays a role in sending Nisus and Euryalus on a dangerous night mission (Book 9). Abas is not mentioned again, Aletes but one more time.

159   *...trident*: Aeolus is king of the winds. In primordial times Saturn's three children, Jupiter, Neptune, and Dis (Pluto), divided up by lot rulership over the world.

160 Aeolus holds the savage rocks, yes—your home, East Wind—
may he throw around his weight in that hall, your Aeolus,
and may he rule that barred prison of the winds!"
                                        So Neptune
spoke and more swiftly than his word he calmed the swollen
seas and scattered the assembled clouds, and he brings
165 back the sun. Cymothoë and Triton° with a common effort
drive back the ships from the sharp rocks. Neptune himself
raises them up with his trident. He makes a way through
the sandbanks, he calms the sea. On light wheels he races
across the top of the water.
                            Just as when, as often happens,
170 among a great people tumult has arisen, and the vulgar crowd
roars in anger, and now they throw torches and rocks—
for madness° gives them arms—then if by chance they see
a man dignified in his noble character [*pietate*] and service,
they fall silent and stand attentive with ears pricked up, listening.
175 And with speech he commands their spirit, and he softens
their hearts. Even so all the roar of the sea fell away as soon
as Father Neptune, borne in a chariot under an open sky,
guides his horses and, flying along, lets loose the reins
of his obedient car.

the fleet's remnants land in Africa

                        The followers of Aeneas, exhausted,
180 strive hurriedly to run toward the nearest shore. They turn
toward the coast of Libya. There in a deep cove is
an island that makes a harbor with the barrier of its sides
that breaks all the waves that come from the deep
and cuts them into receding ripples. On both sides
185 immense cliffs ending in twin peaks loom menacingly
into the sky, beneath whose summit the wide waters
lie silent and safe. Above is a background of shimmering
forest. A grove overhangs the harbor, black with horrid shade.
        Under the crags that fronted the grove was a cave with its
190 overhanging rocks. Inside were fresh water and seats
of natural stone, the house of the nymphs. Here no chains
hold fast the tired ships, no anchor ties them down

---

165 ... *Triton*: Cymothoë is a Nereid, a daughter of Nereus, the Old Man of the Sea; Triton is a merman who commonly accompanies Neptune.

172 *madness*: The Latin is *furor*, a key word in the poem. It is *furor* and *ira*, "anger," that drives Juno to persecute Aeneas in the storm (*furit aestus*, "the flood rages") and, later, in the war in Italy. Turnus, Aeneas' great enemy, often gives in to *furor*, as does Queen Amata, and sometimes Aeneas himself.

with its hooking bite. Here Aeneas drove in with seven
ships he had gathered from all his number.° With a great
love for the earth the Trojans leave the ships and take
possession of the beach they have longed for. They lay
their limbs on the shore, dripping with brine.
                                               The first thing
Achates did was to strike a spark from a flint. The leaves
took fire and all around he set fuel and fanned the flames
to take up the tinder. Then, exhausted from their ordeal,
they take out the produce of Ceres, spoiled by the water,
and the tools of Ceres.° They get ready to parch what grain
they could save and pound it in a mortar.°
                                                In the meanwhile
Aeneas climbs a place of outlook and gazes out over
the wide sea to see if he could make out Antheus, tossed
by the wind, and his Phrygian twin-tiered boats,° or Capys,
or the arms of Caïcus pinned to the high stern. But there
is no ship in sight.
                      He sees three stags walking along the shore,
and behind them follows an entire herd. In a long line
they graze down the valley. At this Aeneas stopped and took up
his bow and swift arrows in his hand, weapons that the faithful
Achates always carried. First he cut down the leaders,
who carried high their branched antlers, then he struck
the herd, and with his arrows he drove them into the midst
of the leafy woods. He did not let up before he had victoriously
laid out seven big animals, as many deer as he had ships.

   From there Aeneas goes to the harbor, and he divides the deer
among all his companions. Then he divides the wine which
the good hero Acestes had loaded into casks on the Trinacrian
shore and gave to them as they sailed off.° He calmed their
mourning hearts with these words: "My companions—we
are hardly ignorant of earlier misfortunes. You who've suffered
worse, a god will put an end to these pains too. You drew near

---

194 *number*: Aeneas had twenty ships when he set out from Troy.

202 *Ceres*: Equivalent to the Greek Demeter, goddess of grain. The tools of Ceres are the tools used for the preparation of food.

203 *mortar*: First the grain is parched, then crushed, then from the meal you make the bread.

206 *Phrygian twin-tiered boats*: "Phrygian," that is, Trojan: Phrygia is an area inland from Troy; "twin-tiered" is anachronistic for the era of the Trojan War, when all boats had a single tier, as was the earlier reference to "hooked anchors" (lines 192–193), not found at so early a time.

220 *...sailed off*: Acestes was a Trojan who had established a settlement in Sicily that Aeneas visited just before getting caught in the storm. Sicily is called Trinacria, "with three promontories," because it is roughly triangular in shape.

to the fury of Scylla, to her deep-resounding crags. You experienced
225 the rocks of Cyclops.° So take back your spirits! Put aside
your worthless fear. Perhaps you will one day recall even these
times with pleasure. Our trip to Latium takes us through
all kinds of misfortunes and many hazards. But Fate destines
peace for us there. There it is fated that Troy rise again.
230 So endure, and save yourselves for a happier day."

        So he spoke, and sick with his great cares he makes his face
look hopeful while suppressing the pain deep in his heart.
The other men gird themselves to cut up the booty for the coming
feast. They flay the hides from the ribs and expose the entrails.
235 Some cut the meat into pieces and fix it, still trembling, on spits.
Some put down bronze cauldrons on the shore, and they light
a fire beneath them. Then they restore their strength
through eating. Spread out on the grass, they take their fill
of old wine and venison running with fat.

                              After the Trojans had satisfied
240 their hunger with the feast and the tables were taken away,
they remember regretfully their lost comrades. Between hope
and fear, they are unsure whether to believe that they still lived,
or had suffered the final doom and no longer heard when called.
And now in silence dutiful [*pius*] Aeneas laments especially the death
245 of courageous Orontes, now of Amycus, now the cruel fate of Lycus,
and the brave Gyas, and the brave Cloanthus.°

Venus intercedes with Jupiter, who prophesies Roman greatness

                                  But there was
an end to it all, when Jupiter, gazing down from the summit
of the sky, looked down at the sea winged with sails,
and the outstretched lands, the shores, and the peoples
250 who occupied wide territories—he paused, resting on heaven's
height and fixed his eyes on the realms of Libya.

        While he considered such cares in his heart, a melancholy
Venus speaks to him, her shining eyes filled with tears:
"O you who rule the affairs of men and gods with eternal
255 commands, you who terrify the world with your thunderbolt—
what great crime can my Aeneas, or the Trojans, have committed

---

225 ... *Cyclops*: The Trojan seer Helenus had warned Aeneas against the barking hounds of the monster Scylla and the whirlpool Charybdis. In Book 3 (not included here) we learn of the Trojans' encounter with Cyclops shortly after Odysseus' famous visit (in *Odyssey* Book 9).

246 ... *Cloanthus*: In fact Lycus and Amycus have survived; they are killed by Turnus in Book 9. Gyas and Cloanthus also survive.

against you so great that all the world is shut off to them
on Italy's account? Surely, you promised that from them
the Romans would one day arise as the years rolled along?
That from them the restored line of Teucer would come 260
to command the sea and all the lands under their sway?
What thought, father, had turned your mind? By this promise
I was comforted for the fall of Troy and its sad ruin
when I weighed happier fates against contrary unhappy ones.
But as it is, the same fortune follows these men who have 265
already been tried by so many calamities. What *end*
do you give to their labor, O great king?
                              "Antenor was able
to escape through the middle of the Achaeans and penetrate
the gulfs of ILLYRIA, and safely pass the inner realms
of the Liburnians, and sail past the springs of TIMAVUS 270
where it passes through nine mouths, a bursting flood,
with a gigantic roar of the mountain, to bury the fields
under the resounding sea.° Nonetheless here he founded
the city of PADUA, a place of settlement for the Teucrians,
and gave his name to the people, and hung up his 275
Trojan arms.° Now he is at peace, settled in tranquility.

    "But we, who are your offspring, to whom you grant
the citadel of heaven,° have lost our ships—it is shocking!
All because of the anger of *one* individual we are betrayed,
we are kept far from the shores of Italy. This is the reward 280
for doing one's duty [*pietatis*]? Is this the way you restore us to power?"
    Smiling at her with the look by which he calms the sky
and the storms, the father of men and gods kissed
his daughter's lips, then he said: "Don't be afraid,
Lady of CYTHERA.° The fates of your children remain 285
unchanged. You *will* see the promised walls of Lavinium.
You *will* raise on high our great-spirited Aeneas to the stars
of the sky. I have not changed my mind. This man—I will speak

---

273   *... resounding sea*: Antenor was a Trojan elder prominent in the *Iliad* who escaped the Greeks and founded Patavium (PADUA, MAP IV) near Venice. Illyria roughly designates the western part of the Balkans fronting on the Adriatic Sea. The Liburnians are a people of Illyria. The Timavus River flows down from the Alps (partly underground) and enters the sea in the Gulf of TRIESTE.

276   *arms*: According to the historian Livy, the area around Padua was called *Troia*. Antenor hung up his arms in a temple as a sign of peace.

278   *of heaven*: Aeneas supposedly did not die, but was taken to heaven, where he joined his mother and became one of the "native gods," the *Di Indigetes*, divinized benefactors like Hercules and Romulus.

285   *Cythera*: After Venus/Aphrodite was born from the sea, she landed on the island of Cythera off the southern coast of Greece, according to some accounts.

frankly because this care gnaws at your heart, and, further
290 unrolling the scroll of Fate, I will tell its secrets—this man
will wage a great war in Italy. He will destroy proud peoples,
and for his followers he will establish laws and walls
until the third summer shall find him ruling in Latium,
and three winters will have passed after the Rutulians
295 are laid low.° Then the boy Ascanius, whose family name
is now Iulus—he was *Ilus* so long as the state of Ilium
was in control—will fulfill in empire thirty great circles
as the months roll by. Then he will shift his rule from the seat
of Lavinium. Great in power, he will build the walls
300 of Alba Longa.
      "Here for three hundred years the kingdom
will endure, ruled by the race of Hector, until Ilia, a royal
priestess, pregnant by Mars, will give birth to a pair of twins.°
Then Romulus, joyful in the golden-yellow coat of his nurse,
a wolf, will take up the line. He will found the walls of Mars°
305 and he will call the people Romans after his own name.
For this people I set no boundary in space nor limits in time.
I have given them empire without end.
      "And the harsh Juno,
who now in her fear harasses the sea and the earth
and the sky, will turn to better counsels. With me she will favor
310 the Romans, lords of the world, the race who wears the toga.
    "So it is decreed. The time will come, as the years slip by,
when the house of Assaracus will subdue Phthia and famous
MYCENAE, and will rule over a conquered Argos.° The Trojan
Caesar will be born from the noble line. He will extend
315 his empire to Ocean,° his fame to the stars—Julius, a name

---

295 *laid low*: That is, Aeneas will be raised to heaven three years after defeating the Rutulians.

302 *...pair of twins*: Aeneas will rule in Lavinium for three years; Ascanius/Iulus in Alba Longa for thirty ("thirty great circles"); then their descendants will rule for three hundred years until the birth of Romulus and Remus. Ilia, usually called Rhea Silvia, was a daughter of King Amulius and a Vestal Virgin (the "royal priestess"). Iulus seems to have been invented as an alternate name for Ascanius in order to connect the family of Aeneas with the Julian clan, which included Julius Caesar and his grand-nephew Augustus, the new Aeneas who is founding a New Rome. However, "Iulus" is trisyllabic (i-**u**-lus), whereas the name of the family (*gens Iulia*) is bisyllabic (**yul**-ya), so the names are not really related.

304 *...Mars*: A wolf nourished the infants Romulus and Remus when they were exposed on the Tiber. Mars is Romulus' father, but also the sponsor of Roman military success.

313 *...Argos*: Assaracus was the father of Anchises, Aeneas' grandfather (see Genealogical Chart). Phthia is Achilles' homeland, as Mycenae was ruled by Agamemnon, king of the Greek host that attacked Troy. Argos was the city of the great Greek warrior Diomedes. In 146 BC the Roman general Mummius sacked Corinth, putting an end to Greek independence, so avenging the destruction of Troy.

315 *Ocean*: The river that surrounds the world.

descended from the great Iulus.° This man you will,
in some day to come, receive in heaven free from care,
loaded with the spoil of the East. He too shall be invoked
with vows.°
      "Then, with wars set aside, the savage age
will soften. Ancient Faith, and Vesta, and Quirinus with his brother   320
Remus will give laws. The gates of war, dire with iron
and tightened bars, will be closed.° Within will sit impious [*impius*]
Rage° on his savage armor, and with his arms bound behind
his back with a hundred knots of brass he will roar,
his ghastly mouth covered with blood."   325

Venus meets Aeneas in the woods

                    So Jupiter spoke.
He then sent the son of Maia° down from on high
so that the land and the new walls of Carthage might open
in hospitality to the Teucrians, and so that Dido, not knowing
what Fate held in store, might not bar them from her lands.
Mercury flies through the magnificent air, rowing with wings,   330
and quickly he comes to rest on the shores of Libya.
At once he does what he was told, and the Phoenicians set aside
their ferocity, obeying the will of the god. Above all the queen
receives a quiet spirit and a kindly mind toward the Teucrians.
But the dutiful [*pius*] Aeneas, rolling over many thoughts in the night,   335
when the nourishing light first appeared, decides to go forth
and explore the strange country to learn what shores the wind
has blown him to—who lives there, man or beast, for all he sees
is wild—then to bring back what he discovers to his companions.
He hides his fleet beneath arching woods, under a hollowed-out   340

---

316   *...great Iulus*: Opinion is divided on whether Vergil is referring to the dictator Julius Caesar or to the emperor Augustus, and we cannot really tell from the Latin. The emperor's original name was *Gaius Octavius*. He became *Gaius Julius Caesar Octavianus* on his posthumous adoption by the dictator Julius Caesar in 44 BC. He received the name *Augustus*, "the one who increases," from the senate in 27 BC. *Julius Caesar* here could refer to either man.

319   *with vows*: That is, Julius Caesar, in addition to Aeneas, will be prayed to in heaven.

322   *will be closed*: "Faith" (*fides*) is a typical personification of a quality, a *numen* (for *numen, numina*, see Introduction). *Vesta* is *numen* of the hearth. *Quirinus* is a *numen* representing the Roman people. The gates of the temple to Janus, the god who looks both ways (hence *January*), located in the Roman Forum, were opened when Rome went to war and shut when the Roman world was at peace. According to legend, they were closed during the reign of the early Roman king Numa (c. 750–670 BC), then reopened under his successor. The Gates of Janus remained open for the next four hundred years until after the First Punic War, when they were closed in 235 BC. They reopened eight years later and did not close again until 29 BC, under the reign of Augustus, following the deaths of Antony and Cleopatra.

323   *Rage*: The Latin is *furor*.

326   *son of Maia*: Mercury (Hermes).

FIGURE 1.2 *Venus Appears to Aeneas*, **1631, by Pietro da Cortona (1596–1669).**
Da Cortona was the leading Italian Baroque painter of the seventeenth century. He worked mainly in Rome and Florence and is best known for his frescoed ceilings, though he was also an accomplished architect. Here Venus, disguised as a huntress, holds a bow and gestures toward her son Aeneas, who is accompanied by Achates, on the shores of Libya. In the lower right-hand corner is a cupid, and a second cupid flies in the air above Venus, drawing his bow; he is soon to infect Dido with love for Aeneas. A third cupid lurks in the trees. The bearded Aeneas wears a cloak over his armor, and Achates, behind him, carries a bow. Behind Achates, the prow of a ship is pulled onto the shore and Trojans unload cargo. Oil on canvas.

rock, shut-in by trees all around and by twinkling shade.
He himself goes forth accompanied only by Achates,
brandishing in his hands two shafts tipped with broad iron.

    His mother went to meet him in the middle of the wood
having the face and appearance of a young girl, and armed   345
like a Spartan girl, or like Thracian Harpalycê who tires out
horses with her running, and outstrips the Hebrus River
with her swift flight.° Like a huntress she had suspended
her handy bow from her shoulders and had given her hair
to the winds to scatter, her knee bare, her flowing robes   350
gathered in a knot.

          "Hallo," she said before he could speak,
"—you youths, point her out, if by chance you have seen
a sister of mine wandering here, girt with a quiver
and the hide of a spotted lynx, or pressing with shouts
on the tracks of a boar covered in foam."   355

                So she spoke,
and the son of Venus said this in reply: "I have neither
heard nor seen any of your sisters—but by what name
should I call you, young lady? For your face does not
seem that of a mortal, nor does your voice seem that
of a human being. Certainly you are a goddess—the sister   360
of Phoebus?° one of the race of nymphs? May you cast
your grace upon us, whoever you are, and lighten our labor.
Tell us beneath what sky, on what coasts of the world
we are cast. We wander not knowing the people or places,
driven by the wind and the huge waves. Many sacrifices   365
will fall on your altars at our hand!"

              Then Venus said:
"By no means am I worthy of such respect. It is the custom
among young Tyrian women° to carry the quiver
and bind their ankles high with the purple boot.
You see the Punic realm, the people of Tyre and the city   370
of Agenor.° But the neighboring country is Libya,
inhabited by a people unconquerable in war. Dido
holds the power, having come from Tyre, fleeing
her brother. Long is the tale of woe, long its winding

---

348   *...flight*: The Hebrus flows into the Aegean through Thrace just opposite the island of SAMOTHRACE. Harpalycê was a Thracian princess who took to living in the woods after her father was deposed from power, according to Servius, a Latin commentator on Vergil.

361   *sister of Phoebus*: That is, Diana (Artemis).

368   *Tyrian women*: The Tyrians are the Phoenicians, Dido and her followers.

371   *Agenor*: Agenor was an ancestor of Dido. The "city of Agenor" is Carthage.

375 course. However I will give you the high points
of the affair.

Dido's story

"She had a husband by the name of Sychaeus,
richest of the Phoenicians in his wide fields, and loved
with a great love by the unhappy Dido. Her father
gave Sychaeus to her, a virgin. He yoked Dido to him
380 under the best of auspices.° But Pygmalion, Dido's brother,
held the power in Tyre, more monstrous in crime than all
others. Rage° arose between them, and Pygmalion impiously [*impius*]
killed Sychaeus at the altar of the household gods, blinded
by the love of gold—secretly, while Sychaeus least suspected
385 the attack, without a thought for his sister's love.
             "For long Pygmalion
concealed the deed. Maliciously pretending this and that,
he deceived the love-sick bride with false hope. But while
Dido slept, the ghost came of her unburied husband.
Raising his pale face in a wondrous way, he laid bare
390 the cruel altars where his breast was pierced by iron.
He revealed all the secret crimes of the house. He persuaded
her to take swift flight from the land of her fathers. As an aid
to her journey he showed her treasures long hidden underground,
a mass of silver and gold known to no one. Moved by this
395 information, Dido made ready a company for her flight.
      "Dido and her followers gather, all those who felt a hatred
or keen fear for the cruel tyrant. They take hold of ships which
chanced to be ready, and load up the gold.° The wealth of greedy
Pygmalion is carried across the sea. The leader of the expedition
400 is a woman. They came to the place where now you see
the huge walls and citadel of new Carthage rising. They
purchased the ground, called 'Byrsa' from the name of the deed,
as much as they could surround with a bull's hide.°
      "But who are you? From which shores do you come?
405 And where are you going?"

---

380 *auspices*: The Romans always took auspices before any important business, and especially before a wedding.

382 *Rage*: The Latin is *furor*.

398 *the gold*: That is, the buried treasure for which Pygmalion had murdered Sychaeus in the first place.

403 *bull's hide*: The Tyrians purchased as much ground as an oxhide (*byrsa*) would cover. Then they cleverly sliced the hide into thin strips to surround a large area. The story arose from a false etymology: the Phoenicians called their citadel *Bosra*, Semitic for "citadel," which sounds like the Greek word for oxhide, *byrsa*.

Aeneas' story

                      To Venus' questions Aeneas answers,
sighing and drawing a deep breath from his breast:
"O goddess, if I were to tell you all that has happened
from the beginning, and you have time to listen to the story
of our labors, the night would close the day before I finished.
"From ancient Troy we come, if by chance you have heard   410
the name of Troy. A storm has driven us by its own caprice
over many seas to the coast of Libya. I am the dutiful [*pius*]
Aeneas. I carry with me in my fleet the Penates snatched
from the enemy. My fame is known in the heavens above.
I seek Italy, the land of my fathers, and a race sprung   415
from Jupiter on high.°
                    "With twice ten ships I sailed
on the Phrygian sea,° my mother showing the way, following
the decrees of Fate. Scarcely do seven ships remain,
shaken by the waves and the East Wind. Myself unknown,
in want, I wander over the Libyan wasteland, expelled   420
from Europe and Asia."
                        Venus did not let him complain more,
but interrupted him in the middle of his lament:
"Whoever you are, you do not draw breath of life as a being
hated by the gods of heaven, for you have come to this
Tyrian city. So go forth, and make your way from here   425
to the queen's palace. For I tell you that your companions
will be restored and your fleet recovered, and brought
to a safe harbor when the North winds turned—unless
my parents have falsely given an augury° for nothing!
"See those twelve swans exultant in a row that the bird   430
of Jove, swooping from the ethereal regions, has harried
in the open air? Now in a long array they seem either
to take their places, or to look down on the places
where the others have settled. Just as they play, having
returned on their whistling wings, and all together   435
have encircled the sky and sung their song, no differently
have your ships and your men reached the harbor,

---

416 *on high*: Dardanus, a famous early Trojan king and a son of Jupiter/Zeus (see Genealogical Chart), supposedly came originally from Italy.

417 *Phrygian sea*: That is, the Aegean Sea near Troy.

429 *augury*: Probably from a root meaning "to prosper," augury was a Roman religious practice in which the will of the gods was determined by observing the flight of birds and other celestial phenomena. The augur was an important official in ancient Rome, and no undertaking in Roman society—public or private, including war, commerce, and religion—went ahead without an augury, or a "taking of the auspices."

or under full sail entered the river's mouth.° So go forth,
and direct your steps where the path leads you."
440 She spoke, and as she turned away, her rose-colored
neck flashed and from her head her ambrosial hair° breathed
forth a divine scent, and her gown fell to the bottom of her feet.
It was clear from her gait that she was a goddess.
                                              When he
recognized that she was his mother, he pursued her with
445 these words as she fled: "Why do you mock your son with
these empty phantoms?—you too are cruel! Why can I not
clasp your right hand and hear, and speak, with heartfelt words?"

Aeneas enters Carthage

      Thus he reproaches her, and he turns his feet toward
the city's walls. Venus hid the Trojans in a dark mist as they went.
450 Being a goddess, she poured around them a thick blanket
of cloud so that no one might see them, so that no one might
touch them or delay them or ask why they had come.
She herself goes off through the high air to PAPHOS,
and joyfully revisits her residence where her temple
455 and its hundred altars burn with Sabaean incense and breathe
with fresh garlands.°
                              In the meanwhile Aeneas and his men hastened up
the road in the direction where the path indicated. And soon
they climbed the hill that loomed large over the city,
looking down from above on the towers turned toward them.
460 Aeneas marvels at the massive structures, once mere huts,
and he marvels at the gates and the din and the paved roads.
The Tyrians eagerly press on, some to draw out a line of wall
or to build up the citadel and to roll stones with their hands,
some to choose a place for a building and to mark it with
465 a furrow. They make laws and choose magistrates and a sacred
senate. Here some dig out the harbor; there, others set in place
the deep foundations for theaters. They cut out huge columns
from the cliffs, suitable decorations for the stage under construction.

---

438 *river's mouth*: Venus points to and explains the omen of twelve swans that, though pursued by an eagle, safely reach land. The swans are Aeneas' ships, and the eagle is the storm. One ship, that of Orontes, was sunk, leaving nineteen of the original twenty ships—the seven Aeneas knows about and the twelve indicated by the omen. The swan was a bird sacred to Venus.

441 *ambrosial hair*: Ambrosia, "immortal," was the food of the gods, but the adjective is often used to mean "fragrant" or "divine," as here.

456 *garlands*: Paphos is in Cyprus, where there was an ancient shrine to Aphrodite/Venus. The Sabaeans were a people of southwest Arabia famous for their production of frankincense.

Even as bees in the early summer go about their business
in the flowery fields beneath the sun, when they lead forth 470
the grown offspring of their race, or when they pack
the liquid honey and strain their hives with the sweet nectar,
or they receive the burdens of the bees flying in, or making
a line of war they prevent the lazy herd of drones from
approaching the folds—the work is hot, and the fragrant 475
honey is scented with thyme—
                      "Blessed are they whose walls
already rise!" said Aeneas, and he looks up at the roofs
of the city.
          Hidden in a cloud, he enters the city and—wondrous
to tell!—he passes through the midst of the crowd, and he
mingles with the men. No one sees him. 480
                                 There was a grove
in the middle of the city, joyful in its shade, just where
the Phoenicians, pummeled by waves and the whirlwind,
first dug up the sign that Juno the queen had showed them,
the head of a spirited horse.° Thus were they to be great
in war and a wealthy people throughout the ages. Here 485
Sidonian Dido was building to Juno a huge temple,
rich in gifts and the power of the goddess.° Its threshold,
rising in steps, was made of bronze, and its lintel beams
were joined with bronze, and its doors of bronze creaked
on the hinges. 490

Aeneas sees a painting of the Trojan War

          In this grove first did a surprising sight
allay Aeneas' fears. Here first Aeneas dared to hope for safety
and to trust in a better outcome to his troubles. For while
waiting for the queen in the huge temple, while he marvels
at the good fortune of the city, he inspects every object,
the handicraft of various artists intermingled and the products 495
of their labor, and he sees the battles of Ilium all in due order,
the war now famous and known throughout the entire world—
the sons of Atreus, and Priam, and Achilles enraged at them both.°

---

484 *spirited horse*: A priest of Juno had told Dido where to build her city. While laying the foundations, the Phoenicians dug up the head of a horse, a sign of future power because the horse is an animal of war.

486–487 *Sidonian Dido . . . the goddess*: SIDON was the other great Phoenician port, along with Tyre. The great goddess of ancient Carthage was Tanit. Her symbol, the design of a woman raising her hands 🙌, is commonly found in archaeological sites of Phoenician settlements.

498 *them both*: Aeneas sees painted scenes from the Trojan War. Achilles, the Greek, is angry at Priam because he is king of the Trojans and at the sons of Atreus because Agamemnon took his girl, the central theme of the *Iliad*'s action.

Aeneas stopped, and weeping said: "What place, Achates,
500 what region on earth is not filled with our sorrow? Look—
there is Priam! Here too honor meets its own rewards.
There are the tears of things,° and mortal destiny touches
the heart. Let your fear go. Your fame will bring you
some safety."°
　　　　　　So he spoke, and he feasts his soul on the insubstantial
505 paintings, moaning all the while, and his face was covered
with tears. For he saw how, as they fought around Pergama,°
the Greeks fled, the Trojan youth pressing on them, and in another
place the Trojans were in rout with the plumed Achilles
running them down in his chariot. Not far from here
510 he recognizes, weeping, the tents of Rhesus with their
white canvas. Betrayed in their first sleep, the son of Tydeus,
covered in gore, laid them waste, with many dead. He turned
the fiery horses toward the Greek camp before they could taste
the Trojan food or drink from the waters of Xanthus.°
515 In another part Troilus has thrown away his armor and is borne
away by his horses—unhappy boy and no match in a fight
with Achilles. Fallen backward, he clings to his empty chariot,
still holding the reins. His neck and hair are dragged on the ground,
and the dust is inscribed by his inverted spear.°
　　　　　　　　　　　　　　　　　In the meanwhile
520 the Trojan women went to the temple of an unfriendly Pallas,
their hair all undone, carrying a robe, sad like suppliants,
beating their breasts with their hands: But the goddess turned away
and held her eyes fixed on the ground.°

502　*tears of things*: The Latin is the famous line *sunt lacrima rerum*, often taken as encapsulating the melancholy tone of the *Aeneid*.

504　*some safety*: Aeneas thinks that the fame of the Trojan War will lead the Phoenicians to help them.

506　*Pergama*: The citadel of Troy, often used as a synonym for the city.

514　*Xanthus*: In *Iliad* Book 10 (the *Doloneia*) Odysseus and Diomedes (the son of Tydeus) sneak into the Trojan camp and murder king Rhesus and his men, newly arrived from Thrace, in their sleep, then drive the horses back to the Greek camp. An oracle said that Troy could never be taken if Rhesus' horses ate the grass or drank the water of Troy. A play, the *Rhesus*, attributed (probably wrongly) to Euripides (480–406 BC), survives on the theme. The XANTHUS is one of the rivers on the Trojan plain.

519　*inverted spear*: Homer only mentions Troilus in passing, the youngest legitimate son of Priam, but the developed theme was the subject of a lost play by Sophocles (497–406 BC) and was illustrated commonly on Greek pottery from the Archaic and Classical periods (700–300 BC). An oracle said that Troy could never fall if Troilus reached the age of twenty, so Achilles ambushed and murdered him as he watered his horses at a well outside Troy. The story of Troilus and Cressida, told by Chaucer and Shakespeare, is medieval in origin.

523　*on the ground*: In Book 6 of the *Iliad* the Trojan women, led by Hecuba, attempt to placate Athena/Minerva by presenting her with a fancy robe, but she does not grant their prayers.

                        Three times Achilles
dragged Hector's body around the walls of Troy and sold off
his lifeless body for gold.° Then he gave a great moan   525
from the bottom of his heart when he saw the spoils,
when he saw the chariot and the body of his friend,
and Priam stretching forth his unarmed hands.
                                                He also
recognized himself among the Achaean captains, and Dawn's
troops and the arms of black Memnon.° The mad Penthesilea   530
leads her troops of Amazons with moon-shaped shields, and rages
in the midst of her thousands, bound with a golden belt
beneath her naked breast—a warrior queen, she dares battle,
a virgin lady fighting with men.°

the Trojans meet Dido

                        While Dardanian Aeneas
was looking at these wondrous scenes, while in amazement   535
he stared fixed in a single gaze, the queen comes to the temple,
the beautiful Dido, surrounded by a large crowd of youths.
Just as on the banks of the Eurotas, or along the hills of Cynthus,
Diana leads her dancing bands, whom a thousand Oreads follows,
grouped on this side and that, and she carries a quiver   540
on her shoulder, overtopping all the goddesses as she goes,
and joy fills the silent breast of Latona°—even so was Dido
as she moved joyously through the middle of the crowd,
urging on the work of her future kingdom.
                                           Then at the doors
of the goddess, beneath the dome of the temple, girded in arms,   545
resting on a high throne, she took her seat.° She gave out rules
and laws to the people. She equally divided the labor
of construction or assigned it by lot.

---

525 *for gold*: In Book 22 of the *Iliad* Achilles pursues Hector three times around the walls of Troy; he later drags Hector's body around the tomb of his dead friend Patroclus. In Book 24 he ransoms the body to Priam.

530 *black Memnon*: Memnon was a son of Dawn (Aurora). In the post-Homeric tradition, he brought his Ethiopian troops from the East, but Achilles killed him in a duel. The story was told in the lost epic the *Aethiopis* by Arctinus (seventh century BC).

534 *with men*: According to another post-Homeric tradition, an army of Amazons came to the Trojan's aid, led by Penthesilea. Achilles killed her too, but as he thrust in his spear he met her eyes and fell in love—so the story goes.

542 *Latona*: The Eurotas is the stream that flows through SPARTA, where there was a shrine to Artemis/Diana. Cynthus is the hill on the island of DELOS where Artemis/Diana was born. Oreads are mountain nymphs. Latona is Leto, the mother of Artemis/Diana.

546 *her seat*: The doors would be at the back of the main hall, which is domed. This is a Roman style of architecture, and the Roman senate often met in such temples.

FIGURE 1.3 *Dido Building Carthage*, **1815, by J. M. W. Turner (1775–1851).** Turner was an English Romantic painter and artist, one of the greatest experts of landscape painting, with an astonishing mastery of light and color. Turner was known as "the painter of light" and his work is seen as a Romantic forerunner to Impressionism. This is one of Turner's best-known works, a classical landscape taken from the *Aeneid*. Dido is the tiny figure on the left, in white, standing by the harbor and directing the builders of the new city of Carthage. The man in front of her, wearing armor and facing away, is probably Aeneas. On a rock to the right of Dido some children play with a small toy boat in the water, suggesting the emerging naval power of Carthage. The tomb of Dido's dead husband Sychaeus is on the right bank. Other buildings in a classical style rise in the background. An intense yellow sunrise dominates the top and center of the painting, symbolizing the dawn of a new empire. Oil on canvas.

                    Then suddenly Aeneas
sees Antheus and Sergestus and the powerful Cloanthus°
and others of the Trojans approaching through the large mob,   550
whom the black storm had scattered on the sea and driven far away
to other shores. Aeneas was amazed, and so was Achates—
with joy and fear. They burned with eagerness to join their hands,
but the uncertainness of the affair confused their spirit.°
They conceal their eagerness. Still enclosed in the enfolding mist,   555
they look to see what is the fortune of their comrades,
on what shore they have left the fleet, and why they have come.

    From all the ships, chosen men have come, begging for kindness,
and with a cry they sought the temple. And when they had entered
and were given a chance to speak to the queen, Ilioneus,   560
the oldest of them, began to speak with a calm demeanor:
"O queen, to whom Jupiter has granted the freedom
to found a city and to reign with justice the insolent tribes,
we beseech you—wretched Trojans, driven by winds over every sea—
please drive off terrible fire from our ships! Spare a pious [*pio*] race!   565
Look graciously on our affairs! We have not come to wreck your
Libyan home with the sword, or to drive stolen booty to the shores.
Such violence is not within us, nor is there such arrogance
in the vanquished.
              "There is a place that the Greeks call Hesperia,
an ancient land, mighty in arms and the richness of its soil.   570
Oenotrians lived there. Now, as they say, a younger race
calls it Italy from the name of their leader.° This is where
we were going when suddenly a stormy Orion,° rising
in flood, carried us into blind shoals, and with ferocious
blasts scattered us amid pathless rocks, far in the midst   575
of waves that surged relentlessly.
                        "We have sailed to your
shores, there being few of us. What race of men are you?
Or, what land is so barbarous as to permit this custom? We are

---

549   *... Cloanthus*: Aeneas had earlier expressed concern for the whereabouts of Antheus and Cloanthus; Sergestus is first mentioned here.

554   *their spirit*: That is, Aeneas and Achates do not know how these other Trojans survived the storm and made it to Dido's court.

572   *... their leader*: "Hesperia" is a Greek word that means "western land." Italus was a legendary king of the Oenotrians, a people of southern Italy.

573   *stormy Orion*: Storms were associated with the rising of Orion in midsummer. Ilioneus does not know about Juno's responsibility for the storm.

barred from the welcome of your beach! Your men stir up
580 wars and prevent us from setting foot on the border of the land.
    "If you despise the bonds of humanity and mortal arms,
then expect that the gods will reward you according
to your deeds. Our king was Aeneas, than whom no one
was more just, nor more dutiful [*pietate*], nor greater in war
585 and in arms. If the Fates preserve the man, if he still
feeds on the air of heaven and does not lie in the cruel
shades, we are not afraid.
    "Nor would you regret to have
competed first in kindness. Sicily too has cities and arms,
and the illustrious Acestes, a Trojan.° Allow us to beach
590 our fleet wracked by the winds, and allow us to cut out
planks in the forest, and fit out oars so that we may
gladly seek Italy and Latium, if it is given us to recover
our companions and our king and to head for Italy.
    "But if our salvation is cut off, and the Libyan sea has taken
595 you—great father of the Trojans!—and there is no hope
for Iulus leading us, at least let us seek the straits of Sicily
from where we have come, and the homes that are prepared
there, and let us have Acestes as our king."
    So spoke Ilioneus,
and all the Dardanians at once shouted their assent.

Dido welcomes the Trojans

    Then Dido,
600 lowering her eyes, speaks briefly: "Don't be afraid, Trojans.
Put aside your worries. Harsh necessity and the newness
of my kingdom compel me to undertake such deeds
and to protect my borders with guards.
    "Who is there who does
not know of the race of the followers of Aeneas? Who does
605 not know about the city of Troy, or about its brave men,
or of the fires of that great war? The Phoenicians do not have
such dull hearts, nor does the sun yoke his steeds so far
from this Tyrian city.° Whether you choose great Hesperia
and the fields of Saturn, or the land of Eryx and Acestes

---

589 *a Trojan*: That is, if Aeneas is dead, the Trojan Acestes can protect them and pay back Dido for any help she can give.

608 ... *this Tyrian city*: That is, we are not so uncivilized, nor do we live so far away, that we have not heard of the Trojan War.

as king, I will send you forth with an escort as protection 610
and I will help you with my wealth.°
                    "Or do you wish
to settle here in this realm with me on equal terms?
The city that I am building is yours. Draw up your ships.
I shall treat Trojan and Tyrian alike. And I wish that your king
himself, driven by the same wind, were here now. For surely 615
I will send trusted men along the shore, and I will order
them to traverse the furthest bounds of Libya to see if,
shipwrecked, he wanders in the forest or in a town."

Aeneas is revealed

    Moved in their spirit by these words, the brave Achates
and father Aeneas had long burned to break free from the cloud. 620
Achates first addresses Aeneas: "Son of a goddess, what
do you think we should do? You see that everything is safe,
the fleet and our comrades restored. Only one is missing,°
whom we ourselves saw drowned in the midst of the flood.
All else agrees with what your mother says."° 625
                    Scarcely had
he spoken, when the cloud around them suddenly parts
and disappears into open air. Aeneas stood forth and gleamed
in the clear light, his face and shoulders like those of a god.
For his mother herself breathed beauty on his locks, and gave him
the radiant light of youth, and on his eyes a joyful luster, even as 630
the grace that the hand adds to ivory, or when silver or Parian stone°
is set in yellow gold.
                    Then he spoke to the queen as follows:
"I am here before you, whom you seek—Aeneas of Troy,
snatched from the Libyan waves! O you who alone have taken
pity on the unspeakable sufferings of Troy, you who grant us— 635
the remnants left by the Danaäns, exhausted on land and sea
by every misfortune, bereft of everything—to be a part
of your city, your home. It is not in our power, nor in the power

---

611 *... my wealth*: After being expelled from heaven by his son Jupiter, Saturn went to Italy, where he established a Golden Age on the fields of Saturn (see Book 8). Eryx, a son of Venus, was a king in western Sicily who challenged Hercules to a wrestling match but was defeated and killed. Nearby Mount ERYX (on which is built the modern town Erice) was named after him. In ancient times there was a temple to Venus there, probably originally dedicated to the Semitic goddess Tanit. Whether the Trojans want to go to Italy or Sicily, Dido will help them, she means.

623 *is missing*: Orontes, whose death Aeneas witnessed (lines 130–136).

625 *mother says*: In lines 426–428, though Venus did not mention the death of Orontes.

631 *Parian stone*: The Cycladic island of Paros was the source of fine marble for statues and buildings.

of anyone who anywhere survives from the Dardanian race,
640 scattered over the whole great earth, to pay you back with sufficient
thanks. May the gods bring you worthy rewards, if any powers
respect those obedient to their duty [*pios*], if there is justice
in the world and a spirit conscious of what is right.
   "But what happy ages have produced you? What glorious parents
645 gave birth to you, so noble a child? While the rivers run
into the sea, while in the mountains shadows run over
the hills, while heaven feeds the stars—for so long will
your honor and your name and your praises last, no matter
what lands summon me."
           Thus Aeneas spoke, and reached out
650 to Ilioneus with his right hand, and with his left to Serestus,
and afterwards the others, stalwart Gyas and stalwart Cloanthus.
   Dido was amazed first at seeing him, then at the immense
misfortune of the man, and so she said: "What misfortune,
O son of a goddess, follows you through so many dangers?
655 What violence brings you to these cruel shores? Are you
that Aeneas whom lush Venus bore by the wave of the Simoeis?
In fact I remember well when Teucer came to Sidon,
driven from the land of his fathers, he sought a new kingdom
with the help of Belus.° My father Belus at that time
660 was laying waste Cyprus, and held it under his sway.
From that time on was known to me the fall of the city
of Troy and your name and the Pelasgian kings.°
Though Teucer was an enemy, he praised the Teucrians
highly, and claimed that he was sprung from the ancient
665 line of the Teucrians.°
             Come then, young men, and pass
within our halls. I also have been driven by a like fortune
through many trials, a fortune that willed that, here
in this land, at last, I might find my rest. Familiar with evil,
I have learned to come to the aid of those in distress."

---

659 *of Belus*: When Ajax was refused the arms of the dead Achilles, he killed himself. When his half-brother Teucer returned from the war to the island of his native Salamis without Ajax's body or armor, his father Telamon exiled him. Teucer fled to Cyprus and there founded a city called Salamis after his homeland. Belus is the Semitic *Baal*, "lord," here Dido's father, but also the name of the Semitic storm-god (equivalent to Zeus/Jupiter).

662 *Pelasgian kings*: That is, Menelaus and Agamemnon. "Pelasgian" refers properly to the pre-Greek inhabitants of the lower Balkans, but Vergil uses it to mean "Greek."

665 *Teucrians*: An ancient king of Troy was named *Teucer*, hence the Trojans are *Teucrians* (see Genealogical Chart). This is not the Teucer, son of Telamon, whose mother was Hesionê, a daughter of Laomedon, a king of Troy: Hercules gave the captive Hesionê to his companion Telamon after sacking Troy in an earlier generation. Hence the Greek Teucer is of Trojan descent!

                              Thus she spoke.
At once she leads Aeneas into the palace, at once she proclaims   670
a sacrifice to the gods. In the meanwhile she sends twenty bulls
to his companions on the shore, and one hundred large swine
with bristling backs, and one hundred fat lambs with their ewes,
joyous gifts of the day.
                    The palace within is adorned in splendid
luxury, and in the midst of the halls they prepare a banquet.   675
There are elaborately embroidered coverlets of a proud purple,
and on the table massive silver plate, and in gold are chased
the mighty deeds of her forefathers, a long series of exploits
traced through many heroes from the first days of her race.°
Aeneas—for a father's love did not allow his heart to rest—   680
sends swift Achates to the ships to report these matters,
to Ascanius, and to lead him to the city: Toward Ascanius
lies all the care of a loving parent. He asks Ascanius to bring
presents snatched from the ruins of Ilium—a cloak stiff
with embroidered figures of gold, and a veil fringed   685
on its edge with a yellow acanthus leaf design, clothes
worn by Argive Helen, which she brought from MYCENAE.
They were a marvelous gift from her mother Leda when she fled
to Pergama and her unlawful marriage. Also, the scepter
that Ilionê, Priam's oldest daughter, once had carried,   690
a pearl necklace, and a double crown decorated with gems
and gold.° Hastening to follow these commands, Achates
hurried to the ships.

Cupid impersonates Ascanius to inflame Dido's passion for Aeneas

                    But the Cytherean° devises new schemes,
new devices in her heart so that Cupid, changing his appearance
and form, might come in the place of sweet Ascanius,   695
and with his gifts inflame the queen with a mad passion,
and light a fire in her very bones. In fact Venus fears
the duplicitous Tyrians, who spoke with double-tongue.
Wild Juno angers her, and at nightfall Venus' worries increase.
Thus Venus speaks to winged Cupid as follows: "Child,   700

---

679 *of her race*: These are drinking vessels of gold and silver carved in relief with the figures of famous men and their deeds. Such vessels were popular in Roman elite circles.

692 *...and gold*: "Mycenae," that is, Greece, because Helen came from Sparta where Menelaus ruled; Agamemnon was king in Mycenae. Jupiter possessed Leda in the form of a swan, who then gave birth to Helen. Ilionê was a daughter of Priam who married a king from Thrace, who then treacherously murdered her brother Polydorus.

693 *Cytherean*: Venus.

my strength, my mighty power—you alone, O child, disdain
my powerful father's Typhoean arrows!° To you I flee!
As a suppliant I beg your godhead. How your brother Aeneas
is tossed around on the sea, off all the coasts, by the hatred
705 of wicked Juno is known to you—and often have you felt
the same pain as I. Phoenician Dido now holds Aeneas and delays
him with soft words, but I dread where Juno's hospitality may lead.
She will not be idle at so great a turning point of affairs.
For this reason I intend first to outwit queen Dido with duplicities,
710 to bind her with the flame of love, so that she may not
be changed by some divine power, so that she might be kept
on my side by her passion for Aeneas. How can you do this?

"Listen to my plan. The princely boy, Iulus, my greatest
darling, prepares to go at the summons of his beloved father
715 to the Sidonian city with gifts that have survived the sea
and the flames of Troy. Him I will put to sleep on high Cythera,
or hide him in my sacred shine of Idalium° so that no one
is aware of the trick or meets him on the way.

"Take on his form
by craft for a single night and, being a boy, assume the boy's
720 familiar face. When a joyful Dido receives you in her bosom,
in the midst of the royal feast and the flowing wine, when she
embraces you and impresses her sweet kisses, you can
breathe into her a secret fire and beguile her with poison!"

Cupid obeys the words of his beloved mother, and he sets
725 aside his wings, and he walks rejoicing in the steps of Iulus.
But Venus pours over the limbs of Ascanius a quiet repose
and, nestled in her bosom, the goddess carries him to the high
woods of Idalium where soft herbs wrap him in flowers
and fragrance-breathing shade.

Cupid went in obedience
730 to his mother's word, carrying the royal gifts for the Tyrians,
happy in having Achates as his guide. When he arrived,
the queen had already taken her place among the splendid
tapestries on a golden couch set in the midst of all.

Now father Aeneas, now the Trojan youth gather,
735 and they lie down on purple coverlets. Servants pour water

---

702 *Typhoean arrows*: The thunderbolts by which Jupiter overcame Typhoeus, a monster of chaos who threatened rule by the Olympians. Venus means that even Jupiter is subject to the power of Love, a familiar theme in ancient literature.

717 *Idalium*: Idalium was a town and shrine sacred to Venus on the island of Cyprus. Venus means she will magically transport Ascanius to one of these places to keep him out of sight.

on their hands, serve out bread from baskets, and offer napkins
of smooth texture. There are fifty serving girls within, whose task
is to arrange in order the long succession of foods, and to magnify
the Penates with fire.° There are a hundred more, and as many
boys again of a like age to load the tables with food and to set out   740
the cups.
        The Tyrians, too, gathered in throngs throughout
the merry halls, summoned to recline on the embroidered
couches. They marvel at the gifts of Aeneas, they marvel
at Iulus, at his rosy face and his words that seemed so human,
and the robe and veil decorated with a golden acanthus.   745
        The unhappy Phoenician, especially, doomed to future ruin,
is unable to satisfy her heart, but catches fire as she gazes.
She is thrilled alike by the boy and the gifts. Once he has
hung in embrace from Aeneas' neck and has satisfied
the great love of his pretended father, he goes to the queen.
She with her eyes, with her whole heart hangs onto him,   750
and again and again fondles him in her lap. Poor Dido,
she does not know how great a god sits there, to her sorrow!
        He, mindful of his Acidalian mother,° gradually begins
to rid her of the memory of Sychaeus, and tries with a living
passion to preoccupy her long-suffering spirit and her heart   755
unused to love. When there came a lull in the feasting,
and the tables were removed, they set up huge wine-mixing
bowls and surrounded the bowls with garlands of flowers.
A din arises in the palace, and voices echo through
the spacious halls. Burning lamps hang down from the coffered   760
golden ceiling and flaming torches expel the night.
        Then the queen called for a cup heavy with gems and gold
and filled it with wine—a cup that Belus and all his line
was accustomed to use.°
                    A silence fell upon the hall:
"Jupiter—for they say that you give laws for host and guests—   765
grant that this be a day of joy for the Tyrians and those who
have set out from Troy, and that our children may remember it.
May Bacchus be here, the giver of joy, and the good Juno.
And you, O Tyrians, celebrate this gathering with a friendly spirit!"
So she spoke, and she poured out a drink-offering on the table.   770

---

739 *with fire*: Images of the Penates, the "spirits of the larder," were placed over the hearth so that to keep up a good fire was to "magnify" them.

753 *Acidalian mother*: Venus and the Graces are said to bathe in the Acidalian fountain in Boeotia (Greece).

764 *... to use*: Not the Belus of line 659, but an ancestor, probably the founder of the line.

FIGURE 1.4 *Aeneas Introducing Cupid Dressed as Ascanius to Dido*, **1757, by Giovanni Battista Tiepolo (1696–1770).** Tiepolo was an Italian Rococo painter and printmaker from Venice, one of the greatest painters of eighteenth-century Europe. Tiepolo did a series of fresco paintings on classical subjects in the Villa Valmarana, Vicenza, in northern Italy, where this painting comes from. Dido, sitting on her throne under a baldachin and robed in precious furs, welcomes Aeneas and Cupid disguised as Aeneas' son, Ascanius/Iulus. The wings and the quiver of arrows point to the true identity of the god of Love. Aeneas wears a helmet and breastplate, and his shield is propped against his thigh. The old man is Achates, who carries a medieval halberd. The architectural backdrop is typical of Tiepolo. Fresco.

She was the first, after pouring libations, to touch the cup
to her lips. Then, prodding him, she gave it to Bitias.° He briskly
drank from the foaming golden cup, and he gulped it down deep.
Afterwards the other lords drank.
                       Long-haired Iopas then filled
the hall with sound from his golden lyre: Great Atlas had taught   775
him his craft.° He sings of the wandering moon and solar eclipses,
from which sprang the race of men and beasts, from which come
the rain and lightning. He sang too of Arcturus and the rainy
Hyades and the twin Bears,° and of why the sun of winter
hastens to dip itself in Ocean, or what delay holds back   780
the slowly passing nights.
                       The Tyrians redouble their applause
and the Trojans follow. No less did unhappy Dido extend
the night with all manner of conversation, and she drank
the draft of everlasting love, asking repeatedly about Priam
and Hector, and about the armor with which the son of Dawn   785
came, and about the horses of Diomedes, and about the greatness
of Achilles.°
    "But come, and tell us from the beginning,
my guest, of the treachery of the Danaäns,° the destruction
of your people, and your wanderings. For already a seventh
summer carries you, a wanderer, over every land and sea."   790

---

772 *Bitias*: Apparently a follower of Aeneas (later killed by Turnus, Book 9).

776 *his craft*: The Titan Atlas was said to have invented astronomy, the subject of Iopas' song. Atlas is also associated with Africa. Today the Atlas Mountains rise in Morocco, Algeria, and Tunisia.

779 *... twin bears*: Arcturus in the constellation Boötes is the brightest star in the northern hemisphere, except for Sirius. The Hyades, "rainers," were the five daughters of Atlas and half-sisters to the Pleiades; after the death of their brother Hyas, the weeping sisters were transformed into a cluster of stars in the constellation Taurus, afterwards associated with rain. The Bears are the Big and Little Dippers.

787 *... of Achilles*: The son of Dawn is Memnon (see note on line 530); Vulcan made his armor. The horses of Diomedes are probably those he stole from the Thracian king Rhesus (see note on line 514). Of course Achilles is a major figure; in the *Iliad* he fights Aeneas.

788 *treachery of the Danaäns*: The Trojan Horse.

BOOK 2. *The Fall of Troy*

A general silence fell over the room, and all gazed intently.
Then father Aeneas began to speak from his high couch:
"O queen, you ask us to rehearse our unspeakable pain,
to tell how the Danaäns overthrew wealthy Troy and our sad
5 kingdom—which sorrowful events I witnessed, and was part
of to a great extent. Which Myrmidon, or Dolopian, or soldier of hard
Ulysses° could hold back from tears in recounting such things?
It is nighttime when the dew falls from the sky, and sinking stars
call us to sleep. But if you desire so much to know the disaster
10 that befell us and, in brief, to hear of the final throes of Troy,
although my spirit shudders to remember and recoils in pain—
still, I will begin.

the Trojan Horse

        "Broken by the war, crushed by bad luck
as the years slipped by, the leaders of the Danaäns build a horse,
thanks to the divine skill of Pallas,° as huge as a mountain.
15 They made its ribs of timbered pine. They pretend it is a ritual
offering for a safe return. They spread this lie abroad. Then
they secretly enclose select men in its dark sides, and they
fill the huge deep caverns of its womb with an armed band.
        "In sight of Troy lies TENEDOS, an island celebrated
20 for its wealth so long as the power of Priam remained, now only
a poor harbor with anchorage scarcely trustworthy for ships.
Here the Greeks take themselves, and lurk just off the deserted shore.
We thought they had gone, sailing for MYCENAE. All of Teucria°
threw off its long agony. The gates are opened. Joyously we go forth

---

7 ... *Ulysses*: The Myrmidons were led by Achilles, the Dolopians by his son Pyrrhus (also called Neoptolemus). Pyrrhus has an important role to play later in this book. Ulysses, the Greek Odysseus, typifies all that is rotten and deceitful in Greek culture, a thorough bad guy in Roman myth.

14 *Pallas*: That is, Minerva (Pallas Athena). She of course supported the Greeks, but is also the patroness of handicrafts of all kinds.

23 ... *Teucria*: Mycenae was the home of Agamemnon, but here just stands for Greece. Teucria is another name for Troy (Teucer was an early Trojan king; see Genealogical Chart).

FIGURE 2.1 *Aeneas Telling Dido of His Misfortunes at Troy*, 1815, by Pierre Narcisse Guérin (1774–1833). Guérin, a French Neoclassical painter, was born in Paris, then worked in Rome and Naples. He was famous for his portrayals of scenes from Greek and Roman myth. In this celebrated painting, Aeneas sits on the left on a chair covered by a leopard skin, wearing a helmet but otherwise unarmed. The crowned Dido relaxes on a couch, her left arm around a naked Ascanius/Iulus, who wears a Phrygian (Trojan) cap. A female attendant stands behind the two figures. A statue of Neptune, holding a trident and a cornucopia, stands on a pedestal in a shrine in the background. In the distance is the Bay of Carthage. Oil on canvas.

25 and see the Dorian° camp deserted, the shore abandoned. Here was
the camp of the Dolopians, here savage Achilles pitched his tent.
Here the boats were pulled up, and here they used to draw up
their line.
    "Others wonder at the deadly gift of virgin Minerva.
They are amazed at the massive horse. Thymoetes° first urged
30 us to lead the horse inside the walls and to set it on the citadel—
either he was a traitor, or the fate of Troy drove him to this!
But Capys°—as did those of better opinion—commanded that we cast
the false gift of the Danaäns into the sea, or set it afire,
or that we probe its hollow womb with piercing spear.
35 The undecided crowd split into factions.

Laocoön and the lies of Sinon

                          "Then Laocoön,°
indignant, standing out before all, came running down
from the citadel, accompanied by a great crowd, and from
far off he cried out: 'Wretched citizens! What is this madness?
Do you believe that the enemy has sailed away? Or do you think
40 that the Danaäns' gift lacks in treachery? Don't you know Ulysses?
Either the Achaeans hide concealed in the horse, or this machine
is built to use against our walls, or spy on our homes, or fall
on the city from above. Or it conceals some trick. Don't trust
the horse, Teucrians! Whatever it is, I fear the Danaäns even
45 bearing gifts!'
    "So speaking, he whirled with immense power
a huge spear into the belly of the beast with its rounded seams.
It stood there trembling, and the hollow caverns of the vibrating
womb gave out a long groan. And if the fate of the gods had not
been ill-disposed, if our own minds were not so deluded, he would
50 have driven us to slaughter the Greeks hidden in the horse,
and you, O Troy, would still be standing. And you, O high citadel
of Priam, would yet remain!
                   "But lo, just then some Trojan shepherds
brought up a youth with hands tied behind his back, and with a great
clamor dragged him to the king. He gave himself up willingly,

---

25 *Dorian*: Dorian designates the division of the Greeks who lived in the Peloponnesus in classical times, but here it just means "Greek."

29 *Thymoetes*: Not mentioned elsewhere.

32 *Capys*: One of Aeneas' men (see Book 1, line 206).

35 *Laocoön*: A Trojan priest of Neptune.

a man unknown to the Trojans, so that he might bring down
Troy and open the gates to the Achaeans. Of firm spirit and ready
for any outcome, either to pull off his trick or to succumb
to a certain death, the Trojan youth rushed in from every side,
eager to see, and they compete in mocking the captive.
"Hear now about the treachery of the Danaäns, and learn from
a single crime how they are rotten all. The object of everyone's
attention, dazed, defenseless, the captive took his stand and regarded
the lines of Phrygians°: 'Alas, what land will take me now?' he said.
'What seas? What road now remains for wretched me? Now I have
no place with the Danaäns, and the furious Dardanians° summon
bloody vengeance down on my head!'

    "Our spirits were turned aside
by his laments, and our urge to strike him was suppressed. We urged
him to speak, to tell of his birth and his mission, and why we should
believe what he, a captive, had to say.

    "And he, at last putting aside
his fear, said: 'I will tell you everything, O King, no matter what happens
to me—and all the truth,' he said. 'And I do not deny that I am a Greek—
this first of all! If Fortune has made Sinon a wretch, nonetheless,
though she is wicked, she will not leave me without honor,
will not make me a liar.

    "'Perhaps in conversation you have heard
the name of Palamedes, the son of Belus—as well as his glory,
famous by report. On a false charge of treason, by conspiracy,
the Greeks condemned him to death, though he was innocent,
because he opposed the war, and now they regret having taken
from him the light.°

    "'To that man my father, a poor man, sent me
as a companion and relative by blood, to take up arms, and come here
even as a youth. So long as his throne endured, and he was vigorous
in the counsels of the kings, we enjoyed a certain reputation

---

63 *Phrygians*: Phrygia is an area inland from Troy, but Vergil uses "Phrygian" as synonymous with "Trojan." In art Trojans are ordinarily shown wearing Phrygian caps, which have a curious forward-curving shape (see Figure 2.1).

65 *Dardanians*: Dardanus was an ancestor of Priam and founder of Dardania, a kingdom in the TROAD. Hence "Dardanians" are Trojans. The DARDANELLES, an alternate name for the HELLESPONT, are named after Dardanus. See Genealogical Chart.

79 *the light*: Palamedes incurred the anger of Ulysses when Palamedes exposed him for pretending madness in order to avoid the expedition to Troy. Ulysses took his revenge at Troy by planting a letter on a Trojan captive that implicated Palamedes in treachery, whereupon the Greeks stoned him to death. Nothing otherwise is known about Palamedes opposing the war. The story is not in Homer, but all the tragedians treated it. Palamedes was the legendary inventor of the Greek alphabet, and perhaps a man of that name did invent it. His father's name "Belus" suggests his Eastern origins.

and honor. But afterwards, because of the spite of that deceitful man°—
I think you know who I mean!—he withdrew from the shores
85 of light.
    "'I dragged on my life, afflicted, in gloom and sorrow,
and I lamented in my heart the fall of my innocent friend.
Like a fool I did not keep my mouth shut. I vowed that if Fortune
should bring me home, if ever I should return to Argos, my fatherland,
a conqueror, I would take revenge. But my words only raised up
90 hatred. From this I first slipped into disaster.
                            "'From this moment
Ulysses kept terrifying me with slanderous accusations.
From this moment he spread subtle lies among the people.
From that moment, conscious of his guilt, he sought to destroy me.
And he did not rest until, with Calchas° as his assistant—but *why*
95 should I go over all this cruel and useless story? Why delay?
If you count all Greeks as the same, is it not enough to have heard
this much? So take the revenge you should have already taken!
That's what the Ithacan° wants, and the sons of Atreus will pay you
dearly for your deed!'
                "Then we burn to know and find out
100 Sinon's motives, never thinking of such huge wickedness nor of Greek
deceit. Trembling, Sinon prattles on, and he speaks with pretended terror:
'The Danaäns, tired of the long war, often wished to flee away
and give up the siege of Troy. Would that they had! Often a ferocious
storm from the sea shut them up in the land, and South Wind
105 terrified them, though they longed to be gone. And especially,
when that horse stood there, made of maple beams, storm clouds
thundered through the whole sky. Anxious, we sent Eurypylus°
to ask Apollo's oracle, and he brought back these gloomy oracles
from the shrine: *With blood and a murdered virgin you appeased*
110 *the winds when first you came, O Danaäns, to the shores of Ilium.*°
You must seek your return in blood, you must sacrifice an Argive.
    "'When this message came to the ears of the crowd, their minds
were stunned. An icy tremor ran through their bones, wondering
for whom Fate prepared this death, who was it that Apollo demanded.

---

83 *deceitful man*: Ulysses.

94 *Calchas*: The principal Greek seer at Troy. He had advised that Iphigenia, the daughter of Agamemnon, be sacrificed so that the fleet could sail to Troy.

98 *the Ithacan*: Ulysses.

107 *Eurypylus*: In the *Iliad* Eurypylus came to Troy with forty ships. When wounded by Paris, he was nursed and cured by Patroclus.

110 *of Ilium*: Agamemnon sacrificed his daughter Iphigenia to Diana (Artemis), who was holding back the Greek fleet at Aulis with contrary winds.

"'At this the Ithacan dragged the prophet Calchas into the midst 115
in a great tumult, demanding to know what was the gods' will.
Already many prophesied to me the cruel wickedness of that cunning
man, and, keeping silent, they saw what was to come. For ten days
Calchas keeps silence, and shut up in his tent refuses to reveal
the secret by his words, or to condemn someone to death. 120

"'But finally,
driven on by the loud cries of the Ithacan, he breaks his silence,
as agreed, and sentences *me* to the altar. Everyone agreed,
and, what each man had feared for himself, each man endured when
turned to the destruction of another—a wretch!

"'And now the unspeakable
day arrived. The rites were prepared, and the salted grain,° 125
and bindings placed around my temples. I saved myself from death—
I admit it! I broke my chains. I hid myself in the bushes of a slimy
lake all night long until they set sail—as in fact they did set sail!

"'And now I have no hope of ever again seeing the ancient land
of my fathers, nor my sweet children or the father that I have 130
longed for. Perhaps they will seek punishment from them because
of my flight, and take vengeance for this crime by putting these
unfortunate ones to death. And so I beg you, by the gods,
and by the powers who are conscious of the truth, and by whatever
faith that still remains inviolable anywhere among men—have pity 135
on my great suffering, have pity on the spirit who endures
undeserved agony!'"

Sinon's explanation of the Horse

"Because of these tears we granted him life,
and we also pitied him. Priam was first to order that the man
be released from his manacles and his tight bonds, and he speaks
to him with friendly words: 'Whoever you are, from this time forward 140
forget about the Greeks. They are lost to you. You will be one of us!
And explain to me truly what I ask: Why have they built this massive
huge horse? Who is responsible? Or what is their purpose?
What object of religion is this, or what machine of war?'"
"He spoke. But Sinon, schooled in deception and the Greek art, 145
raised his palms, released from the chains, to the stars, and said:
'You, O eternal fires, in your invulnerable power, I call to witness,'
that man said, 'and you altars and foul swords that I escaped, and you
bindings of the gods that I wore as a victim—divine law allows me

---

125 *salted grain*: Wheat meal mixed with salt was sprinkled on the head of the sacrificial victim.

150 to break the sacred oaths of the Greeks and to hate those men! and to
carry everything that is hidden into the light!
                              "'I am held by no laws
of their country. Only do you Trojans abide by what you have promised.
Now that Troy is saved, honor your assurances, if what I say is the truth,
if I repay you handsomely.
                              "'The Greeks always placed their hopes
155 and their confidence in beginning the war in the help of Pallas.
But from the moment that the son of Tydeus, Diomedes, and that deviser
of evil [*impius*] Ulysses, approached the fateful Palladium, to snatch it away
from its sacred temple, murdering the guardians of the high citadel,
and dared to seize the sacred idol, and to touch the ribbons of the virgin
160 goddess with bloody hands°—from that moment the hopes of the Danaäns
slipped backwards and ebbed away. Their power was broken!
                              "'The mind
of the goddess was against them. Tritonia° showed clear signs of this,
and with certain portents. Scarcely was the statue put down
in the camp but that flashing fires darted from her upturned eyes,
165 and a salty sweat ran over her limbs, and three times—this *is* amazing!—
she leaped from the ground, holding her shield and her quivering spear!
     "'So right away Calchas proclaims we must attempt a flight by sea,
and that Troy cannot be taken by Argive weapons, unless they first
seek purification at Argos and bring back the support of the goddess,
170 whom they have taken over the sea with them in their curved ships.°
     "And now they are heading with the wind to their native Mycenae.
They are preparing weapons and the friendship of the gods,
recrossing the sea to arrive unexpectedly. Thus Calchas
explains the omens. Warned by them, they have set up this horse
175 as a substitute for the Palladium. They have made this effigy to appease
Minerva's wounded godhead, to make severe atonement for their violation.
     "'Calchas commanded them to raise up this great mass of woven timbers,
to raise it to the sky, so that it could not be taken within the gates,
so that it could not be dragged within the walls, or watch over
180 the people in their ancient rites. For if your hands did violence
to the gifts to Minerva, then great destruction—may the gods
first turn that omen against themselves!—would be sure to come

---

160 *bloody hands*: According to a prophecy, Troy would never fall so long as a statue of Minerva (Athena), called the Palladium, remained in its place. Therefore Diomedes and Ulysses sneaked into the city one night and stole it. But, Sinon says, lying, this bloody theft angered Pallas and caused her to turn against the Greeks.

162 *Tritonia*: An epithet of Minerva (Athena), sometimes said to have been born at Lake Triton in Africa. But the real meaning of the epithet is unknown.

170 *curved ships*: That is, the Greeks have supposedly taken the Palladium back to Greece with them to purify it, evidently in the temple to Juno/Hera at Argos.

to the rule of Priam and the Trojans. But if the horse were to go up
to the city dragged by your hands, then Asia would come in mighty
war to the walls of Pelops, and the same fate would be in store
for our children!'°

"Through such deception, and the skill of the lying Sinon,
we believed it all. We were taken in by his deceits and his pretended
tears, though we were not conquered by Tydeus' son Diomedes,
nor by Achilles from Larissa,° nor by ten years of war, nor by
a thousand ships.

the death of Laocoön

"At this point something greater, much the more
tremendous, happens to us wretches, and shakes our unsuspecting hearts.
Laocoön, chosen by lot as our priest of Neptune, was sacrificing
an immense bull at our sacred altar. But look!—two serpents
with gigantic coils slither over the tranquil sea from Tenedos.
I shudder to tell it!

"Side by side they head for the shore.
Their breasts are raised high over the water, their blood-red crests
wind over the waves. The rest of their body sails through the sea
behind and their huge backs are arched in folds. A roar comes
from the foaming sea. And now they are ashore, their burning eyes
filled with blood and fire. They lick their hissing jaws with flickering
tongues. Terrified, we fled at the sight!

"They go straight for Laocoön.
At first each serpent enwraps the slender bodies of his two sons,
and they feed on their wretched limbs. Then they seize Laocoön
himself, who runs to help them, brandishing his weapons.
They wreathe him in their massive coils. Twice they wrap around
his waist, twice they wind their scaly backs around his throat.
Their heads and high necks tower over him. Laocoön tries to loosen
the knots with his hands, his headband soaked in blood and black poison.
At the same time he raises a terrific shout to the stars, like a bellowing
bull who flees wounded from the altar, shaking the ill-aimed ax
from his neck.

"But the pair of serpents slips away toward the highest
shrines. They seek out the citadel of ferocious Tritonia. There

---

186 *for our children*: That is, if the Trojans carried the horse to Troy, then Troy would defeat the Greeks in war not only in this generation, but in that to come. The "walls of Pelops" is the Peloponnesus ("island of Pelops"), of which Mycenae is the capital, hence, Greece. Pelops was the grandfather of Agamemnon and Menelaus.

189 *Larissa*: Larissa is in Thessaly, Achilles' homeland.

they hide under the feet of the goddess and the round circle
of her shield.° Then a strange terror slips through the shuddering
breasts of everyone. They say that Laocoön has only paid the deserved
price for wounding the sacred oak with his spear, by hurling
his wicked shaft in its back. They shout, 'Pull the statue to her house!
Offer prayers to the goddess's power!'

the horse enters the city

"We breached the wall
and opened up the buildings of the city. Everyone girds himself
for the work. They place gliding wheels under its feet. They stretch
ropes of hemp around its neck. The fatal machine ascends our walls,
pregnant with arms. Boys and unmarried girls sing holy songs around
the horse, and they rejoice to touch the ropes with their hands.

"Up it goes. The horse slips threateningly into the middle of the city.
O my country, O Ilium, house of the gods! And you, the walls
of the Dardanians, famous in war! Four times it stuck on the threshold
of the gate, and four times the arms rattled in its belly. Nonetheless
we pressed on, blind with madness, and we set up the calamitous
monster atop our sacred citadel. Then Cassandra opens her lips
and reveals what is fated to come—but her words are never to be believed,
by order of the god!°

"We wretches—for whom that day was to be the last—
we wrap the shrines of the gods with festive fronds throughout the city.
Meanwhile the heavens turn and night rushes from Ocean, wrapping
the earth and the sky and the tricks of the Myrmidons in its huge
shadow. The Teucrians scattered through the city, the city fell silent.
Sleep enfolds their exhausted limbs.

"And now the Argive troops
come from Tenedos, through the friendly quiet of the silent moon,
with their ships arrayed for battle, in search of the familiar shore,
when the king's galley lit a torch. Sinon, protected by the unjust
fates of the gods, sets free those Danaäns shut up in the womb
of the horse, loosens the bars of pine. Opened up, the horse
releases them to the air. Sliding down a rope let down, the leaders
Thessandrus and Sthenelus, and the dire Ulysses, emerge joyfully
from the wooden cave, along with Acamas and Thoas and Peleus'

---

214 *of her shield*: Statues of Pallas often had serpents at her feet.

232 *the god*: Apollo tried to seduce Cassandra by giving her the gift of prophecy, but when she still rejected him he decreed that no one would believe her prophecies.

FIGURE 2.2 *Laocoön and His Sons,* c. first century BC/AD first century, by anonymous ancient artist. One of the most famous of ancient sculptures, sometimes claimed to be the greatest of all artworks, this statue was excavated in Rome in 1506 and put on view in the Vatican. The statue appears to be the same as one described by the Roman writer Pliny the Elder (AD 23–79). The figures are near life-size. The Trojan priest of Poseidon and his sons are attacked by sea serpents, just as Vergil describes. It is variously dated, but probably comes from the Julio-Claudian period (AD 27–68). It was reworked in ancient times and has undergone numerous modern restorations. Though not mentioned by Homer, the story of Laocoön was the subject of a lost tragedy by Sophocles and is mentioned by other Greek writers. Vergil's description may be later than the sculpture, but many scholars see the group as a depiction of the scene described by Vergil. The Laocoön continued to influence Italian art into the Baroque period of the seventeenth and early eighteenth centuries. Michelangelo was captivated by the work's great size and its sensuous depiction of the male figures. Several of the figures in the Sistine Chapel ceiling were modeled on these figures. Raphael (1483–1520) used the face of Laocoön for his portrait of Homer in his painting *Parnassus* in the Vatican. Titian (c. 1490–1576) echoes the figures in his works, as does Rubens (1577–1640). The original was taken to Paris by Napoleon after his conquest of Italy in 1798 and installed in the Louvre. After Napoleon's fall, it was returned to the Vatican in 1816, where it remains today. Marble.

FIGURE 2.3 *The Laocoön*, **1610–1614, by Doménikos Theotokópoulos (1541–1614), known as El Greco ("The Greek").** After training as a painter of icons in his homeland of Crete, El Greco studied in Venice and Rome, then moved to Spain in 1576. He settled in Toledo in 1577 as a church painter. He became a leading artist in the Spanish Mannerist movement of the sixteenth century, known for his strangely elongated figures. This is El Greco's sole painting of a mythical subject, inspired by the recently discovered sculpture of Laocoön and his sons in Rome. The dying Laocoön, his body twisted in agony as he struggles with a serpent, lies between his two sons, the one on the right already dead and the one on the left tussling with a serpent bent into a bow. Apollo and Artemis (apparently) stand to the right. In the background the Trojan Horse moves toward the city of Toledo, drenched in storm and mystery. Oil on canvas.

son Neoptolemus, and the honorable Machaon, and Menelaus,
and Epeus, the deviser of this trick.°

the ghost of Hector

"They invade the city buried
in sleep and wine. They kill the watchmen and receive all
their companions through the open gates. They join their allied troops.
"It was the time when first sleep begins for tired mortals   250
and steals over them as the most pleasing gift of the gods.
Then in a dream—see! Before my eyes seemed to stand
the saddest Hector,° and to pour forth great tears, dragged
away by the chariot, as once he was, black with bloody dust,
his swollen feet pierced by thongs. Alas, how he looked!   255
How he was changed from that Hector who returned wearing
the armor of Achilles, or when he cast Trojan fire into the ships
of the Danaäns!° His beard was filthy and his hair matted with
blood, bearing those many wounds that he received when dragged
round the walls of his city.   260
"I seemed first to weep, and to address
the man with words of sorrow: 'O light of Dardania,
O truest hope of the Teucrians, what has delayed you?
From what shores do you come? You are expected! I see you,
exhausted as I am from the many troubles of our people
and of the city, after the many deaths in your own family.   265
What cruel events have fouled your gentle face? And why
do I see these wounds?'
"He does not answer, he does not await
me asking foolish questions, but dragging deep moans from the depths
of his heart, he says: 'Ah! Get out, child of a goddess! Tear yourself
from the flames. The enemy holds the walls. Troy falls from her high   270
eminence. Enough has been granted to your fatherland, to Priam.
If my right hand could have saved Pergama, it would have.
Troy gives her sacred relics and its Penates to you. Take them
as the companions of your fate. Find great walls for them that
you will build, once you have at last crossed the sea.'   275

---

247 *... of this trick*: Thessandrus, apparently the son of the Theban Polynices, does not appear in the *Iliad*; Sthenelus is son of Capaneus (one of the Seven Against Thebes) and appears several times in the *Iliad*; Acamas is a son of Theseus, not in the *Iliad*; Thoas is a Greek warrior who fights in the *Iliad*; Peleus is actually the grandfather of Neoptolemus, who is Achilles' son, also called Pyrrhus; Machaon is prominent in the *Iliad*; Epeus is mentioned in the *Odyssey* as the builder of the Trojan Horse. In the *Iliad* Epeus participates in the boxing match at the funeral games of Patroclus.

253 *Hector*: Greatest of the Trojan warriors.

258 *of the Danaäns*: In *Iliad* 15 Hector leads the charge to set fire to the Greek ships.

"So he spoke,
and Hector brings out the holy headbands in his hands from the innermost
shrine of powerful Vesta and her eternal flame.°

Aeneas organizes resistance

In the meanwhile
the city is everywhere confused with lamentation. And more and more,
although the house of my father Anchises is set apart, secluded
and hidden by trees, the sound grows louder and the terror of arms
sweeps over it.
"I shake myself away and climb to the highest rooftop.
I stand there with ears perked-up—as when a fire falls upon a wheat
field driven by the fury of South Wind, or a swift torrent from
a mountain stream levels the fields and scatters the rich crops
and the work of oxen, and brings down the trees headlong,
and the dumfounded shepherd hears the sound from a high rocky peak.
The truth was out, the plot of the Greek revealed.
"Now the house
of Deïphobus was given to ruin, engulfed by fire; now that of Ucalegon
burns nearby. The broad Sigean straits reflect the glare.° Then rises
the clamor of men and the blare of trumpets. Out of my mind,
I take up arms. There is little sense in military action, but my spirit
burns to gather together a band ready for war, to run to the citadel
with my companions. Rage and anger drive me onward, and it seems
to me that it is glorious to die in battle.
"Look, there is Panthus escaping
from the weapons of the Achaeans—Panthus the son of Othrys,
the priest of Apollo on the citadel.° He drags along the holy objects
and the conquered gods and his little grandchild with his own hand.
He runs frantically to my door. 'Where is the main battle, Panthus?
What position of defense should we take up?'
"I had barely spoken
when he answers with a groan: 'The last day is here, the time
for Dardania that cannot be escaped. The Trojans are finished,
Troy is finished, and the great glory of the Teucrians. Savage

---

277 *eternal flame*: In her role as state goddess, Vesta protected the permanent flame that burned on the altar of Vesta at Rome, thought to guarantee the permanence of the state. Aeneas was said to have brought this flame from Troy.

289 *... the glare*: Helen took up with Deïphobus, a brother of Hector, after Paris' death; Ucalegon is a Trojan elder; Sigean designates the waters around Sigeum, a promontory of the Troad.

296 *citadel*: Panthus was brought from Delphi to Troy to serve as priest of Apollo in the temple on the Trojan acropolis (according to the Latin commentator Servius).

Jupiter has carried all to Argos. The Danaäns rule in the burning
city! The horse stands high in the middle of the city and pours
out armed men. The victor Sinon leaps in exultation and stirs up   305
the flames. Others are at the wide-open gates, as many thousands
as ever came from great Mycenae. Still more have blocked the narrow
ways with weapons. A line of steel with flashing points is ready
for the kill. The guards at the gates barely attempt to resist,
and they fight in blind battle.'   310
    "By such words from the son of Othrys,
and by the divine will, I am carried among the flames and the weapons,
where the gloomy Erinys sounds,° where the roar calls out and the clamor
is raised to the sky. Allies joined me—Rhipeus and Epytus, mighty
in battle, and Hypanis and Dymas, clear in the moonlight. They come
to my side, and the young Coroebus, son of Mygdon°—by chance   315
he had come to Troy at just this time, burning with an insane passion
for Cassandra, bringing help as a potential son-in-law to Priam
and the Trojans—poor fellow, who did not listen to the prophecies
of his mad bride!
    "When I saw them gathered, ready to dare battle,
I began like this: 'My men, most brave spirits for a vain hope,   320
if it is your desire to follow me to the bitter end, you can see what
fortune follows our deeds. All the gods by which this empire was
supported have departed, our sanctuaries and altars are abandoned.
You come to the aid of a burning city. Let us die and rush
into the midst of battle. There is one salvation to the conquered—   325
to have no hope for safety.'

exploits of Aeneas' band

    "And so their young spirits were roused
to a fury. Then, like ravening wolves in a black cloud, whom
a vile hunger of their bellies has driven into a cruel fury, and their
young are left behind with dry throats, we wade through weapons,
through the enemy to a certain death. We make our way to the middle   330
of the city. Black night surrounds us in enfolding shadow.
    "Who can
explain the destruction of that night? Who can put in words all that death?
Who can equal our pain with tears? The ancient city falls that ruled
for so many years.
    "Masses of bodies lie here and there lifeless
in the roads, in the houses, and on the sacred thresholds of the gods.   335

---

312 *Erinys sounds*: The Erinys is a Fury, a spirit of rage and vengeance.

315 *... of Mygdon*: These Trojans are known only from this book.

Nor is it the Trojans alone who pay the price with their blood.
From time to time courage returns to the hearts of the conquered,
and the victorious Danaäns die. Everywhere is cruel mourning,
everywhere fear, and every form of death.

          "First Androgeos° comes
340 to meet us, accompanied by a large crowd of Danaäns. He does
not know who we are—he thinks we are allied troops. He calls
to us with friendly words: 'Hurry up, my men! Why so sluggish?
Why do you delay? Others are raping and plundering burning
Pergama. Do you only now come from the tall ships?'

          "He spoke,
345 but right away—because no reply that we gave seemed credible—
he realized that he had fallen into the midst of the enemy. Stunned,
he drew back in silence, like a man who unexpectedly comes
on a snake in rough bush as he strides across the ground. Terrified,
he pulls back as the snake rears in anger, swelling its dark blue neck.

350 "Even so Androgeos, shuddering, tried to get away. We charge
forward and surround them with serried arms and, because they
were ignorant of the layout of the place, and were seized by terror,
we killed them all. So fortune favored our first undertaking.

    "At this Coroebus, exultant with success and courage, says:
355 'My companions, let us follow where fortune first shows the path
to safety, and where she shows herself to our advantage. Let us
change our shields and adopt the emblems of the Danaäns. Deceit
or virtue? Who wonders about that in war? They will themselves arm us!'

    "So he spoke, then he puts on Androgeos' plumed helmet
360 and took up his shield with its fancy blazon. He straps the Greek sword
to his side. Rhipeus does the same, and Dymas too, and all the youth
take delight in it. Everyone arms himself with the fresh spoils.

    "We went forward and mixed with the Greeks, guided by gods
that are not our own, and we closed in many battles through the blind
365 night. We sent many Greeks to Orcus.° Some scatter to the ships,
some run to seek the safety of the shore. Some, in abject terror,
climb back into the huge horse and seek refuge in the familiar womb.
Alas, you should never place faith in something that the gods oppose!

the rape of Cassandra

    "See—Cassandra, the virgin daughter of Priam, was dragged from
370 the temple and innermost sanctuary of Minerva with hair all undone,

---

339 *Androgeos*: Otherwise unknown.

365 *Orcus*: Orcus is one name for the Roman god of the underworld.

raising her burning eyes to the sky—in vain!—her eyes because chains
restrained her tender hands.

"Coroebus, maddened in mind, could not
bear the sight, and he threw himself into the middle of the line,
determined to die. We all follow together and attack with our weapons
packed together. Here at first we are overwhelmed by Trojan weapons   375
thrown from the roof of the temple.° Deathly slaughter arises from
the appearance of our armor and the confusion of our Greek crests.

"Then the Greeks gathered from all sides and, angry because a girl
was being pulled from them, they attack—the ferocious Ajax,
the two sons of Atreus, and the whole band of the followers   380
of Neoptolemus. Just as when at times at the onset of a storm
conflicting winds run against each other—West Wind and South
Wind and East Wind who takes joy in the horses of the East°—
and the forest screams, and Nereus,° wet with brine, stirs up the depths
of the water with his trident.   385

"Even those reappear whom we had scattered
through our trick in the dark of the night and drove through the whole city.
They were the first to recognize our shields and deceiving weapons
and to see that our speech differed from theirs. In an instant we are
overwhelmed by their numbers.

"First Coroebus falls at the altar
of the armed goddess, at the hand of Peneleus.° And Rhipeus goes   390
down, who was the most just of all the Trojans and the finest servant
of right (the gods saw it otherwise!). And Hypanis and Dymas
perish at the hands of the Greeks. Nor can your great devotion to duty [*pietas*],
O Panthus, and your headband of Apollo prevent your downfall!

"O ashes of Ilium, and the death flames of my own people, be witness   395
that at your ruin I did not avoid the Greek weapons or the dangers
of fighting the Greeks! If my fate had been that I fall by my deeds,
I earned it.

battle at the palace

"Then we are separated, Iphitus and Pelias° with me—
Iphitus weighed down by years, Pelias slowed by a wound

---

376 *of the temple*: Aeneas and his band are still dressed as Greeks and so are mistaken by their own men.
383 *of the East*: The Winds were thought to be the children of Dawn (that is, the East). Thought to have intercourse with horses, the winds are often represented as horses.
384 *Nereus*: The Old Man of the Sea, a water spirit, here with the trident of Neptune.
390 *Peneleus*: An Argonaut and a suitor of Helen, he led twelve ships from Boeotia.
398 *Iphitus and Pelias*: Nothing further is known about these men.

FIGURE 2.4 *The Rape of Cassandra*, **1810, by Jérôme-Martin Langlois (1779–1838).** Langlois was trained in the studio of the French Neoclassical painter Jacques-Louis David (1748–1825). Langlois and David worked together on several paintings. Here Langlois shows Cassandra, the daughter of King Priam, leaning naked against an altar on which a fire burns, her hands tied behind her. The statue of Athena (Minerva) is not visible, but the first two letters of Athena's name, AΘ, on the base are visible to the left of Cassandra's robe and belt, thrown over the stone as she was stripped and raped. She looks up to the invisible idol, praying for vengeance, or release. In the dim interior to the right a Greek soldier tears Astyanax, the son of Hector, away from his mother Andromachê. He will cast him from the walls. In the far distance, the city burns. Oil on canvas.

that Ulysses gave him. At once we are summoned by shouting 400
to Priam's palace. We see that there was a great battle there, as if the rest
of the war were nothing, as if no one else was dying throughout
the whole city. We see savage war, and the Greeks rushing
to the palace, and the gate attacked by an advancing roof of shields.°
"Ladders are put against the walls. Right up under the roof beams 405
they climb up by the rungs of ladders. They hold shields
with their left hands defending themselves against the spears.
They grasp the topmost stones with their right hands. In turn
the Trojans pull down the towers and the roof-tiles of the houses.
"They see the end coming, but prepare to defend themselves 410
with these tiles in their final hour. They throw down the gilded roof-beams,
the high glory of their ancient fathers. Others block the doors below
with drawn swords. These they defend in dense formation. Our spirits
were revived to bring aid to the palace of the king and to relieve
our fighting men with our help, to add power to the conquered. 415
   "There was an entrance with hidden doors and a passage connecting
Priam's halls with one another, and a hidden gateway beyond
that the unhappy Andromachê often used, going unattended, to go
to her parents-in-law, to bring the child Astyanax to his grandfather.°
I reached to the top of the roof from which the wretched Trojans 420
were throwing down their missiles—in vain. There was a tower
standing on a sheer edge and reaching from the top of the roof
to the sky from where you could see all of Troy and the familiar ships
of the Greeks and the Achaean camp. Attacking it from the sides
with our swords, where the mortar on the topmost levels was weak, 425
we tore the tower from its high seating and sent it down. Falling suddenly,
it dragged all to ruin with a crash and collapsed over the Greeks,
shattering them. But more came up, and neither the stones,
nor any other kind of weapon ceased to fly.
              "In front of the forecourt
and in the doorway of the palace Pyrrhus° gloats, glittering with 430
his shining bronze weapons—like a snake, having fed on poisonous
grass, that a cold winter has hidden, swollen, under the earth,
that comes forth into the light and now, refreshed and gleaming
with youth, its skin sloughed off, it ripples its slimy back with its breast
raised high toward the sun, and it darts its triple tongue from its mouth— 435

---

404 *shields*: In this Roman military tactic, called the "tortoise" (*testudo*), the attackers locked their oblong shields over their heads to protect them from missiles cast down from above.

419 *his grandfather*: Astyanax is the child of Hector and his wife Andromachê. The grandfather is Priam.

430 *Pyrrhus*: "red-head"; also called Neoptolemus, "new-fighter," the son of Achilles and Deïdamia, raised on the island of SCYRUS. He led Achilles' followers after the death of Achilles.

"The enormous Periphas and the armed Automedon,° who drove
Achilles' horses, and all the youth of SCYRUS advance on the palace
together and cast fire onto the roof. Pyrrhus himself among the front
ranks, wielding a double ax, breaks through the stubborn doors,
440 pulling the bronze doors from their hinges. Then he hews out
the panel and makes a hole in the solid oak. He makes a huge window
with a wide opening. The interior of the palace is revealed and the inner
halls of the ancient kings.
                "The Greeks see armed men on the threshold.
Inside the palace groans are mixed with a wretched tumult,
445 and deep within the vaulted halls women howl. The sound strikes
the golden stars. Terrified mothers wander through the vast building.
They hang on the doorposts, embracing them and kissing them.
        "Pyrrhus presses on with the strength of his father. Neither barricades,
nor guards themselves can stop him. The door collapses under
450 the incessant battering. The posts collapse, torn from their hinges.
The Greeks make their way by violence. They burst an entrance. They
pour through, they cut down the front ranks. They fill the wide places
with their soldiers.
                "Not so violent is a foaming river that floods,
bursting its banks, overwhelming the barriers set against it with
455 its violent torrent, and it roars across the fields in a mass and sweeps
cattle along with their stables across all the plain. I myself saw
Neoptolemus raging on the threshold, and the two sons of Atreus.
I saw Hecuba° and her fifty daughters and fifty daughters-in-law,
and Priam at the altars polluting with blood the fires that he himself
460 had consecrated. The doorposts of the fifty chambers themselves,
so great a hope for offspring, proud with the spoil of Trojan gold,
fall to the ground. The Greeks have hold of what the fire spares.

the death of Priam

        "Perhaps you would like to know what happened to Priam?
When he saw the fall of the city, the palace doors ripped off
465 and the enemy in the midst of the inner chambers, the old man
put on armor, long-neglected, around shoulders that tremble with age,
useless, and he fastens on the vain sword, and he hurls himself,
sure to die, into the thick of the enemy.
                        "In the center of the hall
and under the naked arch of the sky there was a huge altar beside

---

436 *...Automedon*: Periphas is an unimportant fighter in the *Iliad* (Book 5); Automedon appears as Achilles' charioteer in the *Iliad* (Books 16, 17).

458 *Hecuba*: The queen, Priam's wife.

an ancient laurel tree that overshadowed the altar and embraced 470
the Penates with shade. Here Hecuba and her daughters, like doves
tempest-driven, crouched uselessly around the shrine, and, huddled
together, sat down and clung to the statues of the gods.
          "When she saw
that Priam had put on his youthful armor, Hecuba said: 'What madness,
sad husband, his driven you to put on this armor? And where are you 475
running to? The time does not ask that you help in this way, nor put
up a defense, not if my own Hector were right here. Come now!
This altar will protect us together, or we will die at the same time.'
     "So she spoke, and drew the old man to herself and sat him down
on the sacred spot. See!—Polites, one of Priam's sons, had escaped 480
from the slaughter of Pyrrhus. He runs down the long hallways through
the spears, through the enemy, and wounded he crosses the empty
courtyards. Pyrrhus follows him, burning to strike. He grasps
at him now, and now again and presses on him with his spear.
"When at last Polites reached the eyes and gaze of his parents, 485
he falls, and he pours out his life in a gush of blood. At this Priam, although
he was in death's clutches, did not hold back, but he spoke in anger:
'If there is any justice [*pietas*] in heaven that cares for such things,
may the gods pay you back with fit thanks and a just reward for your
wickedness! for what you have dared! who made me see the death 490
of my son so close! You have defiled a father's sight with murder.
But Achilles, whose son you falsely say you are, was not such an enemy
to Priam. He respected the rights and protection of a suppliant,
and gave back the bloodless body of my Hector to be buried,
and he sent me back to my kingdom.'° 495
          "So spoke the old man, and he threw
his worthless spear, without strength. Immediately it bounced off
Pyrrhus' clanging bronze and hung from the center of the shield's
boss. Pyrrhus answered him: 'And so, you can carry the news as a messenger
to my father, the son of Peleus. Remember to tell him of the *degenerate*
Neoptolemus, and of my atrocious deeds! Now die!' 500
               "Saying this,
he dragged the trembling Priam to the altar, slipping in the pool of his son's
blood. He twined his left hand in his hair. Raising the flashing sword
in his right hand, he buried it up to the hilt in Priam's side. This was
the death of Priam. This death came to him by Fate, seeing Troy burning
and Pergama fallen down, once the proud ruler of so many people 505
and Asian lands. A mighty body lies on the shore, the head torn
from its shoulder, a corpse without a name.

---

495 *my kingdom*: In *Iliad* Book 24 Priam successfully beseeches Achilles for the return of Hector's body,
     an incident already referred to in *Aeneid* Book 1.

"Then first a terrible horror
came over me. I stood thunderstruck. The image of my beloved father
rose before me as I saw the king, of a like age, breathing out his life
510 from a cruel wound—and there arose before me too the image
of my forlorn Creüsa,° and the ransacked house, and the fate
of little Iulus. I looked back, taking account of the troops
that were around me. All were gone, exhausted, and had thrown
their bodies to the earth or, sick with misery, had dropped
515 into the flames. Now I was alone.

Aeneas and Helen

"I saw the daughter of Tyndareus,
Helen, near the portal of Vesta,° silently hiding in the hidden shrine.
The bright fires give me light as I wander, looking here and there,
everywhere. She, fearing Trojan anger at her for the fall of Troy,
and fearing the Greek's longing for vengeance, and the fury of the husband
520 she had deserted—she, the common curse of Troy and of her fatherland,
had concealed herself and crouched down beside the altar, a hated thing.

"Fire blazed in my spirit. Anger arose to take vengeance for our fallen
fatherland and to take revenge for her wickedness. 'Will this woman,
unharmed, see Sparta again and her native Mycenae? Will she, a queen,
525 go in triumph? Will she see her husband, her house, her parents,
her children, attended by a crowd of Trojan women and Phrygian slaves?
When Priam has been put to the sword? When Troy has been burned
to the ground? The Dardanian shore soaked so often with blood?

"'This cannot be. Even though there is little memorable in punishing
530 a woman! Victory wins no praise. Still there will be glory in having
extinguished wickedness, in taking punishment that is well deserved.
I will delight to fill my spirit with avenging fire, appeasing the ashes
of my people.'

"I cried these words, and was carried onward
in a maddened state of mind. Then my blessed mother came
535 to my vision, bright as never before to my eyes. She shone with
a pure light through the night, making herself known as a goddess,
in form and stature as she is accustomed to appear to the dwellers
in heaven.

"She took me by the right hand and stopped me, and then
she spoke these words from her rose-colored lips: 'My son, what

---

511   *Creüsa*: Aeneas' wife.

516   ... *Vesta*: Though Helen was the daughter of Jupiter, her earthly father was Tyndareus, the husband of Leda. Vesta as goddess of the hearth was attended in Rome by virgins, emphasizing the outrageousness of Helen's taking refuge there.

pain stirs so great an anger? Why this rage? Where is your care 540
for what is our own? Will you not first see where you have left
your aged father Anchises? And whether your wife Creüsa survives,
and your child Ascanius? Greek troops surround them from all sides.
If I did not give them my care, already the flames would have
carried them off and the enemy swords would have drunk their blood. 545
The face of Helen from Sparta is not so hateful to you, nor is Paris
to blame. It is the brutality of the gods—of the gods!—that brings down
this power, that tumbles Troy from its peak.
        "'Now I will tear away
all the cloud that shrouds your sight and dims your mortal
vision, darkening all with moisture. Do not fear what your mother 550
commands, do not refuse to obey her directions. See, here where
you see broken heaps of stone, and stone ripped from stone, and billowing
smoke mixed with dust—Neptune shakes the walls and rips the foundations
with his trident. He overturns the entire city from its roots. There
the most savage Juno first takes the Scaean Gates,° and with a sword 555
strapped to her side—maddened!—she calls her allies from the ships.
See—Tritonian Pallas sits on the highest towers. She sends lightning
from a storm cloud, raging with her Gorgon breastplate.° Father Jupiter
himself provides the Greeks with their spirit and abundant strength.
He himself drives on the gods against the Trojan army. 560
        "'Flee, my son!
And put an end to your labor. I will never be apart from you, and I will
place you safe at your father's threshold.'
       "She spoke, and hid herself
in the deep shadows of night. Then dreadful shapes appeared, and the huge
powers of gods against Troy. All of Ilium seemed to sink in flames.
The Troy of Neptune° was overturned from its foundations—as when 565
farmers on the tops of mountains compete to dig out an ancient ash tree,
and they strike again and again with a double-blade, and the tree threatens
repeatedly to fall, and it nods with trembling crown until little by little
it is overcome by the blows—and it groans out a last gasp as torn from
the ridge it tumbles down in ruin. 570

Aeneas goes to save his family

      "I descend from the roof, and with a god
leading me I escape the flame and the enemy. The spears give way

---

555 *Scaean Gates*: The "left-hand gates," the principal gate of Troy. It is not clear why they are so named.
558 *Gorgon breastplate*: The Gorgon is the snaky severed head of Medusa that Pallas wore on her breastplate. Even its glance turned one to stone.
565 *Neptune*: Neptune and Apollo built the walls of Troy for Laomedon, Priam's father, who then cheated the gods of their wages. Consequently Neptune hated Troy, though Apollo inexplicably continued to support it.

FIGURE 2.5 *Helen Saved by Venus from the Wrath of Aeneas*, 1779, by Jacques H. Sablet (1749–1803). Jacques Sablet was a Swiss Rococo painter, son of a decorator from Lausanne. He moved to Paris in 1772, where he competed with Jacques-Louis David. He specialized in portraits, genre painting, and landscape painting. In this scene inspired by Vergil's *Aeneid*, Aeneas has drawn his sword and is about to kill Helen when his mother, a naked Venus, appears to him from the sky. Around Aeneas the city burns. In the background, above his head, can be seen a statue of Vesta, in whose temple Helen has taken refuge. Oil on canvas.

and the flames recede. When I reached the threshold of my father's
house and my ancient home, my father—whom I first wanted to carry
to the high mountains, whom I sought out first—he refuses to extend his life
now that Troy had fallen, or to suffer exile. 575
      "'Oh you,' he cried,
'whose blood is unimpaired by age, whose strength stands in full force—
flee! If the heaven-dwellers had wished to prolong my life, they would
have preserved my house. It is enough and more that I saw one destruction
and survived the taking of one city.° So depart, bidding goodbye
to my body lying in state, just so. I will find death in fighting 580
hand to hand. The enemy will take pity on me and look for plunder.
I care nothing for the loss of burial. Already for a long time I have delayed
my death, hated by the gods and useless with my old age, from the time
when the father of gods and the king of men breathed the winds
of his lightning bolt on me and touched me with fire.'° 585
      "So he went on saying,
and he stubbornly remained put. But we on our side, weeping abundantly—
Creüsa my wife and Ascanius and the whole house—wished not that
my father destroy everything along with himself, that he not add
weight to a doom already rushing upon us. He says he won't go,
and he clings to his resolve and his place. I turn again to my arms 590
and, wretched, I long for death. For what plan was of any use to us,
or what chance did we have?
      "'Did you think that I could go off and leave
you behind?' I said. 'How could such an evil thought come from your
mouth? If it pleases the gods to leave nothing from so great a city,
if this is set in your mind, if it pleases you to add yourself and all 595
that you own to Troy that is perishing—well, the door lies open
to that death. Soon Pyrrhus will be here after drenching himself
in the blood of Priam, he who cuts down the son in front of the father,
who kills the father at the altar.
      "'Kind mother, did you rescue me from
the sword, from the fire, so that I could see the enemy in my innermost 600
chambers, so that I could see my father, Ascanius, and Creüsa butchered
side by side, in a pile, in one another's blood? Bring weapons, men,
weapons! The last day summons the conquered. Lead me again

---

579 *one city*: Anchises refers to the earlier destruction of Troy by Hercules. Laomedon planned on sacrificing his daughter Hesionē to Neptune to forestall a monster attacking the city. Hercules rescued her at the last minute and killed the monster. In payment for rescuing his daughter Laomedon had promised magic horses that he had received from Jupiter, but when Laomedon broke his word, Hercules sacked the city.

585 *with fire*: Anchises slept with the goddess Venus. When he bragged of his deed, Jupiter struck him in the thigh with a thunderbolt, crippling him.

to the Greeks. Let me again attain the battle, and renew it! This day
605 we shall not all die unavenged!'

"Again I fasten on my sword.
I slip my left arm through the shield strap. I adjust it and go quickly
from the house. But see, my wife clings to the threshold and seizes
my feet, and she holds up little Iulus to his father.

"'If you are going off to die,
take us with you at all costs. But if you put some hope in the arms
610 you have taken up, that you know so well, first protect this house.
To whom do you abandon this little Iulus, to whom your father—
and me, once said to be your wife?'

"Crying out such words, she filled
the whole house with her groans.

the omen

Then suddenly, an omen—amazing to see!—
appeared. Behold, between the hands and the faces of his sad parents,
615 from the very top of Iulus' head, seemed to shine a gentle light,
and a soft flame, harmless to the touch, licking his hair and dancing
around his temples. Trembling with fear, we tried to shake off
the burning hair and extinguish the sacred fire with water.

"But my father,
Anchises, overjoyed, raises his eyes to the stars and lifts his palms
620 and voice to heaven: 'Jupiter, all-powerful, if any prayers move you,
look at us and grant only this: If we deserve anything for our virtue [*pietate*],
show us a sign, Father, and confirm your omen.'

"The old man had barely
spoken when suddenly it thundered on the left,° and a star, through
the shadows, slid from the sky and, trailing a torch, ran through the heaven
625 in a blaze of light. We watched it glide over the tops of the houses
and hide its brilliance, which marked its path, in the forests of IDA.°
Then the furrow of its long track gives out a light, and far and wide
the place smoked with sulphur.

"At this my father, convinced, raised
himself to the sky. He speaks to the gods and addresses the holy star:
630 'Well now, there will be no delay! I will follow! Where you lead,
there will I be. Gods of my fathers, preserve my family line, preserve
my grandson! This is your omen. Troy lies within your holy protection.
I accept, my son, and I will not refuse to go with you as your companion.'

---

623   *on the left*: A good omen in Roman augury, the foretelling of lucky and unlucky outcomes through the observation of events in the sky.

626   *of Ida*: Ida is a mountain south of Troy.

Aeneas escapes with his family

"He spoke, and now the sound of the fire grows louder through the city,
the blaze rolls its conflagration nearer. 'Come then, dear father, 635
cling to my neck. I will hoist you on my shoulders. The task won't
weigh me down. However things fall out, it will be a shared danger,
and the same salvation will befall us both. Let little Iulus come with me.
Let my wife follow our footsteps at a distance. And you servants,
pay attention to what I say. 640

"'When you get out of the city, there is a mound
and an ancient temple to the forsaken Ceres.° Nearby is an old cypress tree,
protected through so many years by the devotion of our fathers. Let's head
for this one place, coming from many directions. You, father, take the sacred
objects and the Penates of our fathers. It is not permitted for me to touch them,
having just come from the fight and recent slaughter, until I can wash myself 645
in flowing water.'

"Saying these things, I spread a cloak made of the tawny pelt
of a lion over my broad shoulders and my bowed neck. I bend to the task.
Little Iulus winds his hand in my right hand and hastens to follow
his father's long strides. My wife follows behind. We are borne through
the shadows. And I, up to then moved by no shower of spears nor crowd 650
of enemy Greeks, am terrified by every breeze. I am uneasy, and every
sound startles me, afraid for my companion and my burden.

"And now I came close to the gates. I seemed to have passed
the road in safety when suddenly the sound of feet filled my
hearing. Looking through the shadows, my father shouted: 'My son, 655
flee, my son, they are coming near! I can see their burning
shields and their flashing bronze!'

Creüsa is lost

At this some evil spirit scattered
my troubled mind, for while I followed remote paths at a run,
straying from the area of streets that I knew, Alas! my wife Creüsa
was snatched by Fate from wretched me—or she strayed from the path, 660
or she collapsed, exhausted. I could not be sure. I never saw her again.

"Nor did I look back for my lost darling or turn my attention backwards
before we came to the mound and the ancient sacred place of Ceres.
Here, when at last we were all gathered, one was missing, and had not
been noticed by her companions, both child and husband. What man 665
or god did I not accuse in my madness? What was more cruel in this
overturned city?

---

641 *Ceres*: Goddess of the harvest (the Greek Demeter). It is not clear why the temple is abandoned.

FIGURE 2.6 *Aeneas Fleeing Troy,* **1750, by Pompeo Batoni (1708–1787).** An Italian painter inspired by classical antiquity and the work of artists such as Nicolas Poussin and Raphael, Batoni was a precursor of Neoclassicism. He was, known especially for his portraits. Here, in a scene taken from the *Aeneid*, he shows the hero carrying his lame father Anchises over his shoulder while his son Iulus clings to Aeneas' skirt. Anchises holds the Penates, wrapped in fur, in his right hand. Aeneas' wife Creüsa follows behind. In the distance is the burning city of Troy. As an image of the continuity of the Roman family, the scene was often represented in antiquity and was popular in the modern period. Oil on canvas.

"I place Ascanius and my father Anchises and the Trojan
Penates in the care of my companions. I conceal them in a winding valley.
I myself go into the city once more. I bind on my shining armor.
I am determined again to undergo every hazard, to go back again over 670
all Troy, and again to put myself in danger.

                              "First I try to find the wall
and the dark threshold of the gate where I left. I retrace the landmarks
that I followed in the night, scanning them with my eye. Everywhere
the horror in my heart, and the very silence terrify me. Then I go back
to my house, if by chance, by some chance she has gone there. 675

    "Greeks have invaded it, they have taken over the whole house.
Suddenly consuming fire is rolled across the rooftops, driven
by the wind. Flames take hold, the blaze rages to the heavens.
I pass by and I see again the palace of Priam and the citadel.
"Now Phoenix° and the savage Ulysses, chosen guards, watch over 680
the booty in the empty courts of Juno's sanctuary. Here are the Trojan
treasures gathered from everywhere, from the burning shrines—
tables of the gods, bowls of pure gold, and captured robes.
Boys and frightened mothers stand about in long rows.

                                        "I dared to shout
through the shadows and to fill the roads with my cries. Wretched, 685
I called out again and again—hopeless! As I searched endlessly,
raging among the houses of the city, the unhappy phantom and shade
of Creüsa seemed to stand before my eyes in a form greater than
I knew before. I was staggered and my hair stood on end and my voice
stuck in my throat! 690

                   "Then she spoke and lessened my distress with these words:
'O my sweet husband, why do you take pleasure in such mad pain?
These things have not happened without the will of the gods. It is not fated
that you take Creüsa from here as a companion—the great ruler
of high Olympus does not permit it. Your exile will be long, and you must
plow the huge reach of the sea. You will come to the Hesperian land 695
and where the Lydian Tiber° flows in gentle course through the rich fields
of farmers. There happiness and a kingdom and a royal wife is won for you.

   "'Get rid of these tears for your beloved Creüsa. I, a woman of Troy
and daughter-in-law to the goddess Venus, shall not behold the proud
halls of the Myrmidons or the Dolopians, or go as a slave to some 700
Greek mother. But the Great Mother of the gods° holds me on these shores.

---

680 *Phoenix*: The aged tutor to Achilles, prominent in *Iliad* Book 9.

696 *... Tiber*: "Hesperian" is Greek for "Western"; the Tiber separates Etruria to the north, where the Etruscans live, from Latium to the south, where the Romans live. The Etruscans were said to come from LYDIA, southeast of the Troad; hence the Tiber is "Lydian."

701 *of the gods*: Cybelê, worshiped in Phrygia and thus friendly to the Trojans. It is not clear why the Great Mother has kept Creüsa from leaving Troy.

So farewell—and preserve your love for the son we hold in common.'

"When she had spoken these words, she left me, weeping, wishing
to say so many things, and she receded into the thin air. Three times
I tried to throw my arms around her neck, three times her form fled
my hands that reached in vain, like a light breeze, or most like a winged
dream. So at last, when the night was done, I return to my friends.

"And here I find that a great number of new companions had streamed
in—I am amazed—women and men, and young men gathered,
ready for exile—a miserable crowd. They had come in from all sides,
prepared in spirit and with their wealth for whatever land I might wish
to lead them to, across the sea.

"And now Lucifer° rose above
the peaks of Ida and brought the day, and the Greeks held barricaded
the thresholds of the gates. There was no hope of rescue. I gave it up
and headed for the hills, my father on my strong shoulders."

Book 3 is omitted. Aeneas goes on with his story. He tells how the Trojans set forth from the Troad and at first settle in THRACE, until they are warned away by the ghost of Polydorus, the youngest son of Priam. Polydorus had been entrusted to the Thracian king, then was treacherously murdered. They sail south into the CYCLADES and stop at DELOS, where the oracle of Apollo says that they should seek their ancient homeland. Anchises takes this to be Crete. But when they arrive at Crete they are afflicted by plague. A new oracle explains that their ancestor Dardanus did not come from Crete at all, but from ITALY, and that is where they must go. They head north, but Harpies attack them in the STROPHADES ISLANDS. One harpy predicts that the Trojans must one day eat their tables from hunger. Continuing north, they stop in BUTHROTUM in EPIRUS and are received by Helenus, a brother of Hector and a prophet. Helenus is married to Andromachê, the former wife of Hector of Troy. Helenus tells Aeneas that they must go to the west side of Italy. The fleet skirts southern Italy, then along the southern coast of SICILY. They encounter Polyphemus just after Ulysses had been there. Acestes, a Trojan who has settled in DREPANUM, receives them. Anchises, Aeneas' father, dies. They set sail and are engulfed in the great storm sent by Juno that lands them in CARTHAGE, Dido's kingdom. Aeneas has finished his story.

---

712 *Lucifer:* "light-bearer," that is, the planet Venus, the morning star.

BOOK 4. *The Death of Dido*

But the queen, long since wounded by intense love, nourishes
the wound in her veins, and wastes away from a hidden fire.
She goes over and over in her mind the manliness of this man
and the nobility of his race. She cannot get his features or his words
out of her mind. Because of her love, she cannot enjoy gentle sleep. 5

Dido confesses her passion to her sister Anna

    The next day Dawn was lighting the earth with the brilliance
of Phoebus and moving the dewy shadows away from the sky
when Dido, scarcely in her right mind, speaks to her sister, with whom
she was close: "Anna, my sister, what dreams terrify me and hold me
suspended! Who is this strange guest in our house? How well he speaks! 10
How wise his thoughts, how strong his arms! Truly I think—
no empty belief—that he is from the race of gods. Fear makes clear
the base-born soul, but this man—by what mighty fates has he been tested!
What battles, drunk to the dregs, he has spoken of! If I had not made
a firm and immovable decision in my mind not to bind myself 15
in marriage, after my first love was cut short by death—if I were
not tired of the wedding chamber and marriage ... perhaps I might
give in to this weakness of mine.
                      "Anna, I confess it. After the death
of my poor husband Sychaeus, and the Penates splashed by my murderous
brother,° this is the only man who has moved my senses, who has made 20
an impression on my wavering spirit. I recognize the traces
of the ancient flame. But I would rather that the deepest earth
swallow me, or that the all-powerful father would blast me
to the land of shadows with his thunderbolt—the pale shadows
and the deep night of Erebus!° —before, O Shame! ... I violate you 25
or break your laws. He who first joined me to himself took away
my love. May he keep it with him, may he preserve it in the grave!"
    So speaking, she filled her breast with rising tears. Anna answers:
"O you who are more beloved to your sister than the light, will you
waste away, alone and mourning, for your whole youth? Will you 30

---

20 *brother*: Dido's brother Pygmalion killed Sychaeus at the altar so he could take his gold.
25 *Erebus*: The underworld.

never know sweet children, or the pleasures of love? Do you think
that ashes or the buried spirits of the dead care? I grant you:
No suitors in Libya, nor before in Tyre, have ever turned you aside
from your sorrow. Iarbas° was scorned and the other leaders nourished
35 on Africa's land, rich in fame.
                              "Will you fight against a passion that pleases
you? Don't you recall in whose fields you have settled? Here the cities
of the Gaetuli, and people unbeaten in war, and the unbridled
Numidians, and the hostile SYRTES surrounds you. Then there is a region of dry
desert, and the Barcaeans raging all around.° Do I need to mention
40 the imminent war with Tyre, or the threats of your brother?
                                                  "Under divine
auspices, I think, and under Juno's sponsorship the Trojan ships made
their way here with the help of the wind.° How great a city, my sister,
will you see arise, what great power, with a husband like that!
With Trojan arms as allies, there is no end to the heights of Punic
45 glory! Only ask the gods their permission, then after performing
the appropriate sacrifices, be kind to the guest. Spin out reasons
for delay—while the winter, and stormy Orion,° rage on the sea,
while the ships are broken and the weather is intemperate."
                                                           With these words
Anna inflamed Dido's burning spirit with love and gave hope
50 to her doubting mind, and Anna dissolved Dido's sense of shame.

Dido in love

    First they visit the temples and they beg for peace on the altars.
They kill sheep, chosen according to prescribed ritual: to Ceres,
who establishes laws, and Phoebus and to father Lyaeus,°
and above all to Juno, in whose care lay the chains of matrimony.
55 The very beautiful Dido, holding the cup in her right hand,
pours it out between the horns of a white cow, or she walks up before
the face of the gods to the rich altars. She celebrates the day with gifts,
and cutting open the chests of sheep and peering in she consults

---

34 *Iarbas*: An African king, a son of Jupiter, scorned by Dido, who will soon play an important role in the story.

39 *... all around*: The Gaetuli lived to the south of Carthage; the Numidian tribes lived southwest of Carthage; the Syrtes are the dangerous sand banks between east of Carthage; the Barcaeans lived in Barca, a city on the north coast of Africa. The name may also suggest Hannibal, Rome's enemy in the late second century BC, who belonged to the Barca family.

42 *the wind*: It was in fact the terrible storm raised by Juno that brought the Trojan ships to Carthage.

47 *Orion*: Orion sets in November, the beginning of the time of storms.

53 *Lyaeus*: "looser," an epithet of Bacchus/Dionysus.

the steaming entrails.° Alas, the ignorant minds of seers! What is the use
of prayers? What is the use of shrines to the impassioned?   60

                              In the meanwhile
her tender marrow was aflame, and a silent wound lives in her heart.
Unhappy Dido is burning up, and she wanders through the whole city
in a delirium, like an incautious deer that a shepherd, hunting
with his bow while he roams through the Cretan woods, has shot
at long distance in the neck with an arrow, and without knowing   65
he left the winged iron in her.° She flees through the woods
and the groves of Dictê.° The deadly shaft hangs in her side.

   Now Dido leads Aeneas with her around the walls, and she shows
him the riches of SIDON and the city she has built. She begins to speak…
but stops in the middle of a word. Now, when the day was waning,   70
she longs for the banquet, mad again to hear about his Trojan trials,
and again she hangs on every word.

                        Then, when all have departed,
and the dark moon has subdued her light, and the setting stars
encourage sleep, Dido grieves alone in the empty hall. She lies down
on the couch he had occupied. Absent she sees and hears him,   75
the absent one. Or she hugs Ascanius on her lap, captured by this
image of his father—if only she could deceive her silent passion!

   The building of the towers, though begun, now stopped. The youths
no longer drill, or prepare the port and the battlements to make them safe
for war. Works interrupted just hang there, and the huge threatening walls,   80
and the construction cranes reaching to the sky.

Juno and Venus conspire to bring the lovers together

                              As soon as the beloved wife
of Jove saw that Dido was held by such a disease, and that she would not
allow her reputation to interfere with her mad passion, she, the daughter
of Saturn, went up to Venus and said: "You have earned high praise,
and ample spoil—you and your son,° a great and a memorable display   85
of divine power, when a single woman is overcome by the trickery
of two gods! I am surely aware that you have been suspicious of the halls
of high Carthage, fearing our city's defenses. But what will be the end to it?
Where are we going to go with this contest? Why not rather work
on an eternal peace and a wedding pact? You have everything that your   90

---

59   *entrails*: She is performing an extispicy, or divination by examining the entrails to learn, by the configurations, what is the will of the gods.
66   *in her*: Aeneas is like the shepherd—unaware of how he has wounded Dido.
67   *of Dictê*: A mountain in eastern Crete.
85   *your son*: Cupid.

mind sought. Dido is in love, she burns, and she has drawn this madness
into her very bones. So let us rule this people together and with equal
power. May she be a slave to her Phrygian husband, and yield her Tyrians
into your hands as a dowry."

                                      Venus answered her in this way, perfectly aware
95   that Juno had spoken with deceptive intent, so that empire might
be moved from Italy to Libya's shores: "Who would be so mad
as to reject your proposal, or would prefer to contend with you in war,
if only Fortune brings about what you say? But I am borne along
uncertain about Fate, whether it is the will of Jupiter that there
100 be a single city for Tyrians and those who have come from Troy,
or whether he approves that the peoples be mingled, joined together
in federation. For you, Jupiter's wife, it is right to explore
his intentions by asking. Do it, and I will follow."

                                            Then royal Juno replied
to Venus: "Leave that task to me. Now I will explain, in brief, how we
105 can accomplish the purpose at hand. Aeneas and the miserable Dido
are getting ready to go off together into the woods at the first break
of dawn, when Titan° reveals the world with his rays. While the bearers
on horseback are shaking the woods, and they are surrounding the forest
with nets, I will pour out over them a black rain mixed with hail
110 that will make the forest quake, and I will shake the whole sky with
thunder.° The companions will scatter and be covered by dark night.
Dido and the Trojan captain will come to the same cave. I'll be there,
and—if I can be sure of your good will!—I will join them in a firm
marriage and I will call her his own. This will be their wedding."
115 Not opposed to what Juno wanted, Venus agreed, and she smiled
at the deceit she had discovered.°

Aeneas and Dido in the cave

                                    In the meanwhile Dawn, surging
upward, left the Ocean. When the light had come, a select group of youths
come out of the gates. The Massylian horsemen° rush out with their
keen-scented hounds, bringing with them their nets of mesh,
120 both for large game and small, and their hunting spears with broad
points. The Punic princes await their queen at the threshold as she
lingers in her chamber. Her horse Stamper, decked out in purple

---

107 *Titan*: The sun.

111 *thunder*: For the second time in the poem Juno acts very much like her husband, the god of storm.

116 *had discovered*: Venus is aware of Juno's desire to make a great state of Carthage by uniting Trojans and Carthaginians, but she knows that in the end Fate must be fulfilled.

118 *Massylian horsemen*: Horsemen who lived west of Carthage.

and gold, stands there, and ferociously he chews the foaming bridle.

    At last Dido comes forth, a great crowd around her, wearing
a Sidonian cloak with an embroidered edge. Her quiver is of gold, 125
her hair is knotted with gold, a golden broach closes her purple
garments. Her Trojan friends and a happy Iulus come along with her.
Aeneas himself, most handsome of all, goes forward to meet her,
and he joins his crew with her own troops.
                                 Even as Apollo abandons
his winter dwelling in LYCIA beside the flowing Xanthus° and he visits 130
his mother's Delos, and he sets up dances, and Cretans, Dryopes,
and painted Agathyrsi mingle around his altars and shout° —while
he himself strides across the hills of Cynthus,° his flowing hair
decorated with tender leaves and clasped with gold, and his weapons
resound on his shoulders —even so went Aeneas, light on his feet, 135
and with the glory of a god shining from his handsome face.

    After they came into the high mountains and the wild haunts of animals,
they see wild goats, dislodged from their rocky summits,° running down
the slopes. In another place the deer move with speed across open fields
and gather together in dusty flight as they leave the mountains. 140

    But the youth Ascanius rejoices in his fast horse as he rides through
the valleys, passing these riders at a gallop, now those riders.
Ascanius hopes that, in answer to his prayers, a foaming boar might appear
in the midst of these harmless herds, or that a tawny lion might come
down from the mountain. 145
                        In the meanwhile the sky begins to roll
with thunder. Rain follows, mixed with hail, and the Tyrian companions
and the Trojan youth and the Dardanian grandson of Venus in fear
scatter here and there through the fields. Rivers rush down from
the mountains.
                  Dido and the Trojan leader come to the same cave.
Primeval Earth and Juno of the Nuptials° give a signal: Lightning 150
flashed and heaven is witness to their connubial union, and the nymphs
howl on top of the mountain.° That day saw the beginning of destruction,

---

130 *Xanthus*: Apollo had a shrine at a place called Patara near the mouth of the Xanthus River, which runs through the center of Lycia (same name as a river on the Trojan plain).

132 *... and shout*: Crete is south of Delos; the Dryopes are an obscure tribe from central Greece; and the Agathyrsi are a barbarian non-Greek tribe from farther north in SCYTHIA. The point is that adorants have come from near and far to celebrate the god Apollo.

133 *Cynthus*: The only hill on Delos.

138 *dislodged from their rocky summits*: By the beaters.

150 *Juno of the Nuptials*: Juno in her capacity as the goddess who presides over weddings.

152 *... of the mountain*: The language is based on that of a Roman marriage, but suggests the union of cosmic powers, of Heaven (or Sky) descending into Earth in the form of fecundating showers. Juno of the Nuptials (*Pronuba*) functions like the matron who assists the bride. The lightning is like the torches that accompanied Roman marriages, as the nymphs shrieking are the bridal song.

FIGURE 4.1   Aeneas and Dido Embrace, c. 340 AD, Roman mosaic.   This mosaic comes from a Roman villa in southwest England, near Low Ham, discovered by a local farmer in 1938 while digging a hole to bury a dead sheep. The villa has an extraordinary picture cycle depicting the story of Aeneas and Dido. In this panel the couple embrace in the wild. Dido is nude, while Aeneas wears a Phrygian cap and is fully dressed. Other panels show Aeneas sailing to Carthage, Aeneas meeting Dido, the couple out hunting, and Dido left alone after Aeneas' departure. It is the earliest piece of narrative art ever found in England.

it was the first cause of evil. For Dido is not moved by appearances
or reputation, nor does she thinks of it as a secret affair. She calls
it a marriage, and with this label she disguises her fault. 155

Rumor of the affair reaches Iarbas

                                       At once Rumor
courses through the great cities of Libya—Rumor, faster than any
other evil. She flourishes by moving, and acquires strength as she goes.
At first she is small, through fear, but soon raises herself to the sky.
She walks on the ground and hides her head in the clouds. Earth
was her parent. Exasperated by her anger at the gods,° Earth bore 160
Rumor last—so they say—a sister to Coeus and Enceladus,° a horrendous
monster, huge, swift of foot, with rapid wings, who has as many
watchful eyes beneath as feathers on her body above—amazing to say!—
and as many tongues, and as many mouths, and she pricks up as many
ears to listen. 165
            Rumor flies in the night and through the shadows of the world,
screeching. She never closes her eyes in sweet sleep. By day she sits,
a guardian, on the peaks of the highest roof, or on the tall towers,
and she terrifies the great cities, as tenacious of lies and the depraved
as she is a messenger of truth. Rejoicing, she has filled the people
with endless gossip. She sings of real things and unreal alike: 170
that Aeneas has come, a creature of Trojan blood, and the lovely
Dido thinks he is a worthy husband to join with. And now they
are passing the winter in the lap of luxury, no matter how long
it lasts, thoughtless of their royal station, captured by the lust
for fornication. The foul goddess spreads these things on men's lips. 175
           Immediately Rumor slants her course to King Iarbas, and Rumor fires
his mind with words and she fuels his anger. He was a son of Jupiter
Ammon, by a Garamantian nymph who was raped.° Iarbas built a hundred
huge temples to Jove in his broad realms. He set up a hundred altars.
He consecrated ever-living fires, eternal watchmen of the gods, and the soil 180
ran fat with the blood of sacrificial animals. The thresholds were bedecked
with garlands of all kinds of flowers.
                                    And Iarbas, maddened in spirit
and on fire from the bitter rumor—they say that he often prayed to Jupiter,
turning his hands upwards as a suppliant before the altars, in the midst

---

160 *anger at the gods*: Because of their hostility to the Titans, Earth's children.
161 *Enceladus*: Coeus was a Titan and Enceladus a Giant, but Vergil confuses the two.
178 *... who was raped*: In the pre-Vergilian myth, Dido killed herself rather than marry Iarbas. Ammon was an Eastern god usually equated with Jupiter. The Garamantes are tribesmen of the eastern Sahara.

FIGURE 4.2 *Aeneas and Dido*, **1469, from an illustrated manuscript of the commentary on Vergil by Servius.** Servius was a grammarian who lived in the late fourth century and early fifth century AD, the most learned Italian of his generation. His commentaries on Vergil were the first book to be printed at Florence, in 1471. They are the only surviving commentary on a classical author written before the collapse of the western Roman Empire in AD 476. Here the two lovers sit at the foot of a canopied bed. Aeneas is unbearded, wears a cap, and has a sword strapped to this side. He wears a skirt of mail. He holds Dido's right hand. Dressed as a fifteenth-century lady, Dido raises her left hand modestly. Ladies in waiting stand at the back of the room. Paint on vellum.

of the divine powers: "All powerful Jupiter, to whom the Moors° 185
pour out offerings of wine after dining on embroidered couches—
do you see this? Or do we shudder at you for *nothing* when
you throw your thunderbolts, father? And do your aimless lightnings
in the clouds only terrify our spirits and mix with their empty rumblings?
"A woman wandered within my borders and paid for a small town. 190
We gave her lands along the coast to plow and fixed terms for holding
the land, but she has refused me in marriage and has taken Aeneas
into her country as lord. And now *this* Paris with his band of castrati,
wearing a Phrygian cap tied under his chin, his hair dripping with
oil, has taken control of what he has grabbed! In the meanwhile, 195
we load your temples with offerings and we further your empty name!"

Jupiter sends Mercury to warn Aeneas

As Iarbas prayed and clung to the altar, the all-powerful
one heard him, and he turned his gaze to the royal city and the lovers
who had thrown reputation to the wind. He speaks to Mercury
and gives him these orders: "Off you go, my son! Call the winds 200
and glide on your wings. Speak to the Trojan leader now wasting
his time in Tyrian Carthage. He gives no thought to the cities granted
him by the Fates! Carry my words on the quick breezes. This is not
what his most beautiful mother promised, nor why twice she saved
him from the arms of the Greeks.° He was supposed to be one to 205
rule Italy, pregnant with military commands, howling for war.
He would produce a race from the high blood of Teucer
and bring the whole world under the rule of law.
                                    "If the glory of such
a destiny does not inflame him, nor does he labor for his own fame,
still, does the father begrudge to Ascanius the citadels of Rome? 210
What are his plans? With what hope does he stay among an enemy
people, forgetting his Ausonian offspring and the Lavinian fields?
Let him sail! That is the sum of it. Let that be my message."
    He spoke. Mercury prepared to obey the command of his great father.
First he put golden winged shoes on his feet, fastened to the ankles, 215
which carry him high on their wings over the sea and the earth,
as fast as the storm. Then he takes up his wand. With this he calls
up the pale spirits from Orcus, and others he sends beneath to sad

---

185 *Moors*: Native tribesmen of northwestern Africa.

205 *of the Greeks*: Once Venus/Aphrodite saved him from Diomedes (*Iliad* Book 5) and then again at the fall of Troy.

Tartarus.° Mercury gives sleep and he takes it away, and he unseals
220 the eyes of the dead.° Depending on his wand, he drives the winds,
and he flies through the stormy clouds.

Now in his flight Mercury sees the peak
and the steep side of rugged Atlas, who props up the sky on his head—
Atlas, whose pine-covered head is ever bound with dark clouds,
lashed with wind and rain. Fallen snow covers his shoulders.
225 Rivers fall from the chin of the old man, and his bristling beard is stiff
with ice.

There, balancing on even wings, Cyllenian Mercury° first
stopped. Then from Atlas he threw his whole body headlong toward
the waves, like a bird that flies close to the water near the shores,
around the coasts and the rocks filled with fish. So the Cyllenian-born
230 Mercury flew between the earth and heaven to the sandy shore of Libya,
and he cut the winds, coming from Atlas, his mother Maia's father.

As soon as he reached the workers' huts on his winged feet,
he sees Aeneas building towers and renewing roofs. His sword
was studded with reddish-yellow stones that shone like stars,
235 and a cloak hung down from his shoulders blazed with Tyrian
purple, a gift that wealthy Dido had made. She interwove gold
threads with the wool.

Mercury challenges him at once: "Slave to a wife!
do you now establish the foundations of high Carthage? Do you set up
a beautiful city? Ah, have you forgotten your own kingdom, your own affairs?
240 The king of the gods himself, who bends heaven and earth by his will,
sends me down to you from bright Olympus. He himself commands
that I bear these instructions through the swift winds.

"What are your plans?
With what hope do you waste idle hours in Libya? If the glory
of so great an undertaking does not move you, and you do not labor
245 for your own praise, consider Ascanius as he grows up, as Iulus,
your heir, to whom the rule of Italy and Roman earth are owed."

So Cyllenian Mercury spoke, and then he broke off and vanished
from mortal eyes, and far off he disappeared from their sight into thin air.
But Aeneas, stupefied at the vision, was silent. His hair stood up
250 and his voice stuck in his throat. He burns to flee and leave this sweet land,
overwhelmed by such an admonition and command from the gods.

---

219 ... *Tartarus*: Orcus is the same as Dis, lord of the Roman underworld, and by extension the underworld itself. Tartarus is a Greek underworld somehow lower than the house of Hades. The Titans are imprisoned in Tartarus.

220 *of the dead*: Evidently referring to the Roman practice of opening the eyes of the dead as they were placed on the funeral pyre, so they could see on their journey to the other world.

226 *Cyllenian Mercury*: Mercury was born on Mount Cyllenē in ARCADIA in the PELOPONNESUS.

FIGURE 4.3 *Mercury Orders Aeneas to Leave Dido*, c. 1570, by Orazio Samacchini (1532–1577). Samacchini was an Italian painter in the late Renaissance and Mannerist styles. He worked in Rome and his native city of Bologna, painting mostly religious subjects, but here he shows Aeneas at the moment he receives orders from Zeus to move on to Italy. Dido sits demurely, naked, on a bed whose headboard is in the form of a sphinx. She holds a cloth in her left hand. A dog sleeps on the other side of the bed. Aeneas sits on a stool while a cupid works to unbind his left foot resting on a footstool, in preparation for intercourse. A flask of wine stands beside the footstool. Aeneas looks up in surprise at Mercury, who comes down from heaven in the upper right holding his special wand, the caduceus. He wears a winged hat and points accusingly at Aeneas. Two other cupids raise a curtain in the back, revealing two gossips. In the upper left the room recedes into a classical vista. Oil on canvas.

Alas, what should he do? With what speech dare he now go to the raving
queen? How would he begin?
                              Swiftly he turns his mind this way,
then that, and he considers the matter from every aspect, and examines
255 it from every side. This seemed to be the best of the two alternatives.°
He calls to Menestheus and Sergestus and strong Serestus, telling them
to fit out the fleet in silence, to bring all the men to the shore,
and to make ready the tackle. They should hide the reason for the change
in plans. In the meanwhile, because the excellent Dido knew nothing
260 and did not expect that so great a love would be broken, he would find
a way, the gentlest time to speak, a favorable means for these matters.
      They swiftly obey his command, with joy, and they accomplish
what he ordered. But the queen sensed the trick—for who can deceive
a lover?—and she anticipated that he was going to go, fearing even when
265 everything seemed safe.

Dido accuses Aeneas of treachery

                          The same wicked Rumor brought to the maddened
woman the news that they were fitting out the fleet and getting ready
to leave. Her mind weakened, she rages, and on fire she runs wild through
the whole city, like a Bacchant excited by the shaking of the sacred emblems
of the god, when she hears the name *Bacchus*! cried out at the two-year
270 festival, and Mount Cithaeron calls at night with its shouting.°
                                             Of her own
accord she at last addresses Aeneas: "Did you expect to hide, unfaithful one,
that you were capable of so great a wickedness, and that you would leave
my land in secret? Does our love not stop you? Or the oaths that we once
swore? Or Dido who will die a cruel death? Or do you work on your fleet
275 even in winter time? And do you hasten to sail over the deep through
the middle of northern winds—cruel man!
                                    "What if you did not seek foreign
fields and an unknown home, but ancient Troy still stood, would
you seek Troy by taking your fleet across wave-torn seas? Is it *me* you're
running away from? By these tears and your right hand—for I have left
280 myself no other course in my misery—by our marriage, by the wedding
that has just begun . . . if ever I deserved well from you, or if anything
of me was sweet to you, take pity on my house now falling into ruin,
and—I beg you, if there is room in your heart for prayers, change

---

255 *two alternatives*: That is, to tell her right away, or to defer his conversation.

270 *its shouting*: Every two years a Bacchic festival was held on Mount Cithaeron behind Thebes. Sacred objects were shown, and the Bacchants, women inspired by Bacchus/Dionysus, would wander wildly over the mountain.

your mind! On your account the Libyan peoples and Numidian commanders
hate me, and my Tyrians are hostile. On your account too is all shame   285
lost, and all my earlier fame,° by which alone I might reach the stars.

"My *guest*—for this name alone remains of *husband*—to whom do you
give me up now that I'm bound to die? And why do I delay?
Until my brother Pygmalion destroys the city, or Iarbas the Gaetulian
makes me his captive? If only you had fathered some offspring before   290
your flight, if some little Aeneas should play in the halls, whose face
recalls your own, I would not feel so utterly deceived and deserted."

Aeneas explains himself

So she spoke. Aeneas held his gaze steadily on Jove's warnings.
Struggling, he pushed down his love within his heart. At last, he speaks
briefly: "I will never deny that you deserve the most that you can put   295
in speech, O queen. I will not regret remembering you, Elissa,° so long
as I have memory of myself, so long as breath governs these limbs.
But I will speak briefly about your charge.° It was never my intention
to conceal my flight—don't think so!—and I never extended the bridegroom's
torch, or entered into that alliance. If the fates would allow me to lead   300
my life on my own authority, and to solve my problems as I wished,
I would be taking care of a Trojan city, and honoring the dear remnants
of my people. The high halls of Priam would stand again, and with
my hand I would have restored the citadel of Pergama for the conquered.

"But now Apollo of Grynium has ordered that we head for great Italy—   305
it is *Italy* that the Lycian oracles° have commanded! That is my love,°
that is my fatherland. If the citadels of Carthage, and the sight
of your Libyan city holds your gaze—Phoenician woman!—why should
you resent that Teucrians settle in Ausonia? It is right that we too
seek out a foreign kingdom. As often as night covers the earth   310
in dewy shadow, as often as the fiery stars rise upward, the troubled
image of my father Anchises warns and terrifies me in my dreams.°
I am frightened for my son Ascanius and the harm I could do to so dear
a person, cheating him of his Hesperian kingdom and his foreordained fields.

---

286 *earlier fame*: Based on her fidelity to her dead husband Sychaeus.

296 *Elissa*: Her Phoenician name.

298 *charge*: Aeneas speaks as if he were in a court of law.

306 *. . . Lycian oracles*: Apollo had a temple at Grynium in Asia Minor not far from Troy. Apollo was called "Lycian," but it is uncertain whether the word means "wolf-god" or "from Lycia." Helenus gave Aeneas advice from Apollo at Buthrotum, but that is in EPIRUS. Evidently Vergil is characterizing Apollo by giving him recognizable geographical epithets.

306 *my love*: That is, Italy is my love, not you.

312 *my dreams*: We have heard nothing about these appearances.

315 "Now even the messenger of the gods, sent by Jove himself—I swear it
on both our heads!—has brought orders on the swift winds. I myself saw
the god in broad daylight as he came within the walls, and I heard
his voice with these very ears. So stop trying to incite me, and yourself,
with your complaints. I do not go to Italy of my own free will."

Dido's reply

320   She looks at him askance as he says these things. She casts
her gaze here and here and goes over the whole man with silent eyes.
Enraged, she speaks: "Your mother is no goddess! Nor is Dardanus
the father of your race—traitor! but harsh Caucasus gave birth to you
on its rough crags, and Hyrcanian tigers gave you suck!°
                                                       "Why pretend?
325 For what greater wrong am I saving myself? Did he moan when I wept?
Did he turn his eyes away? Did he fall to weeping, overcome?
or did he take pity on his beloved? What shall I put before what?°
        "No, no, neither greatest Juno, nor father Jupiter, the son of Saturn,
views these matters with friendly eyes. Nowhere is faith safe.
330 I took him up when he was tossed on the shore, a beggar, and like
a mad woman I set him up in a part of my kingdom. I saved his lost
fleet, I brought back his friends from death.
                                       "Agh, I am driven, burning,
by the Furies! Now the prophet Apollo, now the Lycian oracles,
now the messenger of the gods sent by Jove himself brings these
335 *horrid* commands through the air. Surely this is a job for the gods!
Care for this matter disturbs their equanimity!
                                       "Well, I do not constrain
you, and I do not refute what you have said. Go, follow Italy on the winds.
Seek out your kingdom over the waves. I only hope, if the righteous [*pia*]
gods can do anything, that you drink the cup of suffering, and that
340 you often call the name of 'Dido'!
                                       "Absent, I will follow you with
dark torches, and when cold death has separated the spirit from
my limbs, I will be present as a shadow, everywhere. I will pay you back,
you wretch! I will hear of it even in the depths of the underworld!"
        With these words she breaks off in the middle of her speech,
345 and, sickened, she flees the light. She turns herself away from his eyes,
going, leaving Aeneas fearful and ready to say more. Slave women take

---

324 *...you suck*: Dardanus is the Italian ancestor of all the Trojans. Caucasus refers to the area beyond the
       eastern end of the BLACK SEA. Hyrcania is a fertile plain in Persia famous for its wolves and tigers.

327 *before what*: Because everything is hopeless, she does not know what word, deed, or thought she
       should put first.

her up, and they carry her back in a state of collapse to her marble
bedchamber and place her on the bed.
                              But dutiful [*pius*] Aeneas, although
he wants to lessen her sorrow by consoling her, and he wants to turn
aside pain with his words, he nonetheless follows the commands of the gods.   350
Moaning loudly, shattered in spirit by their strong love, he returns
to the fleet.

Aeneas is determined to depart

           Then the Teucrians set to. They drag down the swift ships
all along the beach. They float the keels, coated with resin. They bring in leafy
oars and untrimmed staves of oak from the forests, in their eagerness for flight.
You might see them hurrying along, rushing from every part of the city.   355
     Just as when ants despoil a huge pile of grain and, thinking of the winter,
store it up in their house. The black horde goes across the field,
and they carry their booty along a narrow track through the grass.
Part of them pushes against an enormous grain, leaning into it, part puts
the ranks in order and castigates delay. The whole path is fervid with labor.   360
     What did you feel, O Dido, when you saw these things? What groans
did you give when you saw, from the top of the citadel, the shore swarm
far and wide? When you saw the whole sea before your eyes thrown
into confusion by such clamor? Wicked Love! To what will you not drive
the mortal heart?   365
                 Cruel Love: To burst once more into tears, to attempt once
more to persuade him by prayers and as a suppliant to submit her spirit
to Love—so that she not leave anything untried, and die in vain—
     "Anna, you see how there is activity all over the beach. They come
in from all sides. The canvas cries out for the breeze, and the sailors
have joyfully placed garlands on the prows. If I was able to expect   370
(as I *did*) such great pain, then, my sister . . . I can endure it.°
Only do this one thing for me, because I am wretched! That faithless
man befriended you alone, and entrusted you with his private thoughts.
You alone know when it is a good time to approach the man.
                                              "Go, my sister,   375
and speak as a suppliant to the proud enemy. I never swore at Aulis°
along with the Danaäns to destroy the Trojan people. I never sent a fleet
to Pergama, nor did I disturb the ashes and ghost of his father Anchises.°
     "Why does he refuse to hear me out? Where is he rushing off to?

---

371 *endure it*: But we are never told that Dido has expected pain. Probably she is dissembling before her
     sister so that her sister might think that Dido is resigned to the situation.

375 *at Aulis*: Where the Greek fleet gathered for the expedition.

377 *father Anchises*: Anchises is of course buried in Sicily. Dido refers not to an actual crime, but to an
     imaginary one so heinous as to justify the bad treatment she has received.

May he grant this last gift to his lover: May he wait for an easy voyage
and favorable winds. I do not pray for our former marriage, which
he betrayed, nor do I pray that he give up fair Latium or that he abandon
his kingdom. I only seek an empty time, a repose and space in which
my passion may work itself out, until Fortune can teach my conquered
spirit to grieve. I pray for this last favor—pity your sister!—and when
he has given it to me, I will pay it back with interest... at my death."

    So she prayed, and such tears Dido's unhappy sister carried again
and again to Aeneas. But he was unmoved by tears, or receptive to anything
she said. Fate was in the way, and a god stopped the man's gentle hearing.

    Just as when north winds from the Alps compete among themselves,
blowing now here, now there, to uproot an oak, tough because of its great age—
there is a creaking, and the trunk is shaken and the topmost leaves
strew the ground, but it clings to the cliffs, for as far as it stretches its crown
into the sky, so far does it reach with its roots down to Tartarus.
In the same way the hero was knocked on this side and that by Anna's
constant pleas, and he feels the pain in his great heart. But his mind
remains unmoved. All that weeping is for nothing.

Dido is resolved to die

    Then unhappy Dido,
truly terrified by her fate, prays for death. She no longer wants to see
the dome of the sky. And in order that she might accomplish her purpose,
which she had begun to think about, and leave the light, she saw
when she placed offerings on the altar that burned with incense—
horrible to say!—she saw the holy water turn black and the wine poured
out change into vile blood. She told this vision to no one, not even her sister.

    There was in her palace a shrine made of marble for her former husband,
which she honored greatly, bound with snowy wool and festive fronds.
From here she seemed to hear voices and the words of her husband
as he called her, when dark night held the earth and the lone owl on the roof
complained with his funereal cry, drawing out its long call into a wail.

    And predictions of ancient seers horrified her with their terrible
warnings. Fierce Aeneas pursues her, frenzied, in her dreams. Always
she seems to be left alone by herself, to be going on a long journey
without a companion to seek her Tyrian people in a desert land.
Or she seemed like the maddened Pentheus who sees the tribes
of the Eumenides and a twin sun, and Thebes shows itself double.°
Or like Orestes, the son of Agamemnon, who flees his mother armed

---

413 *... itself double*: In Euripides' *Bacchae* (404 BC), Pentheus rejects the new god Bacchus/Dionysus, who drives Pentheus mad so that he sees two suns and a double Thebes. The Eumenides, "kindly ones," is a euphemism for Erinyes, or "Furies."

with torches and black serpents while the avenging Furies sit on 415
the threshold.°
          And so when, overcome by pain, she gave in to madness
and decided to die, she debates in her heart the time and the means.
She goes to speak to her sad sister, concealing her plan with her expression—
calm—with hope on her brow: "I have found a way, my sister—rejoice
with your sister!—which will either bring him back to me, or will release 420
me from my love. Near the end of Ocean,° and where the sun sets, lies
the land of the Ethiopians, the furthest of lands, where the mighty Atlas
turns on his shoulder the heavens studded with blazing stars. I've learned
of a priestess from there, of the Massylian race, a guardian of the sacred
enclosure of the Hesperides, who used to give food to the dragon, 425
and guarded the holy branches of the tree, scattering the damp honeydew
and the soporific poppy.°
          "This woman claims that she sets free the hearts
of whomever she wishes, and sends down cruel pain on others,
and that she stops the water in rivers, and turns back the stars, and wakes
the nighttime spirits of the dead. You will see the earth yawn beneath 430
your feet, and the ash trees come down from the mountains. I swear
by the gods, my darling, and by you, my sister, and your sweet heart,
that all unwilling I arm myself with the magical arts!
          "But in secret build a pyre
in an inner courtyard, open to the sky, and place on it the arms of the man,
which he left hanging in our bedroom—faithless! [*impius*]—and all the clothes, 435
and the bed of our union, by which I perish. I want to destroy every trace
of that evil man, and the priestess commands it."
          After saying these things,
she falls silent, and a paleness comes over her face. Anna could not understand
how her sister Dido veiled her own funeral by these strange rituals,
nor can she conceive in her mind such a great madness. And she does not 440
fear anything worse than at the death of Sychaeus. And so she does what
she is ordered.
          When a huge pyre was erected in an inner court in the open air
of pine and cut oak, the queen hangs the place with garlands, and she crowns

---

416 ... *threshold*: When Orestes killed his mother to avenge the murder of his father Agamemnon, the Furies pursued him, the subject of Aeschylus' famous play *The Eumenides* (458 BC). Here the ghost of Orestes' mother pursues him in the guise of a Fury, evidently inside some building, while the actual Furies prevent his escape by guarding the door.

421 *Ocean*: The river that surrounds the world.

427 ... *poppy*: Massylia is somewhere in Libya, but apparently the priestess is now in Carthage. The Hesperides, "nymphs of the West," and a dragon guarded the Tree of Life, given by Jupiter to Juno as a wedding present and planted in a garden in the far West. Honeydew is a sweet extract that appears on plants, exuded by aphids. It is odd that the Hesperides should feed the dragon on the soporific poppy if his task was to keep awake and guard the tree.

the pyre with funereal fronds. She places his clothes and the sword he left
445 behind and his portrait on the couch, well aware of what was to come.

      Altars stand all around and, now a priestess with unbound hair, she calls
on three hundred gods: Erebus and Chaos and the triple Hecatê, and the three
faces of virgin Diana. She sprinkles water symbolizing the fountains
of Avernus.° Herbs too are brought forth, cut with bronze knives by moonlight,
450 juicy with the dark milk of poison. And a love-charm torn from the brow
of a new-born foal, snatched away from the mother.° Then she herself,
standing beside the altars with holy [*piis*] offering and holy hands,
with one foot unsandaled,° her clothes loosened, calls the gods to witness,
and the stars conscious of Fate, that she is about to die. Then she prays
455 to whatever power, just and mindful, has a care for those who love
in an unequal pact.

      It was night, and throughout the earth weary bodies
fell into a peaceful sleep, and the forest and the savage sea fell quiet
while the stars wheel midway in their motion. All the fields are still
and the herds and brightly colored birds. Both those who live on widely
460 scattered lakes and those who live in the country in the brambles—they were
sunk in sleep in the silent night.

      But not the Phoenician woman, unhappy
in spirit. She does not find the release of sleep, or receive the night into her eyes
or breast. Her cares only double, and her love, again resurgent, rages
as she floats on the great sea of anger.

      She begins in this way, and alone
465 turns it over in her heart: "Agh, what am I doing? Shall I approach my prior
suitors—an object of contempt? Shall I seek as a suppliant marriage with some
Numidian—whom I have so many times thought unworthy as husbands?
Shall I then follow the Trojan ships and every last wish of the Teucrians?
Because they might be delighted in having been helped before?
470 Because gratitude for earlier deeds might be fixed in their memories?

      "But who would let me—supposing I wanted to—come aboard their
proud ships? Who would take on one they hate? Alas, do you not yet know—
abandoned!—the treachery of the race of Laomedon?° What then—shall

---

449 ...*Avernus*: Erebus, "darkness," stands for the god of the underworld. Chaos is a primordial god from which all things came. The triple Hecatê is Luna in the sky, Diana on earth, and Hecatê in the underworld and is symbolized by a three-faced image placed at the meeting of three roads (see Figure 6.3). Witches often called on the triple Hecatê to help them in their nefarious practices. Lake Avernus is near the entrance to the underworld (as we learn in Book 6).

451 *from the mother*: Vergil refers to *hippomanes*, a fleshy mass sometimes found on the forehead of a new-born foal (a remnant from the fetal membrane), thought to have dangerously aphrodisiac properties. The mother would ordinarily bite it away, unless it were snatched up to serve as a love-charm.

453 *unsandaled*: Perhaps so that her bare foot may stay in contact with the earth and its underworld powers.

473 *Laomedon*: The father of Priam.

I go alone among exultant sailors, or packed in among the whole band
of my Tyrian followers? And those whom I barely tore away from Sidon—
shall I drive them again across the sea and order them to spread their sails
to the wind?

      "Just die! As you deserve! Avert pain with the sword!
You, my sister, overcome by my tears—you first burdened me, filled
with passion, with these evils. You threw me to the enemy. I was not allowed
to lead a life without blame, free from the marriage chamber—like an animal!—
and not to know such cares. I have not kept the vow that I made to the ashes
of Sychaeus."

Mercury again urges Aeneas to flee

          Such was the lament that erupted from her heart. Aeneas,
on his ship's high stern, now certain that he was going, was snatching
some sleep after putting everything in order. Then the same form of the god
appeared again to him in his dreams, and again it seemed to admonish him,
similar to Mercury in every way, in voice and color and his yellow hair
and his youthful graceful limbs:
                         "O son of a goddess, do you think you can
go to sleep in the midst of this disaster? Do you not see the danger that
surrounds you? Madman! Do you not hear the favorable West Wind blowing?
She contrives deceptions and dread disaster in her heart, she who is certain
to die, and she is tossed on the turbulent sea of anger. Will you not flee
in haste from here while you can hasten? Soon you will see ships crowding
the water, and you will see savage torches burning, and on the shore
flames will rage if Dawn finds you still delaying in these lands.
Come now, break off delay! A woman is always fickle and changeable."
     So he spoke, and dissolved into black night. But then Aeneas,
terrified by the sudden apparition, rips his body from sleep. He importunes
his men: "Wake up quick, my men, and go to the rowing benches.
Quickly unfurl the sails! A god sent from the deep sky again urges, yes,
that we hasten our flight, that we cut the twisted ropes. We follow you,
holy among the gods, whoever you are, and again we gladly obey
your command. May you be present and help us with a gentle mind,
and may you show stars favorable to us in the heaven."
                                       Aeneas spoke,
and he draws out his lightning sword from its scabbard, and he strikes
the cable with the naked blade. All alike were seized with the same ardor.
They grab up their possessions and run. They abandon the shore.
The water disappears beneath the mass of ships. Leaning in, they churn
the foam and they sweep the blue waves.

the curse of Dido

                            And now Dawn, leaving
the saffron bed of Tithonus,° sprinkled the earth with the first light.
510 When from her tower the queen saw the day first whiten, and the fleet
sailing away under full sail, and she saw that there were no oarsmen
on the shore or in the harbor, three and then four times she struck her lovely
breast with her hand.
                    She tore at her golden hair, and she said:
"Ah Jupiter, will he leave then? Will this stranger mock our realm?
515 Shall my Tyrians take up arms, and follow them out of the city,
and others drag our ships from the docks? Go! Bring fire quick!
Spread the sails! Drive the oars!—What am I saying? Where am I?
What insanity changes my mind? Unhappy Dido,° now your impious [*impia*]
acts touch you.° The right time was then, when you gave him the scepter . . .
520 "Behold the faith and trust of a man who they say carries with him
the Penates of his father, of a man who they say carried around
on his shoulders his father worn out with age. Could I not have seized
him and ripped him apart and scattered the parts on the waves?
Could I not have put his companions to the sword, and he himself—
525 and Ascanius, and served up Ascanius to feast on at his father's meal?!°
      "Of course the fortune of war is always uncertain—Let it have been.
Whom should I have feared, I who am about to die? I would have carried
torches to his camp, I would have filled his gangways with flame,
and I would have destroyed his son and his father along with their
530 whole race. Then I would have flung myself on the pile.
                                        "O Sun,
who illumines the whole world with your flames, and you, O Juno,°
the mediator and witness of these pains, and Hecatê howled to throughout
the cites at the crossroads at night, and you, the avenging Furies,
and you gods of the dying Elissa—listen to these things and turn your
535 divine will to evils that have earned it, and hear our prayers.
      "If it is necessary that that man, whose name I cannot speak, touch port
and sail to the land—and so the fate of Jove demands—Well, that boundary
stands fixed. But let him beg for help, harassed by war and the arms
of a bold people, banished from his territories, torn from the embrace

---

509 *Tithonus*: The Trojan prince who was a lover of Dawn.

518 *Dido*: Dido is the only person in the *Aeneid* to refer to herself by name.

519 *touch you*: Presumably her unfaithfulness to the memory of Sychaeus.

525 *father's meal*: The punishment Dido imagines she might have inflicted on Aeneas and his men reminds us of gory details in Greek myth.

531 *O Juno*: Dido's ignorance of Juno's real role is remarkable.

of Iulus—and may he see the shameful death of his people!   540
"Then, when
he has surrendered himself to a peace under unequal terms,° may he not
enjoy his kingdom or the days he hoped for, but may he fall before his time
and lie unburied on the sand.°
"I pray for this, and I pour out my last
words with blood. Then you, my Tyrians, hound with hatred all the offspring
of the race that is to come! Offer this as a tribute to my ashes. Let there   545
be no love among our peoples! May no treaties come into being.

"Arise, some unknown avenger° from my bones, who will pursue
the Dardanian colonists with fire and sword. Now, or in the future,
at whatever time that his strength shall be given him. I pray that shore
be opposed to shore, waves to water, arms to arms! Let them fight—   550
themselves and their descendants!"°

the death of Dido

So she spoke, and turned her thoughts
in all directions, considering how with all speed to break off this hated light.
Then she spoke briefly to Barcê,° the nurse of Sychaeus (for dark ashes
hid her own nurse in her former country): "My dear nurse, bring
my sister Anna here. Tell her to hurry, and to sprinkle herself with water   555
from the river, and bring the sacrificial animals and the fine offerings.
So, let her come. And you bind your temples with sacred [*pia*] ribbons.
For I want to complete the holy rites to the Stygian Jove° that I have duly
begun, and to put an end to care by giving to the flame the pyre
of this Trojan person."   560
So she spoke, and the old woman hurried off.
But Dido, agitated, maddened by her awful purpose, rolling her bloodshot eyes,
her trembling cheeks stained with red spots, yet pallid with approaching death—
she rushes into the interior house across the threshold and she ascends,
crazed, onto the high funeral pyre, and she unsheathes a Trojan sword, a gift

---

541   *terms*: In Book 12 Jupiter and Juno make an agreement under which the Trojan name will die out as the Italian name predominates.

543   *on the sand*: Some sources say that Aeneas fell in battle after ruling for three years and that his corpse lay undiscovered.

547   *avenger*: No doubt she means Hannibal in the Second Punic War.

551   *...their descendants*: Dying people were thought to have the gift of prophecy. Most of what Dido says will come true, especially the historical animosity between Carthage and Rome that led to the greatest of ancient wars, the Second Punic War (218–201 BC), when the great Hannibal invaded Italy and nearly destroyed Rome.

553   *Barcê*: Barca was the name of the family to which Hannibal belonged.

558   *Stygian Jove*: Dis.

565 not sought for such a purpose.°

As she saw the Ilian clothing and the familiar
bed, she delayed for a moment, weeping and thinking, and then she climbs up
on the bed and speaks her last words: "Sweet remnants, while Fate
and the god allowed it—take now this soul, and release me from these cares.
I have lived, and I fulfilled what course Fortune decreed, and now my august
570 spirit will go beneath the earth. I established a bright city. I saw its walls.
Avenging my husband, I punished a hostile brother. Happy, alas, too happy,
if only the Trojan ships never touched on our shores!"

She spoke, and, impressing
her mouth on the couch, she said: "We will die unavenged, but let us die.
Just so, just so it is pleasing to go beneath the shadows. May the cruel
575 Trojan drink in with his eyes this fire on the high sea, and may he bear
with him the omen of our death."

She spoke, and her companions saw that
in the middle of her speech she had collapsed on the sword, and the sword
was foamy with blood, and her hands were stained with blood. A shout
goes up to the high halls. Rumor dances wildly through the astounded city.
580 The houses resound with lamentation and wailing and the ululation
of women. The sky echoes with great groanings, no different than
if all Carthage or ancient Tyre were falling under the attack
of an invading enemy, and raging flames were rolling over the roofs
of men and gods.

Her sister heard it, nearly fainting, and terrified
585 she ran through the frenzied crowd, digging her nails into her face
and striking her breasts with her fists. As Dido dies, she cries
out her name: "So this is what you meant, sister? Did you set out
to trick me? Was this pyre of yours, these fires and altars, prepared
for my sake? What first should I grieve for, I who am deserted?
590 Did you despise, in your dying, to have your sister as companion?

"You should have called me to the same fate. The same pain
of the sword should have taken the two of us at the same hour.
I even built this pyre with my own hands. Did I call aloud
to our father's gods so that I would be absent—O cruel one!—
595 as you are laid out for burial? You have extinguished yourself,
and me too, O sister, and the people and your Sidonian ancestors
and your city. Here, let me wash your wounds with water and catch
whatever dying breath remains . . ."

While so speaking, Anna had climbed
the high steps. She clasped her semiconscious sister to her breast
600 with a sigh, absorbing the dark blood with her dress. Dido tried

---

565 *a purpose*: Apparently Aeneas has given Dido a sword.

FIGURE 4.4 *Dido's Death*, **c. 1630, by Peter Paul Rubens (1577–1640).** Rubens was a Dutch painter and an advocate of an exaggerated Baroque style that emphasized rich colors, and voluptuous overweight women. He is known for his portraits, landscapes, and historical, mythical, and allegorical subjects. In his large workshop, Rubens hired skilled artists to paint in his own style from sketches that he provided, manufacturing over two thousand works of art. Here Rubens emphasizes Dido's mad passion through the twisting of her plump body and her unruly hair. Dido seems to be seated on the empty tomb of Sychaeus, which Vergil describes. The carved image of its face is seen on the right. Dido raises her eyes to the sky while, naked, she plunges Aeneas' sword into her breast. Oil on canvas.

to raise her heavy eyes, but they rolled backwards. The wound fixed
beneath her breast hisses. She raised herself three times, struggling to lean
on her elbow; three times she fell back to the couch, and with wandering
eyes she sought the light in the high heaven. Finding it, she groaned.
605   Then all-powerful Juno, taking pity on Dido's long suffering and difficult
death, sent down Iris° from Olympus to release the struggling breath-soul
from the limbs that cling to it. For because she had not perished by Fate,
nor by a death she deserved, but miserable and before her time, inflamed
by a sudden madness, Proserpina had not yet cut a yellow lock from
610 the top of her head, and condemned her person to Stygian Orcus.°
    And so Iris, dewy-wet, flies down through the sky on crocus
wings, trailing a thousand different colors across the sun. She takes
her stand above Dido's head: "Under orders, I take this sacred lock
of hair, and I release you from this body of yours."
                                                               So she spoke,
615 and she cut the hair with her right hand. All the warmth slipped
away at once, and Dido's life withdrew into the winds.

Book 5 is omitted. Aeneas and his followers leave Carthage, but a storm drives them into Drepanum *in Sicily, where Acestes again welcomes them. It has been a year since Anchises died, so Aeneas holds elaborate funeral games in his honor. Meanwhile, Juno inspires the women followers, weary after seven years of wandering, to attack the ships with fire, but Jupiter extinguishes the flames with a rainstorm. The ghost of Anchises appears to Aeneas and advises him to leave behind those who just cannot go on. The fleet sets sail for Italy. Venus asks Neptune to assure a good voyage. Neptune agrees but demands a human life in return. Palinurus, Aeneas' helmsman, falls asleep and tumbles into the sea. He swims ashore but is killed by local savages.*

---

606 *Iris:* "rainbow," often Juno's messenger.

610 ... *Orcus*: Proserpina is the goddess of Death (Persephonê). Her need to cut a lock of hair from the dead appears to be Vergil's own invention, based on the practice of cutting hair from a sacrificial animal: Dido is like a sacrificial animal.

BOOK 6. *Descent into the Underworld*

So Aeneas spoke, weeping, and he gave the fleet free rein.
At last he comes to shore at Euboean CUMAE.° They turn
the prows to the sea. Then they fix the ships with the strong
teeth of the anchors, and the curved boats cover the shore.
The band of young men leaps out eagerly onto the Hesperian shore. 5

the doors of the temple at Cumae

Part of them seeks the seeds of fire hidden in the veins of flint,
part raids the woods, the dense homes of wild animals, and they point
out the rivers they have found. But dutiful [*pius*] Aeneas seeks out
the heights over which Apollo rules from on high, and the huge cavern
nearby, the secret place of the awesome Sibyl, in whom the Delian 10
prophetic god inspires greatness of mind and spirit, and opens the future.°
They went through the groves of Trivia and the golden house.°
Daedalus, as the story goes, while fleeing from the kingdom of Minos,
dared to entrust himself to the sky, flying on swift wings,
and he soared on the unfamiliar road to the icy North, 15
and at last stood lightly hovering above the Chalcidian hill.°
First returned to earth here, he dedicated the oars of his wings
to you, O Phoebus, and built an immense temple. On the doors,

---

2 *Cumae*: Cumae was the first proper Greek colony in the West, founded c. 750 BC by Greeks from the cities of Eretria and Chalcis in EUBOEA, the long island east of the Greek coast near ATHENS, who had earlier established a trading station on the island of Pithecusae (modern ISCHIA) in the Bay of Naples. The name Cumae seems to refer to a peninsula in Euboea. The Euboeans brought with them the Greek alphabet, which a Euboean Greek probably invented c. 800 BC. The Etruscans took the writing system from the Euboean Greeks, then the Romans took the script from the Etruscans, whose variation of Euboean script became the Latin alphabet used worldwide today, the very writing on this page.

11 *. . . the future*: An anachronism because the cult of Apollo on the Acropolis at Cumae was not established until 410 BC. There was evidently an earlier cult to Hera on the site. Prophetesses of the god Apollo, "the Delian god," were called Sibyls. There were many in the ancient world. According to the legend, the Sibyl at Cumae sold to Tarquinius the Proud, the last king of Rome (c. 535–495 BC), the Sibylline Books, mysterious documents in Greek that the Romans did consult in times of crisis.

12 *golden house*: Trivia, "she of the three ways," is Hecatê, goddess of the crossroads, witchcraft, and the underworld, identified with Apollo's sister Diana (Artemis) (Figure 6.3). The "golden house" is the temple of Apollo, of which traces remain today.

16 *Chalcidian hill*: After leaving CRETE, Daedalus and his son Icarus flew north. Icarus fell into the sea near SAMOS (the "Icarian Sea"). Then Daedalus flew west to Cumae, in Italy, called the "Chalcidian hill" because it was founded by setters from Chalcis on the island of Euboea.

the death of Androgeus;° then the penalty imposed on the descendants
20 of Cecrops—misery!—to send seven of their sons. There the urn stands,
with the lots drawn out. Facing this, on the opposite door, the land of Crete,
rising from the sea. Here her cruel passion for the bull, and Pasiphaë's
secret intercourse with him—and the Minotaur is there, a mixture of species,
a biform-child, the monument of unspeakable love. Here the building
25 of the palace and its wandering passages from which there is no escape.
But Daedalus himself, pitying the great passion of the queen, unraveled
the deceptive and roundabout twistings of the Labyrinth, guiding
his blind footsteps with a thread.
       And you, too, would have had a large
part in so great a work of art, Icarus, if grief had allowed it! Twice
30 Daedalus tried to show your fall in gold; twice your father's hands fell.

the Sibyl at Cumae

  They would have gone on staring at the work of art if Achates, earlier
sent ahead, had not come up together with the priestess of Phoebus
and Trivia, Deïphobê, the daughter of Glaucus, who speaks to Aeneas
in the following way: "This is not the time for such sightseeing! It would
35 be better if you sacrificed seven bullocks from a herd that has never
done work, and as many two-year old sheep, carefully chosen."
  Having spoken to Aeneas in this way—the men did not delay
to perform the sacrifices as commanded—the priestess calls the Trojans
into the high temple. A cave is hewn into the immense face of the Euboean
40 cliff from which a hundred broad approaches lead, a hundred mouths
from which rush as many voices, the replies of the Sibyl.

---

19 *...Androgeus*: Aeneas is standing in front of the temple to Apollo built by Daedalus, and he beholds the images carved on its doors. Ancient critics called such a passage an *ekphrasis*, Greek for "description," in which we learn of some ancient work of art that the character is looking at. We have already seen an *ekphrasis* in Book 1, where Aeneas and Achates look at images on the temple of Juno in Carthage. According to this story, Minos prayed to Neptune to send a white bull from the sea that he could sacrifice to him, but the bull was so beautiful that he sacrificed another bull instead. To punish him, Neptune made Pasiphaë fall in love with the white bull from the sea. Daedalus built a wooden cow for her to squat in and have intercourse with the bull (see Figure 6.1), and so the Minotaur ("bull of Minos") was conceived. The Minotaur was imprisoned in the Labyrinth, also built by Daedalus. When Minos' son Androgeus was treacherously killed in Athens, Minos ordered Aegeus, king of the Athenians (and descendant of Cecrops), to send an annual tribute of seven young men (and usually seven girls), selected by lot, to be fed to the Minotaur. Aegeus' son, Theseus, volunteered to go with the group. Ariadnê, Minos' daughter, fell in love with him and gave him a ball of thread that he unraveled as he went into the Labyrinth. Theseus killed the Minotaur, then followed the thread back to the entrance. Angered at the turn of events, Minos now imprisoned Daedalus and his son Icarus in the Labyrinth of Daedalus' own construction. Making wings from feathers and wax, the father and son nevertheless flew away, but Icarus flew too close to the sun, the wax melted, and he fell into the sea and was drowned. Daedalus flew on to Cumae in the West.

FIGURE 6.1 *Daedalus, Pasiphaë, and Icarus*, c. AD 60, fresco from Pompeii. Daedalus, the master Athenian craftsman, depicted with a trim beard and balding, shows Pasiphaë the cow he has constructed for her to crouch in. The wooden bull stands on a wheeled platform. Daedalus holds a sheet of papyrus in his right hand, perhaps plans for the manufacture of the wooden cow. Two attendants stand behind Pasiphaë; one points to the cow. In the lower left, Icarus plays with his father's hammer and chisel. The theme of the Minotaur was often shown on Roman houses, pottery, and gems. Fresco.

                                      They had come
to the threshold of the cave, when the virgin said: "It is time to ask the Oracles—
behold the god, the god!"
                    As she said these things in front of the door,
suddenly neither her face, nor her color remain the same, and her hair
45 was loosened, and her breast heaved and her heart swells with a wild madness.
She seems taller, nor does she speak with the voice of a mortal when
the power of the god, now closer, breathes upon her.
                                          "Do you delay to perform
your vows and your prayers," she says, "O Trojan Aeneas? Do you delay?
For until you pray, the great lips of this terrifying house will not open."
50   So saying, she fell silent. An icy shudder ran through the hard bones
of the Trojans, and the king pours forth prayers from the depths of his heart:
"Phoebus, you who have always taken pity on the intense suffering of Troy,
you who guided the hand of Paris and the Dardanian arrow against the body
of Achilles°—I have entered so many seas bordering vast lands with
55 you as guide, penetrating the remote peoples of Massilia and the fields
stretching along the SYRTES.° Now at last we take hold of the shores
of a fleeing Italy. This far, and no further, may Troy's bad luck have
followed us.
         "It is right that all of you° also spare the people of Troy,
and all the gods and goddesses to whom Ilium, and the mighty glory
60 of Dardania, was offensive. And you, O most holy prophetess, who
knows what is to come—I do not ask for a kingdom not owed by Fate—
grant that we Trojans settle in LATIUM, along with the wandering gods
and the storm-tossed powers of Troy. Then I will establish a temple
from solid marble to Phoebus and to Trivia and festival days in the name
65 of Phoebus.°
         "A magnificent inner shrine awaits you, too, in our kingdom.
For there I will set up your oracles and hidden utterances spoken
to my people, and I will consecrate a group of select men—O gracious one!
Only do not utter your oracles in verse on leaves!—or they may fly away,
confused playthings on the winds! Sing them from your own lips."°

---

54 *of Achilles*: Paris shot Achilles in the heel with an arrow guided by Apollo, so killing him.

56 *... Syrtes*: Massilia is part of Numidia, the territory south of Carthage; the Syrtes are the shallow quicksands west of Carthage.

58 *of you*: That is, the gods opposed to Troy: Juno, Neptune, and Minerva.

65 *of Phoebus*: Apparently the reference is to the temple to Apollo built by Augustus in 28 BC on the PALATINE HILL to commemorate his victory over Marc Antony at the battle of ACTIUM in 31 BC.

69 *... own lips*: The Sibylline Books were originally kept in the TEMPLE OF JUPITER on the CAPITOLINE HILL, then moved to the inner sanctum of Augustus' TEMPLE TO APOLLO on the Palatine Hill. There were originally nine Sibylline Books, written in Greek hexameters. When Tarquin the Proud, Rome's seventh and last king, refused to buy all nine, the Sibyl—so the story goes—burned three of them, then asked the same price for the remaining six. When Tarquin still refused, she burned three more. At last Tarquin purchased the

Aeneas stopped speaking. But, not yet submitting to Phoebus, 70
the prophetess rages violently in the cave, trying to shake the god from
her breast. The more she rages, the more he wears out her raving mouth,
conquering her untamed heart, training her by restraint.
                                                          And now
the hundred huge mouths of the shrine opened by themselves,
and they carry the replies of the prophetess through the air: 75
"O you, who at least have finished with the great dangers of the sea!
But even graver dangers await you on the earth. The Dardanians will
come into the kingdom of LAVINIUM.° Put this care from your heart.
Yet they will wish they had not come. I see war, terrible war,
and the Tiber foaming with abundant blood. You will have your SIMOEIS, 80
your XANTHUS, your Greek camp. Already another Achilles is born
in Latium, he too born from a goddess. Nor will Juno, a curse
to the Trojans, ever be absent, while you, a suppliant in trying circumstance—
what races and cities of Italy will you *not* beg for assistance!
                                                     "The cause
of so much evil for the Trojans will again be a foreign bride, again 85
the marriage to a man from another country. Do not give way to these evils,
but go more boldly against them than your fortune allows. The first path
of safety, which you little imagine, will open from a Greek city."°

Aeneas seeks entrance to the underworld

    After saying these things, the Cumaean Sibyl sings terrifying obscurities
from her inner sanctum, and she echoes from the cave, mixing true things 90
with incomprehensible. Apollo shakes the reins of the raving woman,
and he twists the spur beneath her breast.
                                              When the frenzy stops
and her mad lips fall quiet, the hero Aeneas begins: "No new
and unexpected face of suffering, O virgin, rises before me. I've foreseen

---

    remaining three books at the original price. The Sibylline Books were consulted in times of crisis. The
    books did not predict specific events, but gave instructions for rituals of expiation in case of disaster or
    bad omens. The Trojan prophet Helenus had warned Aeneas in Book 3 that the Sibyl's predictions were
    written on leaves that scattered when the doors of the cave were opened, with the result that those
    seeking an oracle went away disappointed. Vergil's own text of the *Aeneid* was used as a source of
    prophetic information as early as the second century AD.

78 *Lavinium*: The first Trojan settlement in Italy, south of Rome on the coast. This is the first time that
    Aeneas has heard the name, although it appears in Book 1 when Jupiter speaks to Venus.

88 *... Greek city*: In her prophecy the Sibyl refers to the Iliadic portion of the *Aeneid*, Books 7–12 as Books 1–6
    are the Odyssean portion, although now the Trojans are the invaders. The other Achilles will be Turnus,
    king of the Rutulians, the son of the goddess Venilia, as Achilles was the son of Thetis. The SIMOEIS and
    XANTHUS are analogous to the TIBER and the Numicus. The camp of Aeneas and his followers is analo-
    gous to the Greek camp. As Helen received Paris as a foreign guest, now Lavinia, the daughter of King
    Latinus, will be betrothed to Aeneas, leading to a savage war. The Greek city that will help the Trojans is
    PALLANTEUM, the city ruled by the Greek Evander from ARCADIA, who will ally himself with Aeneas.

FIGURE 6.2A Passageway to the Sibyl's cave, c. 500 BC. This rock-hewn tunnel, leading to the cave of the Cumaean Sibyl, has "windows" opening out to the sea. The left-hand wall is solid, and the openings are on the right.

FIGURE 6.2B The Sibyl's cave. The Sibyl was one of the major oracles of the ancient Greeks and Romans. This cave at Cumae is unique in Mediterranean archaeology and has never been satisfactorily explained. Constructed at an unknown date, perhaps in the sixth century BC, the inner sanctum is approached by a 450-foot-long corridor cut into the tufa rock that runs inside the face of the cliff, penetrated by triangle-shaped lateral passageways that overlook the sea and let in light through "a hundred mouths" (Figure 6.2a); in fact, there are eight of these passageways. The translator sits on a bench in the trapezoidal inner sanctum from where the Sybil issued her oracles. The cave was only discovered in 1932. Author's photo.

95 all of them, gone over them in my spirit. I ask for one thing.
They say this is the door of the infernal realm, and the shadowy
swamp where Acheron overflows. Let it be my fortune to have sight
of my father, and his face! Show me the road and open the sacred
doors. I carried him on these shoulders through the flames
100 and the thousand pursuing weapons. I brought him from the middle
of the enemy. He was the companion on my journey. He endured with me
all the seas, the threats of ocean and sky—though he was weak,
beyond his strength and the proper lot of old age.
                                    "But he ordered me,
with his prayers, that I should seek you out and humbly seek your
105 threshold. Take pity, O blessed one, on a son and his father—I beg you!
For you can do anything. Hecatê has not set you up over the woods
of Avernus for nothing. If Orpheus could summon the shade of his wife,
dependent on his Thracian lyre and his tuneful strings, and if Pollux redeemed
his brother by dying on alternate days, going back and forth so many times—
110 and what about Theseus? or great Hercules?—My own race is from
the highest Jove too."°

            He prayed in this fashion and took hold of the altar,
when the prophetess said: "O you who are sprung from the blood of the gods,
Trojan son of Anchises, the descent to Avernus is easy. Day and night
the door of black Dis lies open. But to retrace your steps and to return
115 to the winds above—this is a task, this a labor. Some sons of the gods
have done it, whom the just Jupiter loved, or whose blazing virtue raised
to the skies. Woods cover all the intervening space, and Cocytus°
surrounds it, sliding in dark coils.
                            "But if so great a desire compels you,
if your longing is so great—twice to swim the Stygian lakes, twice
120 to see black Tartarus, and it pleases you to indulge in an insane labor—
only listen to what you must first accomplish.
                                    "There lurks in a dark tree
a bough golden in its leaves and its supple stem, said to be sacred
to Proserpina, the Juno of the underworld. All the wood hides it,
and shadows enclose the hidden valleys. But it is not allowed to enter
125 the hidden places of the earth before one has plucked the golden-leaved
fruit from the tree. This—beautiful Proserpina has ordained that it be brought

---

111 *...Jove too*: The Thracian singer Orpheus was allowed to enter the underworld to bring back his wife Eurydicê. Pollux and Castor were sons of Leda, but Pollux was also a son of Jupiter and so immortal. When Castor died, Pollux was permitted to share his immortality with his brother, so the brothers spent alternate days in the underworld and on Olympus. Both Theseus and Hercules descended into the underworld. Aeneas is a grandson of Jupiter because his mother Venus is Jupiter's daughter.

117 *Cocytus*: "wailing," a river of the underworld. Other underworld rivers are Lethê ("forgetfulness"), Acheron ("suffering"), and Styx ("hateful"). In Vergil's account, Phlegethon ("fiery") is the river of Tartarus.

to her as a gift. A second fruit of gold always appears when
the first is plucked, and the stem puts forth leaves of the same metal.
    "Therefore, with your eyes search for it up high, and once you have
found it, take it respectfully in your hand. For it will follow willingly, 130
easily, if the Fates summon you. Otherwise you cannot conquer it by any
force, nor will you be able to cut it with hard steel.
                                      "Furthermore, the lifeless
body of your friend°—I see, you do not know—pollutes the entire fleet
with his corpse while you seek our advice, hanging around our threshold.
First take this man to his resting place and bury him in a grave. 135
Lead up black cattle. Let those be your first offerings of expiation.
Only in this way will you see the groves of Styx and the realms
forbidden to the living."

the burial of Misenus and the plucking of the golden bough

                      She spoke, then fell silent with closed lips.
Aeneas walks away, leaving the cave, with a sad face, his eyes downcast.
He turns over the mysterious outcomes in his mind. His faithful 140
companion Achates comes up to him, and he plants his footsteps
with an equal concern. They debate at some length, in a wide-ranging
discussion—of which ally did the prophetess speak? and which was
the body that needed to be buried?
                              As they walk along, they see Misenus
lying on the dry beach, ruined by a shameful death—Misenus, the son 145
of Aeolus.° No other was more outstanding in rousing the troops
with his trumpet, in enflaming war with music. He was the companion
of great Hector and went with him, distinguished by his trumpet
and his spear.
              After Achilles had beaten Hector and despoiled
him of life, this most brave hero, Misenus, allied himself with 150
Trojan Aeneas, following a man no inferior. But then, when by chance
he made the seas echo with his hollow conch shell—madman!—
and he called the gods to compete in song, his rival Triton°
(if you believe the story) lay in wait and drowned the man
in a foamy wave between the rocks. 155
                                  And so everyone mourned around
the body of Misenus with a great cry, and especially dutiful [*pius*] Aeneas.

---

133 *your friend*: Aeneas is unaware of the death of the trumpeter Misenus, his friend (we learn of this below).

146 *son of Aeolus*: Aeolus here is probably the wind-king.

153 *Triton*: A merman, son of Neptune. Misenus evidently challenged him to a musical contest and paid with his life.

    Then without delay they all hasten, though weeping, to perform
the Sibyl's commands. They hurry to raise up toward the sky
an altar for a funeral made of tree trunks. They enter the ancient
160 forest, the deep lairs of wild animals. The pine trees fall and the red-oaks
resound, struck by axes. Trunks of ash and the fissile hardwood
is split by wedges. They roll huge mountain-ash down from
the hills. Aeneas, too, encourages his companions in the midst
of their labors, and he girds himself with the same tools they use.
165 But he himself turns over these things in his sad heart, viewing
the immense forest, and so he prays: "If only the golden bough
on the tree would show itself to us in the midst of so great a wood!
For the prophetess spoke truly of you—alas, too truly, O Misenus!"
    Scarcely had he spoken, when by chance twin doves came flying
170 from the sky under his very eyes, and they settled on the green grass.
Then the great hero recognizes the birds of his mother,° and joyfully
he prays: "Be our leaders, if there is any path, and lead our way
through the air into the trees where the rich bough casts its shadow
on the fertile soil. And you, my divine parent, do not fail me
175 in my precarious affairs."
        So speaking, he stopped his footsteps, watching
which signs the doves might give, and which direction they might take.
They kept advancing in flight as they fed, just as far ahead as his eyes
could follow. Then when they came to the jaws of stinking Avernus,
they flew up swiftly and, slipping through the clear air, the two birds
180 settled in a chosen spot of a tree from which the variegated radiance
of gold shone through the branches.
        Just as mistletoe—which does not
form a tree of its own—is accustomed in the cold of winter to flourish
with new vegetation, and surrounds the shapely trunk with yellow
growth, such was the appearance of the leafy gold in the dark
185 oak-tree, so did the gold-leaf rattle in the gentle breeze. Aeneas
at once eagerly snatches it, breaking the close-clinging bough,
and he carries it to the cavern of the prophetic Sibyl.
        In the meanwhile,
the Trojans were weeping for Misenus on the shore, and they paid
their last respects to the thankless ashes. First they built a huge pyre,
190 heavy with pitch-pine and cut oak. They wove its sides with dark leaves
and set mournful cypress trees in front, and they adorn it on top
with his shining arms.
        Some of them make ready hot water, boiling
it in bronze cauldrons on the flames. They wash the cold body
and anoint it. A moan sweeps over them. Then they place the lamented

---

171 *his mother*: Doves are sacred to Venus.

limbs on the couch, and they toss purple robes over the corpse, 195
the well-known wrappings. Others shouldered the great bier—a sad duty—
and according to the customs of the ancestors, with averted gaze,
they placed the torch below.° Gifts are placed on the flames—incenses,
the flesh of sacrificed animals, and bowls of poured olive oil.
After the ashes had collapsed and the flames fell quiet, they washed 200
the remnants of the dry bones in wine, and Corynaeus gathered up
the bones and closed them in a bronze urn. Also he carried purifying
water three times around his companions, sprinkling dew from a bough
of a fruitful olive. He spoke the last farewell.
                                But dutiful [*pius*] Aeneas
heaps up a large mound for Misenus' tomb with the man's own 205
equipment, his oar and his trumpet, beneath a high mountain now called
"Misenum" after him, preserving his eternal name through the ages.°

sacrifice to Hecatê

      Having accomplished these things, Aeneas hastily follows
the Sibyl's orders. There was a high cave, huge and gaping, wide,
made of sharp rocks and protected by a black lake and shadowy forest, 210
over which no birds could safely extend their wings—such a breath
poured from its black jaws and was borne up to the overarching sky.
For this reason the Greek called the place "Aornos."°
                                          The Sibyl first of all
tethered four young black bulls. She poured wine over their brows.
Plucking bristles from between their horns, she places the hair 215
on the holy fire as a first offering, and she calls out to Hecatê, powerful
in heaven and in the underworld.
                                    Others cut the victims' throats,
and they catch the warm blood in bowls. Aeneas himself strikes
with a sword a black-fleeced lamb, to Night, the mother of the Furies,
and Earth, her great sister, and a barren young cow to you, Proserpina. 220
Then he ignites the nocturnal altars for the Stygian king. He places
whole carcasses of bulls on the flames,° pouring rich oil on the burning
entrails. Behold, at the first light and rising of the sun, the earth groaned
under their feet, and the wooded hills began to move, and dogs seemed

---

198   *... torch below*: The funeral bed is set on the bier, which is placed on the pyre, which is fired.

207   *through the ages*: Today it is Capo Miseno (ancient MISENUM), a three-hundred-foot-high isolated flat rock forming the northwestern cusp of the BAY OF NAPLES.

213   *Aornos*: "birdless."

222   *... on the flames*: The Stygian king is Dis, lord of the underworld. The burning of whole carcasses, or holocaust, would be an unusual procedure.

FIGURE 6.3 *Hecatê,* **or** *The Night of Enitharmon's Joy,* **1795, by William Blake (1757–1827).** Blake, an Englishman, is best known as a poet, but he was an accomplished artist and pritnmaker, too. Unrecognized while he lived, he is now thought to be an originator of Romantic poetry and art. He lived in London for his whole life. Many of his paintings illustrate his own rather strange poetry, but in this stand-alone representation of Hecatê, also called Enitharmon in Blake's private mythology, he shows the triple goddess as three nude figures huddled together in a nightmarish scene. The sex of the figures behind the dark-haired goddess is not clear. She faces us, holding her hand over a book inscribed with occult signs while looking toward the mountainside, where lurk ill-omened beasts: a jackass munching a thistle, an owl, a crocodile, and, hovering over the three figures, a bat with a cat's face. Hecatê, mentioned several times by Vergil, was a goddess of magic and the crossroads, where anything could happen. Pen and ink with watercolor on paper.

to howl in the shadows as the goddess approached.° 225
"Stand away, O you
uninitiated, stand far away," the prophetess said, "and be absent
from this grove! And you, Aeneas, be on your way, and rip the sword
from its sheathe!° Now you need to be courageous, now you need
a steady heart!"

Aeneas and the Sybil enter the underworld

Having said this, she threw herself raging into the open cave.
He fearlessly keeps up with his guide as she went. O gods, who possess 230
command over the spirits, the silent shades, and Chaos and Phlegethon,
wide silent places of the night, let it be permitted that I speak of what
I heard. May it be lawful to reveal things buried in the deep earth
and the gloom!
On they went through the shadows, hidden in the lonely night,
on through the empty halls of Dis and its vacant realms, as if one were 235
to go his way through a forest in the faint light of the moon, under
a malignant light, when Jupiter has hidden the sky in shadow and dark
night has taken the color from things.
Before the entrance, at the beginning
of the jaws of Orcus,° Grief and vengeful Cares have made their beds,
and pale Sickness lives there, and sad Old Age, and Fear, and seductive 240
Hunger, and squalid Need, terrible to look upon: and Death and Pain,
then Sleep, the brother of death, and Evil Pleasures of the mind,
and death-dealing War on the opposite threshold, and the iron chambers
of the Furies,° and mad Discord, her snaky hair bound with bloody
ribbons. 245
In the center a dark elm, huge, spreads its branches
and its aged trunks—it is the seat that insubstantial Dreams hold,
they say, and they cling beneath every leaf. There are besides many
monsters of varied form: Centaurs are stabled beside the doors,
and biformed Scyllas, and hundred-headed Briareus, and the Lernaean
Hydra, ferociously screeching, and the Chimaera armed with flames, 250
and the Gorgons and the Harpies and Geryon, the triple-bodied shade.°

---

225 ...*approached*: Hecatê, often accompanied by dogs.

228 *its sheathe*: Apparently so he will feel protected, but the Sibyl later prevents him from using it.

239 *Orcus*: Another name for Dis.

244 *Furies*: Though Vergil here places the Furies at the entrance to the underworld, he later says that they inhabit Tartarus.

251 ...*triple-bodied shade*: The Centaurs were half-man, half-horse. Ordinarily there was a single Scylla who lived in the Straits of Messina, half-female with dog-headed tentacles. Briareus was one of the Hecatonchires ("hundred-handers"), allies of Jupiter in his war against the Titans, who usually had

At this Aeneas, seized with sudden fear, takes hold of his sword,
and he presents the naked blade against the creatures as they came on.
If his wise companion had not warned him that these were thin lives
without a body, flitting about under the hollow semblance of form,
he would have rushed at them, and in vain he would have struck
the shadows with his sword.

on the shores of Acheron

From here is the road that leads to the waves
of Tartarean Acheron.° Here, thick with mud, a whirlpool seethes
in the mighty depths and spits all its sand into the Cocytus.
A forbidding ferryman, horrible in his squalor, watches over the waters
and the streams. A mass of white unkempt hair hangs from his chin.
His eyes stand fixed with flame, and a dirty cloak hangs knotted
from his shoulders. He himself poles the boat and he trims the sails,
and he ferries the bodies in his dark boat. He is old—but for a god
old age is vigorous and green.
Here all the crowd was rushing
to the banks, mothers and men, and the lifeless bodies of great heroes,
boys and unmarried girls, and youths laid on the pyre before the eyes
of their parents—as many as the leaves that fall in the forest
at the first frost of autumn, or as many as the birds that gather
on the land from the deep ocean when the cold year drives them
across the sea and sends them to sunny climes.
They stood there,
begging to be the first to cross the river. They held out their hands
in longing for the further shore. But the gloomy boatman takes
now these, now those, and keeps the others far from the sand.
Aeneas, amazed and astonished at the tumult, says: "Tell me,
O virgin, what is the meaning of this crowding at the river? What do
these souls want? By what criterion do some leave the bank, while others
sweep the livid stream with their oars?"
The aged priestess spoke briefly to him:
"O son of Anchises, true offspring of the gods, you see the deep pools
of Cocytus and the Stygian swamp, whose deity the gods fear to invoke,

---

fifty heads. The Hydra had seven or a hundred heads. The Chimaera was part lion, part snake, and part she-goat, killed by Bellerophon. Medusa, whose gaze turned one to stone, was the best known of the three Gorgons and the only mortal one. The Harpies were often represented as birds with female heads (like the Sirens). Geryon was a triple-boded monster killed by Hercules.

258 *Acheron*: The Acheron flows into the Cocytus, then the Cocytus and the Styx come together to form the river over which Charon ferries the dead.

and to deceive?° All this crowd that you see were without means°
and unburied. This ferryman is Charon. Those who cross the river
were buried. Charon cannot take the dead from the terrible shore
across the raging flood before their bones have come to rest in the grave.
They wander for a hundred years, they flit around these shores.   285
Then at last they are admitted, and they visit the pools they have
longed for."
    The son of Anchises stopped and checked his footsteps,
thinking of many things and pitying their unjust fate in his heart.
He sees there Leucaspis and Orontes,° the captain of the Lycian fleet,
grieving and lacking the honor due the dead, whom South Wind   290
overwhelmed as they set off from Troy over the windy waves,
submerging ship and men in the water.

the ghost of Palinurus

                                        Behold, the helmsman Palinurus
made his way toward them, who recently fell from the stern
on the voyage from Libya while he gazed at the stars, cast into
the middle of the waves. Aeneas recognized him, grieving in the deep   295
shadows. Aeneas spoke first, saying: "Which of the gods took you from us,
O Palinurus, and drowned you in the midst of the sea? Come, tell me.
For Apollo, who before was always to be believed, deceived my spirit
by this one response, who prophesied that you would come safely
to the Ausonians° across the sea. Was this promise true?"   300
                                                 But Palinurus
answered: "The tripod of Phoebus did not deceive you,° my leader,
the son of Anchises, nor did a god drown me in the sea. It was by chance
that the tiller was violently torn from me as I clung to it, its appointed
guardian, and guided our course. I dragged it headlong with me.
I swear by the harsh sea that I never feared as much for myself   305
as for your ship, that it might founder among such great surging
waves, robbed of its rudder, torn from its helmsman.
                                             "For three nights
of storm the violent South Wind drove me through the vast seas.

---

281 *to deceive*: An oath sworn by the Styx is unbreakable.

281 *without means*: That is, they lacked the wealth to place a coin between their dead lips as payment to Charon.

289 *... Orontes*: Leucaspis is not mentioned earlier; presumably he was the helmsman of Orontes' ship, which went down in the storm sent by Juno.

300 *Ausonians*: The Ausonians were the native inhabitants of CAMPANIA, the territory south of LATIUM where Cumae is located. This prophecy is not mentioned earlier in the poem.

301 *deceive you*: The oracle at DELPHI sat on a tripod when she gave her oracles, inspired by Phoebus Apollo.

On the fourth dawn I could just make out Italy, rising high
310   on the crest of a wave. Little by little I swam to the land. I was almost
safe, but a barbaric people attacked me with swords, weighed down
as I was with sodden clothes, grabbing onto the sharp tips of rocks,
ignorantly thinking me booty.
                                   "Now the waves have taken hold
of me, and the winds roll me along the shore. Because of this,
315   I beg you by the sweet light of the sky and its breezes, by your father,
and by your hopes for the growing Iulus—save me from this evil,
O unconquered one! Either cast some earth over me—for you can—
and seek again the port of Velia.°
                              "Or if there is some way, if your
divine mother shows you one—for, I think, you would not prepare
320   to sail across such mighty waters, and the Stygian swamp, without
the will of the gods—give your right hand to this wretch! Take me
with you across the waves, that at least I might find rest in a quiet place,
in death."
           So he spoke, and the prophetess began as follows:
"Where does this dire longing of yours come from, O Palinurus?
325   You are unburied—how can you see the Stygian waters and the savage
river of the Furies, Cocytus, or approach the shore unasked?
Give up your hope that you can turn aside divine Fate by prayer.
But be mindful of my words, hold them as a solace in your hardship:
For I tell you that the neighboring peoples, from cities far and wide,
330   driven by prodigies and divine omens, will worship your bones.
They will set up a tomb, and they will send offerings to the tomb,
and the place will have the name 'Palinurus' forever."°
                                                        His anxiety
was eased by these words, and for a little while the pain was driven
from his melancholy heart. He rejoices in the land named after him.
335   And so they continue the journey they have begun, and they come
close to the river.

Charon, the ferryman, takes them across the Acheron

                      When the boatman saw them from the Stygian wave,
going through the silent forest and turning their footsteps to the bank,
already from a distance he attacks them with his speech, and without
being provoked he scolds them: "Whoever you are, who come to our river
340   in arms, come, tell me, why have you come? Speak from where you are!

---

318   *Velia*: A harbor south of Cumae.

332   *...forever*: This place is today known as Capo Palinuro, on the south coast of Italy.

Stop your approach! This is a place of shades, of sleep and dull night.
It is not permitted to transport living bodies in the Stygian boat.

    "I was not pleased to have welcomed Hercules on his journey
across this lake, nor Theseus and Pirithoüs, although they were children
of the gods and unconquered in strength. Hercules sought by violence   345
to place Cerberus in chains, the guardian of Tartarus, and he dragged
him away trembling from beneath the throne of King Dis. Theseus
and Pirithoüs had come to carry off the wife of Dis from her bedchamber."°

    To this the Amphrysian prophetess° said briefly: "We practice
no such deception here. Don't be troubled. Our weapons offer   350
no violence. The huge gatekeeper of the cave may terrify the bloodless
shadows, howling forever, and chaste Proserpina can keep watch
over her uncle's threshold.° Trojan Aeneas, famous for doing his duty [*pietate*]
and his deeds in war, is descending to the lowest shadows of Erebus°
to see his father. If the vision of such great piety [*pietatis*] has no effect   355
on you, then recognize this branch."

    The Sybil shows the branch concealed
in her clothing. Then the anger in Charon's heart subsides. No more was spoken.
Charon, marveling at the venerable gift of the fateful branch, seen after
so long a time, turns the blue stern of his boat and nears the bank.
He expels the other souls who were sitting on the long benches,   360
he clears the gangways. At the same time he takes on the huge Aeneas.
The stitched boat° groans under the weight, and lets in much marsh
water through its chinks.

    At last Charon sets the prophetess and the man
safe across the river on the shapeless mud, in the bluish swamp-grass.
Huge Cerberus makes all these regions echo from the howling   365
that comes from his three throats, crouching gigantic in the cave
opposite them. When the prophetess sees the snakes writhing around
his neck, she throws him a morsel soaked in honey and narcotic grain.
Rabid with hunger, he opens his three throats and seizes what
she threw. He relaxes his immense back, spread out on the ground,   370
and he extends his massive bulk over the whole cave floor.

    When its guard was buried in sleep, Aeneas seizes the entrance,
and quickly he escapes the bank of the river that permits no return.

---

348 *her bedchamber*: One of the labors of Hercules was to bring back Cerberus from the House of Hades. Theseus and Pirithoüs went to the underworld to capture Proserpina, the wife of Dis, whom Pirithoüs wanted to marry. Both were imprisoned in stone chairs, but Theseus was later freed by Hercules.

349 *Amphrysian prophetess*: Amphrysian is an epithet of Apollo, who was forced to serve the Thessalian king Admetus for a year beside the river Amphrysus.

353 *uncle's threshold*: Proserpina is the daughter of Jupiter, the brother of Dis; she is married to her uncle.

354 *Erebus*: "darkness," that is, the underworld.

362 *stitched boat*: It is made of hides sewn together and stretched over a wooden frame.

FIGURE 6.4 *Aeneas, the Sibyl, and Charon*, **c. 1695, by Giuseppe Maria Crespi (1665–1747).** Crespi was an Italian late Baroque painter, known for his religious paintings and portraits, but he also did genre paintings of ordinary people engaged in mundane activities. Here he shows a scene from Vergil's *Aeneid*: Aeneas is about to step into Charon's boat. He holds the Sibyl's hand while he points to the boat, asking if he should in fact climb onboard. The veiled Sibyl carries the golden bough in her right hand. A muscular Charon, old and bearded, is naked except for a loincloth. He holds the punting pole and rests his left leg on the boat's gunwale. Oil on canvas.

Immediately he hears voices, a loud wailing, and the spirits of weeping
infants, whom a dark day carried off, deprived of sweet life, snatched 375
from the breast, drowned in bitter death.
                                    Nearby were those condemned
to death on a false charge. And yet their place is not given without
appointment of a jury by lot: Minos, the judge, shakes the urn,°
he summons a gathering of the silent dead and hears about
their lives and the charges against them. 380
                                The next place is held
by those sad spirits who died by their own hand, innocent of crime.
Hating the light, they cast away their lives. How they now wish
to endure poverty and harsh labor in the upper air! But divine law
forbids it. The gloomy marsh and its hateful waters bind them,
and the nine windings of the Styx holds them in. 385

Aeneas sees the ghost of Dido

                                    Not far from here
they saw the Fields of Mourning, spread out on all sides—that is
what they call it. Here are those whom a hard love has eaten away
with a cruel wasting. Hidden meadows conceal them and a myrtle°
forest covers them around. Their cares have not left them even
in death. In these places Aeneas sees Phaedra and Procris, 390
and sad Eriphylê, displaying the wounds from her cruel son,
and Evadnê and Pasiphaë. With them walks Laodamia,
and Caeneus, once a young man, now a woman, turned back
again into his original form.°
                            Among these women Phoenician
Dido wanders through the great forest, her wound still fresh. 395
When the Trojan hero saw her first and stood beside her,

---

378 ...*shakes the urn*: Minos, a king of Crete, became a judge in the underworld after death. In Roman courts, the names of prospective jurors were written on tablets and placed in an urn that was shaken until one flew out.

388 *myrtle*: Sacred to Venus, goddess of love.

394 ...*original form*: Phaedra was the daughter of Minos and wife of Theseus, who killed herself in despair over her love for her stepson Hippolytus. Procris of Athens spied on her husband Cephalus and was killed when Cephalus mistook a motion in the bush for a wild boar. Eriphylê was killed in revenge by her own son Alcmaeon when she accepted the bribe of a necklace in order to persuade her husband Amphiaraüs to go on the expedition of the Seven Against Thebes, in which Amphiaraüs was killed. Evadnê, whose husband Capaneus was also killed at Thebes, threw herself on his funeral pyre because of her great love. Pasiphaë fell in love with the bull from the sea and begot the Minotaur. Laodamia was the wife of Protesilaüs, the first man to die at Troy; she obtained permission for Protesilaüs to return to life for three hours, then died with him. Caeneus was a young woman whom Neptune raped, then turned into a man so she would never again have to undergo such indignity. Vergil has him changed back into a woman, a victim of cruel love.

recognizing her in the dark shadows like a man who sees, or thinks
he sees, the new moon rise through the clouds, as the month begins—
he wept tears, and he speaks to her with sweet affection:
400 "O unhappy Dido, was then the news true that you had died,
taking your life with a sword? Alas, was I the cause of your death?
I swear by the stars, by the gods above, and by whatever pledge
is valid in the depths of the earth, that unwilling—O queen!—
did I depart from your shores. I went by the commands of the gods,
405 which force me now to go through the shades, through places
thorny from neglect, and the profound night. Nor did I think
that you would bear so great a pain by my departure.
Don't go away—don't remove yourself from my sight!
Whom do you flee? This is the last time that fate allows
410 that I speak with you."
                With such words Aeneas attempted to soften
her burning spirit, and he tried to move her to tears. But she turned
away, her eyes fixed to the ground, her face no more moved
by the speech he had begun than if it were hard flint or a cliff
of Parian marble.° At last she tore herself away and, bitter,
415 fled into the shady wood where her first husband, Sychaeus,
responds to her suffering, and matches her love. Aeneas, no less
shaken by Dido's unjust death, follows her for a distance, weeping,
and he takes pity on her as she goes.

the ghost of Deïphobus

                        From there Aeneas labors along
the appointed path. Soon they reach the furthest fields, set apart,
420 where those famous in war crowded together. Here Tydeus meets him,
here Parthenopaeus, celebrated in war, and the shade of pale Adrastus;
here were the Trojans, much lamented by those still alive, fallen
in war. Aeneas groans when he sees them all in their long ranks—
Glaucus and Medon and Thersilochus, the three sons of Antenor,
425 and Polyboetes, the priest of Ceres, and Idaeus, still holding
his chariot, still in his armor.°
                          The ghosts stand around, crowding
on the right and the left. They are not satisfied in having seen Aeneas
only once, but they delight to linger still, and to walk beside him

---

414 *Parian marble*: The Cycladic island of Paros provided some of the finest marble known to the ancient world.

426 *... still in his armor*: Tydeus, Parthenopaeus, and Adrastus all fought in the war against Thebes, which took place a generation before the Trojan War. The Trojan warriors Glaucus, Medon, and Thersilochus are mentioned in Book 17 of the *Iliad*. Antenor is a Trojan elder. Polyboetes, the priest of Ceres, is not in Homer. Idaeus was Priam's herald and charioteer.

and to learn the causes of his coming. But the Greek princes
and the troops of Agamemnon trembled with a great fear when 430
they saw Aeneas and his arms shining through the shadows.
Some turn their backs, just as once they sought the ships;
part raise a cry—a thin sound: once begun, the shout mocks
their gasping mouths.
                      And he sees Deïphobus, the son of Priam,
lacerated over his whole body, his face cruelly torn, his face 435
and both his hands, his ears torn from his savaged head, his nostrils
cut off by a brutal wound.° Aeneas scarcely recognized the trembling
form, hiding its terrible punishment, but he calls to him unprompted,
with a familiar voice: "O Deïphobus, mighty in arms, descendant
of the high lineage of Teucer, who chose to take such awful 440
punishment on you? Who was allowed to treat you so? I was told
that on that last night, exhausted by the massive killing of the Greeks,
you fell down dead on a confused pile of the slaughtered.
Then with my own hands I set up an empty tomb on the Rhoetean
shore,° and I called out three times to your spirit in a loud voice. 445
Your name and your arms watch over the place. I could not see you,
my friend, to deposit you in the land of your fathers as I departed."
                      The son of Priam said this in reply: "You have neglected nothing,
O my friend. You have paid all that is due to Deïphobus and to the ghost
of the dead. But my own fate and the deadly crime of that Laconian 450
woman° have drowned me in these evils. These are the memorials
that she has left.
                      "You know about the final night, how we were wrapped
in false joy—you must remember it all too well. When the fatal horse
came leaping the high walls of Troy, pregnant with an armed band
of foot soldiers carried in its womb, Helen led the Trojan women 455
in a dance, mimicking with Bacchic cries the sacred revels.
Helen held a huge torch in their midst, signaling the Greeks from
the top of the citadel.° At the time I was in our unhappy bridal
chamber, worn out with care and heavy with sleep, and a sweet
and deep peace, most like quiet death, pressed upon me as I lay there. 460
                      "In the meanwhile that most excellent wife of mine removes

---

437   *... brutal wound*: After Paris' death, Helen took up with Deïphobus, a brother of Paris and Hector. Menelaus and Odysseus killed and mutilated him when Troy fell (but neither Deïphobus' marriage to Helen nor his death is mentioned in Homer).

444-445   *Rhoetean shore*: North of Troy.

450-451   *Laconian woman*: Helen, from Laconia (another name for Lacedaemon, the territory around SPARTA).

458   *citadel*: This account is inconsistent with that given in Book 2, where Helen takes refuge in the temple of Vesta and Sinon gives the signal to the Greeks.

all arms from the house, and had even sneaked my faithful sword
from beneath my head. She calls Menelaus into the house,
and she throws open the doors, hoping—I suppose!—that it would
465 be a fine gift for her lover, and that the infamy of her ancient evil
might be wiped out. Why go on? They rush into the room.
Ulysses the Aeolid° comes as an added companion, an adviser
of wickedness. You gods, pay back the Greeks for their deeds,
as surely as the penalty I ask for comes from a pious [*pio*] mouth!
470 "But, come, tell me in turn—what catastrophe has brought you here
while still alive? Do you come here driven by your wandering across
the sea, or by the advice of the gods? Or what fortune harries you so
that you enter these sad houses that lack the sun, the dwelling of disorder?"

Tartarus described

Amid such an interchange of speech, Aurora, the dawn, had passed
475 in her rosy chariot the central pole in her course across the heavens.°
Now by chance they would have passed all the time allotted them in such
conversation, but Aeneas' companion the Sibyl exhorted him,
and briefly said: "Night rushes on, Aeneas. We waste time in weeping.
This is the place where the road splits in two. The right-hand path
480 leads to Elysium, under the walls of mighty Dis. But the left-hand path
imposes punishment on the wicked, and it sends them to pitiless [*impia*]
Tartarus."
Deïphobus said in reply: "Do not be angry, great priestess,
I will depart. I will fill up the number of ghosts and return to the darkness.
Go, glory of our race—go! May you enjoy a better fate!"
He said
485 so much, and in speaking he turned away. Aeneas looks around
suddenly, and under the left-hand cliff he sees the wide
buildings surrounded by a triple wall, and a swift river flows
around it, of blazing flames—the Tartarean Phlegethon, roiling
with echoing rocks. Facing him was a gigantic gate, and doorposts
490 of solid adamant° so that no strength of men, not the gods themselves,
could bring it down by war. An iron tower stands facing the breeze,

---

467 *Aeolid*: According to one tradition, Ulysses was not the son of Laërtes, as told in the *Odyssey*, but of Sisyphus, son of Aeolus, who seduced Ulysses' mother on her wedding night. Sisyphus was the cleverest man who ever lived; he even cheated death. Ulysses in the *Aeneid* is not the wise counselor and brave fighter, as in Homer, but the proper descendant of Sisyphus, deviser of underhanded and devious deeds, a scoundrel who persuades others to undertake tasks that he will not himself undertake.

475 *... across the heavens*: That is, it is past midday. The central pole is that point around which the heavens seem to revolve.

490 *adamant*: A mythical material of extreme hardness, the source of our word "diamond."

and seated before it Tisiphonê,° girded with a bloody dress, guards
the doorway tirelessly, day and night. Groans come from there
and sounds of the cruel lash. Then the crash of iron, and chains
dragged along. 495

        Aeneas came to a halt, and in terror he drank in the din.
"Tell me, O virgin, what evil goes on here? By what torments are they
oppressed? What is this great sound I am hearing?"

                                                                              Then the prophetess
began to speak as follows: "O famous leader of the Trojans, it is not
permitted to the pure to cross this threshold of crime. But when Hecatê
appointed me to preside over the woods of Avernus, she taught me 500
the torments of the gods, and she guided me through them all.

        "Cretan Rhadamanthus° possesses these cruel realms and he punishes
and hears every confession of deceit and he forces them to admit
their crimes—whoever while still alive, joyful at useless fraud,
has deferred punishment until a tardy death took them. When judgment 505
is given, Tisiphonê the avenger° immediately, armed with her whip,
leaps on the guilty and lashes them. Threatening them with
the ferocious snakes she holds in her left hand, she summons
the savage crowd of her sister Furies.

                                                       "Then, at last, the sacred gates,
screeching in their grating pivots,° are thrown open. Do you see 510
what sort of guardian sits at the door, what shape watches
the threshold?° Still more savage sits within the immense Hydra
with her fifty black gaping mouths. Then Tartarus itself opens up,
falling twice as far into the darkness as when we look upwards
to heavenly Olympus. Here the ancient race of Earth, the Titans, 515
cast down by the thunderbolt, writhe in the depths.°

                                                                         "Here I saw
the enormous bodies of the Aloads, who attempted to tear down
heaven with their hands, to topple Jove in his supernal realms.

        "And I saw Salmoneus paying a bitter punishment for attempting

---

492 *Tisiphonê*: One of the Furies.

502 *Rhadamanthus*: A son of Jupiter and Europa, he was a wise Cretan king and the brother of Minos, also a judge of the dead; that is, they presided over courts in the underworld much as in the upper.

506 *avenger*: *tisis*, the root of Tisiphonê, means "vengeance" in Greek.

510 *pivots*: Ancient doors did not use a modern hinge, but were mounted on protruding posts that turned in a pivot hole.

512 *threshold*: That is, Tisiphonê sits outside the doors, but within is a still more menacing figure.

516 *... depths*: The Hydra is the serpent with many heads that Hercules overcame. Tartarus is as far beneath the House of Dis as the House of Dis is beneath Olympus. There Jupiter imprisoned the Titans after the Titanomachy, having overcome them by his thunderbolt.

520   to imitate the lightning of Jove, and the Olympian thunder.°
      Borne by four horses, shaking a torch, he rode in triumph through
      the Greeks and through the middle of a city of ELIS. He claimed
      for himself the honor due the gods—mad! He mimicked
      the storm-clouds and the inimitable lightning bolt by means
525   of bronze castanets and the sound of horses' hoof-beats.
      But the all-powerful father hurled his lighting from the dense clouds.
      Not for Jupiter were torches or the smoky light from pitch-pine!°
      He drove him headlong with the mighty whirlwind.
                                          "And I saw Tityus°
      as well, the foster-child of the mother of all, whose body lies
530   across nine acres, and a huge vulture with hooked beak feeds
      on his immortal liver and his guts, ripe for punishment.
      The vulture pries open his liver for a feast and hunkers down
      deep in his breast. There is no respite given for the tissue that ever
      renews itself.
                "Why even mention the Lapiths, Ixion and Pirithoüs?°
535   Over them stands a dark crag, always about ready to slip and fall,
      and golden gleam the supports for the high-piled festal couches,
      and meals are made ready before their eyes, fit for a king.
      But nearby the oldest of the Furies crouches and prevents them
      from touching the table with their hands.
                                          "She rises up, brandishing
540   her torch, and she speaks with a voice of thunder: 'Here are those who hated
      their brothers as long as they were alive, or who struck a parent,
      and practiced fraud on their client, or who crouched alone with
      the wealth they had piled up and did not give a part of it
      to their relatives'— these were the largest group—'And those
      who were killed for adultery, and those who pursued civil [*impia*] war
545   and did not fear to break their pledges to their masters—shut in,

---

520 ... *thunder*: The two Aloads, "sons of Aloeus," were the giants Otus and Ephialtes, who piled Mount Ossa on top of Mount Olympus, then Mount Pelion, in an effort to mount to heaven and overthrow the gods. Apollo shot them down. Salmoneus, a king of Elis in the northwestern Peloponnesus, was a brother of Sisyphus who in his arrogance tried to imitate Jupiter.

527 *pitch-pine*: By which Salmoneus attempted to imitate the thunderbolts of Jupiter.

528 *Tityus*: Tityus, a child of Earth and Jupiter, tried to rape Leto after she had given birth to Apollo and Artemis, but Jupiter struck him down with a thunderbolt.

534 *Ixion and Pirithoüs*: Ixion tried to rape Juno, but Jupiter made a cloud in her image and Ixion attacked that instead. His semen fell through the cloud onto the earth, from which sprang up Centaurus, father of all the Centaurs. Usually Ixion is said to be bound to an eternally spinning wheel. Pirithoüs was the son of Ixion and a king of the Thessalian tribe of Lapiths. At Pirithoüs' wedding feast, the Centaurs tried to rape the bride and her attendants, giving rise to the battle between the Lapiths and the Centaurs depicted on Zeus/Jupiter's temple at Olympia in ELIS. The punishment of these figures here is reminiscent of the punishment in Greek literature of Tantalus, imprisoned in a pool of water beneath an overarching cliff.

they await their punishment.'

"Do not seek to learn which punishment,
or what kind of suffering drowns them. Some roll up huge stones,
or then hang stretched on wheels. Unhappy Theseus sits there,
and he will sit forever.° Phlegyas,° the wretch, warns them all,
and testifies in a loud voice through the shadows: 'Learn justice—   550
be warned and don't despise the gods!' This man sold out his country
for gold, and imposed a despot as lord. This one passed a law
and then *re*passed it for a bribe. This one invaded the bedroom
of his daughter and engaged in forbidden intercourse. All dared
to undertake terrible crimes, and did what they dared.   555

"Not if I had
a hundred tongues and a hundred mouths, and a voice of steel, could
I relate all the forms of crime, or give the names of every torment."

the Elysian Fields

After she had spoken of these things, the aged priestess of Phoebus
said: "But come now, let us go and finish the task we have undertaken.
Let us hurry. I see the walls forged in the fires of the Cyclopes and the gates   560
in the arch opposite us, where they command that we deposit
the prescribed gifts."°

She spoke and, walking side by side, they entered
the dark path. They crossed the space between. They came near
the gates. Aeneas gains the entrance, and he sprinkles fresh water
on his body.° He places the branch on the threshold opposite.   565

At last, having accomplished these things, the goddess's task fulfilled,
they came to the joyful places and the pleasant grassy parks
of the Fortunate Woods, and the homes of the blessed. A more
abundant air of a violet light covers these fields, which have

---

549   *...sit forever*: These are mostly crimes against Roman customs. To strike a parent violated the power of the *paterfamilias*, the "father of the family," which power was absolute. The Roman state was an extension of the structure of the family. The *patronus* was supposed to be the protector, sponsor, and benefactor of his clients, who were typically from an inferior social class. In return, the client was expected to offer services as needed. The Romans considered it immoral to hoard wealth and not share it with one's family and friends. The reference to slaves betraying their masters may refer to the civil war with Sextus Pompeius, the son of Pompey the Great, who led an insurrection in 36 BC in which he enlisted slaves. Sisyphus, condemned to roll up a hill a stone that always rolled back, is the model for this punishment, as Ixion bound to a spinning wheel is the model for the other. Theseus and Pirithoüs were trapped in stone chairs in the underworld, according to the usual account.

549   *Phlegyas*: The father of Ixion. He set fire to the temple to Apollo at Delphi.

562   *prescribed gifts*: The gates of Elysium, where they are to deposit the golden bough, were forged by Vulcan, god of fire, and the Cyclopes, the smiths of Jupiter.

565   *his body*: A gesture of ritual purification.

FIGURE 6.5 *Aeneas and the Sybil in the Underworld,* **c. 1530, by the Master of the Aeneid.** Eighty-two plaques picturing scenes from the *Aeneid* in enameled copper survive, by an unknown hand, probably designed to be set in the walls of a small room. It is an unprecedented series. At the upper left of this plaque, Aeneas has just crossed the river Acheron with the Cumaean Sibyl (the figures are labeled). To the right stands the city of Dis, protected by Tisiphonê (labeled), holding serpents in her right hand, and either Cerberus or the Hydra, shown as a many-headed fire-breathing dragon. Beneath Tisiphonê is the crowned Dido and, beneath her, her husband Sychaeus (over him a label, "the lovers"). To his right are perhaps Salmoneus and then the fiery river Phlegethon and Ixion bound to a wheel (labeled). In the water are the Titans. In front of Sychaeus are perhaps the twin Giants, the Aloads, their entrails torn out. In the lower right is Tityus, a vulture tearing at his guts (labeled). To his left, one of the seated figures would be Theseus. In the lower left is Pirithoüs, sitting at a table presided over by a Fury in the form of a human-headed bird, who prevents him from eating. Various demons impose other torments on other sinners. Enameled copper.

their own sun and their own stars. Some exercise their limbs 570
in the grassy field. They contend in games and wrestle on the yellow
sand. Some stamp out dances with their feet and sing songs.
There Thracian Orpheus, a priest in a long robe, accompanies
the rhythm of their song with a seven-note scale, now playing
with his fingers, now striking the strings with an ivory plectrum. 575
Here is the ancient race of Teucer, a most beautiful offspring,
great-spirited heroes born in better times—Ilus and Assaracus
and Dardanus, the founder of Troy.°
                              Aeneas marvels at their arms
from a distance and their ghostly chariots. Their spears are fixed
in the ground and their horses, scattered over the field, graze 580
over the plain. The pleasure they took in chariots and arms while alive,
the care they took in tending to their glossy horses, follows them
when buried beneath the earth.
                          Behold! He sees others to the left and right,
feasting on the grass, singing a joyful hymn of praise in chorus.
They are in the midst of the sweetly scented wood of laurel from where 585
the broad river Eridanus° flows through the woodlands to the world
above. Here is the company of those who suffered wounds fighting
for their country, and those who were chaste priests while life remained,
and those who were pious [*pii*] poets, singers worthy of Apollo,
and those who enriched life by discovering new skills, and those who 590
by merit made others remember them: All these had brows bound
with white bands.
                    As they crowded around, the Sybil spoke to them,
Musaeus° above all, for he stood in the center of the large crowd.
And they all look up to him—his tall shoulders stand out above all:
"Tell me, blessed spirits, and you, O best of prophets—in what region 595
will I find Anchises? Where does he dwell? For we have come across
the great rivers of Erebus to find him."
                              And the hero Musaeus answered
her as follows: "No one has a fixed abode. We live in the dark woods
and dwell on cushions of river banks and in meadows fresh
with streams. But you, if you are so disposed, climb this hill. 600
I will place you on an easy path."

---

578   *...founder of Troy*: Teucer is the traditional ancestor of the Trojans (hence they are called Teucrians), but according to one tradition Dardanus was already in the Troad before Teucer arrived. Ilus, brother of Assaracus, was father to Laomedon and Priam's grandfather; see Genealogical Chart.

586   *Eridanus*: The Po River in northern Italy.

593   *Musaeus*: A legendary poet and musician, like Orpheus.

Aeneas meets Anchises

Musaeus spoke, and he went on
before them. He shows them the shining fields below. Then they
leave the heights of the mountains. But deep in a green valley,
father Anchises assiduously surveyed the spirits enclosed there,
605 destined to go to the light above. He was counting all the number
of his own people and his beloved grandsons, and their fates
and fortunes as men, and their character and deeds.
When he sees Aeneas
coming toward him across the grass, Anchises eagerly stretches out his
hands, his eyes filled with tears, and a cry comes from his mouth:
610 "Have you come at last, and has the sense of duty [*pietas*] that your
father saw in you conquered the harsh road? Is it granted that
I see your face, my son, and that I hear and speak in familiar tones?
"Well, this is what I planned in my mind, what I thought would
happen, counting off the hours. Nor has my trouble deceived me.
615 Having traveled over what lands—and across what great seas—
do I receive you! Tossed by what great dangers, my son! How
I feared that the Libyan kingdom would do you harm!"
And Aeneas answered: "Your sad face, my father—yours!—
so often coming to me, drove me to cross this threshold. My fleet rides
620 the Etruscan sea. Give me your hand—give it, father—and do not
withdraw from my embrace . . ."
So speaking, Aeneas' face was also drowned
in tears. Trying three times to throw his arms around his father's neck,
three times Aeneas clasped in vain, the image slipped from his hands—
like a light breeze, most like a winged dream.

shades to be reborn

In the meanwhile, Aeneas sees
625 in a receding valley a secluded wood, and the rustling thickets of a forest,
and the river Lethê that swims past those peaceful houses. Countless
tribes and peoples flutter around it—just as on a peaceful summer day
bees settle on multicolored flowers and stream around the white lilies,
and all the plain resounds with a murmur.
Aeneas is thrilled at the sudden
630 sight, and not knowing he asks the cause: "What is this river over there?
Who are the men crowding the banks in such great numbers?"
Then father Anchises says: "The spirits who, by fate, will receive
other bodies—they drink from the stream of the river Lethê that removes
all care and provide a lasting forgetfulness. Of these spirits I have long
635 wanted to tell you, and to show you up close, and to number my children's

descendants, so you might the more rejoice in finding Italy."

"O father, must we think that some spirits go from here to the upper air, and that they return again to dull matter? What terrible desire for the light of life afflicts these sufferers!"

"I will tell you these things, nor will I hold you in suspense, my son," said Anchises, and he tells each thing in order. 640

the nature of the universe

"First, a breath from within nourishes the heaven, and the earth, and the watery plains and the shining orb of the moon, and the Titan's stars.° Mind, mingling with its mighty frame, sets in motion the whole mass and mixes itself with the great body. From it comes the race of men and animals, and the life of flying things, 645 and the monsters that the sea bears beneath its marbled waves.

"Fiery is the power of those seeds, and their origin is divine, so long as harmful matter does not impede them, and bodies of earth and mortal limbs do not dull them. From their union with material substance these souls feel fear and desire, and they suffer and rejoice. 650 Shut up in shadow and a blind prison, they cannot see the air above.°

"When life has left them on the last day of life, still all the evil, all the plagues of the body have not completely left wretched men. Necessarily many things, long accumulated, have become deeply ingrained in a wondrous way. 655

"And so they are tortured by their punishments, and they pay the penalty for their ancient evils. Some are hung up, spread wide to the hollow winds. For others the guilty stain is wiped away beneath the huge gulfs, or is burned away with fire. Each spirit must endure its own ghosts.

"Then we are sent through broad Elysium—and a few of us stay 660 in the joyful fields°—until the length of days, the cycle of time

---

643 *Titan's stars*: The sun and the other stars, children of the Titan Hyperion. According to Stoic teaching, the universe is material. It is pervaded by a fiery "soul" (*anima mundi*) from which the human "soul" (*anima*) is detached, until death returns it to its source. This is the fiery spirit that animates all living things, giving them their warmth and vitality.

651 *... above*: According to an Orphic slogan, "the body is a tomb" (*soma sêma*, in Greek). The Orphics were a mysterious group that taught reincarnation and purification through dietary and sexual restraint. They are closely related to the equally mysterious Pythagoreans, whose theories influenced Zeno of Citium (third century BC), the founder of Stoicism, the predominant philosophy among the Roman aristocracy.

661 *joyful fields*: A few souls require only minimal purifications (Anchises, Musaeus, Orpheus) and so are not reborn like the souls that swarm around the river Lethê. They will stay forever in the Elysian Fields.

FIGURE 6.6 *Aeneas and His Father in the Elysian Fields*, **c. 1735, by Sebastiano Conca (1680–1764).** Conca was a Baroque painter born in the Kingdom of Naples. Later he settled in Rome, where he painted for officers of the church, including the pope. Here Aeneas stands in the center, wearing a plumed helmet, with the Sybil just behind him. His father points out the souls to be reincarnated, gathered at the river Lethê. Above them, in the sky, Aeneas' mother Venus sits in a cloud surrounded by cupids and doves, her special bird. Mercury (not in Vergil's account) hovers above her and points in the same direction as Anchises. In the foreground are the inhabitants of Elysium eating grapes and dancing to the flute, tambourine, and pan-pipes. Cupids (called *putti*) everywhere contribute to the pleasure of the scene. On the far left a woman rides joyfully in a chariot. Oil on canvas.

completed, removes the impacted stain, and leaves pure the ethereal
sense and the fire of elemental air.
                                "All these others the god calls
in a great crowd to the river Lethê, after they have rolled the wheel
of time for a thousand years so that forgetting, you see, they may   665
revisit the heavenly vault and begin with a desire to return again
into the flesh."
                    Anchises had spoken, and he draws his son together
with the Sibyl into the middle of the gathering and the murmuring
crowd. He reaches the hill from which he can scan all the long ranks
opposite him and learn their faces as they come by.   670

the future of the Roman race

                                 "Come now, I will
explain to you what glory will follow the descendants of Dardanus,
what children await you from your Italian race, illustrious spirits
who will come in our name, and I will teach you your destiny.
           "You see that boy, who leans on a headless spear—he is fated
to hold a place nearest the light. He will rise first to the upper airs,   675
sharing Italian blood—Silvius, an Alban name, your lastborn
son whom your wife Lavinia will give birth to in the wood
in your old age, a king and the father of kings through whom
your race will rule in Alba Longa.°
                              "Next to him is Procas, the glory
of the Trojan race, and Capys, and Numitor, and he who will recall   680
you by his name, Aeneas Silvius, outstanding like you in piety [*pietas*]
and in arms—if ever he will take on Alba as king!° What young men!
           "See—what strength they display, and their brows are shaded
by the civic crown of oak leaves.° These men will build Nomentum
and Gabii and the city of Fidena, and the citadels of Collatia   685
in the hills, and Pometii and the fort of Inus and Bola and Cora.°

---

679 ...*Alba Longa*: Silvius, "man of the wood," is named after the place of his birth (*silva* is "wood"). He is the son of Lavinia, the daughter of Latinus, the king of Latium. Silvius will succeed Iulus as king of Alba Longa, "long white town" (its exact location is unclear). He was succeeded by Aeneas Silvius and, later, Capys and Procas, whose brother Numitor is the father of Rhea Silvia and grandfather of Romulus and Remus.

682 *as king*: According to tradition, Aeneas Silvius was kept from his kingdom for fifty-two years.

684 *oak leaves*: A crown of oak leaves was given to one who had saved a Roman citizen in war. In 27 BC the crown was awarded to Augustus as a perpetual honor.

686 ...*Cora*: These are Latin towns near Rome, members of the early Latin League headed by Alba Longa. Nomentum is around fourteen miles northeast of Rome. Gabii is east of Rome. Fidenae is five miles to the northeast. Collatia is on the banks of the Anio River, a tributary of the Tiber. Pometii is to the south, as are Cora and Bola. The fort of Inus is south, along the coast.

These will be the names of lands today without a name.
                                                    "Yes,
and a child of Mars, Romulus, will join himself as a companion to his
grandfather, whom his mother Ilia will bear, of the blood of Assaracus.°
690 Do you not see how twin plumes stand on the crest of his helmet,
and his own father Mars already designates him with his own emblem
of the gods?°
            "Look, my son, how under the auspices of Romulus famous
Rome will extend rule over the earth and equal the spirits in heaven
and will surround the seven hills with a single wall, blessed
695 with its race of heroes—just as the Berecynthian mother,
crowned with turrets, is borne in a chariot through the Phrygian cities,
joyful in the birth of gods, embracing one hundred descendants,
all gods, all living in the sky above.°
                                    "Now turn your two eyes here
and gaze on this people, your Romans. Here is Caesar and all the offspring
700 of Iulus who will come to live beneath the great axis of the sky.°
This is the man—this is he!—whom you hear so often promised to you,
Augustus Caesar, son of the divine Caesar,° who will again establish
a Golden Age for Latium in the fields where Saturn once ruled,
and he will extend the empire beyond the Libyans and the Indians,
705 to a land that lies beyond the stars, beyond the roads of the year
and the sun, where sky-bearing Atlas turns the world, inset with
burning stars, on his shoulders.° Even now the Caspian kingdoms

---

689 *of Assaracus*: That is, Romulus will be born while his grandfather Numitor is still alive. Ilia is the Trojan name for Rhea Silvia, the Vestal Virgin who was the mother of Romulus and Remus. Assaracus is brother to the Trojan king Ilus and grandfather of Anchises (see Genealogical Chart).

692 *of the gods*: The meaning of the twin plumes is unclear, but it is clear that Romulus has been marked out to become a god. Romulus was worshiped from early times as Quirinus (possibly, "wielder of the spear"), a *numen* representing the Roman state.

698 *... sky above*: The Phrygian goddess Cybelê was worshiped on Mount Berecynthus in Phrygia. Her cult was transported to Rome in 204 BC. She was called *Magna Mater*, the "Great Mother," because she was identified with the Earth and with Rhea, Saturn's wife and the mother of Jupiter. She is also called *Mater Deum*, "mother of the gods": all the gods descend from her. She was represented wearing a turret for a crown, by analogy here with the wall that "crowned" the seven hills of Rome, as the "race of heroes" with which Rome will be blessed corresponds to the race of gods to which Cybelê was ancestor.

700 *of the sky*: By "Caesar" he means Augustus. Coming just after Romulus as the founder of Rome, Augustus is a new Romulus, presiding over the rebirth of the Roman state and the Roman spirit.

702 *divine Caesar*: Julius Caesar, thought to be a descendant of Iulus, is the adoptive father of Augustus and his great-uncle: Augustus' mother, Atia, was Julius Caesar's niece. After death Julius Caesar was declared to be a god and called *Divus*.

707 *on his shoulders*: Saturn, the Roman equivalent of Cronus, was a *numen* of sowing. He was the husband of Ops ("wealth"). He presided over a Golden Age based on agriculture. After being overthrown by his son Jupiter, he escaped to Latium, supposedly so called because he was able to "hide" (*latere*) there (in the Greek story, Saturn/Cronus was cast into the underworld). Augustus will found a new Golden Age characterized by the agricultural wealth and simplicity of life under Saturn. The Libyans

and the Maeotian earth quake at the divine prophecies of the arrival
of this man, and the seven-mouthed trembling Nile are thrown
into disarray.° 710

"Yes, even Hercules did not cross over so much
of the earth, though he shot the bronze-footed Ceryneian deer,
and pacified the woods of Erymanthus, and shot the Lernaean hydra
with his bow. Nor did the victorious Liber, who guides his chariot
with reins made of ivy vines, while driving his tigers down from
the high peak of Nysa.° Or do we still hesitate to extend our power 715
by our actions, or does fear prevent us from settling the Ausonian land?

"But who is this in the distance, distinguished by carrying branches
of olive and bearing offerings? I recognize the hair and chin bearded
white of a Roman king—Numa, called to the highest command from
little Cures' impoverished earth, who first founded our city under 720
the rule of law. Then Tullus will follow him, who will break
the country's peace. He'll create a stir and call idle men to arms, ranks
now unused to triumphs. Then comes the too boastful Ancus, even now
rejoicing too much in the breezes of popular opinion. Do you also want
to see the Tarquin kings, and the proud spirit of Brutus the avenger, 725
and the *fasces* reclaimed?°

"He will be the first to win the consul's
power and the savages' axes, and the father will punish his sons
for freedom's sake when they incite civil war. Unhappy man, although

---

were the southernmost peoples conquered by Rome; India was thought to lie at the eastern edge of the world. The "lands beyond the stars, the roads beyond the ways of the year and sun" are lands on either side of the ecliptic, which is the northern and southern bounds of the band though which the sun travels in a single year, imagined to have a corresponding band on earth—the world that Vergil knows, in other words. Atlas is a rebellious Titan condemned to carry the world on his shoulders, identified with Mount Atlas in Morocco.

710 *into disarray*: The Caspian kingdoms are lands near the Caspian Sea north of Persia; the Maeotian earth are the lands around the Sea of Azov northeast of the Crimean peninsula in the BLACK SEA (where the ancient Maeotae lived); the seven-mouthed Nile reminds the reader of Augustus' victory over Cleopatra.

715 *...peak of Nysa*: Hercules was famous for his far travels, although the adventures described here all took place in the Peloponnesus. Liber ("free"), that is, Dionysus (because he freed you from care), was raised on Mount Nysa, but no one was sure where that was. He traveled widely, even into India, his chariot drawn by tigers, its reins made of the sacred ivy.

726 *...fasces reclaimed*: Numa Pompilius was the second king of Rome from the village of Cures in SABINE territory (to the east of Latium). The Romans considered Numa the founder of their religious institutions; the olive branches are a symbol of peace, for he was a peaceful king. Tullus Hostilius was the third king of Rome, a warlike leader who destroyed Alba Longa. Ancus Martius was the fourth king of Rome; he subdued the Latins. The fifth and seventh kings were Etruscan: Priscus Tarquinius and Tarquin the Proud. Brutus led a revolt against Tarquin the Proud after Tarquin's son, Sextus Tarquin, raped Lucretia, the wife of Tiberius Collatinus. Brutus and Collatinus restored the right of the Romans to elect their own leaders, and became the first consuls. Before the consuls walked twelve men called lictors carrying the *fasces*, an ax bound in rods symbolizing the consul's power to behead and to whip those who violated Roman law. Its origin is probably Etruscan. Representations of the *fasces* appear on either side behind the podium in the United States House of Representatives.

those to come will acclaim his actions—his love of country and great
730 desire for praise will win out.°

"See over there the Decii and the Drusi
and Torquatus and Camillus rescuing the standards.° Those other souls,
which you see shining in Roman arms, souls in harmony now
and while they are clothed in night—Ah, but what great wars
among themselves, if they attain the light of life, what combat
735 and carnage they will cause!

"Julius Caesar, the father-in-law, coming
down from the Alpine ramparts and the citadel of Monaco—and Pompey,
the son-in-law, equipped with his opposing Eastern forces.° My children,
do not become accustomed in spirit to such great wars, and do not turn
the powerful strength of your country against itself. You be the first
740 to stop—you who take your race from Olympus. Cast the sword
from your hand, you who are of my blood!°

"There is Mummius,
who will drive his chariot to the high Capitol after conquering Corinth,
famed because of all the Greeks he's killed. And Aemilius Paulus—avenging
his Trojan ancestors, he will destroy Argos and Agamemnon's town
745 Mycenae, and Perseus, the Aeacid himself, of the race of Achilles,
mighty in arms, taking revenge for Minerva's violated shrine.°

"Who shall fail to mention you, great Cato, or you, Cossus? Who will
omit the family of the Gracchi, or the two Scipios, two lightning bolts

---

730 ... *win out*: The sons of Brutus led a revolt in favor of the expelled Tarquins. For this crime Brutus had them executed; he stood as witness to their beheading.

731 ... *the standards*: Publius Decius Mus was a name borne by father and son, both consuls, who devoted themselves to death in battle, the first against the Latins (c. 340 BC), the second against the Gauls (c. 295 BC). The Drusi were one of the most famous families in Rome, including Augustus' wife Livia Drusilla. Marcus Livius Drusus was a consul who led Roman troops in victorious battle against Hasdrubal, the brother of Hannibal (207 BC). Tiberius Manilius Imperiosus won fame when he defeated a gigantic Gaul (361 BC) and took the chain from his neck (*torque*), hence he was called Torquatus. Later, when consul (340 BC), he executed his own son when his son engaged the enemy against orders. Marcus Furius Camillus recovered the gold paid to the Gauls (390 BC) to ensure the Gauls' removal from Rome. Vergil has modified the story to make him recover the Roman standards instead of gold, probably referring to Augustus' recovery of Roman standards in 20 BC from the Parthians, captured in 56 BC, a major embarrassment for the Romans.

737 ... *eastern forces*: Pompey, the son-in-law, married Julia, the daughter of Caesar, the father-in-law. Julia died in 54 BC, and war broke out between Julius Caesar and Pompey in 49 BC. Pompey was defeated the next year at a great battle in Pharsalus in northern Greece. Caesar's legions had fought in Gaul (58–50 BC), hence the "Alpine ramparts and the citadel of Monaco." Pompey was associated with the East because of his war against Mithridates (134–63 BC), whose power base was the southern coast of the Black Sea (66 BC), and because of Pompey's settlement of Judea and Syria (63 BC); in fact, most of his troops were recruited in Greece.

741 *of my blood*: For the first time Anchises addresses the ghosts of the future Roman leaders.

746 ... *violated shrine*: Lucius Mummius destroyed Corinth in 146 BC. Aemilius Paulus defeated Perseus, the last king of Epirus (that is, Macedonia), in 168 BC. Perseus claimed direct descent from Achilles, the grandson of Aeacus. Ajax, son of Oïleus, raped Cassandra in Minerva/Athena's temple.

of war, the scourge of Libya, or you Fabricius, powerful in your poverty,
or you Regulus Serranus, sowing your furrow with seed?° O you Fabii, 750
to where do you hasten my steps? You, Fabius Maximus, who alone
by delay restored the state for us.°
                        "Others—I think this—will forge
the bronze breathing more naturally than us and bring out the living
face from the marble, and plead their causes with more eloquence,
and describe the movement of the heavens with a staff etching on 755
the sand, and will tell of the rising of the stars—but *you* remember
to rule the nations with your power, O Roman! This will be your art—
to impose civilization on peace, to be sparing to the conquered,
and to fight down the proud!"°

Marcellus

                        So spoke father Anchises, and he adds
this while they marvel at his words: "See, how Marcellus comes forth, 760
famous because of the supreme prize, and he stands out before all men!
He, a knight, will sustain the Roman state when a great upheaval
strikes it, and will scatter the Carthaginians and the rebellious Gauls,
and for the third time will dedicate captured arms to Quirinus."°

---

750 ... *with seed*: Marcus Porcius Cato died in 149 BC at age eighty-five, a virulent opponent of Hellenization known for his opposition to Carthage. He ended every speech, no matter on what topic, with the words "Carthage must be destroyed" (it finally was, in 146 BC in the Third Punic War). Cornelius Cossus killed the king of Veii in 428 BC. The two most famous Gracchi were Tiberius Gracchus, killed by an aristocratic mob in 133 BC, and his brother Gaius, who was killed in similar circumstances ten years later, beginning the civil unrest that resulted in the destruction of the Roman Republic one hundred years later. But there were other prominent Gracchi. Publius Cornelius Scipio Africanus Maior defeated Hannibal at the Battle of Zama (202 BC). His adopted son (the son of Aemilius Paulus), Publius Cornelius Scipio Africanus Minor, destroyed Carthage in the Third Punic War (146 BC). Cornelius Fabricius Luscinius, consul in 282 and 278 BC during the war against Pyrrhus of Epirus, was famous for his modest lifestyle and vigor as a general; he refused the handsome bribes of Pyrrhus. Gaius Atilius Regulus Serranus, consul in 257 BC, defeated the Carthaginians in a naval battle near the Lipari Islands northeast of Sicily. His name Serranus seems to come from a Latin word meaning "to sow."

752 *for us*: Quintus Fabius Maximus Cunctator ("the Delayer") became dictator after the catastrophic battle at Lake Trasimene (217 BC) against the Carthaginians under Hannibal. His successful strategy was to delay Hannibal's progress by hindering his movements while avoiding a pitched battle, always withdrawing just ahead of the enemy, thus "the Delayer."

759 ... *proud*: These famous lines, often quoted, embody the Roman's sense of his own historical mission as opposed to that of the Greeks.

764 ... *Quirinus*: Marcus Claudius Marcellus was consul five times. He was not a patrician (the class of *patricii*) but belonged to the class of Roman knights (*equites*). In his first consulship (222 BC) he killed the general of the Gauls and so was granted the *spolia opimia*, "best spoils," the armor of the general he had killed. This honor was awarded only three times in Roman history: once to Romulus, once to Cossus, and once to Marcellus. Normally spoils were dedicated to Jupiter Feretrius, "Jupiter who strikes down," but in this case the spoils were dedicated to the deified Romulus, that is, Quirinus, *numen* of the people of Rome. Romulus supposedly built the temple to Jupiter Feretrius. Marcus Claudius Marcellus also fought the Carthaginians under Hannibal.

765   And Aeneas said—for he saw a youth walking with Marcellus,
outstanding in beauty, with shining arms, but with a countenance
lacking in joy, and with downcast eyes: "Who, father, is that man
who accompanies Marcellus as he goes along? Is that his son,
or someone from the long line of his descendants? What a commotion
770 around them! What a bearing he has! But dark night with its sad
shadow flies around his head."
                                Then father Anchises, with tears
welling in his eyes, said: "O my son, do not seek to know the immense
sorrow of your people. The Fates will show this man to the world,
but they will not permit any more. The Roman race would seem
775 too powerful to you, O gods, if such gifts had been permanent.
   "What moaning of men will that Field of Mars grant to the great city,
and what funeral processions will you see, O Tiber, when you glide
past his freshly-made tomb! No boy from the line of Ilia°
will so elevate our Latin descendants so high in hope, nor will
780 the land of Romulus one day ever boast so much about one
of its sons!
   "Alas for excellence [*pietas*], alas for ancient honor
and a hand unconquered in war! No one would have attacked him
with impunity when he was armed, whether he went against
the enemy on foot, or dug his spurs into the foaming flanks
785 of his horse. Alas, a boy to be pitied, if only you might shatter
harsh fate—*you'll be a Marcellus*! Let me scatter lilies, bright flowers
with full hands! Let me at least load the spirit of my descendant
with those gifts, and I will discharge that empty duty."°

the Gates of Sleep

   Thus they wander here and there throughout the entire region
790 over the broad fields of air, and they gaze at everything. After Anchises
had led his son through each place, he fires his spirit with love
of the glory to be, and he tells him of the wars that must come.

---

778   *Ilia*: That is, from Rhea Silvia—Ilia is her Trojan name.

788   ... *empty duty*: Augustus had one daughter, the infamous Julia, later implicated in a sexual scandal of enormous proportions and exiled to a remote island. Before her disgrace, Augustus married Julia to Marcus Claudius Marcellus (42 BC–23 BC), the oldest son of Augustus' sister Octavia and Gaius Claudius Marcellus, a former consul. Hence this Marcellus was Augustus' nephew. He was descended through his father from the famous general of the Second Punic War. Augustus promoted the young Marcellus' political career and groomed him as a possible successor, but Marcellus died at age nineteen in 23 BC. His death was a staggering blow to Augustus and his family, who were trying to establish a respectable succession to power. This eulogy of Marcellus in the *Aeneid* seems to be a personal appeal to the feelings of Augustus and his bereaved sister Octavia. The Theater of Marcellus was dedicated to this young man.

He teaches him about the Laurentine peoples and the city of Latinus,
and how to avoid or endure every trial.
                        There are twin gates of sleep,
of which one is made of horn, where an easy passage is granted   795
to true shades, and the other shines made of white ivory, but through
it the spirits of the dead send false dreams to the upper air.
After speaking, Anchises together with the Sibyl accompanies
his son, and he sends him through the Gate of Ivory.
                                    Aeneas makes
his way to the ship and again sees his companions. Then he sails   800
straight to the harbor of CAIETA, along the shore.° The anchors
are thrown from the prows. The sterns rest on the shore.

---

801   ... *along the shore*: The Gates of Horn and Ivory are mentioned by Homer in *Odyssey* Book 19, where
       Penelope talks about her dreams. The departure of Aeneas and the Sibyl through the gates of sleep
       has been interpreted in many ways, with no certainty. Why does he leave by the Gate of Ivory, the
       gate of false dreams? Perhaps the meaning is that unless Aeneas exerts his own will, all that he
       vwitnessed in the underworld will vanish as in a false dream. Caieta is a place set on a promontory
       seventy-five miles south of Rome and fifty miles north of Cumae.

 BOOK 7. *The Seeds of War*

You, too, O nurse of Aeneas—Caieta—you have given eternal fame to our shores in your dying. Now offerings still protect your grave, and your name marks your bones in great Hesperia, if there is any glory in that.°

But dutiful [*pius*] Aeneas, having duly performed the last rites,°
5 raised up a funeral mound. After the deep sea fell silent, he left the port and sailed away. The breezes blew through the night and the white moon did not deny light for their path. The sea sparkles in the tremulous light.

the Trojans arrive at the mouth of the Tiber

They graze along the shore of Circe's island, where that wealthy daughter of the Sun fills the woods with constant song and burns pungent cedar
10 for light at night in her proud halls as she runs her tuneful shuttle through the thin vertical threads of her loom. From here could be heard the angry roar of lions as they fought against the chains, roaring into the night, and wild swine, and bears raging in cages, and the shapes of great wolves howling, whose human faces that cruel goddess Circe had transformed
15 by means of powerful herbs into the forms of wild animals.°

But Neptune, so that the pious [*pii*] Trojans should not suffer a monstrous fate, borne into the harbor and onto its fatal shore, filled their sails with a favorable wind, allowing them escape, carrying them past the bubbling shallows. Already the sea grew rosy from the rays of the sun, and orangish Aurora, goddess
20 of dawn, shone forth from the depths of the sky in her scarlet chariot. The winds let up, and suddenly every breeze drops, and the oars labor across a leaden ocean.

And now Aeneas sees an immense wood from his place on the sea. Through it runs the TIBER with its pleasant stream, with its swirling

---

4 *... in that*: According to legend the town of CAIETA commemorated Aeneas' nurse, who died near there.

4 *last rites*: For the nurse Caieta.

15 *... wild animals*: Circe, who changes men into animals, is the daughter of the Sun and the sister of Aeëtes, the king of Colchis at the eastern end of the Black Sea, against whom Jason contended. Hence Circe was the aunt of the famous witch Medea, the daughter of Aeëtes. The "island of Circe," halfway between Cumae and the mouth of the Tiber, had by Vergil's day become a promontory, as it is today, called Monte Circeo.

FIGURE 7.1 *The Sibyl Takes Aeneas to His Companions* (top); *Aeneas' Departure from Cumae* (bottom), c. 1220, from the *Eneide* by Heinrich von Veldeke (c. 1150–after 1184). Von Veldeke is the first writer in the Netherlands to write in a vernacular Germanic language instead of Latin. He was born in Belgium sometime around 1150. Veldeke's major work is the *Eneas Romance*, based on the Old French *Roman d'Enéas*, which is based on Vergil's *Aeneid*. Surviving versions of Veldeke's *Eneide* are in Middle High German, although Veldeke's original German dialect is uncertain. Despite the unhappy events of Vergil's story (Dido's suicide and the death of many men), in the end of this courtly romance Aeneas marries Lavinia in a magnificent wedding feast, giving the poem a happy ending. But Veldeke's story of Aeneas remains the story of the foundation of Rome: German rulers thought of themselves as heirs to Roman power and medieval royal houses often traced their families back to the Trojans. The influence of von Veldeke's *Eneide* on later German literature was enormous. In this illustration on vellum from a Middle High German version of Veldeke's poem, made about AD 1220 one hundred years after the poem's composition, the Sybil, in the upper panel, delivers Aeneas back from the underworld to his companions. The figures are labeled. The Sibyl holds a paper strip with words of greeting on it. Aeneas and his companions all look alike. You can tell that the scene is set beside the sea because of the large (blue) patch behind the figures. In the bottom panel the fleet prepares to sail. A soldier comes up the gangplank on the right-hand side, while the steersman Palinurus clings to the steering paddle. Through three holes in the ship's cabin you can see the faces of five men. The wavy lines at the bottom indicate the sea. Paint on vellum.

THE SEEDS OF WAR

rapids filled with yellow sand, bursting to the sea. All different kinds of birds,
25 around and above, accustomed to the banks and the river hollows, delight
the heavens with their song as they fly through the woods. Aeneas orders
his men to turn their prows toward the land, and joyfully they slide into
the dark river.

King Latinus receives an oracle

Now come, O Erato,° I will tell of kings, and of the times,
and the condition of things in ancient LATIUM, when a foreign army first
30 landed on Ausonia's shores, and I will tell of the first beginnings of battle.
You, O goddess, advise your poet! I will tell of horrid war and will describe
lines of battle, and princes driven to death by their courage, and Etruscan
armies,° and all Hesperia forced into total war. A greater order is being born.
I attempt a greater task.
King Latinus, now old, ruled in a long peace the lands
35 and the quiet cities.° We have heard the story how this man was the child
of Faunus and the Laurentine nymph Marica, and that Picus was the father
of Faunus and he, O Saturn, calls *you* his parent, *you* the founder of his
bloodline.°
Because of the fate of the gods, Latinus had no male heir
because his only son died at an early age. Only his daughter Lavinia°
40 preserved the house and so fine a palace. Now she was mature and ready
for a man, of marriageable age. Many sought her hand in marriage
from all the breadth of Latium and from all over Italy. Above all others,
the handsome Turnus seeks her hand, of high standing because
of his ancestors. The wife of King Latinus, Amata, wanted very much to join
45 her daughter to Turnus as her son-in-law, in a wondrous love—but terrifying

---

28 *Erato*: Erato is the Muse of love poetry, appropriate because the story Vergil is about to tell concerns Turnus' love for Lavinia and his refusal to give up his bride to the Trojan stranger. Vergil therefore begins the second half of his poem—the Iliadic half as opposed to the Odyssean adventures in the first six books—with an invocation to the Muse.

33 *Etruscan armies*: He refers to the Greek Evander's enlisting the support of Tarchon the Etruscan on Aeneas' side: see below.

35 *quiet cities*: Latinus' palace is in LAURENTUM, a town south of the Tiber.

38 *bloodline*: In the Greek tradition, Latinus was the son of Circe and Odysseus, or of Circe and Odysseus' son Telemachus. Vergil adopts a Roman story that he was the son of Faunus, usually a Roman woodland spirit equated with the Greek Pan but here an early king of Latium, and a local nymph. Faunus was the son of Picus, "woodpecker," another early king of Latium, and Picus was the child of Saturn, who ruled during the ancient Golden Age.

39 *Lavinia*: She is a colorless character in the poem and never speaks. She is rarely mentioned, but the conflict arising over her betrothal drives the plot forward. She is the namesake of LAVINIUM and is the mother of Silvius Aeneas, who became king after the death of Aeneas' son, Ascanius/Iulus. Silvius Aeneas founds the Alban line of kings.

omens of the gods stood in the way!

There was a laurel tree with sacred leaves
in the high innermost recess, at the center of the house, guarded reverentially
through many years. Father Latinus himself discovered it when he first built
the citadel. He dedicated it to Apollo,° and he took the settlers' name from it—
the *Laur*entines. 50

Now a dense mass of bees—this is amazing to tell—were borne
through the clear air with a mighty buzzing, and they settled on the top
of the tree, and hung there from the green branch, their feet tangled
together, a sudden crowd. Immediately the prophet who served the Laurel
tree said: "*I see that a foreign man has come, and from the same direction
an army seeks this same place, to rule from the high citadel.*"° 55

Then, while he lit
the fire beneath the altar with fresh pine boughs, while Lavinia, a virgin,
stands beside her father, she seems to catch fire in her long hair—bad
omen!—and all her fine clothes are burned in the crackling flame.
Her tresses, coiffed like a queen's, are alight—and her crown studded
with jewels. Then, wrapped in smoke and a yellow light, she scattered sparks 60
around the whole room. They said it was a horrendous sight, an amazing
sight: The omen foretold that Lavinia would be distinguished for her fame
and her fate, but for the people there was a great war coming.

The king,
disturbed by this astounding event, visits the oracle of his prophetic father,
Faunus, and he consults the great woods beneath high Albunea° 65
that echo with the sound of the sacred fountain and from the dark exhale
searing and poisonous vapors. The people from Italy, and all the lands
of Oenotria,° seek answers from here when they are in doubt.
Whenever the priest brought offerings there, and lay down on fleeces
spread from sheep sacrificed in the silent night, he sought a dream. 70
He sees many images fluttering about in marvelous fashion,
and he hears various voices, and he enjoys conversations with the gods,
and he speaks to Acheron in deep Avernus.°

Here then father Latinus came,
seeking a response. He sacrificed one hundred wooly sheep according

---

49 *to Apollo*: The laurel is sacred to Apollo.

55 *high citadel*: The Trojans, like the bees, have come from a distance, and they aspire to the highest power.

65 *Albunea*: Probably "cloudy water," the name of the wood and its associated sulfurous fountain, near Lavinium. Faunus was often associated with oracles.

68 *Oenotria*: "land of wine," another name for Italy. Oenotria was named after a people who once lived in southern Italy.

73 *deep Avernus*: Vergil is describing the rite of incubation wherein the seeker of an oracle falls asleep and dreams the answer to his question. Incubation was widely practiced in the ancient world, especially in cults of healing. Acheron is the underworld river, and Avernus, the entrance to the underworld, stands here for the "underworld."

75 to correct ritual, and he lay down, supported by their skins and fleeces.
Suddenly he heard a voice from the deep wood: "Do not seek to ally
your daughter in a Latin marriage, O my child, and do not trust
in the wedding you have prepared. Sons-in-law from foreign lands
come who will bear our name to the stars by intermarriage. From their
80 race the children will see everything, from where the circling sun
views each Ocean,° overturned and ruled beneath their feet." This reply
of his father Faunus—this warning given in the quiet night—Latinus
did not keep to himself. Rumor ran through the cities of Italy,
flying far and wide.

a prophecy fulfilled

In the meanwhile the children of Troy moor their fleet
85 on the grassy slope. Aeneas and the principal captains and handsome
Iulus let down their bodies beneath the limbs of a high tree. They prepare
a meal. For their dinner they set wheat cakes out filled with the produce
of the field (Jupiter himself inspired them to do this), and they add wild
fruits to these tables made of wheat. When they had eaten the edibles,
90 and the lack of food drove them to turn their bites toward the wheaten cakes,
and to break up the circles of fateful crust with their hands and their
aggressive jaws, and not to spare the cakes cut into quarters—"Hey,"
Iulus said, only jokingly, "we are eating our tables!"

That voice, once heard,
first brought an end to their labors. His father Aeneas, as soon as the words
95 came from his son's lips, snatched them up and stopped him, amazed
at the expression of the divine will. Immediately Aeneas said: "Hail, O land
owed to me by Fate. And you—O faithful Penates of Troy—hail!
This is my home, this is my fatherland. My father Anchises told me
of these secrets about our fate—now I remember, 'Son, when you come
100 to an unknown land, and hunger from lack of food drives you to consume
your tables—then, though exhausted, look for a home. And remember
to set your hand here, and build your first walls here, and here heap up
a rampart around your houses.'

"Well, this is the hunger he talked about, this is
the last thing remaining, the thing that will put a limit to our exile.°
105 So come, then, and with the first light of the sun let us explore in joy
what these places are, to see what men live here, and where are the walls

---

81 *each Ocean*: That is, from one horizon to the other, everywhere. The sun is envisioned as rising out of the river Ocean, which encircles the world, and then setting in Ocean on the other side.

104 *our exile*: The story about Aeneas that Vergil inherited included this odd incident of the prophecy of the Trojans eating their own tables. It has little dramatic force, but was a famous detail in the pre-Vergilian legends about Aeneas.

of this people. Let us go out in all directions from the port. Now pour out
offerings to Jove and call on my father Anchises with prayers, and renew
the wine on the table!"

Having so spoken, Aeneas binds his temples with a green
branch, and he prays to the spirit of the place, and to Earth, the oldest   110
of all goddesses, and to the nymphs, and to the still-unknown rivers.
Then Aeneas calls on Night and the rising constellations of Night and Idaean
Jove and—in this order—the Phrygian mother, then his own two parents,
one on Olympus and one in Erebus.°

At this the all-powerful father thundered
three times from the clear sky and revealed a cloud in the sky burning   115
with rays of light, and with gold, as he shook it with his hand. Rumor soon
spread about through the Trojan encampments that the day at last
had come when they would found their city, the city owed them by Fate.
In competition they celebrate the feast. Joyful because of the magnificent
omen, they set up the wine-mixing bowls and they top-off the wine-cups.   120

Lines 121–229 are omitted. Aeneas sends an embassy to King Latinus in Laurentum to request an alliance and a place to settle. Latinus receives them warmly and mentions that by prophecy his daughter Lavinia is destined to marry a foreigner: This must be Aeneas. The embassy returns to Aeneas and reports the happy outcome.

But Jove's savage wife, coming from Inachean Argos, borne in her chariot   230
through the air, saw the joyful Aeneas and the Trojan fleet all the way
from Sicilian PACHYNUS.° She sees that walls are already being built, that they
are confiding in the land, that they have deserted the ships.

She stood stock
still, pierced by bitter pain. Then, shaking her head, she poured out words
from her breast: "Agh, hated race and the fates of the Trojans, so contrary   235
to my own! Could they not have fallen on the Sigean plains?° Could they
not have been taken captive? Could burning Troy not have burned them
to a crisp? They have found a way through the middle of battle, through
the middle of fire.

"But, I think, my divine powers at last lie exhausted,
or I have come to rest, my hatred satisfied. When they were shaken from   240
their fatherland, I followed them with enmity. I opposed them as refugees

---

114 *... in Erebus*: Aeneas calls on the primordial powers of Earth and Night and the local spirits to verify his right to own the land. Idaean Jove is the Jupiter of Mount Ida behind Troy. The Phrygian goddess is Cybelê, from Phrygia east of Troy. Venus, Aeneas' mother, is on Olympus, and his father Anchises is in the underworld (Erebus).

232 *... Sicilian Pachynus*: Juno is returning from Argos, where she had an important cult, to Carthage. The Inachus is a river, and also its god, that runs through Argos. Pachynus is the southeastern corner of Sicily from where Juno saw what was going on far up the coast in Latium.

236 *Sigean plains*: Sigeum was a promontory near Troy.

on every ocean. The might of the sky and the sea have been wasted on
these Trojans! What use to me are the SYRTES, or Scylla? or vast Charybdis?°
They take refuge in the hollow, so longed for, of the Tiber River, safe
from the sea—and from me.

245
        "Mars had the power to ruin the great people
of the Lapiths, and the father of the gods himself gave ancient Calydon
over to Diana's anger.° But what did the Lapiths or Calydon ever do
to deserve such punishment? But I, the great wife of Jove, who in my misery
could leave nothing undared, who have turned myself in every direction—
I am conquered by Aeneas!

250
       "But if my divine powers are not sufficient,
I won't hesitate to look for help wherever I find it. If I cannot persuade
the gods, I will stir Acheron. I know not to forbid Aeneas the Latin
kingdom, and that Lavinia will remain his bride—this is fixed irrevocably
by Fate. But I *can* drag things out and add delays. I *can* destroy
the people of these two kings!

255
      "May father Latinus and his son-in-law come
together at the cost of their followers' lives. Your dowry will be Trojan
and Rutulian blood, my virgin—and Bellona, goddess of war, awaits
you as bridal attendant. It was not Hecuba alone, Cisseus' daughter,
who was pregnant with a firebrand, who gave birth to a conjugal flame.
Venus' son is the same—a second Paris, a funeral torch for the reborn Troy!"°

260

Juno arouses Allecto to foster war

    When she said these things, she sought the earth in her
ferocity. She rouses Allecto from the house of the terrible Furies,° the bringer
of sorrow, from the shadowy underworld, in whose mind live sad war,
and anger, and plots, and awful crimes. Even her father Pluto hated Allecto,
and her Tartarean sisters hated her—a monster! Allecto has many shapes,
many savage features, and she ripples black with vipers.

265
          Juno roused her
with these words: "Give me a favor of my own, virgin daughter

---

243 ... *Charybdis*: Syrtes are the dangerous quicksands off Libya; Scylla is the monster who lives in a cliff opposite the whirlpool Charybdis and eats men alive.

247 *Diana's anger*: A huge war broke out when the Centaurs, guests at the wedding banquet of Pirithoüs, king of the Lapiths, got drunk and attacked the bride and her maids. Oeneus, the king of Calydon, failed to sacrifice to Diana, and she sent a great boar against the people.

260 *reborn Troy*: Before Paris was born, Hecuba had a dream that she gave birth to a firebrand. Priam ordered that the child be exposed, but a shepherd saved him and Paris grew up on Mount Ida behind Troy.

262 *Furies*: The Fury Allecto, "unceasing [in anger]," is the daughter of Earth and Night and the sister of Tisiphonê ("avenger of murder").

of Night—a service so that our honor and fame are not weakened,
and give way, and so that the followers of Aeneas cannot persuade
Latinus to fill the borders of Italy with a marriage. You can throw loving
brothers to arms, to fight! You can overturn houses with hatred! You can
bring a scourge to the house, the torch of funerals! You have a thousand
names, a thousand arts of harm! Search your fertile breast, shatter
the peace they have concluded, spread accusations that lead to war!
Let the youth in a moment desire arms, demand them, seize them!" 275

infected by Allecto, Queen Amata tries persuasion, then madness

And so Allecto, infected with the Gorgons' poison, first seeks out
Latium and the houses of the Laurentian king. She sits on the threshold
of Queen Amata who, burning with female passion, was distressed,
angry over the arrival of the Trojans, and the threat to Turnus' marriage.
The goddess flings one of the snakes from her blue locks. She plunges 280
it into Amata's breast, to the bottom of her heart so that, driven insane
by the beast, she might stir the whole household. The serpent slips between
Amata's clothes along her smooth breast, twists around unfelt, unknown
to the raging woman, breathing its serpent breath. The huge snake becomes
her twisted necklace of gold, it becomes the coil of her long ribbon. It weaves 285
in and out of her hair and wanders slithering down her limbs. At first
the illness, slipping inside like a liquid poison, attacks her senses and fires
her bones, but before her mind feels the flame in her breast, Amata
speaks softly, in the familiar fashion of a mother weeping abundantly
over her daughter and her impending marriage to a Trojan: "You are 290
her father—will Lavinia be carried off by exiles? Have you no pity
for your daughter Lavinia—or for yourself? You certainly have no pity
for her mother. That faithless man will leave her when the first north
wind blows, seeking the deep water with his stolen virgin as prize.
"Didn't Paris, that Phrygian shepherd, enter Sparta to carry off Helen, 295
the daughter of Leda, to the Trojan cities? What about your sacred vow?
What about your ancient care for your own people, and your right hand
so often given to the man of your own blood—Turnus! If a foreign
son-in-law is sought for the Latins, and the matter is settled, and the commands
of your father Faunus weigh upon you, well then—I consider all the land 300
that is free from our power to be foreign. That is what the gods declare.
And if the first origins of Turnus' house are sought, then his forefathers
are Inachus and Acrisius, and the land around MYCENAE."º

---

303 *...Mycenae:* Inachus is the river that flows through Argos; Acrisius was an early king of Argos,
the grandfather of Perseus. Turnus claims descent from them, hence, according to Amata, qualifies
as a foreigner. Mycenae sits in the middle of the Argive plain.

                                                    But when she sees that
Latinus stands against her, although she tries in vain with words, and when
305 the maddening evil of the snake has slipped deep within her heart
and pervaded her thoroughly, then in truth the unhappy woman goes
quite mad, stirred by terrible horrors without restraint, and she rages
through the immense city.
                              Just as when a spinning top that boys intent
on play drive in a great circle around an empty courtyard under a whirling
310 whip—driven by the lash, the top is carried across the curved space,
and the young crowd is amazed in its innocence, marveling at the spinning
piece of wood, and the blows give it life—even so Amata is driven in a course
no slower through the middle of the city and its daring people.
                                                              Then, pretending
to be in a Bacchic frenzy, Amata flees to the woods, commencing
315 a greater crime, arousing a greater furor, and she hides her daughter Lavinia
in the mountains thick with leaves, hoping to snatch the bride from
the Trojans, to put a stop to the wedding torches. Amata cries out "Euhoê"°
to Bacchus—madwoman!—and shrieking says: "You alone are worthy
of this virgin! For you she raises the friendly thyrsus,° for you she circles
320 in the dance, for you alone she tends her holy hair!"
                                                         Rumor flies. At once
the same ardor drives the mothers of the town, inflamed by insanity,
to seek strange dwellings. They leave their homes, they give their necks,
their hair to the winds, while others fill the air with tremulous shrieks.
Clothed in the skins of fawns, they carry spears wrapped in vines.
325 Amata herself holds a torch of burning pine in their midst, her eyes on fire,
and she sings the wedding song of Turnus and her daughter.
                                                              Suddenly
ferocious, she shouts: "O Latin mothers, listen to me, wherever you are!
If any gratitude toward the unhappy Amata remains in your pious [*piis*] hearts,
if concern for a mother's rights afflicts you—undo the bands from your hair,
330 celebrate with me the rites of the god."
                                             Allecto impels the queen with the Bacchic spur
through the woods, working from every direction, out among the haunts
of wild animals.

Allecto stirs Turnus to war

            When it seemed that she had sufficiently incited
craziness and had overturned the plan of Latinus and his whole house,
the gloomy goddess Allecto flew at once on dark wings from there

---

317 *Euhoê*: A ritual cry standard in Bacchic worship.
319 *thyrsus*: A rod tipped with a pinecone that was held in the rites to Bacchus.

FIGURE 7.2 *Allecto Rousing Amata Against Aeneas*, **AD sixteenth century, woodblock illustration from a version of the Latin Aeneid printed in France.**   All the figures are labeled. The fury Allecto is shown as a woman with large wings and hair of snakes. She appears before a bearded King Latinus on the right, who wears a crown and sits on a podium. Latinus gestures toward the Fury. Amata sits in the center, holding her breast from the fury's assault, and the princess Lavinia stands on the left. In the scene on the far right, the women of Laurentum have gone mad. The woman on the bottom raises her arms; her hair is wild and undone. Above her, in the woods, Amata and Lavinia hold a thyrsus. Above them is another wild woman with a thyrsus. Woodblock print on paper.

335 to the walls of the brave Rutulians. The city, they say, was founded
by Danaë, carried by a driving south wind along with her colonists,
the descendants of Acrisius. Once our ancestors called this place ARDEA,
and Ardea remains a great name—but its glory days are in the past.º

Here Turnus, in the middle of the night, was asleep in his high
340 house. Allecto changed her ferocious appearance and awesome shape
into that of an old woman. She plowed her lewd brow with wrinkles
and colored her hair white and bound it with a ribbon. Then she wove
in a bough of olive.

She became Calybê, the old attendant of Juno
and the priestess of Juno's temple. She presents herself before
345 the young man's eyes with these words: "Turnus, will you endure that
your efforts come to nothing? that your power is handed over to Trojan
colonists? The king denies your bride and the dowry you sought, owed
you by the right of blood. The king seeks a foreign heir to rule his kingdom!
Now go, offer yourself—despicable man—to dangers for which you will not
350 receive thanks. Go, cut down Tuscan fighters!º Protect the Latins
with peace!

"All this that I say, while you lie in the peaceful night,
the all-powerful daughter of Saturn has commanded me to speak openly.
For this reason I have come. Prepare to arm the youth, joyfully march
out from the gates. Burn the painted ships anchored in our lovely river
355 and the Trojan leaders with them! The great power of the gods so commands.
May King Latinus himself feel it—unless he allows your marriage
and obeys his own word. Let him at last experience Turnus in arms!"

At this the young man, jeering at the priestess, arose and answered:
"That a fleet has landed on the shores of Tiber has not, as you believe,
360 escaped my ears. Don't suppose that it makes me afraid. Nor is Juno
unmindful of me. But you, O mother, old age—weak and devoid of truth—
has troubled with a worthless concern. Old age makes fun of a priestess
with an imaginary terror in the midst of kingly wars. Your job is to care
for the statues of gods and their temples. *Men* will conduct war and peace,
365 *men* will fight these wars."

Allecto burned with anger at Turnus' words,
and a sudden tremor seizes the limbs of the youth as he spoke. His eyes
were fixed. The Fury hisses with her many vipers as she reveals herself
in her natural form. Turning her flaming eyes on him, she pushes Turnus
away as he hesitates, as he seeks to say still more. She raises up twin snakes

---

338 *in the past*: According to a Roman legend, Acrisius, the king of Argos (which Inachus founded), cast Danaë, his daughter, into the sea in a box with her baby, Perseus. The box came to shore in Italy, where Danaë founded Ardea, the stronghold of Turnus, king of the Rutulians and a cousin of Latinus (in the Greek tradition Danaë landed on the Aegean island of Syros). Today, Ardea is a town twenty-two miles south of Rome and four miles from the coast.

350 *Tuscan fighters*: Turnus has already been at war with the Etruscans (Tuscans).

in her hair. She cracks her whip and adds this from her rabid mouth: 370
"See me, then, conquered by weakness, *whom old age, devoid of the truth,
mocks in the midst of kingly wars with an imaginary terror*! Consider this:
I come here from the house of the terrible sisters. By my hand I bring
wars and death!"

      With this she cast a torch at the youth, fixing a brand in his chest,
smoking with dark light. A massive fear broke the sleep of Turnus, and a sweat 375
broke from his whole body, running over bones and limbs. Crazed, he calls out
for weapons. He looks for weapons by his bed and in his house. Love
of the sword rages through him, and an insane madness for war, anger
over all—as when burning sticks are heaped around the sides
of a boiling cauldron and roaring loudly the water dances with the heat, 380
and the smoky water burbles inside, and the water froths with foam,
and the liquid overflows, and the black stream shoots into the air.

      And so, the peace shattered, Turnus orders the captains of his young men
to march against King Latinus. Turnus orders that arms be prepared to defend
Italy, to drive the enemy from their shores—for he, Turnus, was coming, 385
a match for both the Trojans and the Latins. When he gave these commands,
and called the gods to witness his vows, the Rutulians vie with one another
in their call to arms. One man is moved by Turnus' youth and handsome bearing,
another by his royal ancestors, and another by his famous deeds.

Lines 390–658 are omitted. Allecto contrives that Iulus shoot a pet deer owned by a local herdsman. A fight breaks out. Using the incident as a pretext, Turnus urges war against the Trojans. Latinus abdicates. Juno opens the Gates of Janus, and the Rutulians gather for war, including the female warrior Camilla:

      In addition came Camilla,
from the Volscian people,° leading a corps of horsemen and troops 660
gleaming with bronze, a female warrior, her feminine hands not trained
to Minerva's distaff, and the basket of Minerva's wool, a virgin toughened
to suffer harsh battle and to outrun the wind on her feet. She might have
skimmed the tips of the unharvested wheat and not damaged the topmost
kernels in her running, or suspended above the swollen wave she might 665
have run across the middle of the sea, so swift that she would not touch
the surface with her feet.

      All the young men pour out from the houses, coming
in from the fields, and the women are amazed at Camilla as she passes,
gaping with open mouths at how the glory of royal purple drapes her smooth
shoulders, how the brooch clasps her hair with gold, how she herself carries 670
a Lycian quiver and a shepherd's staff of myrtle, tipped with an iron point.

---

660 *Volscian people*: Who lived in the hill country of southern Latium.

BOOK 8. *The Shield of Aeneas*

When Turnus raised the signal for war from the citadel
of Laurentum, and the trumpets sang out in a raucous song,
and when he roused his keen horses and clashed his arms
together, all their spirits are stirred at once, and at once all
5 Latium swears together in a restless commotion, and the youth
rages as if gone mad. The principal commanders Messapus
and Ufens and Mezentius, the despiser of the gods, bring
in troops from all sides and strip the broad fields of farmers.

Latium on a war-footing seeks an alliance

      And Venulus is sent to the city of great Diomedes° to seek
10 help and to explain that the Trojans have landed in Latium,
that Aeneas has come borne by his fleet, that he brings his conquered
Penates, that he says that he is king, commanded by the Fates,
and that many peoples join themselves with the Trojan, and that
his name increases far and wide in Latium. What Aeneas has
15 in mind with these undertakings, and what outcome of the battle
he desires—if Fortune shows him favor!—might be clearer
to Diomedes than to King Turnus or to King Latinus. That was
the situation in Latium.
      Meanwhile, Aeneas, the Trojan hero from Laomedon's
line,° seeing all this, floats on a great sea of troubles. Swiftly he casts
20 his mind this way and that. He seizes on different ideas and turns
everything over—just as when the tremulous light off the water
in a bronze bowl, thrown back from the light of the sun
or the moon's radiant image, flits over everything far and wide,
then raises up into the air and strikes the panels of the high ceiling.

---

9 *Diomedes*: After the Trojan War the great Greek hero Diomedes is said to have been expelled from Argos in Greece and to have settled in Apulia in Italy, in the city of Arpi, where Venulus now goes to seek help for the Rutulian cause. We later learn that Venulus comes from Tibur (Tivoli), supposedly an Argive colony, so his choice as ambassador to a Greek king from Argos makes sense.

19 *Laomedon*: In a rather complicated genealogy, Aeneas' father Anchises was the second cousin of King Priam of Troy, the son of Laomedon, making Aeneas Priam's second cousin, once removed (see Genealogical Chart).

Aeneas dreams of Tiberinus

It was night, and throughout the whole land a deep sleep
held the exhausted creatures, both winged and on the hoof,
when father Aeneas lay down on the bank beneath the icy bowl
of the sky, shaken in his heart by the sadness of war. At last
he gave peace to his limbs, when old Tiberinus appeared to him,
the god of this place, rising up from his lovely waters among
the poplar leaves. Finely woven linen covers him in a blue garment,
shadowy reeds cover his hair.
          Then Tiberinus begins to speak as follows,
and with his words he removes all care: "O child of the race of gods
who brings back our Trojan city from the enemy and preserves
eternal Pergamum,° you are expected on Laurentine soil and in the Latin
fields. For sure this is your house, here your Penates are at home—
don't resist it! And do not be terrified by the threat of war,
for the gods have given up all their swollen anger.°

    "And now, so that you do not think all this is the vain
fantasy of a dream, you will find a huge sow lying on the shore
under the oaks, who has given birth to a litter of thirty young—
she is white, lying alone, the white piglets around her teats.
This will be the place for your city, this a sure end to your labors.
From here, after thirty years, Ascanius will found the city of ALBA LONGA°
with its bright name. What I say is true. Now I will make clear
in a few words—pay attention!—how you will emerge as victor
in what is to come.
          "Arcadians have chosen a place on these shores,
a race descended from Pallas, who were the companions of King Evander,
who followed his banner. They built a city in the mountains called
PALLANTEUM° from the name of their ancestor Pallas. They wage
constant warfare with the Latin people. Call them as allies
to your camp, join in an alliance. I myself will lead you between
my banks, straight up my stream, so that as you journey inland
you might overcome the opposing current of the river with
your oars.

---

35 *... Pergamum*: Pergamum is the citadel of Troy. He will "bring back" the city because Dardanus, ancestor of the Trojans, originally came from Italy.

39 *swollen anger*: Actually not true, because Juno still nourishes her anger.

44 *Alba*: Alba means "white."

50 *Pallanteum*: Evander is Greek for "good man." This Pallas was grandfather to Evander (the son of Mercury) and unrelated to others with the name "Pallas." Evander's city, a Greek settlement in Arcadia, was on the site of the future city of Rome. The name of the PALATINE HILL in Rome is probably in some way connected to the legend.

"Get up now, child of a goddess! Just as the first
stars set, pray duly to Juno and overcome her anger and her threats
with your humble vows. As a victor, pay me honor! I am he
whom you see pressing in the banks with my full flow
and cutting through the rich cultivated land—the blue Tiber,
60 a river most pleasing to heaven. Here is my great house.
The fountainhead comes from a region of great cities."°

Aeneas sails to Pallanteum

    He spoke, then plunged into a deep pool, seeking the bottom.
Night and sleep left Aeneas. He gets up and, looking
at the ethereal sun rising in the East, he ritually takes up water
65 in his hollow hands, and he pours out this prayer to the sky:
"O Nymphs, Laurentine Nymphs, from where comes the birth
of rivers,° and you, O father of the Tiber River with its holy flow—
receive Aeneas and protect him at last from danger. In whatever
fountain the waters hold you as you take pity on our sufferings,
70 from whatever soil you come forth, most beautiful, always
you will be held in honor by my tributes. Always you will
be adorned by gifts, O horn-bearing river,° the ruler
of the Hesperian waters. O be you here with me and affirm
your divine power by your presence!"
                                     So Aeneas speaks,
75 and he chooses twin ships from his fleet and fits them out
with oarsmen, and at the same time he fits out his companions
with arms.
    But behold! A sudden marvel appears before his eyes,
amazing to see. They see a white sow gleaming through the wood,
of the same color as her litter, lying on the green bank. Dutiful [*pius*]
80 Aeneas carries the sow, along with her offspring, to the altar
and offers it to you, making a sacrifice, O greatest Juno—to you!
    Throughout that entire night, Tiber calmed the swelling
flood, and silently flowing back on itself stilled its silent waves
and spread the level of his waters gently in the manner
85 of a stagnant, a quiet swamp, so that there was no effort for the oars.
And so with happy rumor they speed along the course,
once begun. The oiled pine slips through the shallows. The waves
marvel, and the wood marvels, unaccustomed to seeing

---

61 *great cities*: In Etruria.

67 *of rivers*: That is, the nymphs of the fountains give birth to the rivers.

72 *horn-bearing river*: Rivers are often represented with the heads of bulls in Roman art.

FIGURE 8.1 *Aeneas and Ascanius Discover the Sow with Thirty Piglets,* c. AD 150, **Roman relief.** In the upper left is the altar of Juno, on which a fire burns. The sow with piglets appears to be in a cave beneath a tree in the lower left. Aeneas holds the sacrificial blade in his right hand, and with his left hand holds the hand of Ascanius, who carries a cudgel. Aeneas wears a breastplate and cloak, but is barefoot. Ascanius is in "heroic nudity," wearing only a cloak. On the far right three of Aeneas' men wait in a boat, and the prows of two more boats are visible above. The purpose of this illustration from Vergil's *Aeneid* is not clear. Roman marble relief.

the far-gleaming shields of men and painted hulls floating
on the river.
            They wear out a night and a day with their rowing.
They navigate long bends. They are darkened by all kinds of trees.
They cut through the green woods on a placid surface. The fiery
sun had climbed to the middle arc of the sky when they see
the walls and the citadel far in the distance and the scattered
roofs of houses—which now Roman power has raised to the sky,
but then Evander possessed a poor affair. They turn their prows
quickly into the bank and come near the city.

Aeneas and Evander

                              By chance on that
day the Arcadian king Evander was making solemn ceremonial offerings
to Hercules, the mighty son of Amphitryon,° and to other gods before
the city in a wood. His son Pallas was with him, and all the foremost
of the young men, and the needy senate all burned incense,
and the warm blood smoked on the altars. When they saw
the high ships, that they were gliding through the dark woods,
the men rowing with silent oars, the king and his men were terrified,
and they all rose up and abandoned their tables.
                                            But audacious
Pallas forbad that they break off the sacred rites and, snatching
up a spear, he flies off to where the Trojans are, and from a distance
he shouts from a hillock: "Warriors, what cause has driven you
to try unknown roads? Where are you going? Who are your people?
Where do you call home? Do you bring peace or war?"
                                            Then father
Aeneas speaks as follows from the high stern, and he holds out
in his hand a branch of the peace-bearing olive: "You are looking
at Trojans and weapons hostile to the Latins—men whom
the Latins have attacked with arrogant warfare, though we
are exiles. We seek Evander. Take this message, and say that
chosen leaders of Troy have come, asking for an alliance in arms."
            Pallas was amazed, struck by so great a name.° "Come out,
no matter who you are, and speak to my father in person, and come
to our Penates as guests." Pallas took Aeneas' hand and he gripped it tightly.
They leave the river and go into the wood. Then Aeneas speaks
to King Evander with friendly words: "O best of the sons of Greece,

---

99 *Amphitryon*: Amphitryon was his worldly father, but his real father was Jupiter.
117 *a name*: That is, "Troy."

you to whom Fortune has determined that I pray and offer branches
wrapped with ribbons—I was not at all afraid that you are a leader
of the Greeks, an Arcadian, and that you belong to the same race
as the twin sons of Atreus. But my own worth, and the holy oracles 125
of the gods, and the fact that our fathers are related—your fame
is spread throughout the earth!—join you to me and bring me
here willingly, fulfilling the demands of Fate.
  "Dardanus,
our first father and the founder of the city of Troy, was born
of Electra the daughter of Atlas, as the Greeks maintain. 130
Dardanus voyaged to the Teucrian people.° The great Atlas
who holds up the world on his shoulders begot Electra.
Your ancestor is Mercury, to whom pure Maia gave birth,
conceived on the frozen peak of Cyllenê. But Atlas begot Maia,
if we believe what we have heard, the same one who raises 135
the stars in the sky. Thus both our races split off from the same
blood.°
  "Depending on these facts, I did not send legates
or attempt prior diplomacy. Instead I give you myself—
me and my own life. I come a suppliant to your threshold.
The same Daunian race° pursues you with cruel war as 140
pursues us. If the Rutulians drive us out, they think that nothing
will stop them from placing all Hesperia completely under
their yoke, and taking possession of the sea that washes the east
and west coasts. Accept my friendship, and give your own.
Our hearts are strong in war. Our spirits and our warriors 145
are proven in action."

Evander offers an alliance

  So Aeneas spoke. Evander scanned with
a gaze Aeneas' face and eyes and his whole body for a long time
while Aeneas was speaking. Then Evander spoke briefly:
"Well, I accept you, most brave Trojan, and I gladly welcome

---

131 *Teucrian people*: In Vergil's account (in Book 3), Teucer was originally from Crete but left during a great famine, taking with him a third of its inhabitants. They settled near the Xanthus river in the Troad. Before Dardanus arrived, the land was called Teucria and the inhabitants Teucrians. After Dardanus' arrival, it was called Dardania, then the Troad.

137 *...same blood*: Dardanus, the founder of Troy, was a son of Jupiter and Electra. Electra was one of the seven daughters of Atlas, raised to heaven as the constellation of the Pleiades. Another of the Pleiades was Maia, the mother of Mercury, and Evander is the child of Mercury and Carmentis, a nymph. Therefore Evander and Aeneas are related.

140 *Daunian race*: Turnus' father was Daunus, from Daunia, an area in APULIA. Here, the term refers to the Rutulians.

FIGURE 8.2 *Aeneas with King Evander and Pallas*, **1654, by Pietro da Cortona (1596/7–1669).** Cortona was a leading Italian Baroque painter of his day (see Figure 1.2). In 1651 he was commissioned to decorate the gallery in the new palace of Innocent X, the Palazzo Pamphili (now the Brazilian embassy). His fresco depicts scenes from the life of Aeneas as recounted by Vergil: the Pamphili claimed to be descended from Aeneas. In this scene a bearded Aeneas, without helmet but wearing a breastplate covered by a cloak, holds out an olive branch to the Greek King Evander. The young Pallas stands at Aeneas' side. Evander sits on his throne surrounded by celebrants of the sacrifice to Hercules. They wear ivy crowns and carry jars of wine and animals to be sacrificed. To the right of the king, a sacrificial fire burns on an altar. Fresco.

you! How I remember the words and voice of your father,
the great Anchises, and his face. For I remember that Priam,
the son of Laomedon, came to see the kingdom of his sister
Hesionê, looking for SALAMIS, and he went on and visited
the icy borders of ARCADIA.°

"Then early youth bloomed on my
cheeks, and I marveled at the Trojan leaders, and I marveled
at the son of Laomedon, Priam himself. But taller than all
the rest went Anchises. My mind burned with a youthful ardor
to speak to the man and to clasp his hand. I went up to him
and eagerly I led him inside the walls of Pheneus.° When
he departed his gave me a fancy quiver and Lycian arrows°
and a cloak embroidered with gold and a pair of golden bits
that Pallas now has.

"And so what you ask I give! I give my
right hand in pledge of alliance, and when tomorrow comes
I will send you off happy for my help, and I will supply you
with provisions. In the meanwhile, favor us by celebrating
this annual festival, because you have come here as our friends—
it is quite wrong to delay it—and have a seat at the tables
of your allies."

After he said these things, he commands that
the food and drink that had been removed be brought back,
and he himself seats the warriors on the grass. He receives
Aeneas as the honored guest and invites him to sit on a maple
throne on a cushion and the skin of a shaggy lion. Then
the altar-priest and select youths compete to carry roasted
entrails of bulls, and they load up the baked bread in baskets
and deal out the wine. Aeneas and the Trojan youth at the same
time feast on the whole back of the ox and the sacrificial entrails.

Lines 177–351 are omitted. Evander tells the story of how Hercules defeated the monster Cacus, who lived in a cave on the Palatine Hill. He points out various features of the future site of Rome.

He spoke and he led great Aeneas beneath the steep roof
of his house. He gave him a mattress stuffed with leaves, and the skin

---

154   *... borders of Arcadia*: Hesionê was a daughter of Laomedon, and sister to Priam, who married Telamon, the father of Ajax and Teucer. Priam, on his way to visit her on the island of Salamis near ATHENS, over which Telamon ruled, evidently stopped in Arcadia in the central PELOPONNESUS.

159   *Pheneus*: A town on the north side of Lake Stymphalus, in northern ARCADIA, near Mount Cyllenê, the birthplace of Mercury.

160   *Lycian arrows*: The Lycians of southern Asia Minor were famous archers.

of a Libyan bear. Night rushes in and embraces the earth in her dark
wings.

Venus seeks arms for Aeneas from Vulcan

But Venus was not a frightened mother for nothing—
disturbed by the threats of the Laurentines° and by ferocious violence.
She speaks to Vulcan, her husband,° in their golden bridal chamber,
beginning as follows and breathing a divine love into her words:
"While the Argive kings laid waste to doomed Troy in the war,
and destroyed the citadels destined to fall to enemy flames,
I did not ask help for my wretched people. I did not ask for armor
made by your art and power, dearest husband, nor did I wish
to exercise your skill in vain—although I owed a great deal
to the sons of Priam, and I often wept about the harsh trials
of Aeneas.
           "And now he has set foot on the shores of the Rutulians
because of the commands of Jove. I come as a suppliant and I,
a mother, ask for arms for my son, from a power sacred to me.
Thetis, the daughter of Nereus, and Dawn, the wife of Tithonus,
were able to bend you with tears.° See, what peoples come
together, which cities are closing their gates and sharpening
their swords against me for the destruction of my people!"
       So she spoke, and the goddess—because he hesitated—caresses
him in her snow-white arms, on this side and that, with a gentle
embrace. At once Vulcan accepts the accustomed flame. The familiar
warmth entered his marrow and ran through his melting bones—
just as sometimes happens when a streak of fire, torn out by thunder,
dashes through the clouds of storm with its flash of light.
His wife felt it, thrilled with her tricks, aware of her beauty.
       Then the father speaks, bound by an eternal love: "Why do you
seek incidents from the past? Where has your trust in me gone,
my goddess? If your concern had been the same then, it would
have been all right for me to have armed the Trojans. Neither
the all-powerful father, nor the fates, had forbidden that Troy
stand for another ten years, or that Priam live that long!
"And now, if you are preparing for war, and have made up your
mind, cease to doubt your powers—beg for whatever care I can

---

356 *Laurentines*: That is, the Latini, from the town of LAURENTUM, allied with the Rutulians from the nearby town of Ardea.

357 *husband*: But in the usual version Vulcan divorced Venus (Aphrodite) after discovering her affair with Mars (Ares).

369 *...with tears*: Thetis persuaded Vulcan to make armor for Achilles; Dawn obtained armor for her son Memnon.

promise in my art, for what can be done in iron or in molten
electrum, as much as fire and bellows are able to produce."
    Have spoken these words, he gave his wife the embrace
they both desired and, sinking into his wife's lap, he sought   390
quiet sleep in all his limbs.

Vulcan forges the weapons

                Then in the middle of the night,
when first rest has expelled the need for more sleep, when
a woman, whose burden it is to endure life by the work
of the distaff and the humble handicrafts that Minerva imposes,
first wakes up the ashes and builds up the sleeping fires, adding   395
hours of the night to her labor, and she works her slaves
by torchlight at their endless gobs of wool that she might
preserve her husband's bed pure and raise her young sons—
even so this master of fire, no sluggard at that hour, rises
from his soft bed to his work at the forge.   400
                            An island rises
steeply near the Sicilian coast, near the side of Aeolian LIPARI,
its rocks smoking.° Beneath it is a cave, and the caverns
of Etna resound,° carved out by the forges of the Cyclopes,
and the strong blows on the anvils are heard reechoing
and booming, and the iron bars of the Chalybes° hiss   405
in the caverns. Fire breathes in the furnaces. It is the house
of Vulcan, called Vulcania.
                      Here then the master of fire
went down from the high heavens. The Cyclopes were
working iron in the huge cave, Brontes and Steropes
and Pyragmon with his bare limbs.° Shaped by their hands,   410
they held a lightning-bolt, half-polished and half still unfinished,
like many of those that the Father casts down on the earth
from every part of the sky. They had added three shafts
of twisted rain, three of watery cloud, three of reddish fire,

---

402 ... *rocks smoking*: One of the Lipari Islands off the northeast coast of Sicily and called in the ancient world Hiera, that is, "sacred" to Vulcan. Today the island is called Vulcano. The island of Lipari, just north of this island, was thought to be the home of Aeolus, the wind-king.

403 *resound*: Apparently the caves are thought to be linked to Mount Etna in Sicily by underground passageways.

405 *Chalybes*: A Greek term for peoples of the Black Sea coast famous for trading in iron.

410 ... *bare limbs*: Brontes is "thunder," Steropes is "lightning," and Pyragmon, unknown before this passage, is "fire-anvil." In Hesiod's account, the third Cyclops is called Arges, "bright."

FIGURE 8.3 *Venus Asking Vulcan for Arms for Aeneas*, **1610, by Bartholomäus Spranger (1546–1611).** Spranger was a Flemish painter and sculptor in the Baroque style. He became a painter in the imperial court in Prague, where he uniquely combined Dutch and Italian artistic conventions. He worked on wall paintings in churches throughout Europe but was known for mythical subjects as well. Here he shows a naked Venus, demurely smiling and standing behind a bearded and naked Vulcan, who sits astride a bench while Venus lovingly caresses Vulcan's head. In the lower right, a naked winged cupid holding an arrow in his right hand and a bow in his left indicates sexual attraction. Vulcan turns away from a spear-point that he is filing, held to the bench by a vise. Other tools lie on the bench at the base of a finished helmet. Above the helmet is a breastplate with a Gorgon's head affixed beneath the collar. In the upper left, two workmen labor at an anvil, forging the shield. Oil on canvas.

and the winged South Wind. Now they mixed in the work 415
horrific lightning bolts and thunder and fear and rage
with pursuing flames.
      In another part they pressed on with
a chariot for Mars and winged wheels with which he rouses
warriors, with which he rouses cities, and a terrifying aegis,°
  the breastplate of Pallas. They competed with each other 420
to fit golden scales on serpents, on the interwoven snakes,
and the Gorgon's head itself on the breast of the goddess,
rolling its eyes with its neck severed.°
        "Away with this!" Vulcan said,
"Give up what you're working on, what you've begun, Cyclopes
of Etna, and turn your attention to this task—you must make 425
arms for a brave man. Now there is a need for strength, now for
swift hands! Now we need all of a master's art. Put an end to delay!"
  He did not say more. Quickly the Cyclopes set to the task.
They shared out the work equally. The bronze and gold flow in streams,
  and steel that deals wounds melts in the huge furnace. They pound 430
out a huge shield, one able to stand against all the weapons of the Latins.
They place seven layers on it, disc upon disc. Some suck
in air in windy bellows and breathe it out again, others temper
the screeching bronze in water. The cave groans from the weight
  of the anvils. The Cyclopes alternately raise their arms in rhythm, 435
and they rotate the mass of metal, holding it in tongs.

Evander suggests an alliance with Tarchon and offers his son Pallas as an ally

            While the Lemnian
Vulcan° father hastens this work on Aeolian shores, the kindly
light rouses Evander from his modest house, and the song of morning
birds beneath the eaves. The old man gets up. He wraps his limbs
  in a tunic, and he puts Etruscan sandals around the soles of his feet. 440
Then Evander binds to his side and shoulders an Arcadian sword,
swirling the panther skin that hung on his left side. Two guard
dogs run before him from the high threshold and accompany
the step of their master. The hero sought out the secluded hut
  of Aeneas, mindful of his words, and his promised help. 445

---

419 *terrifying aegis*: The aegis, Greek "goat-skin," was some kind of magical shield represented in art with serpent tassels and usually worn as a cloak. Affixed to Minerva's shield was a Gorgon's head, which also often appeared on real shields.

423 *neck severed*: The intertwined snakes are the hair on Medusa's severed head. Even sight of this head would turn one to stone.

437 *Lemnian Vulcan*: When Jupiter threw Vulcan from heaven, he landed on the island of LEMNOS, where the local people cared for him (*Iliad* 1.593).

                                                    Aeneas was
no less an early riser. Pallas, Evander's son, accompanied Evander,
while Achates went along as companion with Aeneas. When they came
together, they joined hands and took their seat in the inner courtyard.
They finally enjoy an open conversation.°
                                    The king began first
450 with the following: "Great leader of the Trojans, so long as you
are safe, I will never admit that the Trojan kingdom has been
conquered. But our own strength is small in war, inadequate
to so great a name. On the one side we are shut in by the Tiber
River, and on the other the Rutulians press on us and thunder
455 around our walls with their armor. However, I am preparing
to join powerful people with you, and the wealthy camps
of kings, help that an unpredictable chance reveals. You arrive
at Fate's command!
              "Not far from here is the site of the city
of Agylla built of ancient rock, where the Lydian race, distinguished
460 in war, once inhabited the Etruscan hills.° King Mezentius
then held the city with his proud command and savage arms
during many flourishing years. Why should I retell his unspeakable
murders, the wild acts of this tyrant? May the gods reserve that
for the man himself and his race. He even joined dead bodies
465 to living, fitting hand to hand and face to face, a means of torture,
and thus he killed them in a slow death, in a wretched embrace,
by means of the ooze of disease and decomposition.
                                                "But the weary
citizens at last armed themselves and surrounded this totally mad
man in his palace. They cut down his allies, and they cast fire
470 into the rooftops. In the midst of the carnage, he slipped away
and took refuge in the land of the Rutulians, where he was protected
by his host. And so, all Etruria has risen up with just fury.
They demand the return of the king, for execution, by the threat
of imminent war.
              "I will make you commander of these thousands,
475 Aeneas. For their fleet clamors in dense array on the shore. They
order that the banners be raised, but an aged soothsayer holds them
back, singing of Fate: 'O chosen youth of Maeonia,° the flower

---

449 *open conversation*: The festival on the day before did not allow for public business.

460 *Etruscan hills*: Agylla was the Greek name for the Etruscan city of CAERE (modern Cerveteri). The Etruscans were reputed to have come from LYDIA in ASIA MINOR under the leadership of a king Tyrsenus; thus the Etruscans are often called Tyrrhenians.

477 *Maeonia*: A region in Asia Minor contiguous with Lydia, from where the Etruscans come.

and the manliness of our ancient race, whom a righteous pain
sends against the enemy, whom Mezentius fires with deserved
anger—no Italian can control a people so great as you: Choose
foreign leaders!'
    "Then the Etruscan ranks settled down
on this plain, terrified by the warnings of the gods. Tarchon°
himself sent messengers to me with the crown and scepter
of the kingdom, and he entrusts me with insignia so that
I might come to the camp and take over the Etruscan kingship.
    "But the slow chill of old age—I'm worn out by the years—
and strength too late for brave deeds prevents my accepting the command.
I would exhort my son, except that he is of mixed stock: His Sabine mother
carries one part of his lineage. But you, O bravest leader of the Trojans
and the Italians, whom Fate favors both in your years and in your race,
whom the divine will summons—step up!
    "Furthermore, I will add Pallas
here to you, my hope and solace. Let him become accustomed under
you to tolerate military discipline and the harsh work of war,
and may he perceive your deeds, and admire you from
an early age. I will give him two hundred Arcadian horsemen,
the select strength of our young people, and Pallas will provide
as many to you in his own name."

preliminary alarms

    Evander had scarcely spoken, and Aeneas,
the son of Anchises, and the loyal Achates held their eyes fixed
to the ground as they thought of their many difficulties with a sad heart,
when Cytherea° gave a sign from a cloudless sky. Lightning
came with thunder, shaken unexpectedly from the sky, and suddenly
everything seemed to tumble down, and through the air the clangor
of an Etruscan trumpet° seemed to sound.
    The others were astounded,
but the Trojan hero recognizes the sound and the promises of
his divine parent.° Then he says: "My friend, do not seek to know
what these portents signify. I am summoned by Olympus.
The goddess who bore me said that she would send this sign

---

482 *Tarchon*: An early Etruscan hero, the founder of the city of TARCHNA (Roman Tarquinii).

500 *Cytherea*: Venus.

503 *Etruscan trumpet*: Supposedly an Etruscan invention.

505 ... *divine parent*: Promises that she would obtain armor for him. Venus, however, did not actually promise this.

if war came close, and that she would bring arms from Vulcan
through the air to me.
    "Alas, what great slaughter waits upon
510 the Laurentines, what price you will pay me, Turnus! How many
shields and helmets and strong bodies you will roll beneath
the waves, O Father Tiber! Let them demand battle and so break
their treaties."°
    When Aeneas had said these things, he raises himself
from his high throne. First he renews the sleeping altars
515 of Hercules and gladly he approaches the Lar° and the humble
Penates he had visited on the day before. Evander and the Trojan
warriors likewise slaughter chosen sheep in the ritually correct
manner. After this he goes to the ships and meets again with
his comrades. He chooses out from their number those
520 of superior virtue who might follow him in war.
    The others
go downstream, and they float without exertion on friendly
waters, bringing news to Ascanius about his father and his father's
affairs. Horses are given to the Trojans who are to take
the Etruscan field. They lead out a choice horse for Aeneas,
525 which the yellow skin of a lion covers, gleaming with golden claws.
    Rumor suddenly flies through little Pallanteum, that
horsemen are going fast to the shores of the Etruscan king.
Mothers, in alarm redouble their prayers. Fear comes closer
with the danger. The great image of Mars looms large.

Evander says farewell to Pallas

530 Father Evander grasps the hand of his son as he departs,
and he clings to him, weeping inconsolably, and he says the following:
"O, if only Jupiter would give me back the years that are gone—
I was quite a man when I routed the front lines under the very
walls of PRAENESTÊ, and as victor fired the pile of shields, and sent
535 King Erulus into Tartarus with this right hand.° When he was born,
his mother Feronia—strange to tell!—gave him three lives,
and three weapons to wield, and three times to be brought down

---

513 *treaties*: Those between Latinus and the Trojans.

515 *Lar*: Singular for Lares, guardian deities of households and roadways in ancient Roman religion similar to the Penates, with which they are often confused.

535 *... right hand*: Praenestê is about twenty-two miles east of Rome (modern-day Palestrina). The story about Erulus is known only from this passage.

to death. This very right hand took away all three lives
at one time, and I stripped his armor too.
                                    "I would never be torn as now
from your sweet embrace, my son, nor would Mezentius have   540
rained insults on me, his neighbor, and killed so many with cruel
deaths, and widowed the city of its many citizens.°
                              "But you,
who dwell above, and you mightiest ruler of the gods, Jupiter,
take pity on this Arcadian king and hear a father's prayers.
If your divine power, and Fate, preserve my Pallas, if I live   545
to see him again and be together with him, I beg you for life.
I will suffer whatever task you set.
                                 "But if, Fortune, you threaten
some unspeakable disaster, then now—now, may I break off
from cruel life while the outcome is in doubt, while there
is still an uncertain hope for the future, while you, my dear   550
child, my late and only pleasure, are held in my embrace.
May no evil news wound my ears."
                              These were the words
the father poured out at their last parting. Evander collapsed
and his slaves carried him inside the palace.

Venus' gift of special armor

                              And so the cavalry
went out of the open gates, Aeneas among the first, and the trusty   555
Achates, then others of the elite troops of Troy, and Pallas himself
in the midst of the line, conspicuous from his cloak and in his painted
arms—as when Lucifer, the Morning Star,° whom Venus loves more
than any other of the starry fires, having bathed in the wave of Ocean,
raises his sacred face in heaven and dissolves the shadows.   560
     Mothers stand, afraid, on the walls and they follow with
their eyes the cloud of dust, the troops bright with bronze.
The armed men head off through the underbrush, cross-country.
A shout goes up. They form up and their hooves shake
the dusty ground.   565
               There is a huge wood near the icy river of CAERÊ,
held sacred far and wide through religious ritual. The hollow hills
close it in from all sides and surround the wood with dark fir.

---

542 *many citizens*: Apparently Mezentius has made raids on Pallanteum.
558 *Morning Star*: Lucifer is the planet Venus, special to the goddess Venus (and hence named after her).

The story is that the ancient Pelasgians dedicated this wood
and this festival day to Silvanus, the god of the field and of flocks—
570 the Pelasgians who once first occupied the lands of the Latins.°
  Not far from here Tarchon and the Etruscans were camped
in a safe place. From a high hill it was possible to see
their troops scattered far across the fields. Here father Aeneas
and his band of men selected for war came up and, exhausted,
575 rested their horses and bodies.
        But then Venus came through
the airy clouds, the white goddess, bearing gifts. When she saw
her son from far away, withdrawn in secret to a remote
valley beside a cool stream, she went to him, unasked,
and she spoke the following words:
          "Behold the gifts
580 that I promised, made by my husband's skill, so that you
need not hesitate to call out to battle the proud Laurentines,
or fierce Turnus."
      Cytherea spoke and sought the embrace
of her son, and she placed the shining armor under an oak tree
that was opposite her. Aeneas, delighted at the gifts of the goddess
585 and by so great an honor, cannot get enough of looking at each
object. He admires and turns over in his hands and arms
the helmet, terrible with its crest and disgorging flames,
and the death-dealing sword, the stiff breastplate of bronze—
blood-red, huge—such as when a blue cloud is lit by the rays
590 of the sun and glows from a long way off, then the smooth
shin guards made of electrum and refined gold, and the indescribable
patterns on the shield.

the shield of Aeneas: early days of Rome

        On the shield the lord of fire, versed
in prophecy and knowing about the times to come, fashioned
the history of Italy and the triumphs of the Romans. There was
595 the whole race of future generations descended from Ascanius,
and the battles they were to fight, all in a sequence.
              He also
fashioned the she-wolf who had just given birth in the green cave
of Mars° and was lying on the ground, the twin boys Romulus

---

570 *... Latins*: The Pelasgians were a pre-Greek people, but here they are the Greeks themselves, thought to have lived in Etruria before the coming of the Etruscans. Silvanus, "he of the forest," was a Roman woodland god equated with the Greek Pan.

598 *of Mars*: That is, the cave called the Lupercal beneath the PALATINE HILL.

FIGURE 8.4 *Aeneas Receiving the Arms of Vulcan*, **1668, by Gérard de Lairesse (1640–1711).** The Baroque painter Lairesse was the most celebrated Dutch painter after the death of Rembrandt. His treatises on painting and drawing deeply influenced eighteenth-century painting. In de Lairesse's view, painting should portray grand biblical, mythical, and historical scenes. The purpose of art was to improve mankind, to set an example. Here a naked Venus occupies the center of attention, appearing in a cloud in the air and pointing with one hand to Vulcan's armor while with the other she holds her son's hand. Aeneas steps up on the cliff outcropping where the armor is stacked. He wears a helmet and breastplate and carries a spear, a cloak thrown over his shoulder. On the left-hand side of the painting are five cupids: two play with the shield while the other three stand about the new plumed helmet. The middle cupid holds up a scabbard. In the lower left, leaning against the oak tree that Vergil mentions, a rough Vulcan looks over his handiwork. Oil on canvas.

and Remus playing around her teats, hanging from them,
600 and fearlessly sucking from their foster-mother. And she,
turning back her smooth neck, nuzzled them and licked their
bodies with her tongue, now one, now the other.
              Not far from
this scene he placed Rome and the Sabine women lawlessly
stolen while they were sitting in the circus as great games
605 went on, and the sudden surge of a new war between Romulus'
men and old Tatius and the austere Cures.°
                Next, the same two
kings, having set aside their differences, stand in armor
in front of an altar holding libation dishes, and they sanctify
their alliance by sacrificing a pig. Not far from there four-horsed
610 chariots tore Mettius into pieces (Alban, you should have kept
your word!), and Tullus dragged the liar's guts through the forest,
the scattered briars bedewed with his blood.°
                  There was Porsenna
too, who commanded that Rome admit the exiled Tarquinius,
and he laid a mighty siege upon the city. And the followers of Aeneas
615 picked up their swords to fight for freedom. You could see Porsenna
in the likeness of an angry man, like a threatening man,
because Cocles dared to tear down the bridge, and Cloelia
broke her chains and swam the river.°
                At the top of the shield,
Manlius the guardian of the Tarpeian Rock° stood before the temple

---

606 *... Cures*: The SABINES were a local people living in the foothills of the APENNINE range. Romulus could only attract bandits and runaway slaves for his new city of Rome, so on a festival day the Romans snatched the visiting Sabine women and married them (c. mid-eighth century BC). Titus Tatius, the Sabine king of Cures (**ku**-rēz), then attacked Rome and captured the CAPITOLINE HILL, betrayed by Tarpeia, the daughter of a Roman commander, in exchange for what she thought would be a reward of jewelry. She was instead crushed to death and her body cast from the Tarpeian Rock, named after her. The Sabine women, however, had become resigned to their marriages and convinced Titus Tatius and Romulus to reconcile. Cures was in the Sabine Hills east of Rome and was famous for its austere way of life.

612 *... bedewed with his blood*: Mettius was a ruler in Alba Longa who betrayed the Romans. In a battle between the town of Fidenae and Rome, he retreated to see which force would be victorious; he would then join the winning side. Tullus Hostilius, the third king of Rome, won the battle, and proclaimed that because Mettius was torn between the two sides, so would his body be.

618 *... the river*: Supposedly, in 509 BC the Etruscan king of Clusium, Lars Porsenna, attacked Rome to restore Lucius Tarquinius Superbus to power, an Etruscan and the last king of Rome. Horatius Cocles held the bridge called the PONS SUBLICIUS single-handed against the Etruscan forces until the bridge could be cut down, then swam fully armed back across the river. After peace was made, Porsenna took hostages from Rome, including Cloelia. She swam back across the river, but the Romans returned her. Porsenna was so impressed by her bravery that he released Cloelia and the other hostages.

619 *Tarpeian Rock*: A steep cliff off the southern summit of the Capitoline Hill overlooking the Roman Forum. The treacherous Tarpeia's body was thrown over this cliff.

and defended the high Capitol, and the palace of Romulus bristled
with its covering of thatch. And it was here that the silver goose
flying through the golden gates announced that the Gauls were
at the doorstep. The Gauls were there in the brush and were
reaching the citadel, protected by the dark and the gift of black
night. Their hair was of gold and their clothing was gold,
and they shine in their striped cloaks, and their white necks
are torqued with a gold band. Each carries two Alpine spears
in his hand, and their bodies are protected by long shields.º
    Here on the shield he had beaten out the dancing Salii
and the naked Luperci and the wooly priest-caps they wore and the shields
that slipped from heaven, and chaste mothers in cushioned carriages
carrying sacred objects through the city.º
                                        Far from these he added
the Tartarean realms, the high doors of Dis, and the punishments
for crimes and you, O Catiline, hanging from a threatening cliff,
trembling at the sight of the Furies, and at a distance the pious [*pius*]
Cato giving out laws.º

620

625

630

635

---

628   ...*long shields*: The Gauls were a Celtic people, that is, they spoke a language related to Irish or Welsh. They occupied what is today France, Spain, and northern Italy: TRANSPADANE GAUL ("across the Po") and CISPADANE GAUL ("this side of the Po"). Their warriors were famous for wearing a ring of twisted gold around their necks, open at the throat, called a "torque." In the early fourth century BC a band of Gauls from Transpadane Gaul, near the Alps, occupied a site in Etruria and quickly fell into a war with Rome. The Gauls were better armed than the Romans and used long shields that covered their bodies. In 390 BC the Romans suffered a thorough military defeat at their hands, after which the Gauls marched to Rome and sacked the city. Only the Capitoline Hill held out, defended by Marcus Manlius and a small garrison. When the Gauls attempted to scale the hill, Manlius was roused by the cackling of sacred geese in the temple to Jupiter and threw down the assailants. Later Manlius was disgraced and executed by being thrown down the Tarpeian Rock.

632   ...*the city*: The Salii, the "leaping priests" of Mars, were supposedly introduced by King Numa Pompilius, the third king of Rome. They were armed and wore a spiked headdress. They were in charge of twelve special bronze shields. One of the shields fell from heaven in the reign of Numa, and eleven copies were made to protect the identity of the sacred shield, because prophecy held that so long as that shield was preserved, Rome would be triumphant. The Luperci, "brothers of the wolf," were a group of priests of Faunus who dressed only in goatskins or ran naked through the streets during a spring fertility festival. The matrons in their carriages are mentioned here because during the crisis of the Gallic attack Roman matrons gave up their gold jewelry to support the war effort. Ever thereafter they were allowed to ride in carriages.

636   ...*out laws*: Lucius Sergius Catilina (108–62 BC) was a Roman senator of the first century BC who attempted to overthrow the power of the aristocratic Senate. Cicero (106–43 BC), who was consul at the time, discovered the plot, unmasked Catiline, and illegally had him executed (for which crime Cicero later suffered exile). Cicero is not mentioned in the *Aeneid*, unless this reference to Catiline is a special tribute to him. Marcus Porcius Cato (95 BC–46 BC) is commonly called Cato the Younger to distinguish him from his great-grandfather, Cato the Elder. He was a statesman of the late Roman Republic known for his uprightness, a follower of the Stoic philosophy. He committed suicide when the victory of Julius Caesar seemed certain.

the shield of Aeneas: the Battle of Actium

                        Among these things went the golden image
of a swollen sea, though the waters frothed with a white foam,
and the dolphins in bright silver swept the sea with their tails
in a circle around the central image, cutting through the flood.
640 In the middle you could see ships in bronze, the Battle of ACTIUM,
and you could see all of Leucate° in feverish preparation for war,
and the waves shine in gold. On one side Augustus Caesar stands
leading his Italians into battle along with the Senate and the Roman
People, the Penates and the great gods. His joyful temples spit
645 out twin flames and his father's star is shown at the top
of his head.°
            In another part of the shield, Agrippa, favored
by the winds and the gods, leads the troops. His temples
shine, crowned with the beaks of the naval crown, the proud
650 insignia of war.°
                And over here is Antony with his barbarian
wealth and weird arms, victor over Eastern peoples and the shores
of the Red Sea—he brings Egypt and the strength of the East
and furthest Bactria along with him, and his Egyptian wife
(shame!) follows along.°
                    They all rush in together and all
655 the sea foams, churned by the oars drawn back and the threefold
beaks they had for rams. They head for the deep water.
You might think that the CYCLADES islands were overturned
and were floating on the sea, or that high mountains were
clashing on mountains run together, so huge were the towered
660 ships in which the men moved on one another.

---

641 *Leucate*: A promontory on the island of Leukas in western Greece. The Battle of Actium, a decisive naval engagement between Octavian and the combined forces of Marc Antony and Cleopatra, took place north of here in 31 BC.

646 *at the top of his head*: The great gods are probably Vesta and the Lares, household gods similar to the Penates. The star on Augustus' helmet recalls the comet that appeared at the death of Julius Caesar in 44 BC, thought to be his glorified spirit.

650 *insignia of war*: Marcus Vipsanius Agrippa (64–12 BC) was Augustus' close friend, son-in-law, and the general responsible for Augustus' military victories. He led the forces at Actium against Antony and Cleopatra. Agrippa was also father-in-law of the second emperor, Tiberius, maternal grandfather to Caligula, and maternal great-grandfather to Nero. The crown studded with miniature prows of captured ships was given to Agrippa after a naval battle with Sextus Pompeius (63–35 BC), the son of Pompey the Great (106–48 BC), in 36 BC; Agrippa was the only man ever to wear it. This is the only time in the *Aeneid* where Vergil refers to contemporaries of Augustus, except for the reference to Marcellus (42–23 BC), the nephew and son-in-law of Augustus, in Book 6.

654 *...follows along*: The reference is to Antony's campaigns against the Parthians, a Persian people, in 41–36 BC. Bactria is in northern Afghanistan, the farthest east that Greco-Roman culture penetrated.

                                    Flames of flax,
flying iron weapons are thrown from every side,° and the fields
of Neptune grow red from the fresh slaughter. In the center
the queen signals her troops with her native sistrum, not yet
does she turn to view the two serpents at her back. All kinds
of monstrous gods and a barking Anubis throw weapons against   665
Neptune and Venus and against Minerva. Mars, chased in iron,
rages in the middle of the battle and the grim Furies from the sky,
and Discord in a torn robe strides rejoicing, and Bellona follows
with a bloody whip.°
                            Apollo of Actium, seeing these things
from above, drew his bow. Terrified, all of Egypt and India,   670
all the Arabs, and all the Sabaeans turned their backs.°
The queen herself is depicted giving her sails to the winds
that she has summoned, and now, even now, on the point
of releasing the slackened ropes. Amidst the slaughter Vulcan
had made her pale with her imminent death, carried along   675
by the waves and the northwest wind. Opposite her is the Nile,
mourning with his huge body and, opening its harbors, he spreads
wide water-colored robes and calls the conquered into its blue
breast and its sheltering streams.

the shield of Aeneas: triple triumph of Augustus

                            Next Augustus, entering
into the walls of Rome in a triple triumph, offers his immortal   680
vow to the gods of Italy, three hundred great shrines through
the whole city.° The roads ring with joy, with games, with
applause. In every temple there is a chorus of women,
and a sacrifice on every altar. Slaughtered bullocks cover

---

661 ... *every side*: The reference is to a Roman projectile with a steel shaft at the end of which was affixed
     a mass of flax soaked in pitch. The flax would be ignited and fired onto besieged targets.

669 ... *bloody whip*: The sistrum was a uniquely Egyptian rattle that consisted of horizontal bars loosely
     inserted through an open vertical frame. It was used in the cult of Isis, of which Cleopatra was a
     priestess. The two serpents behind Cleopatra (in the design of the shield) remind us of how she will
     die, bitten by an asp. Anubis was the Egyptian jackal-headed god; the Egyptian tendency to have
     gods with animal biforms was the subject of much ridicule by the Romans. Bellona was an ancient
     Roman goddess of war, sometimes the sister or wife of Mars.

671 ... *their backs*: Apollo had a temple on the promontory of Actium, which Augustus enlarged after the
     naval victory. The Sabaeans are from Sheba, an ancient kingdom in Yemen in the southern Arabian
     peninsula.

682 *whole city*: In 29 BC Augustus celebrated a triple triumph over three days for the Battle of Actium
     and his victories in Dalmatia (modern-day Croatia, on the east coast of the ADRIATIC) and
     ALEXANDRIA. By "three hundred shrines" is meant a large number.

685 the ground before the altars. Augustus himself, sitting
on the snow-white threshold of shining Phoebus, acknowledges
the gifts of nations and he hangs them on the proud posts.°
The conquered peoples march past in a long row—speaking
in how many languages, and how diverse in clothing and arms!
690 Here Mulciber showed the -races of the Nomads and the Africans
who wear gowns without cinches, then the Leleges and the Carians
and the quiver-bearing Gelonians. Euphrates runs now with gentler
waves, and the Morini, the most remote of men, and the twin-horned
Rhine River, and the unconquered Daha, and the Araxes humbled
695 by a bridge.°

    Aeneas marvels at such things on the shield, the gift
of his mother. He rejoices in the images, ignorant of what the future holds,
carrying on his shoulders the glory and the destiny of his descendants.

---

687 *proud posts*: Now the shield shows Augustus sitting before the new TEMPLE OF APOLLO on the Palatine Hill that he dedicated in 28 BC.

695 *... a bridge*: Mulciber is another name for Vulcan. The Nomads are a wandering African tribe who wear flowing gowns (the *galabiya*), as today. The Leleges and Carians are from southern Asia Minor, and the Geloni are from SCYTHIA. The Morini are a people of northern Gaul (France). The rivers appear on the shield as a procession of river-gods: Augustus was successful against the Parthians who live near the EUPHRATES; the Rhine River has two horns because river-gods were often portrayed with a bull's head. The Daha are a Scythian tribe. The Araxes River in Armenia washed away a bridge built by Alexander the Great, but Augustus restored it.

BOOK 9. *Turnus Besieges the Trojan Camp*

Lines 1–151 are omitted. Turnus attacks the Trojan camp but can make no headway. He attempts to burn the fleet in the river, but the ships are changed into sea nymphs and swim away. Turnus and the Rutulians camp on the plain outside the walls of the camp.

Nisus and Euryalus plot a raid

The whole army, sharing
in the dangers, keeps watch over the walls. They serve in turn
to guard any point that needs it. Nisus watches the gate, most fierce
in arms, the son of Hyrtacus, whom the huntress Ida° had sent   155
as a companion to Aeneas. He was swift with the javelin and with
light arrows. Euryalus, his companion, is with him. There was no other
of the followers of Aeneas, or of those who wore Trojan armor,
who was more handsome, a boy whose unshaven face showed
the first bloom of youth. A single love united the two, and they   160
charged into war side by side. At this time they also guarded the gate
at the same post.
                Nisus said: "Do the gods place this fire in men's
hearts, or does every man's fierce desire become a god to him?
My mind has long urged me to battle or to some great adventure.
It is not content with peace and quiet. You see how the Rutulians   165
are confident about the situation. Their campfires are far apart.
They have lain down, overcome by sleep and wine. All around
is silence.
    "Now this is what I am thinking, what I am wondering
about, what purpose surges in my mind. The people and the fathers
demand that Aeneas be returned, and that men be sent who can   170
report to him what is going on. If they agree to what I suggest—
the glory of doing it is enough for me—! I *think* I can find a way
under that hill to the walls and fortifications of PALLANTEUM."
    Euryalus, struck by a great love for glory, was impressed,
and at once replied to his ardent friend with these words: "Nisus—   175
are you against my joining you in these great undertakings

---

155 *Ida*: Ida is a nymph of Mount Ida near Troy.

as your ally? Shall I send you into such great danger alone? Not thus
did my father, Opheltes, accustomed to war, educate me, raised
amidst the terrors of the Greeks and the trials of Troy, nor have
180 I behaved in such a way with you in following great Aeneas
and his perilous fortunes. This—this is my spirit—a despiser of the day,
thinking the honor that you desire well bought even at the price of life!"

And Nisus answered: "For sure I had no such doubts about you.
That would not be right. No! Great Jupiter—or whoever looks upon
185 this action with favoring gaze—would not bring me back safely
if I ever thought such a thing. But if any chance—as one often sees
in such a crisis—if any chance or any god sweeps me to disaster,
I want *you* to survive. Your age makes you more deserving of life.

"But let there be someone to give me to the earth, either snatched from
190 the battle or ransomed for a price, or if Fortune forbids the accustomed
rites of burial, let someone perform them in my absence. May he honor
me with a cenotaph. And may I not be a cause of such great sorrow
to your poor mother, who alone of all the many mothers dared
to follow you, not caring for the protection of the city of Acestes."°
195 Euryalus answered: "You weave your empty objections for nothing.
Nor will my view change, or yield to yours. Let's go!" He rouses
the guards at once, and they come up to take over and maintain
the watch.

Nisus and Euryalus propose a sortie to the council

Leaving his post, Euryalus goes as companion to Nisus
to find Prince Ascanius. All the animals throughout the earth had relaxed
200 their cares in sleep, their hearts relieved of their labors. The principal
leaders of the Trojans, the prime of their youth, were holding council
concerning the highest affairs of the kingdom, what they should do
or who would be the messenger to Aeneas. They stand leaning on their
long spears, holding their shields, in an open space in the middle
205 of the camp. Then Nisus and Euryalus together beg eagerly to be admitted
at once, saying that the matter was of great importance, and worth their
while. Iulus first welcomed the impatient men and ordered Nisus to speak.

Then the son of Hyrtacus said: "Listen with a fair mind, O followers
of Aeneas, and do not judge my words by our youth. The Rutulians
210 have fallen silent, overcome by sleep and wine. We ourselves have
seen a place for a sortie. It opens out in the forked road leading to the gate
nearest the sea. There is a gap in the watch fires where black smoke rises

---

194 *of Acestes*: Acestes welcomed Aeneas when he arrived in SICILY (in Book 3), where the funeral games of Aeneas' father Anchises were held. Those of Aeneas' followers who wished to go no further remained behind, and, together with Acestes' people, they founded the city of Acesta (that is, EGESTA).

to the stars. If you give us permission to take advantage of this chance,
to go after Aeneas and the walls of Pallanteum, soon you will see us return
burdened with spoils after slaughtering many of the enemy. The road 215
will not deceive us as we go. We have seen the outskirts of the city
in our constant hunting in the dark valleys, and we are familiar with
the whole course of the river."

To these words Aletes,° heavy with years
and wise in mind, replied: "Gods of our fathers, under whose protection
Troy ever resides, you do not intend as yet to destroy the Trojans 220
when you bring such courage in our young men, and such brave hearts!"

So speaking, Aletes embraced the shoulders and took the hands
of both men, and he covered his face and lips with tears. "With what
prizes do I think that I can repay you? What is worthy of such glorious
deeds, my men? The gods and the knowledge of your own virtue 225
will give you the first and most beautiful prize. Then dutiful [*pius*] Aeneas
and Ascanius, untouched by age and always mindful of such great
merit, will at once reward you with other things."

Ascanius interrupted:
"But I entreat you both, Nisus—because my welfare depends on my
father's return—by the great Penates and by the Lar of Assaracus,° 230
by the innermost shrine of gray-haired Vesta. All my fortune and hope
I place in your lap. Call back my father, return him to my sight.
There is no sorrow once he is returned. I will give you twin cups
made of silver, embossed with figures, that my father captured when
he conquered Arisbê,° and two tripods, two large talents of gold, 235
and an ancient wine-mixing bowl that Sidonian Dido gave me.

"But if we manage to capture Italy and make it part of our realm
and assign the spoils by lot—you have seen the horse on which golden
Turnus rode, and the arms he wore—well, I will set aside that horse,
and his shield and scarlet plumes as your reward, Nisus. Furthermore, 240
my father will give you twelve chosen women, and male prisoners
with all their armor, and beyond that whichever lands King Latinus
himself owns.

"But I welcome you wholly to my heart, Euryalus,
a boy to be honored, whose age I come close to. I embrace you
as a companion for all occasions. Never will I seek glory in my campaigns 245
without you. Whether in peace or war, you will have my utmost trust
in deeds and in words."

And Euryalus said this in reply: "No day will find
me unequal to bold undertakings—only let good fortune not turn to bad.

---

218 *Aletes*: Mentioned during the storm of Book 1.

230 *Assaracus*: A Trojan ancestor (see Genealogical Chart).

235 *Arisbê*: Arisbê is a town in the Troad, but nothing else is known about Aeneas' sack of this town.

FIGURE 9.1 *Euryalus and Nisus at the Trojan Council,* c. AD 400, from the Vatican Vergil (see Figure 3.1). The important figures are labeled. At the top center Ascanius sits on a chair, with Nisus on the left and Euryalus on the right. Five Trojans with spears and shields stand on either side. Aletes speaks from the lower left. A wall surrounds the Trojan camp. Paint on vellum.

But I ask you for one gift above all. I have a mother from the ancient
race of Priam. Neither the land of Troy nor the walls of King Acestes
held her back, unhappy woman, when I set forth. I leave her now,
ignorant of this danger, whatever it might be. I have not said goodbye.
This night and your right hand bear witness, I could not bear a mother's
tears. But I beg you, comfort her in her helplessness, and help her
in her loss. Allow me to carry with me this hope in you. Then I will
enter every danger more boldly."

    The Trojans wept, struck in their spirit,
and above all the handsome Iulus. This image of a son's love touched
his heart. Then he says: "Be sure that I will do all that is worthy
of your great undertaking. For she will be as a mother to me,
lacking only the name of Creüsa.° Nor will there be small gratitude
for bearing such a son. Whatever will come from your deed, I swear
on my head, by which my father has been accustomed to swear:
What I promised to you on your return, if all things go well—
these prizes will still come to your mother and to your family."

    So he spoke in tears. At the same time he took off his golden
sword from his shoulder, fitted to his hand, which Lycaon of Cnossus
had made with wondrous art, and held in an ivory scabbard.
Mnestheus gives Nisus a skin, the shaggy spoils of a lion. The faithful
Aletes exchanges his helmet.

the raid of Nisus and Euryalus

    Armed, the men leave at once. The whole
band of captains, young and old, conduct them to the gates, saying
prayers. And even the handsome Iulus, with a mind more mature
than his years, doing the duty of a grown man, gave them many
orders to carry to his father—but the winds scatter them away, and give
them to the clouds, useless.

    The two men leave and cross over the ditches
and through the shadow of night they seek the enemy encampment—
though they are doomed!—to be the destruction of many. Here and there
they see bodies scattered on the grass, overcome by sleep and wine,
chariots tilted upwards on the shore, men in the midst of harness
and wheels, arms and jars of wine scattered about.

    Nisus, the son
of Hyrtacus, speaks first: "Euryalus, we must be bold in our attack.
The situation calls out for it. The road is this way. You must guard

---

260 *Creüsa*: Creüsa, "princess," the mother of Ascanius, perished in the sack of Troy (reported in Book 2).

that no hand is raised against us from our backs. Keep careful watch.
I'll do big damage, and I'll cut you a wide path."
                                        Thus Nisus speaks,
then falls silent. At once Nisus attacks the proud Rhamnes with his sword,
285 who by chance was breathing deeply in sound asleep, covered by thick
blankets. A king himself, he was King Turnus' favorite seeing-man—
but unable to avert his own destruction through his seership.
          Nisus kills three of his servants who lie carelessly among their weapons,
and the armor-bearer of Remus and his charioteer whom he found
290 at his horse's feet. With his sword he cuts off their drooping heads.
Then he cuts off the head of Remus himself and leaves the trunk
spurting blood. The earth and the couch grow wet with the black
warm gore. Then he kills Lamyrus and Lamus and the young Serranus,
noted for his good looks, who had gambled late into the night,
295 who lay there, his limbs overcome by much wine—happy, if only
he had played all the night long and continued his play to the dawn!
          Even as a lion roars through a full sheepfold (for an insane hunger
drives him on), and he chews and tears at the gentle flock, mute with fear,
and he rages with bloody mouth: Even so was the slaughter done by Euryalus.
300 He rages, on fire, and amidst the nameless crowd he attacks Fadus
and Herbesus and Abaris, all unconscious, and Rhoetus—but Rhoetus
was awake and saw it all, hiding in fear behind a huge wine-bowl.
          Euryalus buried his whole sword in his chest, coming up close as Rhoetus
rose up, and Euryalus pulled it out, drenched in death. Rhoetus vomits
305 out the dark blood of his life, and wine mixed with blood as he dies.
And Euryalus presses on, eagerly, with his stealthy massacre.
                                        Now he moves
toward the allies of Messapus. There Euryalus saw low lights
of the campfires and the horses securely tethered, grazing on the grass.
Nisus spoke briefly when he saw that Euryalus was carried away
310 by the love of slaughter: "Let's hold off," he said, "for the dangerous
dawn is approaching. We've done enough damage. We have made
a path through the enemy."
                              They leave behind many of the men's weapons,
made of solid silver, and wine-bowls and gorgeous weavings.
Euryalus grabs up Rhamnes' breastplate and his gold-studded belt,
315 which once the wealthy Caedicus had sent to Remulus of Tibur as gifts
when Caedicus wished to join with Remulus in friendship, although
they had never met. When Remulus died, he gave them to his grandson
as his own, and after his death the Rutulians captured them in a battle.
And now Euryalus fits them to brave shoulders—in vain!
320 Then he puts on Messapus' fine helmet with its handsome crest.
They leave the camp and head off to safety.

the death of Nisus and Euryalus

                              In the meanwhile
Rutulian cavalry arrive, sent ahead from the city of Latinus while the rest
of the Latin forces delayed in readiness on the plain. They brought
a reply to Turnus:° There were three hundred men with shields,
with the Rutulian Volcens as commander.
                                      And now they come near
the camp and form up beneath the walls, when in the distance they see
two men turning down a path, on the left. His helmet betrayed
the thoughtless Euryalus in the low shadow of night, reflecting back
the rays of the moon. The shining helmet was not seen in vain.
Volcens shouts from the line: "Hold it, men! Why are you traveling?
Who are you?—armed I see. Where are you going?"
                                            The Trojans gave no answer
in reply, but hastened their flight into the woods, trusting to the darkness.
But the Rutulian cavalry cut off all the byways on every side, so familiar
to them, and surrounded every way out with a guard. The forest spread
wide, dark with brambles and thick with scrub-oak that dense thorns
filled from every side. Only occasionally was the path visible through
the hidden clearings. The shadows of the branches and the burdensome
booty impede Euryalus, and fear confuses his sense of the path's direction.
      Nisus is now away, unaware that Euryalus is not behind him.
He has escaped the enemy. He was at the place later called "Alban"
from the name of Alba°—at this time King Latinus had his great
cattle enclosures there—when Nisus stopped and looked back, vainly,
for his friend. "Unlucky Euryalus, where did we get separated? Where
should I go?" he said, considering all the perplexing ways through
the deceptive forest.
                     At the same time he scans the footprints that lead
backwards, and he wanders through the silent brambles. He hears horses,
he hears the cries and the signals of the pursuers. It was not long before
he hears their shouting and he sees Euryalus, betrayed by the place
and by the night and confused by the sudden onrush.
                                               The whole band
has taken him and are dragging him off, struggling terrifically—uselessly.
What should Nisus do? With what power, with what weapons dare he save
the youth? Or should he throw himself to his death in the middle of their
swords? Should he hasten sweet death through his wounds?

---

324 *to Turnus*: In fact, we have not previously heard of any message sent by Turnus to Latinus.

341 *Alba*: Nothing is known of this place, unless the name comes from ALBA LONGA (but that is a good distance away from the Trojan camp).

                                                                Quickly
cocking his spear arm, and looking upwards, he prays with these words:
355 "You, goddess—you be present! Support our task, the glory of the stars,
keeper of the woods, daughter of Latona!° If ever my father Hyrtacus
carried gifts on my behalf to your altars, if ever I myself added to them
through my hunting, or hung gifts from the dome of your temple,
or fixed them to your sacred eaves—let me throw this troop into confusion.
360 Guide my spear through the air!"
                                He spoke, and putting all his weight behind
it he threw the steel. The flying spear divides the shadows of the night
and strikes the back of Sulmon as he turned. It breaks and the broken
shaft penetrates his heart. Sulmon is spun around, vomiting a hot fluid
from his chest. He grows cold. Long gasps shake his sides. The Rutulians
365 look around in all directions.
                                Behold, still more eager, Nisus balances a second
spear from high up against his ear. While the Rutulians hesitate, the spear
goes hissing through both temples of Tagus and sticks, transfixed, still hot,
in his brain. Savage Volcens rages but he cannot see who is responsible
for the act, nor where he can strike in his ardor.
                                                "In the meantime you will pay
370 me with hot blood for both these men," he said, while at the same time
he runs toward Euryalus, raising his naked sword. Terrified, out of his mind,
Nisus shouts aloud, but he can no more hide in the shadows or sustain
such anguish.
            "Turn your weapons against me—me! I did the deed,
O Rutulians! All the guilt is mine. He dared nothing, nor was he able
375 to accomplish anything. The heavens and the stars testify to this.
He only loved his unhappy friend too much."
                                        Nisus was saying such things,
but the sword, powerfully driven, goes through Euryalus' ribs and breaks
open his white breast. Euryalus turns over in death. The blood runs
over his beautiful limbs, and his neck, drooping, sinks into his shoulders—
380 just as when a dark red flower, cut by the plow, languishes in death,
or a poppy bends over its weary head when a chance shower weighs
it down.
        But Nisus rushes into their midst, seeking Volcens before
all, intent on him alone. The enemy gathers together around him.
They drive against him, close in, on this side and that. Nisus attacks
385 nonetheless. He whirls his sword like lightning until he buries it full
in the face of the screaming Volcens and, as Nisus dies, he takes the life
of his enemy Rutulian.

---

356 *Latona*: The Roman name for Leto, the mother of Artemis, who is here identified with Luna, the moon.

Then, pierced through, Nisus threw himself over
his lifeless friend, and at last found peace in the calm of death. Lucky two!
If my poetry has any power, no day will ever erase you from time's
memory so long as the house of Aeneas stands beside the immobile 390
stone of the capitol, and a Roman father commands the empire.°

Lines 392–710 are omitted. Turnus attacks the camp again. Ascanius kills his first man, then Apollo removes him from the fighting. Turnus is trapped inside the city, kills many, then escapes by leaping into the river.

---

391 … *the empire*: The "house of Aeneas" would be the ruling family of Augustus and the whole of the Roman people. The "Roman father" is presumably Augustus as the head of the Roman aristocracy, taking the title as head of the *patres*, "fathers," and as representative of the *patria potestas*, "the power of the father," that characterizes the Roman family. Thus Aeneas is called *pater*, an indirect compliment to Augustus.

BOOK 10. *The Deaths of Pallas, Lausus, and Mezentius*

In the meanwhile the palace of all-powerful Olympus is thrown
open, and the father of gods and the king of men summons
an assembly to his starry house, from whose heights he sees
all the earth, and the camp of the Trojans, and the Latin people.
5   The gods take their seat in the palace with gates at both ends.

Venus complains that Fate is not allowed to take its way

    Jupiter begins: "Great dwellers in heaven, why have you changed
your decision? Why, *why* do you compete in such a hostile spirit?
I have ordered that Italy not make war against the Trojans!
Why then is there such disagreement, contrary to what I ordered?
10   What fear has persuaded the Trojans and the Italians to take
up arms and pursue war?° The right time for war will come—
don't bring it on!—when savage Carthage, passing through the Alps,°
will one day bring destruction to the Roman strongholds.
Then is the time to compete in hatred, to plunder one another.
15   For now let it go—conclude a treaty in joy, as I have decreed."
    So Jupiter spoke briefly. But golden Venus answers at length:
"O Father, eternal power over men and all affairs! For who else
can I appeal to now? You see how the Rutulians are exultant,
and that Turnus is borne on proud horses through the crowd
20   and rushes on, swollen by his good fortune in war?° Close walls
no longer protect the Trojans. In fact they join battle inside
the gates and on the ramparts of the walls themselves, and the ditches
overflow with blood. Aeneas does not know what is going on—
he is absent!
    "Will you never permit the siege to end? A second
25   enemy, a second army again threatens the walls of a newborn Troy,

---

11 *pursue war*: Jupiter implies that interference by some gods has driven the opposing sides to be fearful and go to war.

12 *the Alps*: The reference is to Hannibal's invasion of 218 BC.

20 *in war*: In fact Turnus did all his fighting on the ground, but Venus is more concerned with rhetorical effect than factual accuracy.

and again Diomedes, the son of Tydeus, from Aetolian ARPI,°
rises against the Trojans. I almost believe that the wounds I received
from Diomedes still await me—and that I, your child, only delay
that mortal's attack.°

                  "If the Trojans have come to Italy without
your permission and against your will, let them pay for their 30
offense—you need not come to their aid. But if they have
followed the many oracles of the powers above and below,°
why should anyone now be able to turn aside your commands
or fashion fresh fates? Why should I remind you of their fleet
burned on the shore of ERYX? Or mention the king of the winds 35
and the furious winds roused from AEOLIA, or Iris sent down from
the clouds?° Now Juno rouses up even the dead—the only province
of the universe left untouched—and Allecto, sent up suddenly
to the upper world, runs wild through the middle of the Italian cities.
I no longer have any care for empire. We had hoped for those things, 40
while Fortune favored us.

                  "But let those be victorious whom
you prefer to be victorious. If there is no land that your hard wife
grants, I beg of you, Father, by the smoking ruins of conquered
Troy, that I be allowed to release Ascanius safely from the war,
that my grandson be allowed to survive. May Aeneas, yes, may 45
he be tossed on unknown seas, and follow whatever path that
Fortune grants, but let me have the power to protect this young
man and to remove him from the dire conflict. I have Amathus,
I have high Paphus, and CYTHERA, and a temple in Idalia.° Let him
put aside his weapons and live out his life there. Command 50
that CARTHAGE, with its great power, crush Ausonia: There will
be no resistance from *there* to the Tyrian cities!° What was

---

26 *Aetolian Arpi*: Diomedes, one of the principal Greek warriors who besieged Troy, migrated to Arpi in southern Italy. In Book 8 we learned that Turnus had sent to him to ask for aid (but Diomedes refused, we later learn).

29 *mortal's attack*: In Book 5 of the *Iliad* Diomedes stabs Aphrodite/Venus in the hand, causing her to bleed *ichor*, the blood of the gods.

32 *above and below*: Aeneas has received repeated prophecies that he must seek Italy: from Mercury and Apollo (the powers above), and from Hector and Anchises (the powers below).

37 *... the clouds*: The rebellious Trojan women burned four of Aeneas' ships outside Eryx in Sicily (Book 5); Aeolus, under Juno's promptings, sent a great storm from his island of AEOLIA (Book 1); Iris, Juno's special messenger, stirred up Turnus to burn Aeneas' ships and to attack his camp (Books 5 and 9).

49 *... in Idalia*: Amathus, Paphos, and Idalia are sanctuaries of Venus on the island of CYPRUS; Cythera is an island off the south coast of Greece where there was a temple to Venus, from which Venus is called "Cytherean."

52 *Tyrian cities*: An ironic pronouncement—Venus implies that Rome would yield to the power of Carthage (founded from Phoenician TYRE) without resistance, something in fact unthinkable.

the point in the Trojans' escaping the plague of war, fleeing
through the middle of Argive fires, enduring the dangers
55 of so many seas, and the vast land, while the Trojans seek
LATIUM and a resurrected TROY? Would it not have been better
that they rebuilt on the last embers of their fatherland, on the soil
where Troy once stood?

                      "Give back XANTHUS and SIMOEIS,
I beg of you, and grant, O Father, that the Trojans live *again*
60 through their disastrous misfortunes!"°

Juno says it is all Aeneas' fault

                                  Then Queen Juno, driven
to a wild frenzy, said: "Why do you force me to break my deep
silence and reveal in words the anger I keep within?
Who of men or gods has forced Aeneas to pursue war
or make himself an enemy to King Latinus? He sought Italy
65 compelled by the Fates, driven by the ravings of Cassandra—
fine! Have we urged him to leave the camp, or to commit his life
to the winds? to turn over the outcome of the war, the Trojan
defenses, to a *child*? to upset the loyalty of the Etruscans,°
or that of peaceful tribes? What goddess, what hard power
70 of *ours* has driven him to harm? Where is Juno in all this,
or Iris sent down from the clouds?

                                  "You say that it is unworthy
that the Italians surround with flames a reborn Troy, and that
Turnus takes his stand on his native soil, whose ancestor is Pilumnus,
whose mother is the divine Venilia°—well, what about the Trojans
75 bringing violence against the Latins with their smoking brands,
or planting their yoke on a stranger's fields and taking away
their plunder? What about their picking whose daughters
they will marry? What about their snatching *betrothed* girls
from their lovers' embrace? They offer peace with one hand,
80 but array their ships with weapons.

                                      "You can steal away Aeneas
from the hands of the Greeks, and offer them a cloud and empty

---

60 ... *misfortunes*: Xanthus and Simoeis are rivers on the Trojan plain. Venus means that after suffering so many troubles in their travels, the Trojans deserve a glorious future; if this is to be denied them, they might as well return to Troy and suffer again the destruction of their city.

68 *Etruscans*: In her exaggerated expressions Juno refers to Mezentius' alliance with Turnus, although there is no reason for the rest of the Etruscans to follow him (in fact the reverse, because Mezentius was expelled from the Etruscan community).

74 ... *Venilia*: Pilumnus was the grandfather or great-grandfather of Turnus, an Italian agricultural god. Venilia was a sea-nymph.

winds° instead of a man. You can turn the fleet into so many nymphs:
Is it forbidden then that *we* give a little help to the Rutulians?
'Aeneas knows nothing about this and he is absent.' Well, let him
be absent and remain in ignorance! You have Paphus and Idalium 85
and high Cythera is yours. Why do you provoke a city pregnant
with wars and ferocious hearts? Is it *I* who tries to overturn
from its base the frail Trojan affairs? Is it *I* who threw up the Greeks
against the wretched Trojans? What reason was there for Europe
and Asia to rise up in arms, to dissolve their compact through 90
treachery?° Did the Trojan adulterer conquer Sparta under my
leadership? Did I give him weapons or foment war because
of his lust?

"Then you should have shown some fear for your affairs:
now, late in the game, you raise unjust complaints. You provoke
ridiculous quarrels!" 95

So Juno spoke, and all the dwellers in heaven
murmured their different views, just as when the first rustlings
of wind sigh, caught in the forest, and they send forth unseen
murmurs, revealing to sailors the storms that are soon to come.

Jupiter says: leave it up to Fate

Then the all-powerful father, the greatest power over all the world,
begins—and as he spoke the high palace of the gods falls silent, 100
and the earth is shaken underground, and the high air is silent,
and the west winds come to a stop, and the sea calms its quiet waters:

"Take my words to heart, and fix them there! Since it is hardly
possible that the Italians be joined in alliance with the Trojans,
and your quarrel has no end, I will draw no distinction between 105
Trojan and Rutulian, whatever is the fortune of each on this day,
or whatever hopes each may pursue—whether the camp is under
siege because of Italy's fate, or because of an evil mistake on the part
of the Trojans, who relied on bad advice. But I do not absolve the Rutulians.
What each has instigated will bring its own pain and its own 110
fortune. Jupiter is king of all, indifferently. Fate will find a way."

He nods his head, swearing by the waters of his brother Styx
and by the banks that seethe with pitch and a black chasm, and he shakes
all Olympus with his nod. Here the speaking ended. Then Jupiter rises
up from his golden throne, and the dwellers in heaven, gathering 115
around him, lead him to the threshold.

---

82   *empty winds*: The reference is to the story in the *Iliad* (Book 5) in which Aphrodite/Venus saves Aeneas from Diomedes and Apollo by concealing him in a cloud.

91   *through treachery*: That is, through Paris' abduction of Helen although he was a guest of Menelaus.

FIGURE 10.1 *Jupiter and Juno*, **c. 1590, by Giovanni Ambrogio Figino (c. 1550–1608).**
Figino was an Italian Mannerist painter from Milan, a member of the so-called Lombard school of painting. He is famous as a draftsman, but he was also an expert portrait painter who here shows Juno and Jupiter conversing with one another in an erotic context, indicated by the cupid at Jupiter's back. At Jupiter's feet, to the left, is an eagle, his special bird; to his right stands a bull, to which Jupiter's power was often compared. To the left of Juno stands a peacock, her emblem, crossed by a rainbow, because Iris "the rainbow" was Juno's messenger. Juno is sexily dressed with a red cloth, the color of passion, thrown over her shoulder. Her head is beautifully coifed. Oil on canvas.

Lines 117–403 are omitted. While the battle at the camp continues, Aeneas nears the camp with his Etruscan allies. Sea-nymphs, formerly his ships, greet him. Aeneas lands and sends his troops against the Rutulians. He and Pallas distinguish themselves in the bitter fight.

                        Still, the master of great Olympus
did not allow Pallas and Lausus° to meet face to face. Their fate awaits
them under a greater enemy. In the meanwhile Turnus' kindly sister,   405
the nymph Juturna, advises Turnus to give Lausus aid, and Turnus cuts
through the ranks between them with his swift chariot. When Turnus sees
his companions, he says: "It is time to pull back from the battle.
I alone will take on Pallas! Pallas is owed to me alone. I wish his father
were here to watch!"   410
                     And his companions pulled back from the field,
as commanded. When the Rutulians pulled back, the young Pallas,
amazed at Turnus' bold command, wonders at seeing him. He casts
his eyes over the huge body. He surveys all of Turnus from a distance
with a savage glance, and he speaks as follows to the king: "I will soon
be praised—either for taking such splendid spoils, or for a famous death.   415
My father is ready for either fate. Forget your threats."
                                   So speaking, Pallas
advances into the middle of the field. Cold blood rises into the hearts
of the Arcadians. Turnus leaps down from his chariot. He readies
to fight in the hand-to-hand, on foot—as a lion rushes down when
he sees from a high outlook a bull far off on the plain, meditating battle.   420
     Pallas came forward first, when he thought that Turnus was within
spear-shot range, hoping that chance would help him against the odds.
Pallas speaks loudly to the sky: "By the hospitality of my father,
and the meals that you shared as a stranger,° I beg you, Hercules—
be present in my great undertakings. May you witness me take   425
bloody arms from this dying man, and may Turnus' dying eyes
behold me as victor!"
                           Hercules heard the youth, and he stifled a great
moan from the bottom of his heart, and he poured forth empty tears.°
Then Father Jupiter speaks to his son Hercules° with friendly words:
"Every man has his day, and the time of life is short and irretrievable   430
for all. The task of virtue is to increase one's fame by deeds.
So many sons of gods fell beneath the high wall of Troy—and together

---

404 *Lausus*: The son of the tyrannical Mezentius.

424 *stranger*: Pallas refers to the hospitality that Evander showed Hercules when he was returning from Spain on his adventures.

428 *empty tears*: Hercules knows that because of Fate he cannot save Pallas.

429 *Hercules*: Hercules was the son of Jupiter and the mortal woman Alcmenê.

with them Sarpedon,° my child. Turnus, too, has his own fate,
and he comes to the turning post of the life that is given him."

435 So Jupiter spoke, and he turned his eyes from the Rutulians.
But Pallas casts his spear with all his might, and he pulls his shining
sword from its hollow sheathe. The spear flies and strikes Turnus where
the top of his breastplate covered his shoulder. Passing through the rim
of his shield, the spear grazed Turnus' powerful body.

                                                                                                       At this Turnus, poising
440 for a long time his shaft with point of sharp steel affixed, casts against
Pallas, saying: "See whether this weapon of ours is better at penetration!"

     He spoke. The point of the spear, with a quivering blow, passes
through the middle of Pallas' shield, penetrating so many layers
of iron, so many layers of bronze, and the layers of bull's hide
445 that covered it with its many folds. It pierces the barrier of Pallas'
breastplate and his powerful breast. Vainly he pulls the hot spear
from the wound. Blood and his life follow at the same time, from
the same path. He falls in his own blood. His arms clang over him.
Dying, he strikes the hostile earth with his bloody mouth.

                                                                                               Turnus, standing
450 over him, says: "Arcadians, take note of this, and carry my words
to Evander. I return Pallas to him as Pallas deserved. I bestow whatever
honor there is in a tomb, whatever solace there is in burying him.
His hospitality to Aeneas will cost him dearly."

                                                                       And saying these things,
he put his foot on Pallas' lifeless body and tore away the huge weight
455 of Pallas' belt, embossed with the Danaïds' wicked crime—the band
of young men foully cut down, and the blood-drenched wedding chambers
that Clonus, the son of Eurytus, had richly chased on the belt in gold.°

     Now Turnus exults at the spoil, rejoicing to have captured it.
How ignorant are men of Fate and of what the future will bring!
460 And how to keep to a moderate path when raised on high by fortunate
events? The time will come for Turnus when he would give anything
not to have touched Pallas, when he will hate these spoils and this day.°

     But Pallas' companions gather together and carry off Pallas with
much moaning and many tears, placing him on his shield. O you who
465 are destined to return to your father, bringing great grief, and yet great glory!

---

433 *Sarpedon*: The famous Lycian warrior, son of Jupiter and Europa, whom Patroclus kills in the *Iliad*.

457 *in gold*: The fifty daughters of Danaüs married the fifty sons of Aegyptus, but on the instructions of Danaüs forty-nine of the women killed their husbands. Only one spared her husband because he had spared her virginity. Part of the story is told in Aeschylus' surviving play *The Suppliants* (c. 470 BC). Nothing is known of Clonus, the artist.

462 *this day*: Because the *Aeneid* ends when Aeneas sees this belt on Turnus and in a rage kills him.

This day first gave you to war, and the same day bore you away—
nevertheless you leave behind huge piles of the Rutulian dead!

the rage of Aeneas

                                                  Now not
merely a rumor of the great evil, but a more certain messenger fled
to Aeneas, reporting that his men were a hair's breadth from death,
and that it was time to come to the aid of his Trojans, turned in rout.   470
      Seeking you, Turnus, proud from your recent kill, Aeneas mows down
those nearest him with his sword and, on fire with rage, he plows a broad
path with his steel through the line of battle. Pallas, Evander—all are
before his eyes, the banquets to which he had come first as a stranger,
and the right hands shaken in oaths.   475
                                    Then he captures alive the four sons
of Sulmo, and as many raised by Ufens,° to sacrifice to the infernal shades,
and to sprinkle the flames of the pyre with the prisoners' blood. Then
he aimed a deadly spear at Magus from a distance, but Magus skillfully
dashed under it and the trembling spear flies past.
                                                     Grasping Aeneas' knees,
he says, a suppliant: "By the spirit of your father and the hope   480
of the growing Iulus, I beg you—preserve my life, for my son and my father.
I have a noble house, and talents of chased silver lie buried within.
I have masses of worked and unworked gold. Victory for the Trojans
does not lie with me, nor will one life make much of a difference."
So he spoke, and Aeneas said in reply: "You speak of many talents   485
of silver and gold—keep them for your sons! Turnus has earlier removed
this sort of trading in war when he took the life of Pallas. The spirit
of my father Anchises thinks this, and so does Iulus." So speaking, Aeneas
holds Magus' helmet in his left hand and, bending Magus' head back
as he begged, Aeneas buries his sword up to the hilt.   490
                                            Not far off
was the son of Haemon,° a priest of Apollo and Diana, his brows
bound by a sacred ribbon, shining in his vestments and his white emblems.
Coming up close, Aeneas drove him over the plain. Then, standing
over him as he fell, covering him with his huge shadow, Aeneas cuts
him down. Serestus takes his armor up on his shoulders and carries it off,   495
a trophy to you, O King Mars!
                                    Caeculus, born of the race of Vulcan,

---

476   ... *Ufens*: Sulmo is mentioned in Book 9; Ufens is part of the Italian forces in Book 7.

491   *son of Haemon*: Not mentioned elsewhere.

and Umbro, who came from the Marsian Hills,° renew the battle against
Aeneas: But the Trojan raged against them. His sword sliced off the left
hand of Anxur°—it fell to the ground with the whole disc of his shield.
500 Anxur had spoken some boast, thinking that words would help him out,
lifting his spirits to the heavens perhaps, and he promised himself
a white-haired old age and a long life.
                      Then Tarquitus, nearby, exultant
in his flashing armor, whom the Nymph Dryopê bore to forest-dwelling
Faunus,° exposed himself to the fiery Aeneas, but drawing back his spear
505 Aeneas pinned together the breastplate and the weight of Tarquitus' shield.
As Tarquitus begs in vain, trying with words to persuade Aeneas,
Aeneas dashes his head to the ground. Rolling over the warm trunk,
he speaks these words from a hostile heart: "Lie there now, most
fearsome one. Your good mother will not bury you in the earth,
510 nor place your limbs in your ancestral tomb. You are left for the wild
birds, or submerged in the sea a wave will carry you, and hungry fish
will lick your wounds."
                    Then Aeneas goes after Antaeus and Lucas
in Turnus' front line, and brave Numa and light-haired Camers,
the son of noble Volcens, the richest man in Ausonia's land, who
515 was king in silent Amyclae.° Like Aegaeon, who they say has
one-hundred arms and one-hundred hands, and that fire flashed from
his fifty mouths and chests when he clashed with the thunderbolts
of Jove, with as many shields, all alike, and as many swords:° Even so
does Aeneas rage victoriously over the whole plain, once his sword
520 grew hot.
    And see, how Aeneas heads toward the four-horse chariot
of Niphaeus, the horses' chests turned toward him. When they saw
Aeneas coming from far off in a wild frenzy, they shied from fear and galloped
away, throwing their driver and dragging the car toward the shore.
    In the meanwhile Lucagus and his brother Liger enter the fight with

---

497 ...*Marsian Hills*: Caeculus, son of Vulcan, and Umbro were mentioned in Book 7. The Marsian Hills are the foothills of the Apennines east of Rome.

499 *Anxur*: We never hear any more about this man or the many other Rutulians that Aeneas now kills.

504 ...*Faunus*: Dryopê was a wood-nymph ("she of the oak"), and Faunus was one of the many rural Italian deities with this name (this is not the Faunus who is the father of Latinus).

515 ...*Amyclae*: Volcens led the Latins in Book 9 and was killed by Nisus. According to the ancient commentary by Servius, Amyclae, a town on the coast, was silent because after many false alarms the town decreed that no one could any longer claim that an enemy was approaching.

518 ...*many swords*: Aegaeon is another name for Briareus, one of the hundred-handers who fought Jupiter in the Titanomachy, the battle between the gods and the Titans prominent in Greek myth. He is present at the mouth of the underworld in Book 6.

two white horses, Liger handling the horses' reins and fierce Lucagus 525
swinging his drawn sword. Aeneas could not endure men raging with
such hotheaded fury. He rushes toward them, and he looms huge with
his spear. Liger says to Aeneas: "You do not see the horses of Diomedes,
nor the chariot of Achilles, nor the plain of Troy:° Now the end of war
and life is yours!"° 530
        Such words fly far from foolish Liger. But the Trojan
speaks not in return. He casts his spear at the enemy. While Lucagus
urges on his horses, leaning over and striking them with the side
of his blade as he readies for battle, his left foot advanced—the spear
passes through the bottom rim of his shining shield and perforates
his left groin. Shaken from the chariot, Lucagus is cast dying onto the field. 535
    The dutiful [*pius*] Aeneas speaks to Lucagus with bitter words: "Well
Lucagus, it was not the flight of your horses that betrayed your slow chariot,
or the empty shadows of the enemy that turned them. You yourself, leaping
from the wheels, gave up the reins."
        Saying these things, Aeneas takes control
of the team. Lucagus' unlucky brother Liger, fallen out, held out his 540
useless hands. "By your own life, man of Troy, and by those parents who
begot you, spare this life! Take pity on a suppliant!"
        And Aeneas answered,
as the man begged: "This is not what you said before. Die, and don't
let a brother abandon a brother!"
        With his sword he sliced open Liger's
chest, the hiding place of life. Such were the deaths that Aeneas, raging 545
like a torrent of water or a dark storm, caused on the plain.
        Now at last the boy
Ascanius and his Trojans, besieged in vain, burst forth and leave the camp.

Lines 547–620 are omitted. Juno creates a phantom in the likeness of Aeneas and lures Turnus onto one of the ships, which she then sets adrift. Turnus is carried back to his hometown of Ardea.

the glory of Mezentius

        But in the meanwhile the fiery Mezentius,
because of Jove's advice, comes into the battle and attacks the jubilant
Trojans. The Etruscan lines close up, and with all their hatred

---

529 *plain of Troy*: In the *Iliad* Aeneas was rescued from Diomedes by Aphrodite/Venus and Apollo (*Iliad* Book 5) and from Achilles by Poseidon/Neptune (*Iliad* Book 20).

530 *... is yours*: That is, you (Aeneas) survived the Greek campaign at Troy, but you won't survive this campaign.

and all their shower of weapons they concentrate on Mezentius alone.
625 Mezentius—like a vast cliff that projects into the vast sea, facing the fury
of the winds and exposed to the sea, suffering all the violence
and the threats of sky and sea, but itself unmoved—he brings
down to the ground Hebrus° the son of Dolichaon. Accompanying Hebrus
were Latagus and fast Palmus, but Mezentius got in first and hits Latagus
630 with a huge stone in the mouth—the fragment of a mountain!—
as Latagus turned toward him, then he cuts Palmus' hamstrings and leaves
him writhing helplessly. He gave Lausus the armor to wear on his shoulders
and the plumes to fix on his helmet.
                                    Mezentius killed Euanthes too, the Phrygian,
and Mimas, the age-mate and companion of Paris, whom Theano bore
635 to his father Amycus on the same night that Hecuba, the royal daughter
of Cisseus, pregnant with a firebrand, gave birth to Paris.° Paris lies
in the city of his fathers, the Laurentine shore holds the unknown Mimas.
    And just as a boar, which pine-bearing Vesulus has protected
for many years, and the Laurentine marshes has nourished in its thicket
640 of reeds,° is driven from the high mountains by snapping hounds,
and he takes his stand after he has come within the hunters' nets,
and he rages ferociously, bristling all along his back, and no one
has the courage to go against him in anger, but all the hunters attack
him with spears and shouts from a distance—and the boar stops, without fear,
645 and he turns in every direction and grinds his teeth, and he shakes
the spears from his back. Even so none of those who were justly angry
with Mezentius had the courage to attack him with drawn sword.
Instead, they assault him from a distance with missiles and with
a huge shouting.
                Acron came from the ancient lands of Etruscan Corythus,
650 a Greek, leaving as an exile, his wedding incomplete. When Mezentius saw
him from a distance, thrown into confusion in the middle of the ranks,
with purple crest and wearing the crimson given by his promised bride,
Mezentius rushes eagerly against the mass of men—like a starving lion
that often wanders the deep hiding-places, for hunger drives him on,
655 if by chance he might see a quick she-goat or a stag just growing
its horns, and he rejoices, gaping mightily, and his mane bristles,
and he hangs crouching over the entrails, and his cruel mouth
is loathsomely covered with blood.
                                    Unlucky Acron goes down

---

628 *Hebrus*: This victim of Mezentius, and the others who follow, are unknown elsewhere.

636 *to Paris*: Hecuba, the daughter of Cisseus, dreamed that she was pregnant with a firebrand before giving birth to Paris.

640 *... of reeds*: Vesulus is a mountain in LIGURIA, the source of the Po River. The Laurentine marshes are of course in Latium.

and strikes the black earth with his heels as he breathes his last.
He covers his shattered weapons with blood.
                                         Mezentius did not
stoop to kill Orodes as he ran away, nor to give him a hidden wound
with a thrust of his spear: He ran up against him and fought him
in the hand-to-hand—Mezentius, a better man than Orodes not by stealth,
but by force of arms! Then he placed his foot on the body to pull out
the spear. He said: "Here lies noble Orodes, no small part of this battle."
     The companions of Mezentius all cry out in a joyful song of praise.
But Orodes says as he dies: "You are not victorious over me—whoever you are—
unavenged . . . you will not rejoice for long. The same fate awaits you
and soon you will lie in the same ground."°
                                         To which Mezentius replied,
grinning with anger: "Now die! As for me, the father of gods and the king
of men will see to that!"
                                         So speaking he pulled the spear from Orodes' body.
A hard solitude and an iron sleep came over Orodes' eyes, and their light
was closed in eternal night.
                                         Now Italian Caedicus cuts down Trojan Alcathoüs,
Sacrator kills Hydaspes, and Rapo kills Parthenius and Orses, enduring
of strength. Messapus° kills Cronus and Ericetes, son of Lycaon, the first
as he lay on the ground, fallen from a horse that had lost its bridle,
and the other on foot.
                            Agis from Lycia had run ahead, but Valerus, steeped
in his ancestor's skill, cut him down. And Salius killed Thronius, but Trojan
Nealces, famous for his use of the javelin and the long-distance arrow,
killed Salcius in turn.°

Aeneas kills Lausus, the son of Mezentius

                                 Now grievous Mars dealt out sorrow and death equally.
The men fell equally on both sides, and equally they killed and were killed,
and flight was unknown to this side and that. The gods in the palace of Jove
pity the empty anger of both armies and that such great trials exist for humans.
Here Venus gazes down, there, opposite, Juno the daughter of Saturn
looks on, and pale Tisiphonê° rages in the midst of the thousands.
     But Mezentius, shaking his huge spear, advances like a whirlwind
onto the plain. As great as Orion when he strides through the great expanses

---

669 *same ground*: Prophecies on the lips of dying men are likely to come true.
675 *Messapus*: Of these Italians only Messapus appears elsewhere.
680 *in turn*: Nealces' killing of Salcius is the only Trojan success in this section.
685 *Tisiphonê*: In Book 6 she is the Fury who guards Tartarus in the underworld.

of the middle of the sea, cutting his path, and Orion's shoulders tower over
the waves, or when he carries an ancient ash down from the top
of the mountains, and he walks the earth yet hides his head in the clouds—
no differently does the giant Mezentius march ahead in his massive armor.
    Aeneas, opposite, catches sight of him in the distant ranks,
and prepares to go against him. Mezentius waits, wholly unafraid,
waiting for his great-spirited enemy. Mezentius stands firm in his might
and measures the space with his eyes, to see if he could throw
that far, and he says: "May this right hand, which is my god, and my weapon
that I lower to throw, bring me luck. I vow that you yourself, Lausus,
shall wear these spoils as a trophy to Aeneas, that I will strip from
that robber's corpse!"°
    He spoke and cast the screaming spear from afar,
but, flying on, it glanced from Aeneas' shield and hit big Antores,
who stood nearby, between his ribs and his groin—Antores, the companion
of Hercules, who followed Evander when sent from ARGOS, then settled
in an Italian city.° Unfortunate man, he fell to a wound meant for another.
Antores looks up at the sky, and as he dies he remember sweet Argos.
Then god-fearing [*pius*] Aeneas casts his spear. It passed through the circle
of Mezentius' shield, concave with triple layers of bronze, through the layers
of linen, through the texture made of three bulls' hides, and it came to rest
deep in his groin—but it failed to drive all the way home.
    Swiftly Aeneas,
jubilant when he sees the Etruscan blood, draws his sword from his thigh
and eagerly presses on the shaken Mezentius. When Lausus saw what
had happened, he moaned heavily from love of his dear father, and tears
ran down his face—And here I will not be silent about your cruel death
and your fine deeds, Lausus, if future time will place any faith in great
actions, nor will I be silent about you, young man, worthy to be remembered—
Mezentius was moving backward, helpless, hampered, dragging
the enemy spear sticking in his shield. Lausus runs forward, plunges into
the fight, just as Aeneas raised his right hand to strike a blow. Lausus took
hold of the sword and held Aeneas back. Lausus' companions follow with
a great clamor and shower Aeneas with spears, forcing him to keep
his distance, until the father can withdraw, protected by his son's shield.
    Aeneas rages but hold himself under cover. Just as when
every plowman and farmer flees from the field when a storm pours hail,

---

699 *robber's corpse*: Ordinarily a trophy would consist of a tree trunk decorated with an enemy's spoils and dedicated to a god (usually Mars), but Mezentius as despiser of the gods will drape the spoils from his son.

703 *an Italian city*: Evander came from ARCADIA to settle in PALLANTEUM on the TIBER; evidently Antores (otherwise unknown) joined him from ARGOS before Evander set out from Greece.

and passersby seek shelter in a protected place under a riverbank, or in the arch
of a high rock while it rains on the earth so they can continue the day's
work once the sun has returned—even so, attacked by weapons from every
side Aeneas endures the cloud of war, waiting for it to expend its fury.

    He scolds Lausus and he threatens Lausus: "Why do you rush
to your death and dare something greater than your strength? Your love
for your father [*pietas*] betrays you to folly!"
                                          But Lausus is mad with fury,
and now savage anger surges high in the Trojan leader, and the Fates
gather together the last threads of the life of Lausus. Aeneas stabbed
his sword with power through the young man's body, burying it to the hilt.
His sword passed through Lausus' shield, armor too frail against one
so threatening, and it through the tunic that Lausus' mother had woven
of gentle gold thread, and the boy's chest filled with blood. Then
his sad life left the body and fled through the air to the spirits below.

    But when the son of Anchises saw the face and lips of the dying boy,
lips pale in a wondrous wise, Aeneas groans in deep pity and stretches out
his right hand as the image of his love [*pietas*] for his own father
comes into his thoughts. "What, O sad boy, can pious [*pius*] Aeneas
give to such a nature, something that is worthy of your glorious deeds?
You keep the armor in which you delighted, and—if you worry about this—
I will give back your body to the ashes and shades of your ancestors.
And this too should bring you solace, my unhappy one, for your
wretched death—that you fell to the hand of great Aeneas."

    He rebukes Lausus' comrades too, who hang back, and he raises
the boy from the earth, where his well-kempt hair is soiled with blood.

Aeneas kills Mezentius

    In the meanwhile the father, Mezentius, dried out his wounds
by the water of the Tiber, and renewed his body, leaning against a tree trunk.
Nearby his bronze helmet hung from the branch of a tree, and his heavy
armor lies peaceful on the meadow. His chosen warriors stand about him.

    Feeling ill, Mezentius eases his neck, panting, as his beard streams
down his chest. He asks again and again about Lausus, and he many times
sends men to take the commands of a sorrowing father, to call him back.
Then his weeping companions carry in the lifeless Lausus upon his armor,
a great man overcome by a great wound.
                                       Mezentius' mind, foreknowing evil,
recognized their sighs from far off. He mars his white hair with dust
and he reaches forth his two hands to the heaven and he clings to the body.
"Did so much pleasure in living possess me, my son, that I let you come
against the right hand of an enemy in my place, you whom I begot?
Does this father of yours survive through your death, alive through

FIGURE 10.2 *Aeneas Kills Lausus*, **unknown date, by Wenceslas Hollar (1607–1677).**
On the left is the Etruscan Mezentius, who has been wounded by Aeneas. His son Lausus rushes in to protect his father, his spear raised, but Aeneas stabs him through his shield. Aeneas' own shield is decorated with a scene showing his fleet. At Aeneas' feet lies one of Mezentius' victims. The Latin text of this scene appears at the bottom. Woodblock print on paper.

your wounds? Alas, now at last my exile is wretchedly driven home,
now my wound, deeply!
                         "My son, I have also polluted your name
by my crime, driven in hatred from my father's throne and his royal power.
I needed to pay the penalty to my country and to the hatred of my people.   765
I should have given up my guilty life to any kind of death! Now I still live . . .
I do not leave men and the light. But I *will* leave."
                                         At the same time as he said
these things, Mezentius raised himself up on his sick thigh and, although
slowed by pain from the deep wound, he is not cast down. He commands
that his horse be brought. This his glory, this his solace—on it he has ridden   770
from every battle in victory.
                         He speaks to the grieving creature in these words:
"Rhaebus,° we have lived a long time, and if any thing is long lasting
for mortals, we have lived it. Today you will bring back, as a victor, the head
of Aeneas and his bloody spoils, and you will avenge with me the pains
of Lausus—or, if no power opens a way, you will fall along with me.   775
For, brave creature, I don't think it's right that you suffer a stranger's
commands, or the Trojans as your masters."
                                         So he spoke, and mounting the horse,
he settled his limbs in the usual way. He took up in both hands sharp
javelins, his bronze helmet shining on his head, bristling with its horsehair
crest. He drove swiftly into the middle of the fray. In one heart a vast   780
flood of shame mixes with an insane grief. And he calls out Aeneas three
times in a loud voice.
             Aeneas recognized him, and joyfully Aeneas prays:
"Thus let the father of the gods decree it, thus may great Apollo!
May you begin the fight!"
                         So speaking, Aeneas runs up against Mezentius
with his deadly spear. And Mezentius replies: "How can you frighten me,   785
you savage who have taken away my son? This was the only way you could
destroy me. We do not fear death, nor do we halt for any god. Give it up—
for I come here to die, but I first carry to you these gifts . . ."
                                             Mezentius spoke. He spun
his spear against Aeneas—then he landed another, and another, wheeling
in a wide circle. But the golden shield of Aeneas withstood them. He rode   790
three times to the left° around Aeneas, casting javelins from his hand—
three times the Trojan hero drags around a huge thicket of spears stuck
in his brazen shield.
                 Then when Aeneas had delayed enough, tired of plucking

---

772 *Rhaebus:* "bow-legged" in Greek.
791 *to the left:* So that his shield held in his left hand would protect him.

spears from his shield, burdened by an unequal fight, Aeneas carefully
795 considers, then breaks free and throws his spear between the curved temples
of the war horse. The horse rears, beats the air with his hooves and, throws
his rider, then follows Mezentius down from above, entangling him. The horse
lies upon Mezentius with its head foremost, its shoulder dislocated.
The Trojans and the Latins light the sky with their clamor.

               Aeneas runs up and draws
800 his sword. Standing over Mezentius, he says: "Where now, brave Mezentius . . . ?
where is that wild strength of spirit?"

            And the Etruscan replies, as he looks up
at the sky and gulps the air, and recovers his clarity of thought: "Bitter enemy,
why do you taunt me, and threaten me in death? There is no crime in killing.
I did not come to the war thinking so. Nor did Lausus make any such compact
805 with you. I ask only one thing, if there is any indulgence to a conquered
enemy: Permit my body to be covered with earth. I know that the bitter
hatred of my peoples surrounds me. Protect me, I pray, from this anger.
Let me be buried with my son."

             He said these things as, fully aware, he received
the sword in his throat. He pours forth his life onto the plain in a flux of blood.

BOOK 11. *The Glory of Camilla*

*L*ines 1–415 are omitted. Aeneas sets up a trophy from the arms of Mezentius, then mourns for the dead Pallas. Aeneas proposes peace. Evander mourns for his son Pallas. A truce is set for the burning of the dead. King Latinus proposes a compromise, but there is discord among the Latin officers. Turnus says that he will meet Aeneas in single combat. He prepares an ambush.

Turnus arms himself
for battle, raging for the fight. Already he has put on his bright-red breastplate,
which bristles with bronze scale, and he covers his legs with golden armor,
his temples still naked. He binds his sword to his side. He shone golden
as he ran down from the high citadel, exultant in spirit. He looks forward   420
to the enemy in hope—even as when a horse flees free from its stall,
its tether broken, free at last, and master of the open plain it either heads
for the pasture and the herds of mares or, used to bathing in a familiar river,
it gallops away and with its head held high it neighs with delight,
and its mane plays over its neck, over its shoulders.   425

Camilla and Turnus divide the command

Camilla speeds to meet
him, accompanied by her Volscian troops. A queen, she leaps down
from her steed beneath the gates. All her company imitates her, sweeping
down to the earth from their horses.
She speaks as follows: "Turnus, if the brave
may rightly have confidence in themselves, I dare, and I promise, to meet
Aeneas' followers and, alone, to go against the Etruscan cavalry. Let me try   430
the dangers of war first with my hand while you stay on the walls
and guard them."
Turnus replied, fixing his eyes on this amazing virgin:
"O virgin glory of Italy, how should I attempt to thank you or repay you?
But since your courage goes past all bounds, share this task with me.
Aeneas, as rumor reports and the scouts that I have sent out—that dog!—   435
has sent forth light cavalry to search the fields. He himself climbs
the ridge of the mountains and comes to the city over the steep deserted places.
I am preparing a secret ambush on the overarched path of the woods.
I will block the two openings of the gorge with a troop of armed men.
You await the Etruscan cavalry with your banners raised. Brave Messapus   440

will be with you, and the Latin troops, and the band of Tiburtus.° You take
over as our leader."

So he spoke, and with like words urges Messapus and all
the allied generals to battle. He moves against the enemy. There is a valley
with a curved bend, suited for deceit and the stratagem of war.
445 A dark wall of dense leaves presses from both sides, through which
leads a narrow path. Confined going out, dangerous going in,
above it, on the top of the mountain, lies a hidden plain and a safe
shelter, whether you want to attack from the right or the left, or take
your stand on the ridge and roll down large rocks.

The warrior Turnus hurried
450 to go here, by familiar paths. He took up position in the treacherous forest.

Diana tells of Camilla's background

In the meanwhile, in heaven's seat, Diana, daughter of Latona,
gives orders to swift Opis, one of her sacred band of virgins, and spoke
these sad words: "Camilla is entering this cruel war, virgin, and takes up
my arms in vain.° She was beloved to me in times past, before all others.
455 This is no new love, as you know, that comes to Diana,° or moves
my spirit with a sudden sweetness. When Metabus was driven from his ancient
city of Privernus° because of hatred for his rule and his tyrannical power,
fleeing in the midst of war, he took his child as a companion in exile,
and altering the name of her mother Casmilla, he called her Camilla.
460 "Carrying her in front of him at his breast, he sought out the long ridge
of the solitary woods. Savage weapons pressed in from all sides,
and an army of Volscians hovered over him. Behold! in the middle
of his flight the flooding Amasenus° foamed to the top of its banks,
so much rain had fallen from the clouds. Preparing to swim, he was held back
465 from love of his child and fear for his precious burden. Quickly debating
with himself every option, he decided with reluctance on the following:
The warrior bound his daughter to the huge spear that he carried,
stiff with knots and of hardened oak. He wrapped her in the bark of a cork
tree from the woods, binding her neatly to the middle of the shaft.
470 "Then balancing the spear in his huge right hand, he speaks to heaven:
'I, the father, dedicate this, my child, to you, kind virgin daughter of Latona,

---

441 *Tiburtus*: The brother of the twins Coras and Catillus.

454 *... in vain*: That is, Camilla is armed with a bow and quiver, Latona's typical weapons.

455 *Diana*: She speaks of herself in the third person.

457 *Privernus*: About sixty miles southeast of Rome, in Latium. The story of Camilla is not known before Vergil and is evidently his own invention.

463 *Amasenus*: A river near Privernus.

guardian of the woods. It was your weapon that she clasped as she fled
the enemy, a suppliant, through the air. Accept her as yours, O goddess!
I beg you, she whom I now commit to the uncertain winds!'

"He spoke,
and drawing back his shoulder he threw the spinning shaft. The waves
resounded. Unhappy Camilla flies on the whistling spear across
the swift river. But Metabus, as a large troop now pressed closer on him,
casts himself into the river. Victoriously he plucks the spear along
with the young girl from the grassy turf, a gift to Diana. No city would
accept him within its walls, no houses would take him, and because
of his savagery he would not, in any event, have consented.

"Metabus passed
his time among the shepherds and on the lonely mountains. Here he raised
his daughter among the brush and the bristling dens of wild animals
with the udder of a mare from the herd, on wild milk, squeezing the teats
between her tender lips. And when the child first began to walk,
he placed a sharp javelin in her hands, and he suspended bow and arrows
from the shoulder of the little girl. Instead of a golden tie for her hair,
and a long trailing robe, the skin of a tiger hangs from her head, down
her back. Even then she hurled a child's spears from her tender hand,
and she slung a sling made of a smooth leather around her head, bringing
down Strymonian cranes° and white swans.

"Many mothers wished
her to be their daughter-in-law—in vain!—she, pure, happy with Diana
alone, nourished her love of weapons and her chastity. I wish she had not
been swept up in her love for war, and that she had not challenged the Trojans.
She would be a dear companion to me now, one of my own.

"But come,
because she is urged on by bitter Fate, go off now from the sky, nymph,
and seek out the Latin borders, where sad ill-omened battle is joined.
Take these weapons, take out an avenging arrow from the quiver.
If anyone harms her sacred flesh by wounding her, Trojan or Italian,°
let him pay the price by an equal punishment in blood. Then I will carry
the body and untouched weapons of the poor girl in a hollow cloud,
and the unspoiled arms, to a tumulus, and I will bury her in the land
of her fathers."

So Diana spoke, but Opis slipped with a whirring sound
through the clear air of the heaven, her body surrounded in a black cloud.

Lines 505–546 are omitted. There is fighting before the city. Camilla comes to the fore.

---

491 *Strymonian cranes*: The cranes of the Strymon River in THRACE were famous.

499 *Italian*: That is, one of the Etruscan or Arcadian allies of Aeneas.

FIGURE 11.1 *Camilla and Metabus Escaping into Exile*, c. 1474, from a German translation by Heinrich Steinhöwel of the Florentine Giovanni Boccaccio's *De mulieribus claris*. King Metabus, on the left (labeled), wearing a crown, holds the young Camilla bound to a spear as he casts it across the river. In the middle, Camilla as a grown woman (labeled), her hair streaming beneath her medieval helmet, strikes an enemy with her lance. *De mulieribus claris* ("On Famous Women") is a collection of 106 biographies of historical and mythical women, first published in 1374 and distributed in handwritten copies. It is the earliest collection of the biographies of women in western literature. The book had wide influence, including on Chaucer's *Canterbury Tales*. It was translated from the original Latin into many languages, in this example German, one of the earliest books to be set in Gutenberg's revolutionary movable type. Boccaccio takes his story directly from Vergil's *Aeneid*. Woodblock on print paper.

But in the middle of the slaughter, the Amazon exults,
Camilla with her quiver, one breast bared for the battle. Now she throws
volley after volley of her vibrant spears, scattering them; now she seizes
her strong ax in a tireless right hand. The weapon of Diana, a golden bow, 550
rattles on her shoulder. Even attacked from behind, when she retreated,
she reverses the bow while fleeing to shoot her arrows.° Around her were
chosen comrades, the virgin Larina, and Tula, and Tarpeia wielding
her bronze ax, the daughters of Italy, whom the godlike Camilla herself
chose as her glory, excellent servants in peace or war. 555
                                    Such are the Amazons
of Thrace, when they pound the rivers of Thermodon and fight with painted
weapons, either around Hippolytê, or when Penthesilea, daughter of Mars,°
returns from the battle in her chariot, and the ranks of women exult
with their lunate shields, ululating in a grand tumult.
                                                Who first did you strike
with your spear, who last, O harsh virgin? Or how many bodies did you 560
pour out over the earth?
                          First she struck down Eunaeus,° son of Clitius,
whose exposed chest she pierced with her long pine shaft as he came up
against her. Vomiting, he pours out rivers of blood, and he bites the bloody
earth, and dying he writhes around his wound.
                                      Then she kills Liris
and Pagasus too, the one as he gathers the reins of his wounded horse, 565
rolling from beneath it, the other while he stretched out his defenseless
hand to the man as he fell, and they were flung headlong together.
    Then she adds to them Amastrus, the son of Hippotas, and leaning
forward to throw she strikes with her spear Tereus and Harpalycus,
and Demophoön and Chromis. As many spears as the virgin sent 570
spinning from her hand, just so many Trojan warriors fell.
    In the distance the huntsman Ornytus rode on his Iapygian
horse,° in unfamiliar armor as he went into battle, whose broad shoulders
were covered by a skin taken from a young bull, and the huge
gaping head of a wolf, and its jaws with the white teeth covered 575
his head. He held a rustic hunting spear in his hand and rides through

---

552 *her arrows*: This maneuver refers to an actual military tactic of the Parthians (from Persia), called a "Parthian shot."

557 *... daughter of Mars*: The Thermodon River runs into the southern coast of the BLACK SEA. Hippolytê and Penthesilea were legendary queens of the Amazons. Hippolytê fell in love with the Athenian hero Theseus and bore him a child, Hippolytus. Penthesilea joined the Trojan alliance and was killed by Achilles. The Amazons carried crescent-shaped shields.

561 *Eunaeus*: The Trojan and Etruscan victims of Camilla's moment of glory are not mentioned elsewhere.

573 *Iapygian horse*: That is, from Iapyx, a part of APULIA in southern Italy.

the center of the troops, a full head above the others.
                              She caught him
and pierced him—it was easy in the routed ranks—and towering over
him she speaks with a bitter heart: "Do you think that you are chasing
580 wild animals through the forests, my Etruscan? The day has arrived
that proves your words mistaken—and by a woman's weapons!
All the same, you will carry no small name to the shades of your ancestors,
that you fell to the spear of Camilla!"
                         Next she kills Orsilochus and Butes,
two of the largest of the Trojans. She stabs Butes in the back with her spear
585 between his breastplate and helmet, where the rider's neck gleamed
and the shield hung from his left shoulder. Fleeing from Orsilochus,
driven in a wide circle, she eludes him, then wheeling around
she pursues the pursuer. Raising up high, she brings the mighty
war-ax down again and again on the man, cutting through his armor
590 and through his bones as he begged, as he prayed in desperation.
The wounds rained brains on his face.
                              Now the warrior son of Aunus
meets her. He pulls up, terrified at the sudden sight. He was from
the Apennines, not least of the lying men of LIGURIA, so long as Fate
allowed him to practice his deceptions.° And when he sees that
595 he can no longer evade the battle by turning, or avoid the attacking
queen, he tries to devise a trick through wit and cunning, and he says:
"Why is that such a great thing, if as a woman you trust to a strong horse?
Give up flight and trust yourself to fight me on level ground!
Arm yourself to fight on foot! You will soon know this whole windy
600 boasting is an illusion!"
                    He spoke. In a rage, and incensed by a savage
resentment, she hands her horse over to a companion. She takes
her stand with equal weapons, on foot with a naked sword, fearless
with a plain shield.
                 But the youth, thinking that he has tricked her,
flies away without delay, pulling his reins together and taking to flight,
605 pricking his swift horse with iron spurs.
                                   "Stupid Ligurian! Puffed-up
in your proud spirit—for nothing! You've tried your slippery native
tricks in vain. Cunning won't carry you back safe to your deceitful
father Aunus!" says the virgin.
                             As fast as fire she intercepts the path
of the horse on her quick feet. She takes the reins of the horse from
610 in front, tackles the son of Aunus, and takes revenge on the hated blood—

---

594 *...to practice his deceptions*: The Ligurians were known for their immoral behavior.

FIGURE 11.2 *Camilla Slaying the Son of Aunus*, **unknown date, by Wenceslas Hollar (1607–1677).** The dismounted virgin queen Camilla, her lunate shield suspended from her back, kills the son of Aunus, plunging her sword into the Ligurian while he tries to flee. In the background, the Latins and the followers of Aeneas struggle against one another.

as light as a falcon, the sacred bird of Apollo, when it swoops from a high
rock and takes a dove flying high in a cloud, and holds it in her crooked
talons and tears out its guts. The gore and torn feathers fall from the sky.

Lines 614–642 are omitted. Jupiter stirs the Etruscans to battle. The Etruscan Arruns schemes to take down Camilla.

                    Then Arruns, whose life was owed
to the Fates, circles around the swift Camilla with his spear, and skillfully
645 with cunning he tries for the easy chance. Wherever the maddened
virgin went in the ranks, there Arruns comes from behind, and in silence
he dogs her tracks. Wherever she returns in victory and pulls back
from the enemy, here the youth secretly turns his swift reins. Arruns tries this
approach and that, and goes around the whole circuit, from every side.
650 Relentlessly Arruns brandishes his sure spear.
                                      By chance the Trojan Chloreus,
once a sacred priest of Cybelê, shone forth in the distance, splendid
in Phrygian armor. He was spurring on his foaming horse, protected
by a hide of bronze scales interlinked with gold, that looked like
plumage. He, glorious in dark red and foreign purple, shot Gortynian
655 arrows from his Lycian bow.° His bow was golden on his shoulders
and the helmet of the seer was golden too. He had fastened his cloak
of a saffron color and its rustling folds of linen into a knot with a golden
brooch, his shirt and barbarian pants were embroidered with the needle.
      This man Chloreus the virgin huntress blindly pursued out of all
660 men in battle, either that she might hang his Trojan arms in a temple,
or that she might adorn herself in captured gold. Recklessly she raged
through the battle with a woman's love for booty and spoils.
                                                      Arruns, seizing
his chance, raises his spear from ambush and prays to the gods as follows:
"Highest of gods, Apollo, guardian of holy Soractê!° We are your chief
665 followers, for whom the blaze of the pine-tree fire is fed, who as devotees
place our steps on the flaming coals, confident in our piety [*pietate*]°—
Grant, father, that this shame be removed by our arms, all-powerful one!
I seek no prize, no trophy of the defeated virgin, or any other booty—
other deeds will bring me fame. Only let this ghastly plague fall wounded
670 by my blow, and I will return without glory to the city of my fathers."
      Phoebus heard Arruns and granted that, in his decision, half the prayer
succeed, but half be dispersed to the passing winds. He agreed to Arruns'

---

655 ... *Lycian bow*: Gortyn was a city in CRETE famous for its archers; LYCIA, too, was known for its bowmen.

664 *Soractê*: A mountain in Etruria with a temple to Apollo.

666 *our piety*: A reference to the ancient practice of fire-walking.

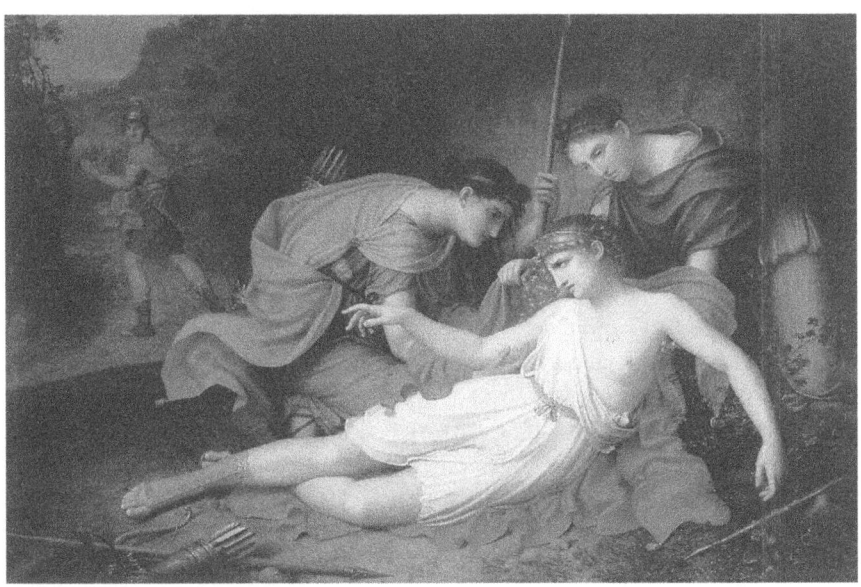

FIGURE 11.3 *The Death of Camilla*, 1810–1814, by Gaspare Landi (1756–1830). Landi was an Italian Neoclassical painter. Here, based on Vergil's description, he shows a scantily clad Camilla, one breast exposed, in her death throes, comforted by Acca and another warrior-woman in a rustic setting. She points languidly to her killer Arruns, who in the left part of the canvas sneaks away. A quiver of arrows lies at her feet, and her spear is just off her left hand. Oil on canvas.

prayer that he lay out Camilla, surprised by a sudden death, but he did not
grant that his noble country should see him return. The gusts carried
Arruns' words away into the south wind.
                                    And so as the spear sounded when it sped
through the air, cast from his hand, all the Volscians turned their eyes
and minds intently toward the queen. She herself was unmindful of the breeze
or the sound of the weapon falling from the sky, until fixed beneath
her naked breast, driven deep, the spear drank her virgin blood.
Her companions run up with trepidation. They take up their queen
as she falls. Arruns, more frightened than anyone, flees, his joy mixed
with fear, not daring to trust further in his spear nor to meet the virgin's
weapons.
            And just as a wolf that has killed a shepherd, or a great bullock,
immediately hides himself out of the way in the high mountains before
the hostile spears can reach it, aware of its audacious deed, and tucking
its tail between its trembling legs it heads for the woods—even so Arruns
in confusion steals out of sight, happy to flee away, and he mixes with
the other soldiers.
                    As Camilla died, she pulls out the spear with her hand,
but the iron point is fixed between the bones on her side in a deep wound.
She sinks backwards, bloodless, and her eyes sink too, cold with death.
The color, once radiant, left her face. Then, giving up her last breath,
she speaks to Acca, one of her peers, faithful to Camilla before all the rest,
the only one with whom Camilla shared her views.
                                                Camilla speaks as follows:
"So far, my sister Acca, has my strength held out. Now the bitter wound
wears me down. All around me grows dark with shadow. Flee, and carry
this last news to Turnus. He must take my place in the battle and keep
the Trojans from the city. And so—farewell."
                                            With these words she let
go the reins, letting them fall helpless to the earth. Then little by little,
growing cold, she let her body go, and she lay down her drooping neck
and her head, seized by death. They release her arms and her life flees
with a groan, complaining, to the shades below.
                                                And then an immense
shouting rises and strikes the golden stars. Once Camilla had fallen,
the battle swells. At once the mass of Trojans, and the Etruscan captains,
and the Arcadian squads of Evander rush on in a dense formation.

Lines 705 to end of Book are omitted. The nymph Opis kills Arruns in revenge for the death of Camilla, but the Latins are forced to take refuge behind the walls of Laurentum. Turnus, learning of Camilla's death and of the city's investment, gives up his ambush and returns to the city.

BOOK 12. *The Death of Turnus*

Lines 1–383 are omitted. Turnus arrives at Laurentum. He now agrees to go ahead with the single combat he had agreed to earlier. However, Juno urges Turnus' sister Juturna to ruin the treaty and stop the duel. Turnus and Aeneas swear an oath but Juturna, disguised as a Rutulian, incites the Latins to defend their hero. Aeneas is treacherously wounded, leaving Turnus to rage with a free hand. Venus heals Aeneas of his wound. He prepares to return to battle.

Aeneas went out from the gates, majestic, shaking a huge spear in his hand.
At the same time, Antheus and Mnestheus rush into the dense battle-line   385
and a mass of men flows out of the camp. Then the field is covered
by blinding dust, the earth trembles, stirred by the tramp of feet. Turnus sees
them coming from the other side of the battle. The Latins see them and a cold
tremor runs through the marrow of their bones. First Juturna, before
anyone, recognizes the sound and takes cover in fear. Aeneas   390
flies ahead. He leads his dark ranks at high speed over the open field.
As when a cloud moves to the land, passing over the middle of the sea
and cutting off the sun's light—Ah, the miserable farmers know it from
far and shudder, for the storm will ruin the trees and ravage the crops,
flatten everything far and wide—and the winds run before the storm,   395
roaring to the shore: Even so the Trojan leader drives his line against
the enemy as they gather in thick serried ranks.
                                                Thymbraeus strikes powerful
Osiris with his sword, Mnestheus hits Archetius, Achates cuts down Epulo,
and Gyas kills Ufens. Even Tolumnius the augur falls, first to throw his spear
against the opposed enemy.° A shout is raised to the sky and the Rutulians   400
turn around and show their backs in dusty flight as they race across the plain.
    Aeneas himself does not bother to cast down in death those running
away, nor to attack those who meet him on foot, or those throwing spears
from a distance. He looks for Turnus alone, circling in the dense gloom.
He seeks to fight him alone.   405

---

400   ... *the opposed enemy*: Of the victorious Trojans, Thymbraeus is not heard of elsewhere; Mnestheus and Achates are often mentioned; Gyas is a contestant in the ship race in Book 5. Of the Italians, Osiris, Archetius, and Epulo are mentioned only here. Ufens appears several times (for example, in Book 7), as does Tolumnius.

Juturna thwarts Aeneas

The wild woman Juturna, shaken by fear
in her heart, knocks Metiscus, Turnus' charioteer, from between the reins°
so that he slipped from the beam. She left him far behind. She herself
takes Metiscus' place and guides the waving reins with her hands, taking on
Meticus' voice, form, and weapons—everything.
                                    Just as when
410 a black swallow flies over the great house of a rich Lord and circles
the high halls, gathering small crumbs and bits of food for its noisy
young, and now it twitters in the empty courts, now by the pools of water—
even so Juturna is borne on her horses and, flying in her chariot, ranges
over the plain, now here, now there, displaying her triumphant
415 brother, but not permitting him to fight in the hand-to-hand.
       Aeneas follows her winding course, eager to take on Turnus.
He tracks him, calls with a loud voice through the scattered ranks.
But as often as he sees his enemy and attempts to match the flight
of Turnus' swift-footed horses, just so often Juturna wheels the chariot
420 in the other direction.
              Ah, what should he do? In vain Aeneas floats
on the tumbling tide. Diverse anxieties pull his spirit in different
directions. Messapus, who happened to be carrying two spears with iron
points in his left hand, comes towards him, lightly running along.
Messapus aims and casts with certain aim. Aeneas stops, crouched behind
425 his shield, sinking down on one knee. Nonetheless the speeding spear
takes off the top of his helmet, knocking off the plumes from its crest.
       But then Aeneas' anger truly rose. Incited by this treachery, seeing
that his enemy's horses had turned around and that his chariot was driven
back, Aeneas calls repeatedly on Jove and the altars of the broken treaty
430 as witness. He plunges into the middle of the troops. Aided by Mars,
he yields to terrible, savage slaughter, killing everyone he can, giving
full rein to his rage.

slaughter on both sides

       What god will tell me now of the bitter suffering?
Who can tell in song of the various deaths and the destruction of captains
whom now Turnus, now the Trojan hero, drove over the entire field?
435 Did it please you, O Jupiter, that people who would live in eternal
peace should clash together in so great a conflict?
                                    Aeneas, in the first battle
that held up the charging Trojans (though briefly), drove his cruel sword

---

406 *reins*: That is, as he held the reins on each side of his body.

FIGURE 12.1 *Aeneas in Combat*, c. 1220, by Heinrich von Veldeke (c. 1150?–c. 1190?), illustration in a vellum manuscript of van Veldeke's *Eneas Romance* (see Figure 7.1). In this beautifully illustrated Berlin manuscript of c. 1220, the illustrator has shown the mailed Trojan hero in the upper panel, riding his medieval charger and smashing an opponent on the head with his sword. Aeneas' head is crowned by a helmet that bears a panel showing a royal lion; two lions rampant stand on side panels, and the word "graf" ("prince") is written on the panel. A rampant lion also appears on Aeneas' shield. His enemy has an eagle emblem, perhaps indicating that it is Messapus. Two mounted warriors appear behind Aeneas. In the lower panel, wearing the same emblems, Aeneas is about to put to death Turnus, who wears an eagle emblem and carries a shield with two rampant lions. Paint on vellum.

through the ribs of the Rutulian Sucro,° through the cage of his chest,
where death is most swift.
                          Turnus strikes down Amycus and his brother
440 Diores,° knocked from their horses, attacking them on foot, getting
the first as he came on with his long spear and getting the other with his sword.
Then Turnus cut off the heads of the two men and hung them from his car.
He carries them away, dripping blood.
                              But Aeneas sends into death Talos
and Tanaïs and brave Cethegus, three in one assault, and sad Onites too,
445 with a Theban name, whose mother was Peridia. Turnus killed two brothers
sent from LYCIA, the fields of Apollo,° and Menoetes from ARCADIA,
who had hated war—in vain! His way of life and his poor home was near
the fish-filled streams of Lerna,° never knowing the attendance on men
of power, and his father plowed rented land.
                                  And just as fires set burning
450 on opposite sides of a parched forest into thickets of rustling laurel,
or when foaming rivers make a roar in a rapid descent from the high
mountains and run out toward the sea, each leaving its own path of destruction,
so Aeneas and Turnus with no less vehemence rush through the lines
of battle.
        Now anger surges within, now breasts that know not defeat
455 are bursting, now with all their strength they move toward deadly combat.
Aeneas hits Murranus headlong with a stone, with the whirlwind of a huge
rock as Murranus bragged of the ancient names of his forefathers,
and all his race traced back through the Latin kings. Aeneas lays him out
on the ground—the wheels roll him around beneath the reins and yoke
460 and the horses' hooves, forgetful of their master, trample him down
with repeated blows.
                    Turnus goes against Hyllus as Hyllus charges at him,
yelling loudly and with spirit. Turnus casts his spear at Hyllus' temples,
covered in gold. The spear goes through his helmet and fixes in his brain.
            Nor did your right hand save you from Turnus, O Cretheus, bravest
465 of the Greeks! Nor did your own gods protect Cupencus° from Aeneas.
Cupencus placed his chest in the path of the steel, and the protection
of his bronze shield was of no use to the wretched man. You, too, the Laurentine
fields saw fall, O Aeolus, sprawled out far on your back on the ground.
You fell, whom the Argive battalions were not able to kill, nor Achilles,

---

438   *Sucro*: This figure appears only here.

440   ...*Diores*: Amycus is mentioned several times in earlier books, but without characterization. Diores participated in the foot race in Book 5.

446   *of Apollo*: Apollo had a famous shrine in Lycia (at Patara).

448   *Lerna*: Near ARGOS in the Peloponnesus.

465   ...*Cupencus*: Hyllus, Cretheus, and Cupencus do not appear elsewhere.

who overturned the kingdom of Priam. Here you found the boundaries
of death. Your noble house was beneath MOUNT IDA, that noble house
at LYRNESUS, but your grave is in Laurentine soil.
            And so all the armies
were engaged, both the Latins and all the Trojans, Mnestheus and brave
Serestus, Messapus, the master of horses, and strong Asilas, and the phalanx
of the Etruscans, the Arcadian wings of Evander, each man struggling
for himself with all his strength. There is no rest, no respite, and they
press on in a vast struggle.

Aeneas attacks the city

        Now the most beautiful mother of Aeneas set
in his mind that he might go against the walls and turn his army swiftly
on the city, to confuse the Latins with sudden ruin. While Aeneas tracked
Turnus through the varied ranks, he turned his gaze here and there,
and he sees the city untouched by the great war, quiet, unharmed.
Immediately the picture of a greater war inflames him. He calls the captains
Mnestheus and Sergestus and brave Serestus, and he takes possession
of a hillock where the rest of the Trojan army assembles, not putting
down their shields or their spears.
          Standing in the middle on a high mound,
Aeneas says: "Let nothing oppose my commands. Jupiter is with us.
Let not anyone advance more slowly because of the suddenness of this
undertaking. Today I will destroy that city, the cause of the war, the very
kingdom of Latinus, and lay its smoking roofs level with the ground—
unless they accept the yoke and as a conquered people to obey us!
Should I wait until Turnus will meet me in battle, until he chooses to fight
me again though I have defeated him before? This city is the source,
O citizens, the cradle of this unspeakable war. So quickly bring fire,
reestablish the treaty with fire!"
        Thus he spoke, and they formed up
in a wedge, and with their hearts all striving together in competition
they moved in a mass toward the walls. In an instant scaling ladders
and sudden fire appeared. Some run to the gates to cut down any advance
fighters, others throw spears, with their weapons they darken the sky.
  Among the forefighters, Aeneas raises his right hand beneath
the walls. In a loud voice he accuses Latinus. He calls the gods as witness
that he was again forced into battle, that the Italians were enemies
for a second time, that a second treaty was broken.° Discord arises
among the frightened citizens. Some command that the city be opened

---

502 *was broken*: The first time a treaty is broken is in Book 7, where Latinus accepts the Trojans' peaceful
   overtures but his people brush them aside and rush into war.

and the gates thrown wide to the Trojans. They drag the king himself
505 out to the walls, while others hurry to defend the ramparts.
It was as when
a shepherd has tracked bees hidden in a dark rock, and he has filled
it with acrid smoke: The bees inside, frightened at what is happening,
spin around through their fortress of wax and sharpen their anger with
a strident buzzing, and a black stench rolls around the hive while the rocks
510 echo inside with a blind humming and smoke goes up into the empty air.

Queen Amata commits suicide

Now further misfortune comes to the exhausted Latins, which with anguish
shakes the whole city to its foundations. When the queen saw from
her palace the enemy coming and that the walls were attacked, that
fire flies over the roofs, that there was no opposing army of Rutulians,
515 that Turnus had no forces—the unhappy queen thought that Turnus
was killed in the war—and, disturbed in her mind by an intense pain,
she cries out *she* is the cause, the guilty party, the source of evil.
Speaking many words in the frenzy of her grief, wishing to die
by her own hand, she shreds her purple garments. She fastens a noose
520 of hideous death from the high beam.
As soon as the wretched Latin
women learn of this catastrophe, first her daughter Lavinia falls into
a frenzy, tearing her yellow hair with her hands and her rosy cheeks,
then the rest of the crowd does the same. The house echoes far and wide
with their lamentation. Unhappy rumor travels throughout the city.
525 Spirits sink.
Latinus comes, his vestment torn, devastated by the death
of his wife and the ruin of the town. He fouls his white hair with clouds
of filthy dust. He loudly accuses himself, who did not earlier accept
the Trojan Aeneas and recognize him as his son-in-law, on his own
authority.

Turnus learns of Amata's death

In the meanwhile, Turnus, fighting at the edge of the plain,
530 follows the few stragglers, but now more slowly, now rejoicing less
and less in the advance of his horses. The breeze carried to him a clamor
mixed with blind terror, and the gloomy sounds of a city in trouble
strike his straining ears. "Alas for me! Why are the walls disturbed
by shouting? What is this clamor that rushes from the distant city?"
535 Thus Turnus spoke, and beside himself he pulled at the reins
and stopped the car. At this his sister, who controlled the chariot, horses,
and reins in the form of his charioteer Metiscus, faces him, saying:

"This way, Turnus! Let us chase the Trojans where victory opens a way—
there are others to defend the houses by hand. Aeneas is attacking
the Italians and he stirs up the war. Let us deal bitter death to the Trojans   540
with savage hand! You will not leave the field of battle inferior in glory
or the numbers you have killed!"
                              Turnus replied: "O sister, I recognized
you long ago, when you upset the first treaty through trickery and gave
yourself to war. Now too you hide your divinity in vain. But who
wanted to send you down from Olympus to suffer such labors? So that   545
you could see the cruel death of your miserable brother? What should
I do? What chance promises salvation? I myself have seen Murranus
overcome before my own eyes, crying out loudly. No one more dear
still survives—a mighty man, killed by a mighty wound. The unhappy
Ufens fell, so that he might not see my shame. The Trojans took   550
his body and armor! Shall I permit our houses to be destroyed—that
one disaster has not happened!—and shall I not deny the words of Drances
with my right hand?° Shall I turn my back? Will this land see Turnus run?
Is it so bad to die? Be good to me, you spirits of the underworld,
because the gods above have turned away. I will descend to you, a holy   555
spirit, ignorant of blame, not unworthy of my great ancestors."
       Scarcely had he spoken when Saces° flies through the thick
of the enemy, borne on a foaming horse, wounded in the face by an arrow,
and he called on the name of Turnus as he goes by: "Turnus! In you is our
last hope. Have pity on your men. Aeneas storms in arms, and he threatens   560
to cast down the citadel of the Italians and give them to destruction.
Already fire flies toward the roofs. The Latins turn their faces, their eyes
toward you. King Latinus mutters to himself, unsure whom he should call
a son-in-law, or to what alliance he should turn.
                                   "Furthermore the queen,
most loyal to you, has taken her own life and in terror fled the light.   565
Messapus and brave Atinas alone sustain the army before the gates.
Around them stand dense squadrons on either side, a harvest of steel
that bristles with drawn swords—while you drive your car over empty grass!"
       Turnus was astounded, confused by the shifting picture of things,
and he stood, silently gazing. A monstrous shame swells in his lonely heart,   570
and an insanity mixed with grief, and a love tormented by frenzy,
and the knowledge of his own manhood. As soon as the shadows dispersed,
and the light returned to his mind, he turned his gaze with blazing eyes
to the walls and looked back from his chariot to the great city. Behold!
a spiraling tongue of flame fixed on a tower, rolling to the sky through   575
its stories, a tower that he himself had raised with jointed beams, then added

---

553   *with my right hand*: Drances had earlier, in an omitted passage, insulted Turnus in open assembly.
557   *Saces*: This figure is not mentioned before.

wheels and provided with high ramparts.

"Now, now, sister, Fate is victorious!
Cease from delay. Where god and harsh fortune calls, let us go there!
I must meet Aeneas in the hand-to-hand. I must suffer death, however bitter.
580 You shall no longer see me without honor, my sister. Allow me, I beg you,
to show this last madness, before the end!"

Turnus spoke, and swiftly he leaped
from the chariot to the ground. He ran through the enemy spears, deserting
his mournful sister. In his rapid course he breaks through the middle
of the ranks.

And just as when a rock rushes headlong from a mountain top,
585 torn off by wind, or loosened by a tempest, or its underpinnings
washed away over years by time, and the uncontrollable mass
is borne downwards in a great rush, and it bounces over the ground,
rolling trees and flocks and men with it—even so Turnus runs through
the scattered ranks to the walls of the city, where the earth is soaked deep
590 with the blood that has been shed and the air is strident with spears.

the duel will go forward

He signals with his hand and at once he begins in a loud voice:
"Stop now, Rutulians! And hold back your spears, Latins! Whatever luck
will have, that is mine. It is better that I atone for the broken treaty on your
behalf—and decide the contest with steel!"

All drew back, making a space
595 in the middle. But father Aeneas, when he heard the name of Turnus,
leaves the walls, the high citadel, throws aside all delay, breaks off
every labor, thrilling with delight, and ferociously he clashes his weapons—
huge like Mount Athos or Mount Eryx, or huge as father Apennine° himself
when he roars through the shining mountain oaks and rejoices in lifting
600 his snowy peak into the sky.

Now truly all turned their eyes, the Rutulians
and the Trojans and all the Italians, both those who occupied the ramparts
and those who struck the bottom of the walls with a ram, and they stripped
their armor from their shoulders. Latinus himself is astounded that these
great men, begotten in opposite ends of the world, are coming together
605 to decide the issue by the sword.

As soon as the field opened up on the open
plain, the two men dash quickly together, throwing their spears from
a distance, clashing their shields and the resounding bronze. The earth

---

598 ...*Apennine*: Athos is at the tip of the easternmost finger of the triple peninsula of Chalcidice in northern Greece; Mount Eryx is in northwestern Sicily; the APENNINES are the central mountain chain that runs down the peninsula of Italy.

groans. They double the rain of blows with their swords. Chance
and valor mingle.

     Just as when two bulls run together head to head in mortal
conflict on great Sila, or on high Taburnus,° and the frightened herder
stands back, and the herd is mute with fear, and the heifers mutter to see
who will command the forest, whom the whole herd will follow, and they
deal wounds to one another with great force, butting and goring and bathing
necks and shoulders in a massive outpouring of blood, and the forest
moans with their bellowing—thus did the Trojan Aeneas and the Italian
hero attack one another with their shields.

     An immense crashing fills the sky.
Jupiter himself holds in a scale two pans equally balanced, and he places
in them the opposite fates of the two men, to see whom the struggle might
condemn, and on which side death might sink down with its weight.
Turnus leaps forward, thinking he is safe, and raising his body full height
with uplifted sword, he strikes. The Trojans shout and the excited Latins,
and both sides are aroused. But the treacherous sword shatters. The eager
warrior would have been left defenseless in mid-blow had not flight
saved him. He flees swifter than East Wind, when he sees the unfamiliar
sword-hilt in his unarmed right hand.

     The story is that when in haste Turnus first
mounted behind his yoked horses for battle, he left behind his father's
sword and took the sword of his charioteer Metiscus. And this sufficed
for a long time while the straggling Trojans turned their backs, but when
he came up against the armor of the god Vulcan, the mortal sword
was shattered like useless ice under a blow. The fragments gleamed
on the golden sand.

     And so the maddened Turnus flees this way and that,
over the plain, and he winds an erratic course, now here, now there.
But on all sides the Trojans imprisoned him in a dense circle, and on one
side was a vast swamp, on the other steep walls close him in.
Aeneas, although his knees were slowed by the arrow wound°
and deny him speed, follows, eagerly pursuing his anxious enemy,
step by step. As when a dog in a hunt presses on a stag, running after him
and barking, a stag shut in by a river or cut off by a rope with red feathers°—
the stag, terrified by the trap and the high banks of the river, flees a thousand
ways, here and there, but the eager Umbrian° closes in, its mouth gaping,
and now he almost has him, and he snaps his jaws as if he does

---

610 ... *Taburnus*: Sila and Taburnus are mountain peaks in southern Italy.

635 *arrow wound*: Earlier treacherously received, healed by Venus (in an omitted passage).

638 *red feathers*: The reference is to a Roman hunting device in which feathers were attached to a rope to frighten the prey.

640 *Umbrian*: That is, a hound from UMBRIA, the territory north of LATIUM and east of ETRURIA.

but the dog bites empty air and the stag gets away. A shout
arises, and the banks and lake respond and the sky sounds with a tumult.
   As Turnus flees, he complains to the Rutulians, calling each man
645 by name, demanding his own familiar sword. But Aeneas threatens death
and destruction to anyone coming near. He terrifies his enemies, threatening
to destroy the city, and though wounded Aeneas presses on. They complete
five full circles and as many again in the opposite direction—for they
do not seek meager prizes at the games, but struggle for the life and blood
650 of Turnus.

Juturna helps Turnus

   By chance a wild olive tree had once stood there, sacred
to Faunus, with bitter leaves, a tree revered by sailors in the old days,
accustomed when saved from the sea to hang up their gifts to the Laurentine
god, and their votive clothes;° but the Trojans had removed the sacred trunk,
sparing nothing, so that they might fight on an open field.
                                                 Here was Aeneas'
655 spear, where the force of his cast had carried it and fixed it in the tough roots.
The Trojan pulled at it, wishing to recover the weapon with his hand
and to pursue Turnus, whom he could not overtake by running.
                                                 But then Turnus,
crazed with fear, said: "O Faunus, I pray to you—take pity, hold the iron
in your earth, if I have honored your rites that the followers of Aeneas
660 have profaned by war."
                              He spoke, and he did not call the god's assistance
for nothing. Though he wrestled long and lingered over the tough trunk,
Aeneas was not able with all his might to break the strong bite of the tree.
While he tugged and strained fiercely, Juturna, the daughter of Daunus,
changed back into the form of the charioteer Metiscus, runs up and returns
665 the sword to her brother. Venus, incensed that the audacious nymph
was allowed to do this, comes up and pulls the spear from the deep root.
The warriors, refreshed in arms and courage—Turnus trusting his sword,
Aeneas bold and towering with his spear—stand face to face, breathing hard
in the contendings of Mars.

Jupiter makes concessions to Juno

670 In the meanwhile, the all-powerful king of Olympus
speaks to Juno in her golden cloud as she watches the fight: "How will this
end, my wife? What is left for you? You yourself know, and you

---

653 *votive clothes*: It was Roman custom for sailors saved from the sea to dedicate their clothes to a god, usually Neptune, but here to Faunus, the local god of Laurentum (Latinus' father).

admit you know, that Aeneas is destined for heaven as god of his nation,
that by Fate he is to be raised to the stars. What are your plans? What hope
do you cling to in the chill of heaven? Was it right that this god be defiled 675
by a mortal's wound? Or that a missing sword—for what could Juturna
do without you—be returned to Turnus, that strength be increased for
the conquered?

"Cease at last! Yield to our prayers so that a great sadness
does not devour you in silence, and so that your sad cares do not come back
to me again and again from your sweet lips. We have come to the end. 680
You were able to drive the Trojans over land and sea, to incite unspeakable
war, to wreck a house, to mix marriage with sorrow. I forbid you to try
anything more!"

So Jupiter spoke. And the daughter of Saturn said in reply
with a submissive expression: "Because I knew it was your will, great Jupiter,
all unwilling I left Turnus and the earth. Nor would you see me alone now, 685
on a heavenly seat, enduring the just and the unjust, but bound by flames
I would be standing in the battle line itself, drawing the Trojans into
destructive war.

"I persuaded Juturna to come to the aid of her wretched
brother—I confess it—and I approved greater acts of daring to save his life,
but not that Juturna might contend with the spear or bow. I swear 690
by the implacable fountainhead of Styx, the one religious sanction held
in awe by the gods above. And now I yield and leave behind the battles
that I loathe.

"I only beg this of you, for the sake of Latium, for the sake
of the greatness of your people°—because it is not forbidden by any law
of Fate when they celebrate peace with happy marriages—let it be so!— 695
when laws and treaties join them, do not order the native Latins
to change their name and be made Trojans, or be called Teucrians,
or change their language, or their clothing. May Latium go on, may
the Alban kings last for ages, may Roman offspring be powerful with
Italian virtue. Troy has fallen, may you allow her to stay fallen, along 700
with the name of Troy."

Smiling, the creator of men and all things said: "You are
Jove's sister, the second child of Saturn. Such anger surges in your heart!
But come, give up the rage that you began in vain. I grant what you wish.
I relent, willingly conquered. The Ausonians will cling to their ancestral
speech and customs, and their name will be as it is. The Trojans will sink, 705
mingling in stock only. I will add the custom and method of worship,
and I will make them all Latins, speaking a common tongue. From them
you will see a race mixed with Italian blood that surpasses men and gods
in piety [*pietate*], nor will any people celebrate your honor with equal devotion."

---

694   *your people*: Because Latinus was descended from Jupiter's father Saturn.

710 Juno agreed and joyfully altered her purpose. She withdrew
from the sky and left her cloud. Having accomplished these matters, the father
turns over something else in his mind, and he prepares to release Juturna from
her brother's side.

Jupiter calls off Juturna

Men speak of twin plagues called the Dread Goddesses,
which timeless Night begot in a single birth from Tartarean Megaera, crowning
715 them equally with writhing serpents and adding wings swift as the winds.°
They wait beside the throne of Jove on the threshold of the savage king,
and they sharpen fear for weak mortals whenever the king of the gods
prepares horrific death, and plagues, or terrifies guilty cities with war.
Jupiter sent down one of these from the highest heaven, commanding
720 her to appear to Juturna as an omen. She flies and is borne to the earth
in a swift whirlwind—no different than an arrow loosed from a bowstring
through the clouds that a Parthian or a Cydonian° has fired, hissing, leaping
unseen through the swift shadows, armed by the bile of a savage poison,
a shaft without a cure. Even so sped the daughter of Night, seeking the earth.
725 As soon as she saw the Trojan lines and the troops of Turnus,
she changed her shape, suddenly shrinking herself into the form of that
small bird that perches late at night on tombs, or on deserted rooftops,
and sings an ill-omened song—the fiend changed into this shape.° She flies
again and again, shrieking, flapping in the face of Turnus, beating his shield
730 with her wings. A strange torpor dissolved his limbs with terror, his hair
stood up in horror, and his voice stuck in his throat.
But when his unhappy
sister Juturna recognized the cry and wings of the Dread Goddess,
she tears her loosened hair, scratching her face with her nails, and her breast
with her fists: "How now, O Turnus, can your sister help you? What is left
735 for me who have suffered greatly? With what skill can I prolong your life?
Can I oppose such a prodigy? Now, now I leave the battle line. O you
ill-omened bird, do not frighten me who am already afraid! I know your
wing-beats, their lethal sound, and I do not mistake the proud command
of great-hearted Jove. Is this what I get for remaining a virgin? What
740 is the point of having eternal life? Why is mortality taken from me?
Then I could at least put an end to my great pain and go as companion
to my sorry brother through the shades! Am I really immortal? What will
be sweet to me, my brother, without you? O what earth could gape deep

---

715 *...the winds*: They are Allecto and Tisiphonê, daughters of Megaera, identified with the Furies.

722 *...Cydonian*: The Parthians of Persia and the Cydonians from Crete were famous for their archery.

728 *shape*: That is, an owl.

enough for me and send me, a goddess, to the lowest shades?"

So saying
she covered her head with a dark-blue robe and, howling loudly, she sank   745
into the deep river.

the death of Turnus

Aeneas presses on, and he flashes his spear, huge like
a tree, and he speaks from his angry heart: "Why do you delay? Why do
you hold back, Turnus? We must fight in the hand-to-hand with our fierce
weapons, not by running with savage arms. Change yourself into every
form. Gather whatever courage and skill you can. Choose to follow   750
the high stars with wings, or bury yourself shut up in the hollow earth."

And Turnus replied, shaking his head: "Your fancy words do not
frighten me, madman! The gods frighten me, and my enemy Jupiter."

He said no more, but sees a huge stone, an ancient stone, that lay
on the plain, set up as a marker to distinguish the borders of the field in dispute.   755
Scarcely twelve chosen men, men of such a form as the earth produces today,
could have lifted it on their shoulders, but the hero took it up quickly.
He rose to his full height, and swiftly threw it at his enemy. But he did
not know himself, running, moving, or raising the huge rock in his hands.
His knees wobbled, and his cold blood froze in his veins. The stone,   760
spun by the man through the empty air, did not cover the whole space
and did not strike with force.

Just as in sleep when quiet presses the eyes, we seem
to want to follow in vain our eager path, and we collapse in the midst
of our efforts, helpless, and the tongue has no power, and the usual strength
in our body is lacking, nor does voice or words come out—even so, with   765
whatever courage Turnus might seek a way out, the Dread Goddess° denied
him success.

Then different visions spin out in his brain: He sees
the Rutulians, the city, he falters in fear, he trembles at the death that is near.
He sees no path of escape, nor strength to fight the enemy, nor does
he anywhere see his chariot or his sister charioteer.   770

As he delays, Aeneas
shakes his fatal spear at him, seeing a favorable chance. With all his might
he casts from a distance. Stones shot from a siege engine never roared
so loudly, nor did such thunder ever leap from a bolt of lighting. As from
a black whirlwind, bearing dread death, the spear flies on and pierces
the outer circle of the sevenfold shield and the outer rim of the breastplate.   775
The spear went screaming through the middle of his thigh.

Under the blow

---

766 *Dread Goddess*: That is, the Fury.

FIGURE 12.2 *The Death of Turnus*, **1688, Luca Giordano (1632–1705).** Giordano was an Italian Baroque painter and printmaker. Born in Naples, he also worked in Rome, Venice, and Florence, painting flowing and ornate frescoes that celebrated the Medici family. He worked in Spain too, decorating the sacristy of the Toledo cathedral. His paintings often depict allegorical figures and mythical episodes. In this painting of the death of Turnus, the Italian hero has fallen to the ground. Aeneas, sword in hand, stands over him and points angrily to the sash of Pallas. Above him, Venus floats in a cloud, accompanied by her doves and cupids, while Juturna flies off to the right, the ill-omened owl beneath her. Achates and Iulus watch the duel from the right, and behind them King Latinus sits on his throne. In the far background is the Castle Sant'Angelo, once the mausoleum of the emperor Hadrian (AD 76–138), one of the most prominent landmarks in Rome. Oil on canvas.

Turnus fell to the earth on bended knee. The Rutulians rise up and moan, and all the hills around groan, and from the distance the high forest sends back the sound.

Turnus, humbled, begging with his eyes, extended his right hand and, beseeching, said: "Surely I have deserved this, and I do not complain—make use of your good fortune. But if any care for my wretched father can touch you, I beg—you too had such a father in Anchises—take pity on Daunus' old age and send me—or if you want, my body, robbed of the light—home to my people. You have won, and the Ausonians have seen me beaten, seen me extend my palms. Lavinia is your wife. Do not go farther in your hatred."

Aeneas stood there, savage in his arms, rolling his eyes, and he hesitated with his right hand. Gradually Turnus' words began to turn him aside, he hesitated, when he saw the unlucky sword-belt of the young Pallas slung across Turnus' high shoulder, an emblem of the enemy. Pallas' strap shone with its familiar decorations—he whom Turnus had lain low with a blow.

As soon as he had drunk in the trophy, memorial of his savage pain, incensed with fury and terrible in his anger, Aeneas said: "Will you be saved from my grasp, you who wear the spoils of my friend? It is Pallas, Pallas who sacrifices you with this stroke, and takes vengeance on you from your accursed blood!"

So saying, aflame, he buries the iron in Turnus' breast. His limbs are loosed in cold death and his life flees with a groan, angrily, to the shades below.

Bibliography

SOME COMMENTARIES

Conington, J., and H. Nettleship, eds., *The Works of Virgil* (London, 1858–1853, three volumes).

Ganiban, R., C. Perkell, J. J. O'Hara, J. Farrell, and P. A. Johnston, eds., *Aeneid 1–6* (Newburyport, MA, 2013).

Page, T. E., ed., *Virgil's* Aeneid (London 1894, 1900, two volumes).

Williams, R. D., *Virgil:* Aeneid (London 1972–1973, two volumes).

COMPANIONS AND ENCYCLOPEDIAS

Farrell, J., and M. C. Putnam, eds., *A Companion to Vergil's* Aeneid *and Its Tradition* (Oxford, 2010).

Horsfall, N., *A Companion to the Study of Virgil* (Leiden, 1995).

Martindale, C., ed. *The Cambridge Companion to Vergil* (Cambridge, UK, 1997).

Page, T. E., *Aeneid* (London, 1900, two volumes).

Putnam, M. C. J., ed., *A Companion to Vergil's* Aeneid *and Its Tradition* (Malden/Oxford, 2010).

Thomas, R. F., and J. M. Ziolkowski, eds., *The Virgil Encyclopedia* (Malden/Oxford, 2013, three volumes).

CRITICAL STUDIES

Adler, E., *Vergil's Empire: Political Thought in the* Aeneid (Lanham, MD, 2003).

Anderson, W. S., *The Art of the* Aeneid (Wauconda, IL, 2006, second edition).

Bailey, C., *Religion in Vergil* (Oxford, 1935).

Cairns, F., *Virgil's Augustan Epic* (Cambridge, UK, 1989).

Clausen, W., *Virgil's* Aeneid *and the Tradition of Hellenistic Poetry* (Berkeley, 1987).

Conte, G. B., *The Poetry of Pathos: Studies in Vergilian Epic* (Oxford, 2007).

Feeney, D. C., *The Gods in Epic: Poets and Critics of the Classical Tradition* (Oxford, 1991).

Galinsky, K., *Aeneas, Sicily, and Rome* (Princeton, 1969).

Gransden, Karl, *Virgil's Iliad: An Essay on Epic Narrative* (Cambridge, 1984).

Hardie, Philip R., *Virgil's* Aeneid*: Cosmos and Imperium* (Oxford, 1986).

Heinze, Richard, *Virgil's Epic Technique* (Berkeley, 1993).

Jenkyns, R., *Virgil's Experience* (Oxford, 1998).

Johnson, W. R., *Darkness Visible: A Study of Vergil's* Aeneid (Berkeley, 1979).

Otis, B., *Virgil: A Study in Civilized Poetry* (Oxford, 1964).

Perkell, C., ed., *Reading Vergil's* Aeneid*: An Interpretive Guide* (Norman, OK, 1999).

Pöschl, V., trans. G. Seligson, *The Art of Virgil: Image and Symbol in the* Aeneid (Ann Arbor, MI, 1962).

Quinn, K., *Virgil's* Aeneid*: A Critical Description* (London, 1968).

Reed, J., *Virgil's Gaze* (Princeton, 2007).

Syme, R., *The Roman Revolution* (Oxford, 1939).

Thomas, R. F., *Virgil's Augustan Reception* (Cambridge, 2001).
Ziolkowski, J. M., and M. C. J. Putnam, eds., *The Virgilian Tradition: The First Fifteen Hundred Years* (New Haven, CT, 2008).

SOME MODERN TRANSLATIONS

Ahl, F. (trans.), *Virgil, The* Aeneid (Oxford, 2007).
Fagles, R. (trans.), Aeneid *by Virgil* (New York, 2008).
Fairclough, H. R., and G. P. Goold, eds., *Virgil*, Eclogues, Georgics, Aeneid 1–6, Loeb Classical Library (Cambridge, MA, 2001).
Fairclough, H. R., and G. P. Goold, eds., Aeneid *Books 7–12, Appendix Vergiliana*, Loeb Classical Library (Cambridge, MA, 2001).
Fitzgerald, R. (trans.), *Virgil, The* Aeneid (New York, 1990).
Lombardo, S. (trans.), *Virgil:* Aeneid (Indianapolis, 2005).
Mandelbaum, A. (trans.), *The* Aeneid *of Virgil* (New York, 1971).

Credits

I.1 Musée National du Bardo, Tunis, Tunisia © Gilles Mermet / Art Resource, NY
I.2 Courtesy of MA-SHOPS.com
1.1 Kimbell Art Museum, Fort Worth, Texas / Art Resource, NY
1.2 Erich Lessing / Art Resource, NY
1.3 National Gallery, London, UK / Bridgeman Images
1.4 De Agostini Picture Library / A. Dagli Orti / Bridgeman Images
2.1 © RMN-Grand Palais / Art Resource, NY
2.2 HIP / Art Resource, NY
2.3 Erich Lessing / Art Resource, NY
2.4 © RMN-Grand Palais / Art Resource, NY
2.5 Digital Image © 2015 Museum Associates / LACMA. Licensed by Art Resource, NY
2.6 Gianni Dagli Orti / The Art Archive at Art Resource, NY
4.1 Somerset County Museum, Taunton Castle, UK / Bridgeman Images
4.2 Bridgeman-Giraudon / Art Resource, NY
4.3 © RMN-Grand Palais / Art Resource, NY
4.4 Erich Lessing / Art Resource, NY
6.1 Gianni Dagli Orti / The Art Archive at Art Resource, NY
6.2a Werner Forman / Art Resource, NY
6.2b © Barry B. Powell
6.3 Tate, London / Art Resource, NY
6.4 © Heritage Image Partnership Ltd / Alamy
6.5 © Fitzwilliam Museum, Cambridge / Art Resource, NY
6.6 Private Collection / Bridgeman Images
7.1 bpk, Berlin / Staatsbibliothek zu Berlin, Stiftung Preussicher Kulturbesitz / Ruth Schacht / Art Resource, NY
7.2 Digital Image © 2015 Museum Associates / LACMA. Licensed by Art Resource, NY
8.1 © The Trustees of the British Museum / Art Resource, NY
8.2 © Araldo de Luca/Corbis
8.3 © Heritage Image Partnership Ltd / Alamy
8.4 Museum Mayer van den Bergh, Antwerp, Belgium
9.1 Album / Art Resource, NY
10.1 Gianni Dagli Orti / The Art Archive at Art Resource, NY
10.2 The Thomas Fisher Rare Book Library, University of Toronto
11.1 "Incunables Collection. Kislak Center for Special Collections, Rare Books, and Manuscripts. University of Pennsylvania Libraries."
11.2 The Thomas Fisher Rare Book Library, University of Toronto
11.3 Mondadori Portfolio / Electa / Art Resource, NY
12.1 bpk, Berlin /Staatsbibliothek zu Berlin, Stiftung Preussicher Kulturbesitz / Ruth Schacht / Art Resource, NY
12.2 © Heritage Image Partnership Ltd / Alamy

Index/Glossary

Included are all names that appear several times; excluded are names that appear a single time, usually as victims of war or obscure place names. I do not include such commonalities as "Rome," "Italy," "Aeneas," or "Troy." I give the pronunciation in parentheses, if it is not obvious, and something about the name.

A

Acestes (a-ses-tēz), a Trojan who established a settlement on Sicily, son of the river-god Crinisus (*Aen.* 1, 2, 4, 9) 12, 25, 40, 76, 100, 174, 177

Achaeans (a-**kē**-ans), a division of the Greek people, Homer's word for the Greeks at Troy (*Aen.* 1, 2) 18, 27, 37, 50–51, 60, 65

Achates (a-**ka**-tēz), Aeneas' most trusted advisor (*Aen.* 1, 6, 8, 12) 23, 25, 30, 31, 36, 39, 41, 43, 44, 46, 102, 109, 162, 163, 165, 209, 222

Acheron (**ak**-er-on), "sorrowful," river of the underworld (*Aen.* 6, 7) 108, 114, 116, 126, 141, 144

Acrisius (a-**kris**-i-us), father of Danaë, killed accidentally by Perseus (*Aen.* 7) 145, 148

Admetus (ad-**mē**-tus), king in Thessaly, whom Apollo served (*Aen.* 6) 117

Adrastus (a-**dras**-tus), king of Argos, sole survivor of the Seven Against Thebes (*Aen.* 6) 120

Aeacus (ē-a-kus), father of Peleus, king of Aegina, judge in the underworld (*Aen.* 1, 6) 22, 134

Aeëtes (ē-ē-tēz), "man of earth," king of Colchis in Aea, brother of Circe, father of Medea (*Aen.* 7) 138

Aegean (ē-**jē**-an) Sea, between Greece and Turkey xviii (map) (*Aen.* 1, 7) 31, 33, 148

Aegeus (ē-jūs), father of Theseus, a king of Athens (*Aen.* 6) 102

aegis (ē-jis), "goat-skin," a shield with serpent border used by Minerva and Jupiter (*Aen.* 8) 161

Aegyptus (ē-**jip**-tus), brother of Danaüs, father of the fifty sons who married the fifty daughters of Danaüs (*Aen.* 10) 188

Aeolia, floating island of the wind-king Aeolus xix (map) (*Aen.* 1, 8, 10) 19, 159, 161, 183

Aeolus (ē-o-lus), king of the winds 12 (*Aen.* 1, 6, 8, 10, 12) 19–20, 21, 23, 24, 109, 122, 159, 183, 212

Aeschylus (ē-ski-lus, **es**-ki-lus) (525–456 BC), Athenian playwright (*Aen.* 4, 10) 93, 188

Aethiopis, a lost epic poem by Arctinus that told the story of Memnon (*Aen.* 1) 37

Aetolia (e-**tō**-li-a), district north of the Corinthian Gulf, where Diomedes came from to found Arpi in Italy (*Aen.* 10) 183

Agamemnon (a-ga-**mem**-non), son of Atreus, brother of Menelaus, leader of Greek forces at Troy (*Aen.* 1, 2, 4, 6) 28, 35, 42, 43, 48, 52, 55, 92, 93, 121, 134

Agenor (a-**jēn**-or), Phoenician ancestor of Dido (*Aen.* 1) 31

Ajax, (1) son of Telamon, the "Greater Ajax," half-brother to Teucer, ruler of Salamis (*Aen.* 1, 2, 5, 8, 11) 34, 57, 78, 161, 334, 345; (2) son of Oïleus, the "Lesser Ajax," ruler of the Locrians, raped Cassandra at altar of Pallas Athena/Minerva (*Aen.* 1, 3, 6, 11) 34, 108, 205, 334

Alba Longa (**al**-ba **lon**-ga), city in Latium founded by Iulus, son of Aeneas xix (map), 4 (*Aen.* 1, 6, 8, 9) 17, 28, 131, 133, 151, 168, 179

Alexandria, city in Egypt founded by Alexander the Great, capital of Cleopatra xvii (map) (*Aen.* 8) 171

Allecto (a-**lek**-tō), a Fury (*Aen.* 7, 10, 12) 144–149, 183, 220

Aloads, Otos and Ephialtes, gigantic sons of Aloeus and Neptune who stormed heaven (*Aen.* 6) 123–124, 126

Amazons, a race of warrior women (*Aen.* 1, 11) 37, 203

ambrosia, "immortal," food of the gods (*Aen.* 1) 34

Ammon, Egyptian god equated with Jupiter (*Aen.* 4) 83

Amphiaraüs (am-fē-a-**rā**-us), a seer, one of the Seven Against Thebes (*Aen.* 6) 119

Amphitryon (am-**fit**-ri-on), descendant of Perseus, husband of Alcmena, mortal father of Hercules (*Aen.* 8) 154

Amulius, king of Alba Longa who took power from his brother Numitor and oppressed Ilia (Rhea Silvia) xxiii (*Aen.* 1) 28

Amycus (**am**-i-kus), a Trojan, killed by Turnus (*Aen.* 1, 10, 12) 26, 192, 212

Anchises (an-**kī**-sēz), prince of Troy, lover of Venus/Aphrodite, father of Aeneas xxiii, 4 (*Aen.* 1, 2, 4, 6, 7, 8, 9, 10, 12) *passim*

Andromachê (an-**drom**-a-kē), wife of Hector, mother of Astyanax, taken captive by Neoptolemos at end of the Trojan War (*Aen.* 2) 64, 65

Antenor (an-**tē**-nor), a Trojan elder (*Aen.* 1, 6) 27, 120

Aphrodite, Greek goddess of sexual attraction, equated with the Roman Venus 11 (*Aen.* 1, 4, 8, 10) 18, 22, 27, 34, 43, 85, 158, 183, 185, 191

Apollo, xx, 11 (*Aen.* 2, 4, 6, 7, 8, 9, 10, 11, 12) *passim*

Apollonius (a-pol-**lōn**-i-us) of Rhodes (third century BC), author of the *Argonautica* 13

Arcadia (ar-**kād**-i-a), mountainous region in the central Peloponnesus, scene of pastoral poetry xviii (map), 12 (*Aen.* 4, 6, 8, 10, 12) 86, 105, 151, 157, 194, 212

Arctinus, composer of the lost epic *Aethiopis* (*Aen.* 1) 37

Arges (**ar**-jēz), "bright," one of the three Cyclopes (*Aen.* 8) 159

Argonauts (**arg**-o-notz), Jason and his companions on the *Argo* (*Aen.* 2) 63

Argos, "plain," city in the Argive plain in the northeastern Peloponnesus xii, xvii (map), 18 (*Aen.* 1, 2, 6, 7, 10, 12) 28, 52, 54, 61, 134, 143, 145, 148, 150, 194, 212

Ariadnê (ar-i-**ad**-nē), "very holy one," Cretan princess, daughter of Minos and Pasiphaë who helped Theseus defeat the Minotaur (*Aen.* 6) 102

Arisbê, a town on the Hellespont on the banks of the Selleïs River (*Aen.* 9) 175

Arruns, a Trojan ally who killed Camilla (*Aen.* 11) 206–208

Ascanius (as-**kān**-i-us), another name for Iulus, son of Aeneas (*Aen.* 1, 2, 4, 7, 8, 9, 10) *passim*

Assaracus (as-**sar**-a-kus), an early king of Troy (*Aen.* 1, 6, 9) 28, 127, 132, 175

Astyanax (as-**tī**-a-naks), "king of the city," son of Hector and Andromachê, thrown from the walls of Troy (*Aen.* 2) 64, 65

Atlas, a Titan, father of Maia, holds up the sky (*Aen.* 1, 4, 6, 8) 47, 86, 93, 132–133, 155

Atreus (ā-trūs), king of Mycenae, son of Pelops, brother of Thyestes, father of Agamemnon and Menelaus (*Aen.* 1, 2, 8) 35, 52, 63, 66, 155

augur (**ow**-gur), Roman seer (*Aen.* 1, 2, 12) 33, 72, 209

Augustus (ow-**gus**-tus) (63 BC–AD 14), originally called Octavian, first Roman emperor xi–xii, xx, xxii, 1, 2, 4, 6–7, 9, 10, 13 (*Aen.* 1, 6, 8, 9) 28, 29, 104, 131–134, 136, 170–172, 181

Aulis (**ow**-lis), port in Boeotia from which the Trojan expedition set sail (*Aen.* 2, 4) 52, 91

Aurora (ow-**ror**-a), Roman goddess of dawn, equated with Greek Eos (*Aen.* 1, 6, 7) 37, 122, 138

Automedon (ow-**tom**-e-don), "self-ruler," the charioteer of Achilles (*Aen.* 2) 66

Aventine (**a**-ven-tīn), one of the seven hills of Rome xx

Avernus (a-**ver**-nus), "birdless," an Italian lake regarded as the entrance to the underworld (*Aen.* 4, 6, 7) 94, 108, 110, 123, 141

B

Baal (**bā**-al), "lord," a Levantine storm-god (*Aen.* 1) 42

Bacchae (**bak**-kē), female followers of Dionysus; a play by Euripides (*Aen.* 4) 92

Bacchus (**bak**-kus), another name for Dionysus, preferred by the Romans 11 (*Aen.* 1, 4, 7) 45, 78, 88, 92, 146

Batoni, Pompeo (1708–1787), an Italian painter inspired by classical antiquity 74

Bellerophon (bel-**ler**-o-fon), Corinthian hero, grandson of Sisyphus, tamed Pegasus and killed the Chimaera (*Aen.* 6) 114

Belus (**bē**-lus), Semitic "lord," father of Dido (*Aen.* 1, 2) 42, 45, 51

Black Sea, also called Pontus xvii (map), xviii (map) (*Aen.* 4, 6, 7, 8, 11) 90, 133, 134, 138, 159, 203

Boccaccio (bo-**katch**-i-o), Giovanni (1313–1375), Italian author 202

Boeotia (bē-**ō**-sha), "cow-land," region north of Attica, where Thebes was situated xviii (*Aen.* 1, 2) 45, 63

Boötes (bo-**ō**-tes), "plowman," a constellation (*Aen.* 1) 47

Boucher, François (1703–1770), a French painter 21

Briareus (bri-**ar**-e-us), one of the Hecatonchires (*Aen.* 6, 10) 113, 190

Brontes, "thunderer," one of the three Cyclopes (*Aen.* 8) 159

Brutus, "stupid," (1) Lucius Junius, liberator of Rome from Tarquin the Proud (*Aen.* 6) 133–134; (2) Marcus Junius (85–42 BC), assassin of Caesar xxi, 2, 6

C

Cacus (**kā**-kus), "bad man," monster who lived at the future site of Rome, killed by Hercules (*Aen.* 8) 157

caduceus (ka-**dū**-se-us), a wand with two intertwined snakes, carried by Mercury 87

Caesar, Julius (100–44 BC), Roman general and politician, assassinated by his friends xi, xx, xxi, 1, 2, 4–6, 9 (*Aen.* 1, 6, 8) 28–29, 132, 134, 169, 170

Calchas (**kal**-kas), prophet of the Greek forces at Troy (*Aen.* 2) 52–53, 54

Calydon (**kal**-i-don), main city in Aetolia in southwestern mainland Greece, site of the Calydonian boar hunt (*Aen.* 7) 144

Calypso (ka-**lip**-sō), "concealer," nymph, daughter of Atlas, who kept Ulysses for seven years on her island 13

Camilla (ka-**mil**-la), warrior maiden allied against Aeneas 14 (*Aen.* 7, 11) 149, 199–208

Camillus (ka-**mil**-lus), hero of early Rome (*Aen.* 6) 134

Capaneus (**kap**-a-nūs), one of the Seven Against Thebes (*Aen.* 2, 6) 59, 119

Capitoline Hill, one of the seven hills of Rome, where Jupiter's temple stood xx (*Aen.* 6, 8) 104, 168–169

Carians, Trojan allies from south of the Troad (*Aen.* 8) 172

Carthage, Phoenician city in modern Tunisia, kingdom of Dido, enemy of Rome xvii, xviii, 5, 14 (*Aen.* 1, 4, 6, 7, 10) 17–18, 23, 29, 31, 32, 34, 35, 38, 49, 78, 79, 80, 82, 85, 86, 89, 93, 97, 98, 102, 104, 135, 143, 182, 183

Cassandra (ka-**san**-dra), prophetic daughter of Priam and Hecuba, raped by Oïlean Ajax (*Aen.* 1, 2, 6, 10) 19, 56, 61–62, 64, 134, 184

Cassius (first century BC), one of the conspirators who killed Caesar xxi, 6

Castor, mortal son of Tyndareus and Leda, brother of the immortal Pollux and of Helen and Clytemnestra xx (*Aen.* 6) 108

Cato (95 BC–46 BC), Roman statesman, enemy of Julius Caesar (*Aen.* 6, 8) 134–135, 169

Caucasus Mountains, at the eastern end of the Black Sea (*Aen.* 4) 90

Cecrops (**sē**-krops), first king of Athens (*Aen.* 6) 102

Centaurs (**sen**-towrs), half-human, half-horse creatures (*Aen.* 6, 7) 113, 124, 144

Centaurus (sen-**tau**-rus), child of Ixion and an image of Hera/Juno, father of the Centaurs (*Aen.* 6) 124

Cephalus (**sef**-a-lus), "head," Athenian son of Mercury, killed his wife Procris by mistake (*Aen.* 6) 119

Cerberus (**ser**-ber-us), multiheaded monster who guards the entrance to the underworld (*Aen.* 6) 117, 126

Ceres (se-**rēz**), *numen* of the grain harvest, equated with the Greek Demeter 11 (*Aen.* 1, 2, 4, 6) 25, 73, 78, 120

Chalcis, "bronze," "copper," the principal settlement (with Eretria) on the island of Euboea (*Aen.* 6) 101

Chalybes (**kal**-i-bēz), an iron-working people of the southeast coast of the Black Sea (*Aen.* 8) 159

Chaos (**kā**-os), "chasm," the first thing that came into being (*Aen.* 4, 6) 94, 113

Charon (**kā**-ron), ferryman of the dead (*Aen.* 6) 114–117, 118

Charybdis (ka-**rib**-dis), dangerous whirlpool opposite Scylla, said to be in the Straits of Messina (*Aen.* 1, 7) 26, 144

Cicero (106–43 BC), Roman politician and orator (*Aen.* 8) 169

Circe (**sir**-sē), "hawk," enchantress who entertained Ulysses for a year on her island 13 (*Aen.* 7) 138, 140

Cithaeron (si-**thē**-ron), mountain south of Thebes, where the Bacchae roamed (*Aen.* 4) 88

Classical Period, 480–323 BC 4 (*Aen.* 1) 36

Cloanthus, a follower of Aeneas (*Aen.* 1) 26, 39, 42

Cnossus (**knos**-sus), principal Bronze Age settlement in Crete, where labyrinthine ruins have been found, associated with Minos and Daedalus xvii (map) (*Aen.* 9) 177

Cocytus (kō-**sīt**-us), "wailing," river in underworld (*Aen.* 6) 108, 114, 116

Coeus (**sē**-us), a Titan, father of Leto (*Aen.* 4) 83

Colchis (**kol**-chis), city at eastern end of Black Sea, where Jason sailed to find the Golden Fleece (*Aen.* 7) 138

Collatinus (col-la-**tīn**-us), Tarquinius, husband of Lucretia who was raped by Sextus Tarquin (*Aen.* 6) 133

Corinth (**kor**-inth), city on isthmus between central Greece and the Peloponnesus xvii (map) (*Aen.* 1, 6) 28, 134

Cressida (**kres**-i-da), beloved by Troilus in medieval legend (*Aen.* 1) 36

Crete, largest island in the Aegean, birthplace of Jupiter xvii (map), xviii (map) 58 (*Aen.* 4, 6, 8, 11, 12) 79, 81, 101–102, 119, 155, 206, 220

Creüsa (kre-**ou**-sa), Aeneas' first wife, perishes in sack of Troy xxiii (*Aen.* 2, 9) 68–69, 71, 73, 74, 75, 177

Cronus (**krō**-nus), child of Sky and Earth, equated with Roman Saturn 11 (*Aen.* 1, 6, 10) 18, 132, 193

Cumae (**kū**-mē), site of earliest Greek colony in Italy, north of the Bay of Naples, where Aeneas descended to the underworld xvii (map), xviii (map), xix (map), 4 (*Aen.* 6) 101–102, 105, 106, 107, 115, 126, 137, 138, 139

Cumaean (ku-**mē**-an) Sibyl, prophetess who led Aeneas into the underworld (*Aen.* 6) 105, 106, 107

Cupid, "desire," spirit of sexual attraction, son of Venus, equated with Greek Eros 12, 21, 30 (*Aen.* 1, 4) 43–44, 46, 79, 87, 130, 160, 167, 186, 222

Cyclades (**sik**-la-dēz), "circle islands," around Delos in the Aegean Sea xviii (map) (*Aen.* 8) 170

Cyclopes (sī-**klōp**-ēz), "round-eyes," one-eyed smiths who forged Jupiter's thunderbolt (*Aen.* 6, 8) 125, 159, 161

Cyllenê (si-**lēn**-ē), mountain in Arcadia where Mercury/Hermes was born (*Aen.* 4, 8) 86, 155, 157

Cynthus, the hill on the island of Delos where Diana/Artemis was born (*Aen.* 1, 4) 37, 81

Cyprus, large island in eastern Mediterranean, home of Venus/Aphrodite xvii (map) (*Aen.* 1, 10) 34, 42, 44, 183

Cythera (**sith**-e-ra), island south of the Peloponnesus, sometimes said to be the birthplace of Venus/Aphrodite xviii (map) (*Aen.* 1, 10) 27, 44, 183, 185

Cytherea (si-ther-**ē**-a), another name for Venus (*Aen.* 1, 8, 10) 43, 163, 166, 183

D

dactylic hexameter, the meter of Homer and Vergil, six feet per line 4, 7–8

Daedalus (**dēd**-a-lus), Athenian craftsman, builder of the labyrinth, father of Icarus (*Aen.* 6) 101–102, 103

Danaäns (**dān**-a-anz), descendants of Danaüs, one of Homer's names for the Greeks (*Aen.* 1, 2, 4) 18, 41, 47, 48, 50–52, 54, 56, 59, 61–62, 91

Danaë (**dān**-a-ē), daughter of Acrisius, mother of Perseus (*Aen.* 7) 148

Danaïds (**dān**-a-idz), fifty daughters of Danaüs, who killed their husband, the sons of Aegyptus, on their wedding night (*Aen.* 10) 188

Danaüs (**dān**-a-us), brother of Aegyptus, father of the Danaïds (*Aen.* 10) 188

Dardanelles (= Hellespont), straits between the Aegean Sea and the Propontis (*Aen.* 2) 51

Dardanians, the inhabitants of Dardania, near Troy (*Aen.* 1, 2, 4, 6) 40, 42, 51, 56, 97, 105

Dardanus (**dar**-da-nus), son of Electra and Jupiter, early king of Troy, after whom the Trojans were called Dardanians xxiii (*Aen.* 1, 2, 4, 6, 8) 33, 51, 90, 127, 131, 151, 155

David (da-**vēd**), Jacques-Louis (1748–1825), French painter 64, 70

Dawn, goddess of the early morning, same as the Latin Aurora or the Greek Eos (*Aen.* 1, 2, 4, 8) 37, 47, 63, 77, 80, 95–96, 158

Deïphobus, brother of Hector, took up with Helen after death of Paris (*Aen.* 2, 6) 60, 120–122

Delos (**dē**-los), "clear," tiny island in the center of the Cyclades, where Apollo and Diana/Artemis were born (*Aen.* 1, 4) 37, 81

Delphi (**del**-fī), sanctuary of Apollo at foot of Mount Parnassus xvii (*Aen.* 2, 6) 60, 115, 125

Demeter (de-**mēt**-er), daughter of Saturn, equated with Roman Ceres 11 (*Aen.* 1, 2) 25, 73

Diana, Roman goddess of the hunt, equated wth Greek Artemis 11 (*Aen.* 1, 2, 4, 6, 7, 10, 11) 31, 37, 52, 94, 101, 144, 189, 200–203

Dictê (**dik**-tē), mountain in Crete (*Aen.* 4) 79

Dido (**dī**-dō), "virgin," Phoenician queen of Carthage who loved Aeneas and committed suicide when abandoned 12–15 (*Aen.* 1, 4, 6, 9) *passim*

Diomedes (dī-ō-**mēd**-ēz), son of Tydeus (who fought in the Seven Against Thebes), a principal Greek warrior at Troy (*Aen.* 1, 2, 4, 8, 10) 22, 28, 36, 47, 54, 55, 85, 150, 183, 185, 191

Dis (dis), "wealth," Roman god of the underworld, equated with Greek Pluto 11 (*Aen.* 1, 4, 6, 8) 23, 86, 97, 108, 111, 113, 117, 122, 123, 126, 169

E

ekphrasis, "aside," a self-consciously elaborate description of a physical object, for example, the shield of Aeneas (*Aen.* 6) 102

Electra, daughter of Atlas, mother of Dardanus xxiii (*Aen.* 8) 155

Elis, a territory in the northwestern Peloponnesus xviii (map) (*Aen.* 6) 124

Elissa, another name for Dido (*Aen.* 1, 4) 18, 89, 96

Elysium (e-**liz**-i-um), the Elysian Fields, a paradisiacal land, part of Vergil's underworld (*Aen.* 6) 122, 125, 129, 130

Epeus (e-**pē**-us), builder of the Trojan Horse (*Aen.* 2) 59

Ephialtes (ef-i-**al**-tēz), a giant who stormed heaven, one of the Aloads (*Aen.* 6) 124

Erebus (**er**-e-bus), "darkness," a region of Tartarus, or Tartarus itself (*Aen.* 4, 6, 7) 77, 94, 117, 127, 143

Eridanus (e-ri-**dān**-us), a mythical river identified with the Po in northern Italy (*Aen.* 6) 127

Erinys (**er**-i-nis), a Fury (*Aen.* 2) 61

Eriphylê (er-i-**fī**-lē), sister of Adrastus, wife of Amphiaraüs, killed by her son Alcmeon (*Aen.* 6) 119

Erymanthus (er-i-**man**-thus), mountain in Arcadia, haunt of the Erymanthian boar (*Aen.* 6) 133

Eryx, city in western Sicily xviii (map), xix (map) (*Aen.* 1, 10, 12) 40–41, 183, 216

Ethiopians, "burnt-faced," a people who dwell in never-never land in the extreme south (*Aen.* 4) 93

Etna, Mount, volcano in eastern Sicily xix (*Aen.* 8) 159, 161

Etruscans (ē-**trus**-kans), inhabitants of Etruria, north of Rome 3, 5, 7, 9, 11 (*Aen.* 1, 2, 6, 7, 8, 10, 12) 20, 75, 101, 133, 140, 148, 162–163, 166, 168, 184, 191, 213

Euboea (yū-**bē**-a), long island east of Attica, site of vigorous Iron Age community where the alphabet seems to have been invented xvii (map), 4 (*Aen.* 6) 101, 102

Eumenides (yū-**men**-i-dēz), "the kindly ones" (= the Furies), the third play of Aeschylus' *Oresteia* (*Aen.* 4) 92, 93

Euripides (yū-**rip**-i-dēz) (480–406 BC), Athenian playwright 13 (*Aen.* 1, 4) 36, 92

Europa (yū-**rōp**-a), daughter of Agenor, brother of Cadmus, mother to Minos (*Aen.* 6, 10) 123, 188

Eurotas (yū-**ro**-tas), the stream that flows through Sparta, where there was a shrine to Diana/Artemis (*Aen.* 1) 37

Euryalus (yū-**rī**-a-lus), Trojan fighter, younger of buddy-pair with Nisus, killed in night raid against the Rutulians 13 (*Aen.* 1, 9) 23, 173–180

Eurydicê (yū-**rid**-i-sē), beloved of Orpheus, who tried to bring her back from the underworld (*Aen.* 6) 108

Evadnê (e-**vad**-nē), wife of Capaneus, who threw herself into his funeral pyre (*Aen.* 6) 119

Evander (e-**van**-der), Greek king in Italy from Arcadia, father of Pallas, ally of Aeneas 12, 14 (*Aen.* 6, 7, 8, 10, 11, 12) 105, 140, 151, 154–157, 161–165, 187, 188, 189, 194, 199, 208, 213

F

fasces (**fah**-sēz), a bundle of rods enclosing an ax, the symbol of *imperium* 5 (*Aen.* 6) 133

Fate, that which is spoken, like the Stoic logos 2, 9, 14, 15 (*Aen.* 1, 2, 4, 6, 7, 8, 10, 11, 12) *passim*

Faunus (**fa**-nus), "kindly one," Roman *numen* of the forest, equated with Greek Pan 11 (*Aen.* 7, 8, 10, 12) 140–142, 145, 169, 190, 218

G

Ganymede (**gan**-i-mēd), son of Tros, beloved of Jupiter, cupbearer of the gods xxiii (*Aen.* 1) 18

Geryon (**jer**-i-on), three-bodied monster killed by Hercules (*Aen.* 6) 113–114

Giants, "earth-born ones," sprung from the blood of Sky that fell on Earth (*Aen.* 6) 124, 126

golden bough, plucked by Aeneas before he entered the underworld (*Aen.* 6) 109–111, 118, 125

Gorgon, terrifying head of Medusa (*Aen.* 2, 8) 69, 160, 161

Gorgons (**gor**-gonz), three female monsters whose look turned one to stone (*Aen.* 6, 7) 113–114, 145

Gortyn, city in south-central Crete (*Aen.* 11) 206

Graces (Charites), attendants of Venus, imparters of feminine charm (*Aen.* 1) 45

Greek alphabet, invented c. 800 BC 3–4, 7, 12 (*Aen.* 2, 6) 51, 101

Guérin, Pierre Narcisse (1774–1833), a French painter famous for his portrayals of Greek and Roman myth 49

H

Hannibal (247–183 BC), "mercy of Baal," who fought Rome 5 (*Aen.* 4, 6, 10) 78, 97, 134–135, 182

Harpies, "snatchers," winged storm-spirits who attack Aeneas and his men (*Aen.* 6) 113–114

Hebrus (**hēb**-rus), (1) river in Thrace (*Aen.* 1) 31; (2) victim of Mezentius (*Aen.* 10) 192

Hecatê (**hek**-a-tē), goddess of the crossroads and witchcraft (*Aen.* 4, 6) 94, 96, 101, 108, 111–113, 123

Hector, greatest of the Trojan warriors, married to Andromachê, killed by Achilles xxiii, 10 (*Aen.* 1, 2, 6, 10) 22, 28, 37, 47, 59, 60, 64, 65, 67, 109, 121, 183

Hecuba (**hek**-u-ba), Roman form of Hecabê, the wife of King Priam xxiii (*Aen.* 1, 2, 7, 10) 36, 66–67, 144, 192

Helen, daughter of Jupiter and Leda, husband of Menelaus, lover of Paris 13 (*Aen.* 1, 2, 6, 7, 10) 18, 43, 60, 63, 68–69, 70, 105, 121, 145, 185

Helenus (**hel**-e-nus), Trojan prophet, brother of Hector, married Andromachê after war. migrated to Buthrotum (*Aen.* 1, 4, 6) 26, 89, 105

Hellespont, straits between the Aegean Sea and the Propontis (= the Dardanelles) (*Aen.* 2) 51

Hercules, Roman form of "Heracles," son of Jupiter, greatest Greek hero xx, 11 (*Aen.* 1, 6, 8, 10) 27, 41, 42, 71, 108, 114, 117, 123, 133, 154, 156, 157, 164, 187–188, 194

Herodotus (her-**od**-o-tus) (c. 484–425 BC), Greek historian x

Hesiod (**hēs**-i-od) (eighth century BC), Greek poet, composer of *Works and Days* and *Theogony* (*Aen.* 8) 159

Hesionê (hē-**sī**-o-nē), daughter of Laomedon, sister of Priam, rescued by Hercules, married to Telamon (*Aen.* 1, 2, 8) 42, 71, 157

Hesperia, "western land," that is, Italy (*Aen.* 1, 2) 39, 40, 75

Hesperides (hes-**per**-i-dēz), "daughters of the West," who protect a magical tree with golden apples (*Aen.* 4) 93

Hippolytus (Hippolytos) (hip-**pol**-i-tus), "horse-tamer," son of Theseus and an Amazon queen (*Aen.* 6, 11) 119, 203

Homer (eighth century BC), composer of the *Iliad* and the *Odyssey* x-xiii, 4, 7–8, 11 (*Aen.* 1, 2, 6) 17, 18, 19, 36, 51, 57, 120–122, 137

Horatius Cocles (ho-**rāsh**-us **kōk**-lēz), "Horatius the one-eyed," defended bridge over Tiber single-handed (*Aen.* 8) 168

Hyades (**hī**-a-dēz), "rainers," a star cluster (*Aen.* 1) 47

Hydra (**hī**-dra), "water-snake," many-headed serpent killed by Hercules at Lerna (*Aen.* 6) 113–114, 123, 126, 133

Hyperion (hi-**per**-ion), "he who travels above," Titan, father of the sun and moon (*Aen.* 6) 129

I

Icarus (**ik**-a-rus), drowned when he disobeyed his father Daedalus' instructions not to fly close to the sun (*Aen.* 6) 101–102, 103

Ida (**ī**-da), Mount, (1) on Crete xviii (map); (2) another mountain near Troy xviii (map) (*Aen.* 2, 7, 9, 12) 72, 76, 143, 144, 173, 213

Ilioneus (il-**ī**-o-nūs), one of Aeneas' trusted commanders (*Aen.* 1) 23, 39, 40, 42

Ilium, another name for Troy (*Aen.* 1, 2, 6) 20, 22, 28, 35, 43, 52, 56, 63, 69, 104

Illyria, the northeast coast of the Ionian Sea (coast of Albania, Montenegro, Croatia) (*Aen.* 1) 27

Ilus (**ī**-lus), early king of Troy, son of Tros, grandfather of Priam xxiii (*Aen.* 1, 6) 28, 127, 132

imperium, supreme authority in Rome, power to conduct war and to execute enemies of the state 5, 6–7

Inachus (**ī**-na-kus), river near Argos, father of Io (*Aen.* 7) 143, 145, 148

incubation, "sleep-in," to determine the god's will (*Aen.* 7) 141

Indo-European language, the hypothetical language of the prehistoric Indo-Europeans 10

Iphigenia (if-i-jen-**ī**-a), daughter of Agamemnon and Clytemnestra, sacrificed by her father at Aulis (*Aen.* 2) 52

Iris (**ī**-ris), "rainbow," messenger of Juno (*Aen.* 4, 10) 100, 183, 184, 186

Isis (**ī**-sis), Egyptian goddess, adored by Cleopatra (*Aen.* 8) 171

Italus, an early king of the Oenotrians, a people of southern Italy (*Aen.* 1) 39

Ithaca, off the northwest coast of Greece, home of Ulysses, one of the Ionian Islands

Iulus (**ī**-ū-lus), son of Aeneas, also called Ascanius, ancestor of the Julian clan xi, 4, 5 (*Aen.* 1, 2, 4, 6, 7, 9) 28–29, 40, 44–45, 46, 49, 68, 72–73, 74, 81, 86, 97, 116, 131, 132, 140, 142, 149, 174, 177, 189, 222

Ixion (ik-**sī**-on), father of Centaurus, tried to rape Juno, bound to a wheel in the underworld (*Aen.* 6) 124–125, 126

J

Janus (**jā**-nus), *numen* of gates, bridges, and archways 10 (*Aen.* 1, 7) 29, 149

Jason, son of Aeson, husband of Medea, leader of the Argonauts 13 (*Aen.* 7) 138

Jove, another name for Jupiter 10 (*Aen.* 1, 4, 6, 7, 8, 10, 12) 19–20, 33, 79, 83, 89–90, 96, 97, 108, 123–124, 143–144, 158, 190, 191, 193, 210, 219, 220

Judgment of Paris, when Paris had to judge who was most beautiful: Juno, Minerva, or Venus

Julius Caesar, see Caesar, Julius

Juno, Roman counterpart of Greek Hera, enemy of Aeneas 3, 8, 11 (*Aen.* 1, 2, 4, 6, 7, 8, 10, 12) *passim*

Jupiter, Roman counterpart of Greek Zeus, king of the gods (*Aen.* 1, 2, 4, 6, 8, 12) 23, 26, 41, 68, 71, 72, 78, 83, 85, 90, 96, 117, 124, 132, 165, 210, 219

Juturna, twin sister of Turnus (*Aen.* 10, 12) 187, 209–210, 218–220, 222

L

Labyrinth (**lab**-e-rinth), "house of the double-ax," Cretan maze, home of the Minotaur (*Aen.* 6) 102

Lacedaemon (las-e-**dēm**-on), the Eurotas furrow in the southern Peloponnesus (*Aen.* 6) 121

Laconia (la-**kōn**-i-a), same as Lacedaemon (*Aen.* 6) 121

Laocoön (lā-**ok**-o-on), priest of Neptune, struck Trojan Horse with his spear, strangled by serpents (*Aen.* 2) 50–55, 57, 58

Laodamia (lā-ō-da-**mī**-a), wife of Protesilaüs (*Aen.* 6) 119

Laomedon (lā-**om**-e-don), early king of Troy, father of Priam (*Aen.* 1, 2, 4, 6, 8) 42, 69, 71, 94, 127, 150, 157

Lapiths (**lap**-iths), Thessalian tribe that defeated the Centaurs (*Aen.* 6, 7) 124, 144

Lares (**lar**-ēz), Roman protective spirits of the household 10 (*Aen.* 8) 164, 170

Larissa, a town in Thessaly (*Aen.* 2) 55

Latini (la-**tīn**-ē), early inhabitants of Latium 4 (*Aen.* 8) 158

Latinus (la-**tīn**-us), early king in Latium 11, 14 (*Aen.* 1, 6, 7, 8, 9, 10, 11, 12) 23, 105, 131, 137, 140–149, 150, 164, 175, 179, 184, 190, 199, 213–216, 218, 219, 222

Latium (**lā**-shum), homeland of the Latins, in central Italy 4, 10, 11 (*Aen.* 1, 2, 4, 6, 7, 8, 10, 11, 12) 17, 18, 26, 28, 40, 75, 92, 104, 105, 115, 131, 132, 133, 140, 143, 145, 149, 150, 184, 192, 200, 217, 219

Latona, the Roman Leda, mother of Apollo and Diana/Artemis (*Aen.* 1, 9, 11) 37, 180, 200–201

Lausus, son of Mezentius, killed by Aeneas (*Aen.* 10) 182, 187, 192, 193–198

Lavinia (la-**vin**-i-a), Aeneas' bride in Italy 4, 14 (*Aen.* 1, 4, 6, 7, 12) 17, 85, 105, 131, 139, 140–141, 143–146, 147, 214, 223

Lavinium, town in Latium founded by Aeneas, named after his wife xviii (map), xix (map), 4 (*Aen.* 1, 6, 7) 17, 27, 28, 105, 140, 141

Leda (**lē**-da; Roman Latona), wife of Tyndareus, mother of Helen, Clytemnestra, Castor, and Pollux (*Aen.* 1, 2, 6, 7) 43, 68, 108, 145

Leleges (**le**-le-jēz), allies of the Trojans from southern Asia Minor (*Aen.* 8) 172

Lemnos, island in the northern Aegean (*Aen.* 8) 161

Lerna, in the Argive plain, where the Hydra lived (*Aen.* 6, 12) 113, 133, 212

Lethê (**lē**-thē), "forgetfulness," a river in the underworld (*Aen.* 6) 108, 128–129, 130, 131

Leto (**lē**-tō), mother of Apollo and Artemis, the Greek Latona (*Aen.* 1, 6, 9) 37, 124, 180

Liber (**lē**-ber), "free," *numen* of wine, equated with Greek Dionysus 11 (*Aen.* 6) 133

Libya, a fertile land in North Africa (*Aen.* 1, 4, 6, 7, 8) 18, 24, 26, 29, 30, 31, 33, 39, 40, 41, 78, 80, 83, 86, 89, 93, 115, 128, 132, 135, 144, 158

Ligurians, inhabitants of what is today southern France (*Aen.* 11) 204, 205

Lipari (li-**par**-ē) Islands, north of Sicily (*Aen.* 1, 6, 8) 19, 135, 159

Livius Andronicus (c. 284–204 BC), earliest Latin poet, wrote Latin version of the *Odyssey* in a meter called Saturnian 7

Livy (59 BC–AD 17), Roman historian (*Aen.* 1) 27

Lucifer, "light-bearer," the planet Venus (*Aen.* 2, 8) 76, 165

Lucretia (lu-**krēsh**-a), virtuous Roman matron, raped by a Tarquin (*Aen.* 6) 133

Lycia (**lish**-i-a), region in southwest Anatolia, home to the Trojan hero Glaucus (*Aen.* 4, 10, 11, 12) 81, 89, 193, 206, 212

Lydia, a region in western Anatolia (*Aen.* 2, 8) 75, 162

M

Machaon (ma-**kā**-on), son of Asclepius, physician at Troy (*Aen.* 2) 59

Magna Mater, the Roman "great mother" goddess xx (*Aen.* 6) 132

Maia (**mī**-a), "midwife," a daughter of Atlas, mother of Mercury, one of the Pleïades (*Aen.* 1, 4, 8) 29, 86, 155

Marc Antony (83–30 BC), Roman general xxi, 2, 6, 13, 14 (*Aen.* 6, 8) 104, 170

Mars, Roman war god, equated with Greek Ares, father of Romulus and Remus by Rhea Silvia xx, 10, 11 (*Aen.* 1, 6, 7, 8, 10, 11, 12) 28, 132, 136, 144, 158, 161, 164, 166, 169, 171, 189, 193, 194, 203, 210, 218

Medea (me-**dē**-a), witch from Colchis, daughter of Aeëtes, wife of Jason, murdered her children 13 (*Aen.* 7) 138

Medusa (me-**dūs**-a), "[wide]-ruling," one of the three Gorgons, beheaded by Perseus (*Aen.* 2, 6, 8) 69, 114, 161

Melpomenê, "singer," muse of tragedy 3

Memnon, king of Ethiopia, a son of Dawn, who fought for the Trojans; in post–Homeric epic, killed by Achilles (*Aen.* 1, 8) 37, 47, 158

Menelaus (men-e-**lā**-us), king of Sparta, son of Atreus, husband of Helen, brother of Agamemnon (*Aen.* 1, 2, 6, 10) 42, 43, 55, 59, 121–122, 185

Menestheus (men-**es**-thūs), one of Aeneas' trusted followers (*Aen.* 4) 88

Mercury, Roman god of commerce, equated with Greek Hermes 11, 12 (*Aen.* 1, 4, 8, 10) 29, 85–86, 87, 95, 130, 151, 155, 157, 183

Messapus, Latin commander, enemy of Aeneas (*Aen.* 8, 9, 10, 11, 12) 150, 178, 193, 199–200, 210, 211, 213, 215

Messina, Straits of, between Sicily and the toe of Italy (*Aen.* 6) 113

Metabus, father of Camilla (*Aen.* 11) 200–201, 202

Mezentius (me-**zen**-shus), brutal Etruscan leader, enemy of Aeneas 14 (*Aen.* 8, 10, 11) 150, 162–162, 165, 182, 184, 187, 191–198, 199

Michelangelo (1475–1564), Italian sculptor and painter 57

Minerva, Roman equivalent of Athena 11 (*Aen.* 1, 2, 6, 7, 8) 18, 19, 36, 48, 50, 54, 62, 64, 104, 134, 149, 159, 161, 171

Minos (**mī**-nos), Cretan king of Cnossus, son of Jupiter and Europa, husband of Pasiphaë (*Aen.* 6) 101–102, 119, 123

Minotaur (**mīn**-o-tar), "bull of Minos," half-man, half-bull offspring of Pasiphaë and a bull (*Aen.* 6) 102, 103, 119

Muses, the inspirers of song 3 (*Aen.* 1, 7) 17, 140

Mycenae (mī-**sēn**-ē), largest Bronze Age settlement in the Argive plain, home of the house of Atreus xii, xviii (map) (*Aen.* 1, 2, 6, 7) 28, 43, 48, 54–55, 61, 68, 134, 145

Myrmidons (**mir**-mi-dons), "ants," followers of Achilles (*Aen.* 2) 48, 56

myth, "word, plot," a traditional tale with collective importance xi, 7, 12–13, 15 (*Aen.* 2, 4, 6, 10) 48, 49, 58, 83, 96, 99, 122, 160, 167, 190, 202, 222

N

Naples, "new city," a Greek colony in southern Italy xviii (map), 4 (*Aen.* 1) 18, 49, 130, 207, 222

nectar, drink of the gods (*Aen.* 1) 35

Neoptolemus (nē-op-**tol**-e-mus), "new-fighter," son of Achilles, also called Pyrrhus, "red" (*Aen.* 2) 48, 59, 63, 65, 66, 67

Neptune, Roman equivalent of Poseidon, lord of the sea 11 (*Aen.* 1, 2, 6, 7, 8, 10, 12) 23–24, 49, 50, 55, 63, 69, 71, 102, 104, 109, 119, 138, 171, 191, 218

Nereids (**nē**-re-idz), "daughters of Nereus," nymphs of the sea 21

Nereus (**nē**-rūs), son of Pontus and Earth, wise Old Man of the Sea (*Aen.* 1, 2, 8) 24, 63, 158

Nero (**nē**-rō) (AD 37–68), Roman emperor (*Aen.* 8) 170

Nestor, garrulous septuagenarian Greek at Troy, chieftain of Pylos, who owned a famous elaborate cup 4

Nisus (**nī**-sus), son of Hyrtacus, older of buddy-pair Nisus and Euryalus 13 (*Aen.* 1, 8, 10) 23, 173–181, 190

Numa Pompilius, early Roman king (*Aen.* 6, 8) 133, 169

numen (pl., *numina*), "nodder," an invisible power in Roman religion 9–11 (*Aen.* 1, 6) 29, 132, 135

Numitor (**num**-i-tor), brother of Amulius, father of Rhea Silvia xxiii (*Aen.* 6) 131, 132

nymphs, "young women," spirits of nature 12 (*Aen.* 1, 4, 7, 8, 9, 10, 11, 12) 20, 21, 24, 31, 37, 81, 83, 93, 140, 143, 152, 155, 173, 184–185, 187, 190, 201, 208, 218

Nysa (**nī**-sa), mythical land that received the infant Dionysus (*Aen.* 6) 133

O

Ocean, river that surrounds the world (*Aen.* 1, 2, 4, 7, 8) 28, 47, 56, 80, 93, 142, 165

Octavian, see Augustus

Odyssey, poem by Homer x, xiii, 7, 8, 13 (*Aen.* 1, 2, 6) 17, 19, 26, 59, 122, 137

Oeneus (**ē**-nūs), king of Calydon (*Aen.* 7) 144

Oïleus (ō-i-**lūs**), father of the Lesser Ajax, king of Locris (*Aen.* 1, 6) 19, 134

oligarchy, "rule by the few" 2, 5, 6

Olympus, Mount, in north Greece between Thessaly and Macedonia (*Aen.* 2, 4, 6, 7, 8, 10, 12) 75, 86, 100, 108, 123–124, 134, 143, 163, 182, 185, 187, 215, 218

Opis, nymph who kills Arruns in revenge for death of Camilla (*Aen.* 11) 200, 201, 208

Orcus (**or**-kus), "the place that confines," Roman equivalent of Hades 11 (*Aen.* 2, 4, 6) 62, 85, 86, 100, 113

Oreads (**or**-e-adz), mountain nymphs (*Aen.* 1) 37

Orestes (or-**es**-tēz), son of Agamemnon and Clytemnestra, who killed his mother and her lover Aegisthus to avenge his father (*Aen.* 4) 92–93

Orion (ō-**rī**-on), a hunter, lover of Dawn, turned into a constellation (*Aen.* 1, 4, 10) 39, 78, 193–194

Orpheus (**or**-fūs), son of Apollo, musician, tried to bring back his wife Eurydice from the dead (*Aen.* 6) 108, 127, 129

Ossa, mountain in Thessaly bordering Macedon, piled on Olympus and Pelion by the Aloads in order to reach heaven (*Aen.* 6) 124

Otus (**ō**-tus), a giant who stormed heaven (along with Ephialtes) (*Aen.* 6) 124

P

Palamedes (pal-a-**mēd**-ēz), clever enemy of Ulysses (*Aen.* 2) 51

Palatine Hill, one of the seven hills of Rome xx, 13 (*Aen.* 6, 8) 104, 151, 157, 166, 172

Palinurus (pal-i-**nur**-us), helmsman of Aeneas who drowned 13 (*Aen.* 6) 115–116, 139

Palladium, protective Trojan statue of Athena (*Aen.* 2) 54

Pallas (**pal**-as), (1) an epithet for Athena 11 (*Aen.* 1, 2) 19, 36, 48, 54, 56, 69; (2) son of Evander, ally of Aeneas 9, 13 (*Aen.* 8, 10, 11, 12) 151, 154, 156, 157, 161–165, 182, 187–189, 199, 222, 223

Paphos (**pāf**-os), city in Cyprus, sacred to Aphrodite/Venus xvii (map) (*Aen.* 1, 10) 34, 183

Paris, son of Priam and Hecuba, lover of Helen xxiii, 11, 13 (*Aen.* 1, 2, 4, 6, 7, 10) 18, 49, 52, 60, 69, 70, 85, 104, 105, 121, 144, 145, 185, 192

Paros, one of the Cycladic islands (*Aen.* 1, 6) 41, 120

Pasiphaë (pa-**sif**-a-ē), "all-shining," daughter of Helius, wife of Minos, mother of the Minotaur (*Aen.* 6) 102, 103, 119

Patroclus (pa-**trok**-lus), Achilles' best friend, killed by Hector (*Aen.* 1, 2, 10) 22, 37, 52, 59, 188

Pelasgians, "peoples of the sea," an unknown people or peoples who lived in Greece before the Greeks came; loosely, the Greeks (*Aen.* 1, 8) 42, 166

Peleus (**pē**-lūs), grandson of Jupiter, husband of Thetis, father of Achilles (*Aen.* 2) 56, 59, 67

Pelion, coastal mountain on the Magnesian peninsula in southeastern Thessaly near Iolcus (*Aen.* 6) 124

Peloponnesus (pel-o-po-**nēs**-us), "island of Pelops," the southern portion of mainland Greece linked to the north by the narrow Isthmus of Corinth xviii (map) (*Aen.* 1, 2, 4, 6, 8, 12) 18, 50, 55, 86, 124, 133, 157, 212

Pelops (**pē**-lops), son of Tantalus, father of Atreus and Thyestes, grandfather of Agamemnon and Menelaus (*Aen.* 2) 55

Penates (pe-**nat**-ēz), Roman protective spirits of the household, often confused with the Lares 10 (*Aen.* 1, 2, 4, 7, 8, 9) 17, 20, 33, 45, 59, 67, 73, 74, 75, 77, 96, 142, 150, 151, 154, 164, 170, 175

Penelope, "duck," mother of Telemachus, faithful wife of Ulysses (*Aen.* 6) 137

Penthesilea (pen-thes-i-**lē**-a), Amazon queen who attacked Troy, killed by Achilles (*Aen.* 1, 11) 37, 203

Pentheus (**pen**-thūs), Theban king who opposed Dionysus, torn to pieces by followers of Dionysus (*Aen.* 4) 92

Pergama, the highest point of the citadel of Troy where there was a temple to Apollo; Troy itself (*Aen.* 1, 2, 4) 36, 43, 59, 62, 67, 89, 81

Perseus (**per**-sūs), Greek hero who killed Medusa the Gorgon (*Aen.* 6, 7) 134, 145, 148

Phaedra (**fē**-dra), "bright," daughter of Minos, wife of Theseus, stepmother of Hippolytus (*Aen.* 6) 119

Phlegethon (**fleg**-e-thon), river of the underworld (*Aen.* 6) 108, 113, 122, 126

Phoebus (**fē**-bus), (*Aen.* 1, 4, 6, 11) 31, 77, 78, 101, 102, 104–105, 115, 125, 172, 206

Phoenicia, the coast of the eastern Mediterranean, modern-day Lebanon xvii (*Aen.* 1) 18, 35

Phoenicians, "red-men," from the dye that stained their hands, a Semitic seafaring people living on the coast of the northern Levant 3 (*Aen.* 1, 4, 6) 29, 31, 32, 35, 36, 40, 44, 45, 89, 94, 119

Phoenix (**fē**-niks), aged tutor to Achilles (*Aen.* 2) 75

Phrygia (**frij**-a), region in Asia Minor, home of fertility religions xvii, xviii (*Aen.* 1, 2, 6, 7) 25, 51, 75, 132, 143

Phrygians, Anatolian allies of the Trojans (*Aen.* 2, 4) 51, 68, 80

Phthia (**thī**-a), region in southern Thessaly, home of Achilles (*Aen.* 1) 28

pietas (**pē**-e-tas), Roman value of dutifulness toward father, gods, and country 11, 12, 13, 15 (*Aen.* 1, 2, 6, 10) 17, 63, 67, 128, 131, 136, 195

Pirithoüs (pī-**rith**-o-us), king of the Lapiths, foe of the Centaurs, friend of Theseus (*Aen.* 6, 7) 117, 124, 125, 126, 144

Pluto, "wealth," another name for Dis 11 (*Aen.* 1, 7) 23, 144

Polites (pol-**ī**-tēz), a son of Priam, murdered before his eyes (*Aen.* 2) 67

Pollux, immortal brother of Castor, Helen, and Clytemnestra xx (*Aen.* 6) 108

Polydorus (pol-i-**dōr**-us), son of Priam and Hecuba (*Aen.* 1) 43

Polynices (pol-i-**nīs**-ēz), son of Oedipus, brother of Eteocles, buried by Antigonê (*Aen.* 2) 59

Polyphemus (pol-i-**fēm**-us), "much famed," the Cyclops blinded by Ulysses (*Aen.* 3) 76

Pompey (**pom**-pē), the Great (106–48 BC), Roman statesman and general, enemy of Julius Caesar xx, xxi, 2, 6 (*Aen.* 6, 8) 125, 134, 170

Porsenna, Lars, Etruscan ally of the Tarquins in Roman legend (*Aen.* 8) 168

Poussin, Nicolas (1594–1665), a leading French painter 74

Priam (**prī**-am), king of Troy, son of Laomedon, husband of Hecuba, father of Hector and Paris xxiii (*Aen.* 1, 2, 4, 6, 7, 8, 12) 19, 35–37, 43, 47, 48, 50–51, 53, 55, 59, 61, 62, 64, 65–69, 71, 75, 89, 94, 120–121, 127, 144, 150, 157, 158, 177, 213

Procris (**pro**-kris), daughter of Erechtheus, king of Athens; wife of Cephalus, who killed her accidentally (*Aen.* 6) 119

Proserpina (pro-**ser**-pi-na), the Latin form of Persephonê, goddess of the underworld 11 (*Aen.* 4, 6) 100, 108, 111, 117

Protesilaüs (prō-tes-i-**lā**-us), first man to die at Troy (*Aen.* 6) 119

Punic (**pū**-nik) Wars, between Carthage and Rome, third and second centuries BC xxi, 5 (*Aen.* 1, 4, 6) 18, 29, 97, 135, 136

Pygmalion (pig-**māl**-i-on), Dido's brother who murdered her husband Sychaeus out of greed (*Aen.* 1, 4) 32, 77, 89

Pyrrhus (**pir**-us), "red-head," another name of Neoptolemus, son of Achilles (*Aen.* 2, 6) 48, 59, 65–67, 71, 135

Q

Quirinus (kwi-**rīn**-us), a *numen* representing the Roman people, sometimes assimilated to Mars, Janus, or Romulus (*Aen.* 1, 6) 29, 132, 135

R

Remus (**rē**-mus), twin founder of Rome xxiii, 4, 10 (*Aen.* 1, 6, 8, 9) 17, 28–29, 131, 132, 168, 178

Renaissance, period of cultural ferment mostly in Italy, in the fourteenth through sixteenth centuries AD 14, 87

res publica (rās **pub**-li-ka), "public matter," the oligarchic government at Rome before 30 BC, when Augustus defeated Marc Antony and Cleopatra 5

Rhea Silvia (**rē**-a **sil**-vi-a), daughter of Numitor, impregnated by Mars, mother of Romulus and Remus xxiii (*Aen.* 1, 6) 28, 131, 132, 136

Rhesus, a Thracian ally of Troy (*Aen.* 1) 36, 47

Romulus (**rom**-yu-lus), twin founder of Rome xxiii, 4, 10 (*Aen.* 1, 6, 8) 17, 27–28, 131–132, 135, 136, 166, 168–169

Rubens, Peter Paul (1577–1640), Dutch painter 57, 99

Rumor, an important *numen* in the *Aeneid* 11 (*Aen.* 4, 7, 8, 11, 12) 83, 88, 98, 142, 143, 146, 152, 164, 199, 214

S

Sabines (**sā**-bīnz), Italic tribe east of Latium (*Aen.* 6, 8) 133, 163, 168

sacrifice, "making separate" 9, 12 (*Aen.* 1, 2, 4, 6, 7, 8, 10, 12) 31, 43, 52, 78, 102, 111, 141, 144, 152, 156, 171, 189, 223

Salmoneus (sal-**mōn**-ūs), son of Aeolus, thought he was Jupiter (*Aen.* 6) 123–124, 126

Samos (**sā**-mos), "hill," island in the east Aegean xviii (map) (*Aen.* 1, 6) 18, 101

Samothrace, island in the north Aegean xvii (map) (*Aen.* 1) 31

Sarpedon (sar-**pēd**-on), a son of Jupiter, Lycian prince, ally of Troy, killed by Patroclus (*Aen.* 1, 10) 22, 188

Saturn, Roman agricultural god, equated with Greek Cronus xx, 11 (*Aen.* 1, 4, 6, 7, 10, 12) 18, 23, 40, 41, 79, 90, 132, 140, 148, 193, 219

Scaean (**skē**-an) Gates, "left-hand" gates, the principal gate at Troy (*Aen.* 2) 69

Scipio, Africanus (236–183 BC), Roman general during the Second Punic War (*Aen.* 6) 134–135

Scylla (**sil**-la), "puppy," many-headed monster who lived opposite Charybdis in the Straits of Messina (*Aen.* 1, 6, 7) 26, 113, 144

Scythia (**sith**-i-a), territory north of the Black Sea (*Aen.* 4, 8) 81, 172

Semitic, referring to the "descendants of Shem," a son of Noah; peoples of the Near East speaking a language with triconsonantal roots, including Assyrians, Babylonians, Hebrews, and Phoenicians 5 (*Aen.* 1) 18, 32, 41, 42

senate, "body of old men," governing body in ancient Rome 2, 5 (*Aen.* 1, 8) 29, 34, 37, 154. 169, 170

Sextus Tarquin, son of Tarquin the Proud, raped Lucretia (*Aen.* 6) 133–134

Sibyl, a prophetess (*Aen.* 6) 101, 102, 104–105, 106, 107, 110, 111, 113, 118, 122, 126, 131, 137, 139

Sibylline Books, collection of oracles held at Rome (*Aen.* 6) 101, 104–105

Sidon (**sī**-don), Phoenician city in the Levant xvii (map) (*Aen.* 1, 4) 35, 42, 44, 79, 95, 98

Silvanus (sil-**vān**-us), "forestman," Roman *numen* of the forest (*Aen.* 8) 166

Simoeis (**sim**-o-ēs), a river in the Troad xvi (map) (*Aen.* 1, 6, 10) 22, 42, 105, 184

Sinon (**sī**-non), Greek who tricked the Trojans into accepting the wooden horse (*Aen.* 2, 6) 50–56, 61, 121

Sisyphus (**sis**-i-fus), son of Aeolus, perhaps the father of Ulysses (*Aen.* 6) 122, 124, 125

Sophocles (497–406 BC), Greek playwright (*Aen.* 1) 36, 57

Sparta, city in the southern Peloponnesus xviii (map) (*Aen.* 1, 2, 6, 7, 10) 37, 43, 68, 121, 145, 185

Stoicism, Greek philosophy that taught submission to natural law 13 (*Aen.* 6, 8) 129, 169

Stymphalus (**stim**-fa-lus), lake in the Peloponnesus, where Hercules killed the Stymphalian birds (*Aen.* 8) 157

Styx (stiks), "hate," a river in the underworld (*Aen.* 6, 10, 12) 108, 109, 114, 115, 119, 185, 219

Sychaeus (si-**kē**-us), first husband to Dido 13 (*Aen.* 1, 4, 6) 32, 38, 45, 77, 89, 93, 95, 96, 97, 99, 120, 126

Syria, the territory surrounding the upper Euphrates xvii (map) (*Aen.* 6) 134

Syrtes, quicksands off the coast of North Africa (*Aen.* 1, 4, 6, 7) 22, 78, 104, 144

T

Tantalus (**tan**-ta-lus), an early king of Lydia who fed his son Pelops to the gods (*Aen.* 6) 124

Tarchon (**tar**-kon), Etruscan leader 14 (*Aen.* 7, 8) 140, 161, 163, 166

Tarpeia (tar-**pē**-a), treacherous daughter of a Roman commander, betrayed the Capitoline Hill to the Sabines (*Aen.* 8, 11) 168, 203

Tarpeian Rock, on the Capitoline Hill, down which criminals were thrown, named after Tarpeia (*Aen.* 8) 168, 169

Tarquin the Proud, last king at Rome (*Aen.* 6) 101, 104, 133–134

Tartarus, place for punishment in the underworld (*Aen.* 4, 6, 8, 10) 86, 92, 108, 113, 117, 122–123, 164, 193

Telamon (**tel**-a-mon), father of Greater Ajax (*Aen.* 1, 8) 19, 42, 157

Telemachus (tel-**em**-a-kus), "far-fighter," son of Ulysses and Penelope (*Aen.* 7) 140

Tenedos (**ten**-e-dos), an Aegean island near Troy xvi (map) (*Aen.* 2) 48, 55, 56

Teucer (**tū**-ser), first king of Troy xxiii (*Aen.* 1, 2, 4, 6, 8) 19, 27, 42, 48, 85, 121, 127, 155, 157

Teucrians, the Trojans, descendants of Teucer (*Aen.* 1, 2, 4, 6, 8, 12) 19, 27, 29, 42, 50, 56, 59, 60, 89, 91, 94, 127, 155, 219

Theano, wife of Antenor and priestess of Athena (*Aen.* 10) 192

Thebes (thēbz), principal city in Boeotia, unsuccessfully attacked by seven heroes, destroyed by their sons (*Aen.* 2, 4, 6) 59, 88, 92, 119, 120

Theseus (**thē**-sūs), son of Neptune, father of Hippolytus, killer of the Minotaur (*Aen.* 2, 6, 11) 59, 102, 108, 117, 119, 125, 126, 203

Thessaly, region in Greece south of Mount Olympus xviii (map) (*Aen.* 2) 55

Thetis (**the**-tis), a daughter of Nereus, wife of Peleus, mother of Achilles (*Aen.* 6, 8) 105, 158

Thrace, region northeast of Greece xvii (map), xviii (map) (*Aen.* 1, 11) 31, 36, 43, 201, 203

thyrsus, phallic staff carried by followers of Dionysus (*Aen.* 7) 146, 147

Tiber, river in Italy xix (map), xx (map), 3, 4, 5 (*Aen.* 1, 2, 6, 7, 8, 10) 18, 28, 75, 105, 131, 136, 138, 140, 144, 148, 152, 162, 164, 194, 195

Tiburtus, Latin commander, enemy of Aeneas (*Aen.* 11) 200

Tiepolo, Giovanni Battista (1696–1770), an Italian painter and printmaker from Venice 46

Tisiphonê (ti-**sif**-o-nē), "vengeful destruction," a Fury (*Aen.* 6, 7, 10, 12) 123, 126, 144, 193, 220

Titanomachy (tī-tan-**om**-a-kē), "battle of the Titans" with the Olympians (*Aen.* 6, 10) 123, 190

Titans (**tī**-tans), offspring of Sky and Earth, the generation of gods before the Olympians (*Aen.* 1, 4, 6, 10) 47, 80, 83, 86, 113, 123, 126, 129, 133, 190

Tithonus (ti-**thōn**-us), son of Laomedon, brother of Priam, beloved of Dawn (*Aen.* 4, 8) 96, 158

Titus Tatius (**tit**-us tā-shus), king of the Sabines, who fought the Romans (*Aen.* 8) 168

Tityus (**tit**-i-us), tortured in the underworld by vultures because he attacked Leto (*Aen.* 6) 124, 126

Triton (**trī**-ton), son of Neptune and a sea nymph, a merman (*Aen.* 1, 6) 24, 109

Troad, the area around Troy, at the entrance to the Dardanelles xvi (map) (*Aen.* 2, 6, 8, 9) 51, 60, 75, 127, 155, 175

Troilus (**troy**-lus), son of Priam, killed by Achilles (*Aen.* 1) 36

Tullus Hostilius, an early king of Rome (*Aen.* 6, 8) 133, 168

Tunis, a town in North Africa (*Aen.* 1) 18

Turner, J. M. W. (1775–1851), an English painter and artist 38

Turnus, Italian leader killed by Aeneas 9, 12, 14 (*Aen.* 1, 6, 7, 8, 9, 10, 11, 12) *passim*

Tydeus (**tī**-dūs), father of Diomedes, fought at Thebes (*Aen.* 1, 2, 6, 10) 22, 36, 54, 55, 120, 183

Tyndareus (tin-**dar**-e-us), Spartan king, husband of Leda (*Aen.* 2) 68

Typhoeus (tī-**fō**-ūs), monstrous offspring of Earth overcome by Jupiter (*Aen.* 1) 44

Tyre, Phoenician city in the Levant, original home of Dido xvii (map) (*Aen.* 1, 4, 10) 17, 18, 31, 32, 35, 78, 98, 183

Tyrian, an inhabitant of Phoenician Tyre, Dido's hometown; a Carthaginian (*Aen.* 1, 4) 31, 32, 34, 40, 41, 43–45, 47, 80, 81, 89, 92, 95–97

U

Ufens, Latin commander, enemy of Aeneas (*Aen.* 8, 10, 12) 150, 189, 209, 215

Ulysses, Roman name for Odysseus 11 (*Aen.* 2, 6) 48, 50–51, 52, 54, 56, 65, 75, 122

V

Venus, Roman goddess of love, equivalent to Greek Aphrodite xi, xx, xxiii, 5, 10–12 (*Aen.* 1, 2, 4, 6, 7, 8, 10, 12) *passim*

Vesta, Roman goddess of the hearth, equivalent to Greek Hestia xx, 10 (*Aen.* 1, 2, 6, 8, 9) 29, 60, 68, 70, 121, 170, 175

Vestal Virgins, attendants of Rome's sacred fire 10 (*Aen.* 1, 6) 28, 132

Vulcan, Italian fire god (= Greek Hephaestus) xii, 11 (*Aen.* 1, 6, 8, 10, 12) 47, 125, 158–161, 164, 167, 171, 172, 189, 190, 217

X

Xanthus, "yellow," a river on the Trojan plain xvi (map) (*Aen.* 1, 4, 6, 8, 10) 36, 81, 105, 155, 185

Z

Zeno (**zē**-nō) (334–262 BC), founder of Stoicism (*Aen.* 6) 129

www.ingramcontent.com/pod-product-compliance
Ingram Content Group UK Ltd.
Pitfield, Milton Keynes, MK11 3LW, UK
UKHW021317180426
11947UKWH00015B/1293